THE MIRROR KING

THE MIRROR KING

AN ORPHAN QUEEN NOVEL

JODI MEADOWS

KATHERINE TEGEN BOOKS

An Imprint of HarperCollins Publishers

ALSO BY JODI MEADOWS

Incarnate

Asunder

Infinite

Phoenix Overture, a digital novella

The Orphan Queen

The Hidden Prince, a digital novella

The Glowing Knight, a digital novella

The Burning Hand, a digital novella

The Black Knife, a digital novella

Katherine Tegen Books is an imprint of HarperCollins Publishers.

The Mirror King
Copyright © 2016 by Jodi Meadows
Part opener photograph © iStockPhoto

Library of Congress Control Number: 2015943596
ISBN 978-0-06-231741-4

Typography by Torborg Davern
17 18 19 20 PC/RRDH 10 9 8 7 6 5 4 3 2
❖
First Edition

For my sister, Sarah.
Close to my heart, no matter the distance between us.

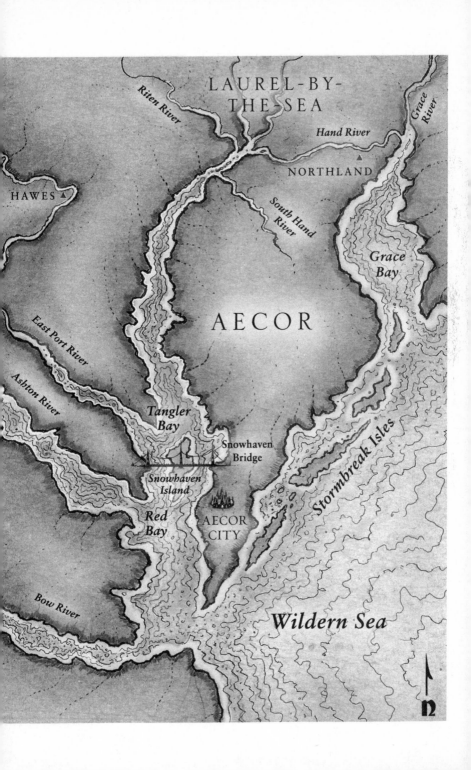

PART ONE

THE
INUNDATED
CITY

ONE

THE PRINCE'S BLOOD was on my hands.

Screams from the courtyard below pounded through my ears, through my head, but I was blind to all but Tobiah's motionless form. He was so still. So pale. His skin was like paper. The guards cut away his clothes, revealing the black bolt protruding from his gut. Blood splashed like angry ink, pooling around him.

"Tobiah." The whisper splintered from inside me. My hands were on his face. His head rested on my knees.

"*Trust Wilhelmina,*" he'd told his guards. "*Protect her.*"

And then, "*I don't want to fight.*"

"But that's all we ever do." My fingers curled over the contours of his cheek. His skin felt icy, but maybe it was my imagination.

Only half aware of the cacophony below, and guards

shooting toward the assassin on a nearby rooftop, I bent until my cheek brushed Tobiah's nose. I held my breath and listened for his.

Gasp.

Rattle.

Sigh.

It was weak, and I could almost hear the blood flooding his lungs in a crimson tide. Flecks of wetness dotted my cheek, but I didn't move.

Gasp.

Rattle.

Sigh.

I'd learned a little about injuries from tutors the Ospreys had hired, and from the boys who were interested in medicine. Though I'd always been more concerned with causing damage, I knew about herbs and binding wounds and how quickly people could slip into shock—even those who hadn't been hurt.

But with every one of Tobiah's weak exhales, everything I'd been taught flew from my mind. Wet little puffs of knowledge, flying away with his gasps and rattles and sighs.

Except for one fact: Crown Prince Tobiah was unlikely to survive this injury.

Gasp.

Rattle.

Sigh.

If he didn't get *real* help, he would die.

Only I could find it for him.

* * *

The world came crashing back in a rush of screams and shouting. The twang and whack of crossbows punctuated the voices.

"What is she doing?" Blood stained the guard's hands as he pressed a cloth onto the prince's wound. The men surrounding him looked up, toward me.

"Get the princess out of here," James barked. He was a familiar face: the crown prince's bodyguard and cousin, and my friend. I should be able to trust him. "Get her inside."

"No!" I clung to the prince's shoulders as someone grabbed around my middle, and another darted in to cushion the prince's head as I was dragged away. "No! Don't touch me!"

Even half standing, I could barely see the rooftop where the shooter had stood with his crossbow, and the boy made of wraith not far from him, following the last command I'd given him: pursue Patrick.

A soldier's fingers dug into my ribs as I struggled. "No!" I elbowed him, and through a gap in the wall of men, I caught sight of the wraith boy returning: a flash of white against the blue sky and brown buildings.

"Wilhelmina!" he cried.

Guards shouted and one took my arms. "Come on!"

But I couldn't move under the weight of their hands, because a memory stole over me, paralyzing.

Hands on my arms. And legs. And chest.

Less than a week ago, I'd been wearing black trousers and boots, rather than one of the exquisite gowns expected of a proper lady. I'd been caught, accused of being the vigilante known as Black Knife, accused of assassinating King Terrell in

5

his sleep, and accused of impersonating a foreign duchess.

Dawn had just been brushing the sky, and the Indigo Order surrounded me. James had been there. Someone had cuffed me, and then the others came.

Touching.

Groping.

Reaching for places they had no right, until James called them off.

They'd claimed they were searching for weapons, but my skin still bore the yellow marks of fading bruises.

The phantom sensations that had haunted me since were real now.

I had to escape.

With a feral scream, I yanked myself away from the guard and landed hard on my knees. Pain flared, but I forgot all about it as the chaos below intensified, and an enormous white horror leapt over the edge of the balcony, knocking aside the men as though they were dolls.

The wraith boy's body had elongated, his face stretched until his mouth was wide and gaping, and his pale eyes were oval and enormous. "Release my queen." His voice boomed like thunder as he shrank and strode across the balcony, stepping around the fallen prince at the last moment. "Do not touch her."

Ten guards backed away from me, leaving me to kneel by Tobiah's head.

The guards who'd been knocked over stood now, their weapons aimed at the wraith boy. Others still scanned the rooftops for the assassin, while many focused on the prince, bleeding to death in front of my eyes.

The wraith boy reached for one of the guards who'd grabbed me.

"Stop!"

The wraith boy froze in a half lurch, waiting for my permission to move again. The guards hesitated.

I fought to steady myself, grabbing my gown into bunches. "He thought I was in danger. Focus on Tobiah. He needs help."

"She's right." James shouted orders, and guards moved in to assist, giving the statue-still wraith boy a wide berth.

Carefully, they pushed the limp prince into a sitting position. Blood saturated his jacket and shirt as they peeled off his clothes and tossed them aside. Blood-soaked wool hit the stone with a *splat*.

The crossbow tip protruded from his back, slick and shining with blood. A hooked barb made the bolt impossible to remove without causing more damage.

If he was even still alive.

"Knife!" shouted a guard. "Cut off the tip."

The screaming below had softened, now that the assassin was gone and guards had emerged to control the crowd. The roofs across the courtyard were filled with soldiers hunting for the shooter.

One of the men lowered his knife to begin cutting the shaft just below the barb, but his hand shook with nerves. The life of his future king rested in those trembling fingers.

Breathlessly, I leaned forward and batted him aside. "*Wake up*," I said, touching the bolt. The magic made my thoughts fuzz, but I hardly noticed. "*Do this carefully and gently: break just below the tip and remove yourself from the prince. Leave no pieces inside him. Cause no additional harm.*"

"Is she using magic?" someone whispered. Soldiers drew back, as if being too close to me would contaminate them, but they held their prince as the crossbow bolt followed my instructions.

The wood snapped and the tip clanked against the floor. One of the men dropped a cloth over it and snatched it up, as though containing a wild animal.

Slowly, the shaft pulled itself from the wound; whatever sound it made was covered by the gasping of soldiers nearby, and the noise of people being corralled in the courtyard below.

"Flasher," someone muttered. "It's true."

In my peripheral vision, I caught the wraith boy's rapt attention, his eyes unnaturally wide as he watched the crossbow bolt drop onto the prince's lap. Tobiah's hands rested limply on the stone floor, drenched in his own blood.

Please. Please.

As soon as the bolt was out, men pressed bandages to the wound, and I reached around to tap the offending object. "*Go to sleep.*"

It was inanimate again.

"Now," said James. "Get His Highness into his quarters. Send for a physician. Have the entire city searched." He turned to me. "Was that Patrick Lien?"

My stomach knotted. Patrick had always intended to be the liberator of Aecor, our conquered homeland. But while we had the same goals, his methods made him the enemy now. "Yes.

8

Trying again, after he failed the other night."

James passed a hand over his stomach, the ghosts of pain and confusion flickering across his face. "All right. I'll need a description. A drawing, if you can manage."

Around us, guards constructed a stretcher to transport Tobiah. This didn't feel real.

"I can." My head buzzed with magic and horror, but there was so much to do. "I can send him to search for Patrick." I nodded toward the wraith boy, still caught in that half lurch. "You can stand now," I told him.

He shot me a quizzical look as he straightened and assumed normal proportions. He was blindingly white, still wearing Tobiah's Indigo Order jacket from the night of the Inundation, though the cloth was torn and dirty.

James glanced from me to the wraith boy. "He's under your control?"

"He is." Saints, I hoped he was.

The captain gave a curt nod. "Tobiah trusts you. I do, too. But I don't think it's a good idea to send him into the city."

The wraith boy, perhaps sensing my reluctant agreement, grew smaller, more placid. His indigo jacket hung down to his knees as he lowered his eyes.

My blood-soaked gown dragged heavily as I stepped toward James, keeping my voice low. "There's no way Tobiah can survive that wound."

Neither of us said what we both must have been thinking: James had survived an almost identical injury.

He kept his voice soft. "What do you propose?"

9

It felt like betrayal, giving up someone else's secret, but he would understand. He would be protected. "I have a friend who can heal."

James's eyebrows shot up. "Magically?"

I nodded.

The captain shoved his fingers through his hair, leaving streaks of Tobiah's blood. "The other day, did you bring your friend to me?"

"No."

He pressed his mouth into a line. "What are the chances of us both mysteriously healing?"

"Are you willing to take the risk?"

"Definitely not," he said. "Where is your friend? I'll have him sent for immediately."

"I should look for him. The Ospreys won't trust a messenger."

"No." James watched as the men transferred Tobiah to the stretcher and moved him inside. "No, that's not a good idea. Not with the people calling you the wraith queen, or after what you did during the Inundation. It's too much. They'd panic. We can't risk it."

It was a risk I was willing to take if it meant saving Tobiah's life. But James held all the power here, so I just nodded. "I'll write a message. I'll draw Patrick's face, and I'll tell you anything you need to know. I want him caught, too."

"And what about your pale friend?" James's jaw flexed as he settled his glare on the wraith-white figure, now no bigger or differently shaped than any other seventeen-year-old boy. "I can't allow him to roam the palace, but I doubt a cell would hold him."

"I'll put him somewhere safe."

"Will you be all right?" James reached for my arm, but stopped short of contact. The wraith boy might see it as a threat.

I touched his arm instead. "When Patrick is in the deepest dungeon, the wraith vanishes, and all of my friends are safe: then I will be all right."

TWO

BY THE TIME the clock tower chimed seventeen, I'd sent messengers to the Peacock Inn and half a dozen other Osprey hideouts in the city. The messages contained orders for all four of my Ospreys to come to the palace immediately; the other four were with Patrick, including my best friend, Melanie.

Saints, I hoped they were safe. Even the ones who'd left me.

Especially the ones who'd left me, because Patrick wasn't always concerned about whether they survived the missions he assigned. We'd lost so many friends through his leadership, and I'd never challenged it. Not until it was too late.

Now, I sat at a table in Crown Prince Tobiah's parlor, finishing the last strokes of a sketch of Patrick's face: close-cropped hair, a hard scowl, and a scar above one eyebrow. Even from paper, he commanded attention.

"That's the last one for you." James took a chair next to me and met my eyes. "We have scribes and messengers copying your drawings for the police and bounty notices. You don't need to make more. That isn't your job."

"What *is* my job? Pacing the palace and hoping Patrick slips up? Because that's the only way he'll be caught."

James's mouth pulled into a frown. "The queen regent is offering five thousand crowns for Patrick's capture."

"You've just persuaded me to go find him myself."

His smile was tolerant, like I'd made a joke. "It's been suggested that you offer a reward, as well."

"Even if I knew what the Aecorian treasury looked like, I don't have access to it. Strip Prince Colin of his overlord title and we'll continue that conversation."

"Would that I could."

He'd been awake for only hours, and was recently injured himself. He didn't need my derision on top of everything else. I made my tone gentler. "How is Tobiah?"

"Same." James lowered his eyes. "The physicians are with him. They said the bolt came out cleanly, which will help the healing process. But they told me not to expect miracles."

We fell quiet, neither of us willing to bring up James's miraculous healing this morning. Why shouldn't we expect miracles from Tobiah, too? But the questions were there, hanging between us. We'd have to talk about it sometime.

Anyway, where was Connor? What about "come immediately" lacked urgency?

"What about him?" James tilted his head toward the wraith boy standing in the corner, where he'd been the whole time I worked. He was hunched over like a scolded hound, waiting for attention.

"He can't do anything." After the shooting, he'd refused to leave my side. I could have ordered him somewhere else, but where? "Wraith is destruction, not healing."

At my words, the wraith boy turned his head, and a thin smile sliced across his face, widening until he showed teeth and gums.

I shivered as he turned back to the corner. James paled and angled himself away from the wraith boy.

"And you?" I touched the back of his hand. "Are you all right?"

"I'm fine." James drew a deep breath. "I should have saved him."

"But you—"

He shook his head. "I should have seen Patrick. I should have been watching the rooftops more closely. Tobiah rushes into what he thinks is best and forgets to look out for danger. He can be reckless."

I closed my eyes, recalling the black-clad boy with a sword sheathed at his back. Easily, I could picture the way he leapt off rooftops and ran toward the crash and growl of danger. Glowmen, wraith beasts, or ordinary criminals: it didn't matter what it was or who was involved; he would intervene to rescue victims and drag perpetrators to the nearest police station. "I remember."

"That's why I'm here," James said. "To look after Tobiah. So that he can be who he is without worrying about danger."

It seemed to me James was being too hard on himself. Tobiah wasn't easy to look after, given his vigilante habit. James wouldn't be reassured, though. His sense of duty wouldn't allow it.

"Why don't you wash up?" He motioned to the bloodstains on my gown. "There's nothing else you can do until your friend arrives."

"I hate feeling powerless." I wiped clean my pen and closed the bottle of ink. "I hate not being able to help."

James's jaw clenched as he glanced toward the prince's closed door. If anyone understood, he did. "Sergeant Ferris will escort you to your quarters." He looked at one of the indigo-jacketed men in the sitting room. "Sergeant, attend Princess Wilhelmina."

I stood and lifted an eyebrow. "Who is being guarded?"

"You, Your Highness." James rose to his feet again, too. "Patrick risked you today. What if his aim had been off? What if the wind had picked up? The queen regent and Lady Meredith are being guarded closely, as well."

As closely as I? *They* were probably permitted knives at meals. "Very well."

James leaned close. "Now that you've identified yourself, you'll simply have to get used to a bodyguard following you at all hours. Do you think Tobiah *enjoys* my constant company? It is the duty of a member of the royal family to stay alive."

A darkness flashed through his eyes: his failure today, the failure of King Terrell's bodyguards not even a week ago. He needed me to obey, to take the guard and keep myself safe. And with the wraith boy in the palace, we all needed to be even more alert.

He was correct. But that didn't mean he wasn't also guarding the rest of the palace from me.

"Only because you asked so nicely." I grabbed the leather-bound notebook I used as a diary and strode after the young sergeant James had indicated. A moment later we were out the door, the wraith boy following at a short distance.

It wasn't a long walk from Tobiah's apartments to mine. Both suites were located in the Dragon Wing, the area typically reserved for Indigo Kingdom royalty. My presence here was indicative of both the respect Tobiah held for me, and the respect he had for my dangerous abilities. He kept me close because he needed to watch me.

Sergeant Ferris led me in silence, though he cast a few curious looks toward me.

As we approached my door, I made my expression stony. "Yes, Sergeant?"

He ducked his head. "Pardon, Your Highness."

"If you have a question, ask it."

He hesitated, but curiosity won over. "*You* are Black Knife?"

Though an afternoon of sitting over writing materials had made every muscle in my shoulders and neck stiff, I drew myself up to my full height, nearly even with my guard. "What do you think, Sergeant?"

He snapped to attention at my door and held his position. "Your Highness."

I entered my sitting room, allowing myself to feel a sliver of satisfaction—at least until I remembered the wraith boy trailing in after me, a white shadow jacketed in indigo.

"Stay in the corner," I told him. He obeyed, hands clasped in front of him, head slightly bowed.

I moved toward the table to lay down my notebook, but stopped. Something was different.

When Tobiah had summoned me to his quarters this morning, I'd run off quickly, not bothering to close the jars of ink, or clean my pens. Now, the bottles were corked or capped, and the ink-stained nibs soaked in a shallow cup of water, rusting.

A folded paper was pinned beneath a bottle of blue ink, a quick W scrawled on the corner.

Someone had been in my rooms. Or still was.

I snatched a clean pen off the table and clutched it like a knife, moving through the room without stealth; any intruder already knew I was here.

One by one, I opened doors and scanned the shapes and shadows of the music room, the game room, and the dressing room for hints of the intruder. But there was nothing untoward. Just the same opulent suite I'd become intimately acquainted with in the days since the Inundation. The same brocade silk curtains, the same glossy, wood-paneled walls, and the same gleaming brass knobs and hinges and other finishings. There were no strange shapes in the pockets of darkness by full bookcases, or under the ornately carved tables, or in the curtain surrounding the tub in the washroom.

Everything was quiet. The windows here faced the back of the palace, giving me a view of the ruined gardens and woods beyond. Protesters' cries were muted, and I heard no scrape of shoes on rugs or brush of clothes on wood.

Whoever had been here was gone now.

My fist relaxed around the pen, and I lit a candle when I returned to the table.

After King Terrell had been assassinated, Tobiah had told me that people always wanted to kill kings. Now that my identity was out—as well as my magical ability and the way I'd allegedly spent time as a vigilante—I had to be careful, too. Particularly since I was alone here. Had Melanie stayed with me—

Well, she wasn't here.

I brought the candle close to the paper, but found no traces of powder. There were no unusual scents, either.

It was probably safe.

I slipped the paper from beneath the bottle and unfolded it. The note was in Tobiah's handwriting. A strained laugh escaped my throat. All that work, and the intruder turned out to be a boy dying just a few doors down the hall.

> *Wilhelmina,*
>
> *I'm sorry I didn't visit you after the Inundation. I should have.*
>
> *Please forgive me for what I'm about to do; know that it is duty and honor that compel me to act against my true feelings. You were correct when you said I need to decide who I am.*
>
> *No matter where my heart leads, I must become who my kingdom needs me to be.*
>
> *With greatest affection,*
> *Tobiah Pierce*

My heart twisted, and tears in my eyes made halos grow around the words.

He must have written this right before he announced the date of his wedding to Meredith—winter solstice—during the minutes he'd left James's side to deliver a list of places in Aecor Patrick might have gone.

Unfortunately, Patrick had been on his way here.

To shoot Tobiah.

Maybe I hated the prince, but I loved the vigilante, and now he was dying.

My feelings had been complicated enough when I'd believed they were separate people, but now that Tobiah Pierce was Black Knife . . .

Black Knife was Tobiah Pierce . . .

And *where* was Connor?

My breath came hard and fast as I placed the letter on the table once more, and smoothed out the corners. My weapons had been taken away, but not my clothes.

I glanced at the window. Nearly dark.

"Wraith boy."

In the corner, he perked up and tilted his head. "Yes, my queen?"

"From the balcony, can you lower me to the ground?" Being on the third story, I wasn't keen to climb down without my grappling hook and line. My first night in this suite, I'd checked the outside wall for any footholds, but without tools, there'd been nothing but a high probability of two broken legs.

"It isn't for me to question my queen, but"—he shifted his weight—"can't you simply walk out? Are you a captive?"

I glanced at the letter on the table, the beautiful room that had been my prison for three days, and the crown prince's blood staining my gown. Black Knife's blood. "Can you do what I asked?"

"Yes."

"Good. Then you're going to help me escape."

THREE

IN MY BEDROOM, I stripped off the bloodied gown and hunted through a wardrobe until I found a dark shirt and trousers. Finally, the haunting sense of internment lifted. James said I shouldn't leave the palace, but this was something I needed to do.

Because as much as I disliked the prince, I was relying on Tobiah to help me reclaim my kingdom.

If he died, I would truly be a hostage here.

Resolved, I moved toward the front door and rested my fingers on the lock. Just then, footfalls slammed through the hall, toward the crown prince's apartments. I held my breath as they shouted for another physician, but there was no word on his condition.

I twisted the lock, and the bolt fell into place with a heavy *thunk*. A breath went by before Sergeant Ferris noticed and began rattling the handle, but I was halfway to the balcony already. "Help me to the ground," I told the wraith boy. "Then I want you to hide under the bed"—surely he couldn't hurt anything there—"and if anyone asks where I went, just tell them I will return soon."

He followed me to the balcony. Stars crowded the sky, their faint shine glowing across the woods at the back of the palace. Gleaming remnants of the king's glasshouse shimmered below. Cold air blew in from the west, buffered by the palace.

"Do you remember my instructions?"

"Yes, my queen." He'd grown bigger outside, ready to follow orders. The acrid stink of wraith came off him, making my eyes water. "I will hide under the bed. I will tell anyone who asks that you'll return soon."

"Good."

"Princess!" Sergeant Ferris was knocking at the door. "What's going on?"

"Hurry." I scrambled over the balcony rail so I faced out, my heels on the very edge, my calves and thighs pressed against the wrought iron. "Quickly, but carefully. Remember, if I die, you'll be inanimate again." As far as I could guess anyway. "I assume you have some sense of self-preservation?"

He sniffed, almost an offended sound, as he gently took me around the waist. Suddenly I was in the air.

My toes stretched for the ground, touching nothing as air whooshed around me. I was dropping.

Dropping.

Very.

Slowly.

Inside the room, the door banged open and James shouted

something, but finally my toes touched the ground. The wraith boy's hands slipped off my sides and the odor of wraith retreated.

"What are you doing?" cried James.

"My queen will return soon."

When I looked up, I could just see James striding toward the edge of the balcony. I stepped beneath it where he couldn't spot me. Not yet.

"Wil!" James leaned over the balcony, scanning the gardens.

If Melanie had stayed, she'd have covered for me. She'd have known just what to say to distract James and his guards while I slipped away.

"Ferris." James's tone was hard. "Get a small team together and search for Her Highness. Keep this quiet. Last thing we need is for everyone to know she's broken out."

"She'll return soon!" added the wraith boy.

"Yes, Captain." Ferris's voice grew softer as he left the balcony.

"And where are you going?" James asked.

"Under the bed until my queen returns."

I stretched my senses, straining to hear footfalls and breathing and the catch of clothes on buildings or brush. Carefully, quietly, I kept to the shadows and slipped around the perimeter of the palace. When patrols strode by, I held still and silent. The surge of adrenaline in my head felt real and right as I darted through the once-extravagant courtyards, leaving the palace for the first time since the Inundation.

There wasn't much of a difference between the King's Seat and Hawksbill; the two ran together and their boundaries weren't marked. So there was no way to tell as I moved from one district to the other, but a rush of relief poured over me as I prowled around the wraith-twisted statues and trellises of nobles' gardens, keeping beyond the glow of the gas lamps lining the streets.

Steadily, I moved westward, past the Chuter mansion and toward the Bome Boys' Academy that sat along the Hawksbill wall. The school was four stories high, with a brick face and dozens of windows. Where there'd once been glass, now the holes were boarded up or covered with heavy wool blankets. Last I'd heard, the students had been sent home; during the Inundation, some of the doorways in the school had grown teeth and begun chewing.

Just past the school, I came to the wall.

It wasn't impassible by any means, but without my grapple it would be a challenge to climb. The stone was smooth, even after the flood of wraith had changed the city.

Low voices sounded, and lanterns flared in the darkness between streetlamps.

I had to hurry, but without my tools, I had only one option.

"It's for Black Knife," I whispered, pressing my palm to the wall. "*Wake up. Make a passage to the other side big enough for me to walk through.*"

Under my hand, the stone warmed and began to ripple. Blackness paraded around the edges of my vision and I swayed. This was a mistake. I hadn't awakened the *entire* wall, had I?

"There!" The soldier's voice came from close by. "I see someone!"

"Is it the princess?"

"*Hurry,*" I whispered to the wall, and my vision blanked as the stone split open with a low rumble and groan. I struggled to breathe, to tell up from down. My groping hands fell on the edges of the new tunnel through the wall. Narrow. But I could squeeze through.

"Flasher! Saints, she's using magic!" A light fell over me, too bright. "Get a patrol on the other side. Run!"

A pair of boots thumped off, leaving two men running for me.

But I was already in the tunnel, which was barely wide enough for me to move through sideways. I scooted as fast as I dared, jagged edges of stone catching on my clothes and hair.

An arm reached in. Fingers scraped my elbow. My stomach turned and I wanted to tell the wall to close after me, but I couldn't with him reaching through. Shouldn't. I'd have to leave it open.

"*Go to sleep.*" My hands scraped over the stone. "*Go to sleep.*"

Just as the soldier started to squeeze in after me, fingers twisting around my sleeve, I threw myself out the opposite side of the wall. He let out a frustrated growl.

"By Captain Rayner's orders, you must return to the palace!" The guard shouted through the hole, but I was already sprinting into Thornton before the rest of the patrol caught up. "You won't be harmed!"

I was gone, down a street and keeping close to the shadows, and finally behind a bakery where I leaned against a wall and let my breath squeeze from my lungs in silent gasps. Cold slithered into my chest.

That had been close.

And the *magic*. That had been stupid. Dangerous. Even if I'd animated only a section of the wall, it had still been too much. I should have found a trellis or something to climb.

But there hadn't been time. And Black Knife was still dying.

I gave myself another long, silent breath as I listened for the patrols, and then I found a stack of crates by a fence where I could climb to the rooftops.

And I got my first look at the nighttime city since the Inundation.

The dark was overwhelming.

In Hawksbill and Thornton, streetlamps glowed like stars and hope, but in Greenstone and the Flags farther south, there was nothing. Just flat blackness.

Only days ago, there'd been mirrors on every west-facing surface in the city, catching sunsets and moonlight. All seven districts of Skyvale had been lit with faint reflected light.

But when the wraith came, every mirror in the city was destroyed. Glass windows, glass shields over lamps: those were shattered, too.

Legend had it that King Terrell the Second, Tobiah's great-grandfather, had been called the Mirror King when he'd had mirrors hung all over the city. While it ultimately became just another way for people to display their wealth, it had been intended to frighten the wraith from ever invading Skyvale.

The truth ended up being a lot more complicated.

My wraith, what was now the boy, certainly didn't *like* mirrors; it had stopped chasing me at West Pass Watch because of them. But in Skyvale, it had shattered the mirrors rather than retreat. How? Because I'd brought it to life?

I gave the dark, unfamiliar city one more look before I threw myself into it.

For hours, I moved from Osprey hideout to Osprey hideout, searching for signs of my friends. I kept an eye out for Patrick as well, but what would I do if I found him? I was unarmed, and as much as I wanted to catch Patrick and punish him for what he'd done, that wouldn't help the prince.

It was almost midnight when I approached the Peacock Inn in White Flag—or what was left of the inn. It hadn't been much to look at before the Inundation, but now boards had warped and bricks over the front of the building had melted over windows.

I stood at the corner of a nearby building, watching the inn for signs of the patrols James had sent after me. Three of my last stops had had a police officer lurking about, which meant James knew where I'd gone—and why.

Usually, the inn was loud with drunks and thugs, but the whole city was quiet. The few people who braved the debris-filled streets skittered from place to place, keeping their heads low. Prey, waiting for a predator to strike.

Sounds from the taproom were muted. No one felt festive tonight.

If there were any officers here, they weren't showing themselves. I dropped to the street and moved for the front door; the window I usually entered by wasn't there anymore.

The front door opened and Melanie strode out.

We stopped and stared at each other for a heartbeat, and then her arms were around my shoulders and she gave a faint, relieved cry. "Saints, Wil!"

"Mel!" I hugged her back, then ushered her into a narrow alley. A dull *crack* sounded under her boot; we both froze, but the dirt and old papers that concealed the glass also muffled the noise.

We both exhaled.

"What are you doing?" she whispered. "Why are you here?"

"What are *you* doing here?" I glanced toward the top floor, dark and eerie without the mirrors. "Are they here? Connor and the others?"

"They're sleeping." She leaned closer, smelling faintly of fire and something warm and damp. "There are people looking for you. Soldiers. The police. Looking for *Princess Wilhelmina*. Everywhere I go, I hear your name. Someone said you're a flasher. What did you do?"

"Nothing. I broke out of the palace. I have to get Connor."

"Are you a prisoner there?"

There wasn't really a good answer to that question.

"Why Connor?" she pressed.

"I need to take him back to the palace." Melanie didn't know that Connor was like me. No one did.

"Are you afraid that I'm going to tell Patrick?"

My heart gave a painful lurch. "*Are* you?"

"No," she breathed, looking hurt. "Saints, no, Wil. I only went with him because you need someone to keep you informed. You know that, right?"

"You couldn't inform me that he planned on assassinating Crown Prince Tobiah?" Stupid Tobiah, standing out there on the balcony only days after the first assassination attempt.

Less than a week after his own father had been killed. Stupid, stupid boy.

At least, if he'd been just Prince Tobiah, I could have blamed ignorance or arrogance, but he was also Black Knife, and for that I could only assign reckless need to do what he viewed as right.

"This is the first time I've been able to get away." Her shoulders slumped. "He suspects why I went with him. There's no proof, of course, and as far as he knows, we're still"—she swallowed hard—"together. But he's kept a close eye on me. The only reason I was able to get out tonight was because we need supplies. We're leaving tomorrow."

"To go where?"

"Aecor. Where else?"

Where else indeed? "Why tomorrow?"

"He's certain the wound Tobiah took will be fatal."

"It is a mortal wound." The words scraped my throat. "He won't survive it." Not without Connor.

"We'll be out of the city by dawn. He aims to reach Aecor before the week is up."

"Where have you been? Where is he hiding out?"

She sighed and glanced toward Greenstone. "Everywhere. The warehouse district, the riverside, neighborhoods you and I would hesitate to venture into. He's got us moving every hour, and he doesn't tell us where the next place will be."

"So where are you meeting him when you go back with supplies?"

"Fisher's Mouth. That's actually where I came from. It's the first time we've stayed still since this morning." Her expression hardened. "You intend to send the police after him?"

"Of course. He assassinated Terrell. He tried to kill Tobiah twice." I couldn't say when he'd decided murder was an option, but it had never been one for me.

Her shoulders lowered with acceptance. "I'll keep him there as long as possible, but he's so paranoid right now I'm afraid to appear suspicious."

"I understand. Do what you can." Cold wind sang through the alley, making me shiver. "Maybe we can put a stop to this before it gets even more out of control."

She brushed back a strand of hair. "The plan hasn't changed, Wil. Even without you, Patrick will go to Aecor and rally the people to your name. He's more determined than ever to retake Aecor by the anniversary of the One-Night War."

That was only a few months off. "And when people ask why I'm not with him?" I could already hear the answer, even before she spoke it.

"He'll tell them the Indigo Kingdom is holding you hostage."

Exactly as I suspected. "Come back with me. Let's get the others and go to the palace."

She shook her head. "You need me with him. I can temper him. Pull him back when he goes too far by reminding him that you're going to be the one ruling Aecor, and whatever he does will reflect on you."

"Like regicide?"

"Say it again," she muttered. "I have to go now. He'll ask questions if I'm gone too long."

She was my best friend. I'd years ago memorized her face and the way I felt complete when she was nearby, but until recently I'd always known when I'd see her again. We'd never been separated for more than a few days, but now the future gaped with uncertainty.

"Be safe." I hugged her tight, squeezing until the clock tower chimed midnight and we both pulled away. There was still so much to do. "I love you, Mel."

"You too, but stop walking around unarmed. This is a dangerous city." With a faint smile, she pulled a small knife from her belt and handed it to me. "I'll contact you as soon as I can."

I snapped and thumped my chest.

She saluted, too, and with a brave grin, she sauntered down the alley, spinning a second knife in her hands. Her form vanished into the shadows, and I swallowed back the threatening tears. I didn't have time to miss my friend now.

Thanks to Melanie, I knew Patrick's location. I could go after him—with a score of police and Indigo Order men to back me up—or get Connor and go back to the palace.

Was it even really a choice?

I slipped the knife into my belt and headed into the inn. Dying flames in the fireplace glowed across the taproom, which was filled with dozens of lumps of sleeping people. Some snored, while others groaned and huddled into corners. The faint light caught the whites of eyes; a few people watched as I picked my way through the room and toward the stairs. A renewed sense of urgency chased me as I paused at our usual door to listen for voices.

When I pushed the door, the oiled hinges didn't make a sound. Only a lantern warmed the small, cramped space.

All four of them were sleeping: Connor and Carl on the bed, and Theresa and Kevin on pallets on the floor. How they'd managed to keep the room to themselves, I could only guess, but I was relieved to find they were alone.

I let the door shut with a *clunk* behind me. At once they were all sitting and reaching for weapons.

"Wil!" Connor abandoned his knife and bounded across the creaky bed, onto the floor, and to me. "You're all right." He skidded to a halt and swallowed so hard his throat jumped, then he smiled. He was small for his age, with bony shoulders and sunken cheeks.

"We heard the prince had kidnapped you." Theresa climbed to her feet and dusted off her trousers. "And that was why Patrick shot him."

"And we heard that you're Black Knife and that's why the prince kidnapped you." Carl rolled his eyes and twisted his little finger at the rumors. "They're saying you controlled the wraith and led all the beasts into the city, and you're responsible for the Inundation."

"Oh." I kept my face impassive. "Is *that* what they're saying?"

Theresa and Kevin stood, and after hugs, Carl and Connor explained how they'd helped during the Inundation and returned to the city with the residents who'd been forced out by the wraith creatures that had rioted through the streets, killing everything in their paths.

"There was blood *everywhere*," Carl said. "And monsters, all dead. We came here and helped clean up to earn our room. Rees went to Laurence's Bakery a few times to help in trade for food."

"Have you gotten enough to eat?"

Carl shrugged. "More than some others who aren't strong enough to earn it. Connor makes us share sometimes."

Connor glanced downward, but his generosity didn't surprise me. I squeezed his shoulder.

"It's bad out there," Kevin said. "Everyone is hungry. Thirsty. Most people don't have anywhere safe to sleep. We were lucky. The refugee camps are empty. A few refugees might have sneaked into the city with the returning residents, same as we did, but most kept moving east. They didn't want to stay here, where it's so dangerous."

It was hard to blame them. "All right, we need to go. Connor, at least. The rest of you can follow tomorrow, if you want to stay here the rest of the night."

"Where?" Connor asked.

"To the palace. That's where we're going to stay."

"Why do you need me right now?" That sounded suspiciously like a whine, but when I frowned, a look of understanding unfolded over his face. "I'll get my bag."

The others looked as though they wanted to ask "Why Connor," too, but they just gathered their belongings instead. While they were busy, I took an envelope off the small desk. It was sealed with red wax and a thumbprint, and the front bore my name in Melanie's handwriting.

The Ospreys hadn't noticed her earlier. They'd been sleeping when she'd come to deliver the letter, and even when they'd awakened, none of them had noticed something new in the room. What if it had been dangerous? They could have been hurt, or worse.

But when I looked up to find them watching me, they all wore closed, embarrassed expressions. I stuffed away my need to scold. In the days since the Inundation, I'd been miserable in my pretty cage, but they'd been hungry, and cold, and hurt. While this was an especially dangerous time to be unguarded in the city, I couldn't blame them for their exhaustion.

"Did a messenger come for you today?" I placed the letter in my pocket and headed into the hall.

"Yes." Theresa slipped her bag over her shoulder. "Were they really from you?"

I nodded.

"We didn't know. We couldn't be sure."

"Don't worry, Rees. That's why I came to get you."

The five of us moved downstairs silently, picked our way through the dim taproom, and went outside to find a dozen men—police and Indigo Order officers—waiting for us.

Sergeant Ferris stepped forward. "Princess."

"Oh good. An escort." I grinned and let my hand drift toward Melanie's knife, but didn't draw it. The gesture was merely a reminder. "Send your best people to Fisher's Mouth in Greenstone. You'll find Patrick Lien there."

People scrambled to follow *that* particular order.

I could go with them. Leave Connor with instructions and go apprehend Patrick myself. But the words wouldn't come. I needed to be somewhere else.

"In the meantime, take me to Captain Rayner and Prince Tobiah."

FOUR

"WHERE DID YOU get a knife?" James didn't bother to greet me as I entered the prince's bedchambers. The gas lamps were dark, but the wood-paneled walls gleamed in the candlelight.

"It just appeared." I touched the handle; my escorts had tried to take it from me, but I'd asked if they'd seen what I'd done to the Hawksbill wall and they spent the rest of the silent ride eyeing me warily.

There was a question in the way James lifted an eyebrow: had I *made* it appear?

I snorted. That would have been a handy magic. "Someone gave it to me." I shut the door behind me and moved toward Tobiah's bed. He was still and sallow, barely breathing. Brown curls fanned across his forehead, and strain carved a line between his eyes. He was *so* still. "Has he awakened at all?"

"No." James walked up beside me, his elbow brushing mine. If anyone knew what happened between Black Knife and me in the breezeway, it was James. "The physicians have made him as comfortable as possible, but it's only a matter of time. Hours. Perhaps minutes."

"Good thing I brought help."

James shifted his attention to Connor, who'd been hovering by the door with a feigned look of meek amazement at the splendor surrounding us. As though the last thing on his mind was which items to pocket and fence.

I gave a small shake of my head. I'd *taught* him that look. "I need you to do anything you can to save Crown Prince Tobiah."

His manufactured expression faded into honest surprise. "Anything?" And the implied word: *magic?*

"If he dies, there will be a war and no way to stop it. Aecor will be crushed, and we will be prisoners or worse. He *must* live."

Connor swallowed hard and moved toward the bed. He peeled down the blankets concealing Tobiah's chest and stomach, revealing clean bandages and dark veins spiderwebbing his too-pale skin. Shadows circled his eyes. His lips were ashen.

"You brought a ten-year-old to heal the future king?" James didn't quite scowl, but the uncertainty was there.

"I'm twelve," Connor said.

"Well that makes all the difference." James stared at his cousin, expression hard. He must have been terrified; he wasn't usually mean. "Can you help?"

"I'm not sure." Connor closed his eyes and seemed to search; whatever he saw made him shudder. "He's really bad."

"Try anyway." My voice sounded hoarse.

"I'll do what I can." He rested his hands on the bandages. "This will take a while."

"Another of the infamous Ospreys." James pulled away from the bed as Connor grew as still as the prince. "And another flasher."

"We aren't all flashers. Connor's the only other one." As far as I knew. And it was only an accident I knew about Connor. Even among friends, we had to be careful.

"A healer and an animator. Powerful duo." At my sharp look, James smiled a little. "Tobiah told me about a girl he'd met during the One-Night War. When your identity was made public, I figured it out. Besides, I already knew you're a flasher."

"I see." I motioned at a chair near the bed, a basket of yarn and needles beside it. "Does the prince knit?"

James shook his head. "The queen regent has been in and out. Lady Meredith visited briefly."

"And his uncles?"

"They were here long enough to see Tobiah's condition and begin memorial preparations."

Disgust turned my stomach. "He's not dead."

"There's no reason to expect him to live."

"But he will. He must." I glanced at Connor and Tobiah, neither boy moving. "No one can know about this."

"Count on silence from all quarters." James excused himself to speak with the stone-faced soldiers in the parlor, and through the closed door I heard orders for discretion, an oath, and someone ask what was happening.

Which meant the only thing they knew was that the foreign flasher princess had brought in a boy in the middle of the night, and they were being sworn to never speak of it again.

As though *that* wouldn't evoke more curiosity.

I paced the room, weary but restless as I listened to footsteps thudding in the other rooms of Tobiah's apartments. Guards and maids and physicians. Connor muttered to himself, something about arteries and ligaments and organs. Sweat formed and dripped down his face.

This was taking so long. True, I'd seen Connor use his magic only once, and that was to heal a rabbit's broken leg—nothing nearly like this—but shouldn't he be finished by now?

I moved toward the oak bookcases. Gilt-lettered spines shone behind small curios: a golden spyglass, an aged wooden box with intricate carvings on the lid, and a framed paper behind glass. The paper was yellowed, and the writing so exact and regular it couldn't have been made by hand.

"Pre-wraith artifacts," James said, returning to the room. "Tobiah is fascinated by the things people created with magic a hundred years ago. Common things, like paper and clothes and trinkets. There were bigger things, too, of course: trains, faster methods of communication, and ways of clearing the land for farming. But it's the smaller items that really intrigue him. Everyday conveniences we've abandoned."

"I didn't know that about him."

"It's not exactly material for polite discussion these days." James checked the bed, but there was no change. "Tobiah hides a lot of who he is. You can understand, I'm sure."

"You're very perceptive, Captain."

He indicated a stack of framed ink drawings leaning against the bookcase, waiting to be hung. They must have been delivered this morning. "I finally got to see some of your artwork."

He pulled out a drawing of Black Knife, sword in hand.

My heart thumped as my eyes followed the lines of ink, remembering the way my pen had slid across the paper without instruction from my head. I'd *hated* Black Knife when I'd started that, but he'd recently saved Connor from a glowman, and our following encounters had been . . . not bad.

"You're talented." James put the drawing into the stack again, hiding it between flowers and landscapes—other things that were more appropriate for a young lady to have spent her time creating. "Which I knew, having inspected your forged residency documents."

Connor gasped and stepped away from the prince. "That's it." He blinked a few times, as though to clear his vision from whatever he'd been seeing. "That's all I can do."

"Thank you, Connor." I stuffed down my disappointment; there was no change in the prince's appearance. "James, is there somewhere for Connor and the other three to stay? I left them in the front hall under guard, but who knows what they've done by now."

He heaved a sigh. "For the sake of my security teams, are they all like you?"

Able to sneak in and out of guarded buildings, fight opponents twice their size, and pocket valuables without anyone noticing? "I helped train them."

"I was afraid of that."

"Connor," I said, "you can trust Captain Rayner. He's a friend."

After James and Connor left, I paced the room for a few

minutes, trying not to check Tobiah for signs of life. Finally, I sat at his writing desk and dug through his pens and ink and paper. I settled on a stiff nib, heavy blue ink, and plain palace stationery.

> *Tobiah,*
>
> *Thank you for the letter you so quickly left in my room. In response to your request for forgiveness: there's nothing to forgive.*
>
> *We had masks and secret lives, and it was so easy to forget our obligations while we both wore black and met in the dark. Wherever our futures are, you've helped shape mine for the better.*
>
> *With gratitude,*
>
> *Wil*
>
> *Postscript: What do you think about this handwriting? I found it on a man in Thornton who was copying valuable books and selling them as though they were originals. You might want to have someone look into that, if he lived through the Inundation.*

Quick and light. That was all I could manage with him barely breathing mere feet away.

The boy I loved existed beyond his black mask, a fact I hadn't fully reconciled. But no matter my muddled feelings, he was meant for someone else. She didn't love the part of him that was Black Knife—she didn't *know*—but she cared for the prince; he'd been warm toward her.

I wanted Black Knife. She wanted Tobiah.

He'd decided who he needed to be.

While the letter dried, I cleaned the pen and organized his jars of ink by color and shade. James returned just as I folded the letter and tucked it under the golden spyglass on the bookcase. "They're settled in?" I asked.

"Yes. They ate everything in sight and had the silverware in their pockets before anyone noticed. You're sure this is a wise idea? I will have to answer to the queen regent about their presence."

"They're all that's left of Aecorian high nobility." We both glanced at Tobiah, still pale, but his breath was more even and deep, as though he slept easier. "They've fought all their lives to reclaim Aecor and this"—I gestured around the room—"sort of world that was taken from them. There's bound to be an adjustment period. They will learn."

"I'm assigning guards on them at all times."

"That's probably not a bad idea."

"You didn't tell me you gave Ferris the location of Patrick Lien and the others."

In my haste to get Connor to Tobiah, I'd forgotten to bring it up. "Was he arrested?"

James shook his head. "Fisher's Mouth was empty. If he was there, he left no trace. Where'd you get your information?"

"Same place I got my knife." I touched the handle. Had Melanie told Patrick we'd spoken? Or had he left Fisher's Mouth so quickly because he was paranoid? I didn't bother to hide my disappointment while James described how many soldiers and police officers had been pulled from other duties to chase this lead, probably giving Patrick and his half of the Ospreys space to slip out of the city.

"You should go to bed." James motioned toward the door. "You look exhausted."

And I was exhausted, but I wasn't leaving. I marched across the room and took the chair near Tobiah's bed. I'd tried to make two things right tonight, and already failed at one. If I'd gone after Patrick myself . . . but I'd made a choice.

I had to see it through.

FIVE

"WAKE UP, NAMELESS girl."

Dawn seeped around the curtains, lighting the dark room into gray. Candles had drowned their flames or been put out—I couldn't remember—and the smothering air of encroaching death had lifted.

Tobiah was still lying on his back, but he'd turned his head and hints of color lit his skin. When our eyes met, his were bright and alert, and so, so familiar.

I sat straight, heart pounding with hope. "You're alive."

"My dear Wilhelmina, you're amazingly accomplished at stating the obvious." His voice was groggy, deep with the remnants of his long slumber.

"And you're well enough for sarcasm. I think you'll live."

His grin was all Black Knife. Because of the mask, it was an expression I'd only sensed before, never seen, but I knew it just the same: the lift of his cheeks, the light in his eyes, and the way the world seemed to pause.

This was the boy I'd fallen in love with.

Please forgive me for what I'm about to do; know that it is duty and honor that compel me to act against my true feelings.

Forgive me.

I took a ragged breath. "I should send for your mother. She has no idea you're—" Alive. Awake. He'd been so close to death just hours before.

"In a few minutes." He closed his eyes. "Just give me a few minutes before I have to be . . . what they all need me to be." He went still, as though he'd drifted off again, but then he smiled. "You're the one with the no-talking-or-get-stabbed rule. Not me."

How did he not have a million questions? Maybe he was saving them. "How do you feel?"

His hand moved beneath his blankets, as though touching the bandages or testing the wound. "Like I got shot a month ago."

"It was yesterday."

"Yesterday?" He started to sit, biting back a grunt and gasp as blankets fell around his waist. Bandages covered his stomach, but his chest and shoulders were bare, exposing muscles built from years of sword fighting. "Wilhelmina." His tone turned serious as he took in my appearance: the trousers, the disheveled hair, the knife tucked into my belt as though Patrick might strike again. "How did I recover?"

"How do you think?"

Light grew around the curtains. With a soft groan, Tobiah swung his legs off the bed; trouser hems brushed the tops of his feet. His dark eyes were wide and warm. "What did you do, Nameless Girl?"

"I couldn't let you die."

He leaned his whole body toward me, shoulders and chest and face. A hand slipped forward on his knee, almost reaching. "You never fail to amaze me."

It took everything in me to stay put. Not move. He was for someone else, and for all the questionably moral things I was willing to do, that was a line I could not cross.

The bedroom door swung open and the gas lamps hissed to life, saving me from temptation. James strode in with Francesca and Meredith behind him.

Tobiah tugged on the blankets to cover himself.

The queen regent gave a little shout and hurried to embrace him. Meredith pressed her hands to her chest. Only James didn't seem shocked, but for a whole second he sagged with naked relief.

I moved toward the writing desk, a safe distance away from the reunion. James bent his head toward mine.

"How long has he been awake?"

"A few minutes."

Across the room, Tobiah was reassuring his mother that he felt fine, and he wasn't going to die. Meredith perched on the edge of the chair I'd slept in, leaning forward with her hands still clasped by her heart. The flush of someone who'd cried herself to sleep was brightening into hope.

"Where were you?" I asked James. "I expected you to be hovering."

"I had work to do. If you recall, I was made head of palace

security and there was an assassination attempt five minutes later. Then you escaped." James shook his head. "Apparently, I have a big job ahead."

He had a point. "So you didn't warn the queen regent and duchess about Connor?"

"I intercepted them on my way here. The royal physicians insisted Her Majesty be, ah, *helped* to sleep last night, and this morning she decided she wasn't happy about it."

"Hard to blame her," I muttered.

"Anyway, I thought you were plenty capable of protecting my cousin while I looked into securing the palace. Even if you couldn't, there are half a dozen men of the Indigo Order in the next room."

"Patrick might have killed Terrell in his sleep, and with nothing more than a knife, but twice now he's attacked Tobiah from a distance."

"Which is why the windows are shut and there are guards on the balcony. But all of our intelligence suggests Patrick has left the city."

"That's my thought, too." The guilt churned in me.

"What are you two talking about over there?" Tobiah lifted his voice, looking beyond his mother, who sat on the bed beside him. "And James, grab a shirt for me. It's chilly."

James fished through a wardrobe and handed his cousin a solid black shirt before beginning his account of the search for Patrick. And though I wished he wouldn't, he included my involvement with drawings and telling the Indigo Order to search Fisher's Mouth.

"So." Tobiah finished shrugging on the shirt—Meredith

demurely turned her head—and began buttoning while he spoke. "Lien has yet to be captured." His gaze cut to me for a heartbeat, then went back to James. "I hope you're still making your best effort."

"Of course. And while it's likely he's left the city by now, confident of your death, the palace remains on high alert."

"This brings me to the first of many questions." Francesca stood and smoothed her gown as she took her place beside Meredith. "Who were those people you brought here last night, Wilhelmina?"

James stilled.

"Captain, do you think I *don't* know when a small gang of youths appropriates one of the best rooms in the palace? They ate through almost a quarter of residents' breakfast before anyone caught them."

Oh, saints. They'd found the kitchens.

"Of course not." Somehow, James kept his tone light. "I just didn't expect you to know quite so soon, and without preparation."

The queen offered a thin smile and turned toward me, waiting for an explanation.

I fumbled. Haughty? Solemn? Kind? I didn't know which mask to put on, so I didn't use one. I exhaled and let her see how much they meant to me. "They're what's left of Aecorian high nobility, kidnapped during the One-Night War. At first, there were nineteen of us. Now there are ten, split down the middle. The night of the Inundation, four came with me, and four went with Patrick."

"The ones eating their way through the kitchens are yours."

I nodded.

"Let me make sure I understand correctly. Patrick Lien was once part of your group. You knew he'd killed my husband, yet did nothing to bring him to justice?"

I pressed my mouth into a line. "The wraith had just reached the city. Trying to deal with that and Patrick at the same time would have been impossible. I made a choice that would save lives."

Francesca's voice flattened. "Your choice nearly cost the lives of my son and nephew."

The accusation twisted my heart, but I held my posture stiff.

"To be fair," Tobiah said, "she did tell me yesterday about Lien. We were already in pursuit after the first attempt on me, though." He glanced at James. "And I think Her Highness would have told me about Father's assassination if I'd bothered speaking to her instead of keeping her confined to her quarters."

Meredith, silent all this time, granted him a deep smile, like she was proud he'd remembered to be courteous. He ignored her.

"All right," said the queen. "Allowing that, why did we not know of Lien's location until last night, when Wilhelmina was apprehended outside an inn in White Flag?" She looked at me. "Isn't that when you told Sergeant Ferris to go to Fisher's Mouth?"

"It was at the inn I learned of his location."

James lifted an eyebrow; he'd been waiting to hear about this, too.

"On my way to fetch the Ospreys, Melanie and I met. She told me where to look."

"Do you think she warned him?" James's tone was neutral,

but the comment stung. "She did side with him when you split."

As if I could forget. "Patrick is paranoid; he probably left Fisher's Mouth as soon as she returned. The entire city is hunting him."

"Let's remember we're not interrogating Her Highness." Meredith's voice was soft, but everyone looked at her. Francesca's expression warmed. "While questions must be answered, let's not forget that Princess Wilhelmina is our guest."

"That does lead to another question, though." Francesca faced me again, a challenge in her eyes. "Why was it that you chose last night to sneak out of the palace and fetch your Ospreys?"

I glanced at James. He nodded.

"Your son wasn't going to live, Your Majesty." I couldn't make myself look at Tobiah, but even from the corner of my eye I could see his expression of impassive boredom. It was a mask. That face always had been, and I hadn't been able to see through it. But he was listening to every word, every breath, every hesitation. Earlier, he'd asked what I'd done. Here it was: "One of my Ospreys is a healer. A flasher with the power to heal."

The room went silent.

Tobiah pressed his palm over the bandages and the princely mask dropped away, revealing confusion and betrayal and wonder. "Magic."

Meredith's eyes were wide.

"I was told you'd sent for a friend." Queen Francesca's words were soft, but cutting. I'd always thought her meek before, but now I knew that was as much of a mask as anything Tobiah and I wore. "I didn't think much of it. But magic." She sucked in a deep breath. "Why wasn't I informed?"

Neither James nor I answered.

"Which Osprey is this? Had he ever used it before? Did either of you consider that what you did is *illegal*? The wraith is already so close."

"I did consider that." I pulled myself to my full height. "But I am neither a citizen of the Indigo Kingdom—I was kidnapped almost ten years ago, if you recall—nor have I ever been overly concerned with the law when the law prevents me from doing what is necessary. Remember that last night, my friend was the only thing standing between your son and death. Your son, who is now sitting up and scowling. Alive. And just hours ago, he was slipping toward the saints."

The queen regent turned her eyes to her son and acquiesced. "And your friend? Had he ever done anything like that before?"

If she was asking about James's miraculous recovery, she didn't give a hint.

"Once. When he was young and didn't know better, he saved a rabbit. We've been hiding his power ever since. There are people who would exploit his gift." Or arrest him for it. Just months ago, Black Knife would have been one of those people. If caught, Connor would have been taken to the wraithland and sentenced to die by the creatures out there. "He's well read and practiced in more traditional medicine. He knew what he was doing."

"Very well. Thank you for your part in saving my son." Francesca seemed to collect her thoughts. "But we will not speak of this again. None of us. Tobiah, we'll tell everyone that you are recovering thanks to the physicians, but you'll need to stay confined until a reasonable amount of time has passed for you to truly heal."

Tobiah shook his head. "The law is clear. One week of mourning for the old king, and the new king should be crowned the following day, or risk being challenged. If we delay, either of my uncles could contest my enthronement. Many of Uncle Colin's men are coming from Aecor, so they can attend the memorial and coronation. But if I miss the date and my uncle claims I'm not fit to rule, that means he has thousands of armed supporters at his command."

"But you're their king. Future king. Would they support him over you?" Meredith's eyes were wide.

"It's a possibility I won't dismiss." The prince gave a deep nod. "The challenger doesn't even have to be direct family, though they're more likely to have the support they need if they're high in the line of succession. How do you think the Pierces took the throne from the Gearys?"

"So," said Meredith, "two days until the memorial, and three until the coronation. Few people will believe you've healed so quickly, naturally."

No one quite looked at James.

I lifted my voice. "Unless you claim the prince knew an attack might happen, and was armored beneath his clothes. You can say this was a ploy to draw out Patrick, and that you allowed everyone to believe the prince's injuries were so grave in order to make him believe he'd succeeded."

"Dozens of guards saw the bolt go through," said James.

"They *are* under your command."

"Give the order." Tobiah ran his fingers through his hair,

making the strands stand on end. "My recovery doesn't have to be miraculous. I'll play the invalid and rule from bed when I must, but we cannot delay the coronation."

The crown prince left no room for argument.

"Very well." The queen regent didn't look happy, but her acceptance caused a sliver of relief to ripple through the room.

In this, at least, we were all five united.

We all had our reasons for needing this: a mother's grieving heart, a fiancée's elevation to queen, a cousin's duty and friendship.

And my reason?

Too complex to name.

"One more thing before I go to share the news that Tobiah will live." Francesca looked to me. "You could have sent your friend here and gone to find Patrick with the Indigo Order."

Meredith gasped. "She could have been hurt!"

Francesca waved that away. "Perhaps, though she is a capable young woman and she'd have had a score of guards to protect her."

I hated where this was going.

"Would you have been able to track Patrick, assuming he'd truly been there?"

Behind my back, I curled my hands into fists. "Possibly."

"Why didn't you go?" When I didn't answer immediately, she added, "I'm not asking anything that my husband's brothers won't. There are still those who believe you cut my husband's throat, and without proof that Lien did it—your word that he confessed holds very little weight after your impersonation of Lady Julianna—there's little to keep suspicion off you. Even if there were proof, Lien is still an Osprey and was under your command during the time of the assassination. So why, a second time, did you allow Patrick to escape?"

"Would you have acted any differently, Your Majesty?"

The queen regent drew back, her eyes cutting to her son, and the answer was clear.

Tobiah slipped off the edge of the bed, using the chair arm for support. Meredith reached up, as though to help, but never quite touched him. "You should have gone after Lien," Tobiah said. "Your presence wasn't required here. You'd have been more useful tracking him."

Before I could form any sort of response, a knock sounded and a wiry man in messenger livery came in.

With owl-wide eyes, the stranger glanced around the room and seemed to take in his mistake all at once. The queen. The crown prince. The princess. The duchess. And the Indigo Order captain.

He swung back to the prince standing on his own.

The prince, who should have been on his deathbed.

Our secret was out before it'd even begun.

Tobiah sighed. "What is it?"

"Refugees, Your Highness. Majesty. Highness. Hundreds of refugees are approaching Skyvale."

"Refugees from which direction?" If they were from the east, that simply meant those who'd left during the Inundation were coming back. If they were from the west, more Liadians—and people from kingdoms beyond—might have made it through the wraithland.

"From the south. They're from Indigo Kingdom villages all along the wraithland border."

"What does that mean?" Meredith's hands were knots of white knuckles.

The messenger's reply came gravely. "It means the wraith is moving again. Faster."

SIX

ACTIVITY EXPLODED ACROSS the room.

James, Tobiah, and I started for the messenger. Meredith looked to the crown prince for guidance. Francesca turned her glare on me, as though this were my fault; maybe it was.

But Tobiah could barely stand, let alone walk, so with a pained groan he crumpled. James switched trajectories and the queen regent rushed around Meredith to help move the prince back to his bed.

While the others were busy, I approached the messenger. "What else do you know about the wraith? How fast is it coming? What towns? How many refugees?"

"Nothing. That's all I heard."

I grabbed the messenger and shoved him against the wall. His head thudded. I held my knife to his throat and growled, "What kind of messenger doesn't get important details and then barges into the crown prince's chambers? Do you work for Patrick?"

His eyes widened.

"You're too incompetent to be an assassin. Are you trying to lure Tobiah into public so someone else can kill him?"

Meredith let out a peep of surprise, like she hadn't even considered that, but then she saw my knife. "Captain Rayner," she breathed.

From the corner of my eye, I could see everyone looking at me.

"That's a little excessive, Wil." James spoke as though I were a spooked animal. "I know him. He's no assassin and he doesn't work for Lien." He met Tobiah's eyes for a heartbeat, nodded, and came to take the messenger from me. "It's all right."

The man's face seemed caught between fear and excitement. His wide owl eyes darted around the room, taking in the details.

I stepped aside for James, not putting away my knife. "I don't trust him."

"You don't trust anyone." James opened the door to escort the messenger out. "This way, Alain. We—and all of these men—need to have a talk about the crown prince's quarters. . . ."

The door shut behind them, leaving me alone with Tobiah, his mother, and his fiancée. A moment later, muffled yelling came from the other room as James dressed down every guard by name.

I shifted my weight to one hip. "I don't think Alain will keep his mouth shut. The secret is out." I leveled my eyes on Tobiah. "He saw you standing. A second miracle in as many days."

"How *did* James heal?" The queen's eyebrows drew in. "Princess?"

"I was locked in my quarters." My glare landed on Tobiah, who'd managed to sit up straight, but his skin was ashen with the effort. "I was allowed to believe James was dead."

"Regardless," Meredith said, her cheeks red as she attempted to forestall another fight, "Princess Wilhelmina is correct. The secret is out. There's nothing we can do right now but hope Alain takes Captain Rayner's request for silence seriously."

Good luck.

"In the meantime, we'll need to make sure there's room in the shelters for the new refugees."

"You think we should let them into the city?" Tobiah looked at her across the small distance, his face bland. "The shelters are already so full and food is scarce."

"They're Indigo Kingdom citizens."

"Would you feel differently if they were refugees from another kingdom?"

Her lips parted with affront or indecision—I couldn't tell. "Of course not. They're people in need, regardless."

Tobiah nodded. "Still, with a few noble exceptions"—he motioned at me—"my father didn't allow refugees into the city."

"You are not your father and the wraith had not touched the Indigo Kingdom while he was in power."

The crown prince offered a shallow nod. "The gates will be open, my lady."

Meredith glowed with her triumph. "Thank you."

Tobiah pressed one palm to his stomach, over the shirt and bandages beneath. A shadow crossed his face. "Now, if you don't mind, I'd like to rest before the next emergency. My father's memorial is in two days and I plan to be fully recovered by then."

"I'll leave you to your rest, then." I replaced my knife and started for the door.

"Wilhelmina?"

I looked over my shoulder to find Tobiah's glare mixed with something like distaste.

"Please change your clothes into something more becoming of a lady of your station. Parading around the palace like that is . . . unseemly."

I let my voice thin. "If Your Highness wishes to control my wardrobe as well as my movements throughout the palace, consider supplying something more to your taste."

He gave a bored sigh and roll of his eyes.

I slipped out of the room and through the busy parlor, and headed into the hall. My fingernails carved crescents into my palms.

Meredith caught up with me a minute later. "He shouldn't be so mean to you. Not only did you help save his life, you're a princess."

I halted in the middle of the hallway and studied her guileless face. She deserved a true answer. Not the whole truth, but some truth, nonetheless. "It's my rank that's part of the problem." Saints, I wished Melanie were here. "The last thing he expected when I was unmasked, so to speak, was to discover the heir to the vermilion throne. He's already dealing with the wraith problem and his ascension to the throne. I complicate everything."

"Still," she said. "It's no excuse for his poor behavior."

"I'm inclined to agree with you, Lady Meredith."

Sergeant Ferris followed me. Was he a bodyguard? Spy? Did it even matter? His sidelong looks were skepticism and distrust, with a dash of superiority. *He* was who he claimed to be, while I exchanged one identity for another, as quickly as changing clothes.

I doubted Sergeant Ferris would judge his crown prince so harshly.

But with the death of King Terrell, Black Knife would never go out again. If I didn't know his identity, I wouldn't know why he'd disappeared. I'd have looked for him a few more times, and accepted that he'd been called to do something else. He would have remained a mystery, a dark and lovely memory who haunted my dreams.

Forgive me, his note had said. *Forgive me.*

"Your Highness." Sergeant Ferris hauled open the door to my suite, as though I didn't have the strength to do it myself. "Please let me know if you need anything else."

I ignored him and went into my room.

The wraith boy was exactly where I'd ordered him: under my bed, his pale face peeking out from beneath the blankets hanging over the sides. His chest was pressed against the hard-wood floor, not quite on the nearby rug of lamb's wool that warmed my feet every morning.

"You're still here."

"You told me to wait for you." His voice was like wind, hollow and ageless, and dangerously powerful.

"I know, but—" Saying I'd hoped he would have left didn't seem wise. "Well, get out from under the bed."

He shimmied out and jumped to his feet, as though spending the night under my bed hadn't left his limbs stiff or his muscles sore. The tattered indigo jacket hung on his lean frame, not quite covering enough.

We stood there a moment, both of us waiting for my next command. I couldn't look away from him, this strange creature in my quarters. He was wraith, part of the toxic cloud smothering the continent in a white mist that changed the fundamental laws of nature. I'd seen trees growing upside down, and roads rising in the air with nothing to hold them aloft. I'd seen people and beasts that couldn't maintain a size or shape. I'd seen innocents trapped in something clear and solid, just heartbeats away from escape.

Wraith was terrible stuff, of that I had no doubt. But in the shape of a boy, with a voice and a consciousness, was it any different?

I had no idea what to do with him.

But I had to start somewhere. A pile of men's clothing had been delivered; it waited on a cedar chest near the door.

I grabbed underclothes, a shirt, and trousers, and strode across the room, not taking my eyes off his. "What's your name?"

His shrug was a too-fluid ripple. "Do things name themselves in your world?" He cocked his head, lizard-like. Though he'd been completely hairless the night of the Inundation, when I ordered the white mist invading the city to become solid, he now had a fine white fuzz covering his skull. He was somewhere between comical and cute, at least until I remembered his feral grin and the way his fingers elongated into claws when he attacked. But now, his tone was soft. The way he hunched his shoulders, like a child enduring punishment, was almost sweet and sad. "I had hoped you would name me. You gave me life."

A frown pulled at me. "I didn't intend it."

"Didn't you?"

Definitely not. My magic wasn't supposed to work like that. Animating objects wasn't the same as giving them life. This had never happened before, so why now? "What *are* you?"

"I don't know." The wraith boy shrank a little. "Do I have to put on those pants?"

"Yes." As if being Black Knife, the lost Princess of Aecor, and a known flasher wasn't damaging enough to my reputation. I couldn't have a half-naked boy in my suite. "Here." I shoved the bundle at his elbow. "Don't put them on in here. Go into the music room to dress."

He took the clothes and sighed, but I couldn't tell whether it was the thought of putting on pants or the need to leave the room to do it that exasperated him so much. Beneath his borrowed jacket, his shoulders slumped. "I am a mystery, my queen."

Chills swept through me. I retreated to the table and lowered myself into the nearest chair. "Explain."

The wraith boy tugged at his jacket, as though it suddenly wasn't big enough. "You gave me life, but you're unsatisfied. In the changing place, you asked me to save you. And I did. I smothered the locusts. Then I followed you because I wanted to be with you, but you ran. You hid behind the reflections, so I went around. At last I discovered where you had been. I could feel your presence all through the city, but couldn't find you. Not with the mirrors. So I broke them. And then you came and ordered me to become solid. I hoped to please you. But again, you seemed unsatisfied."

My breaths came shallow, but I managed the words. "Go on."

"Though you are responsible for me, I'm not what you want. I could change—do or become anything that you order—but I don't think anything would satisfy you. So I am a mystery, given life for no purpose at all."

"You had a purpose."

"To save you from the locusts? To save your city from changing?" The wraith boy spread his arms wide, his clothes dropping with a soft *whumph*. The jacket opened to reveal his chest; I kept my gaze high. "One was over so quickly it hardly matters, while the other was just delaying the inevitable." He cocked his head. "I told you there would be consequences."

"What are those consequences?"

He went very, very still. "You might think you've slowed the advance of change. Of wraith, as you call it. But you haven't. It's coming faster to meet with me."

My stomach and chest knotted.

"Why is it coming to meet you? If you're the wraith that was in the area when I animated it, wouldn't that mean there's less wraith now? You're alive. And solid. You're real."

"I am those things. I am what you want me to be." He lifted a hand and pointed an overlong finger toward the door. "Your breakfast is coming. Smells good."

I barely had time to follow the shift in subject when the knock sounded. "Enter!" I motioned the wraith boy toward the music room. "Go in there and get dressed. Don't mess with anything."

"Yes, my queen." He took his clothes and slipped away, just as the door opened and a maid came inside with a tray. She placed my breakfast on the table and after a quick curtsy and inquiry as to whether I needed anything else, excused herself. She was the same maid I'd had since announcing my identity, and I still didn't know her name; she hardly spoke at all.

I sat at the table, famished after missing dinner last night. I hadn't lived in the palace so long that food was expendable, and for any Osprey, wasting food was the highest of crimes, right up there with betraying Aecor by befriending anyone from the Indigo Kingdom.

Well, no one was perfect.

Hours later, James arrived bearing a large leather and canvas bag. The contents thunked as he hefted it onto the table. The strap dangled off the edge. "Your evening wear and accessories, my lady."

"Truly, you're a man of miracles."

His smile was strained. Haunted. "If I cautioned you to stay in tonight, would you listen?"

Inside the bag, there were several black shirts and trousers, a pair of knee-high boots, masks, and most importantly: weapons. "This will do."

James sighed. "That's what I was afraid you were going to

say. Where's your pale friend? I have more orders."

"He's in the music room. What else, besides delivering my wardrobe?"

He ticked off the items on his fingers. "One: deliver your clothes. Two: ask you to please put the wraith boy in a safer location. Three: assist you in drafting a letter to the people of Aecor announcing your stay here, and the treasonous acts of Patrick Lien."

"I was already going to do that. I've spent the morning writing notes and a draft."

"Good. That way it will sound like it actually came from you."

Who would know, though? For almost ten years, everyone in Aecor believed I was dead.

"Do you want to start with the letter or the transfer? I've already had a nearby space cleaned out, since I don't think he'd stand to be very far from you."

"Let's move him first."

"For the best, I think. With the prince's recovery, it won't be long before talk turns to you and this creature. *I* know you slept on Tobiah's chair last night—a scandal on its own—but as far as anyone else is concerned, you slept in your rooms while the wraith boy was here, too."

Then surely the damage was already done. No matter how I felt about it, my reputation *did* matter. People of the Indigo Kingdom already had so little respect for me, and one day I'd have to marry for the good of Aecor—assuming I ever got back my kingdom and the wraith didn't destroy everything first.

"I'm shocked I have any reputation left to tarnish." I

shrugged and jerked a thumb toward the music room door. "But to protect my delicate sensibilities, will you make sure he's dressed before we go in?"

James wrinkled his nose. "You think he's naked?"

"I told him to put on his clothes, but that was this morning."

"Great." James knocked on the music room door and entered.

A loud *whack* hit the wall: wood crashing. "What are you? You don't belong." The wraith boy's voice rose an octave. "Leave!"

I threw open the music room door to find the piano bench in pieces and a gash torn in the wall paneling. James stood just a step away from the demolished bench, his chest heaving. "Wil." He spoke between clenched teeth. "I think you should send Ferris for more guards."

The wraith boy's posture shifted with unnatural quickness. One moment, he was huge and hunched, ready to grab the piano and hurl it at James. The next moment, he resumed his normal size and shape, and bowed his head. "My queen. Hello."

"What's going on?" I forced the shaking out of my voice, keeping it low and dangerous.

"This"—the wraith boy bared his teeth at James—"*man* is not what he says he is. He's deceiving you, my queen. He's not *real*."

I moved inside the room and stood beside James. Splinters of wood caught in my day dress, scraping the floor. "James is my friend, and he's in charge of palace security. If he sees you as a threat, he will not hesitate to force you to leave."

The wraith boy sniffed. "Only my queen commands me."

"And I would agree with him. Behave." I spun and exited the room, head high, but my heart thudded painfully against my ribs.

James closed the door after him, softly. "This is a problem. No one bothered him last night once he hid under your bed, but what if they had? What would he have done?"

"I don't know." My head buzzed with adrenaline. "What do you think he meant about you? You're not who you say you are? As far as I can see, you're the only one of us who is exactly what he says."

"I wish I knew." Worry and confusion crossed his eyes, but he said nothing more. I wasn't his confidante, after all. "Give me a moment while I have the hall cleared. Then let's get this over with."

SEVEN

DEAD QUIET. THE hallway through the Dragon Wing had never known such silence.

Men wearing Indigo Order uniforms lined the walls, their faces hard and drawn. Swords gleamed in the bright light, every blade lifted and angled in a guarded stance. The steel was polished to a mirror finish, and none of the men so much as moved as James, the wraith boy, and I strode down the hall. Sergeant Ferris came behind us.

A canvas sack covered the wraith boy's pale head, since some of the soldiers were superstitious about his eyes.

They were too unreal, too wraithy.

One look and he could turn you into a wraith beast, or a glowman.

If your eyes met his, you'd go blind.

James had related all the rumors while we prepared the wraith boy for transfer, and now we walked on either side of him, daggers pressed against his throat. Of course, the daggers were just for show because I had no idea if being cut or stabbed would hinder him at all. He wasn't *human*.

"One, two, three, four . . ." The numbers were muffled under the wraith boy's sack.

"Stop it." I elbowed the wraith boy.

"I'm counting the weapons," he murmured, as though it were completely natural.

"Do it silently." It wasn't as if he could see the weapons through the sack, right?

He sighed, but was quiet as we continued through the hall.

Twenty paces ahead, a pair of guards opened a plain, almost hidden door. They waited with their hands on their swords, expressions stoic.

Seventeen paces to go. A soft, breathy noise came from under the sack, like someone exhaling in quick bursts. Like smothered laughter.

Fourteen paces.

"Not real." The sack twisted as though the wraith boy was looking at James. "Not real."

Ten paces.

"Shall I order you to stop speaking?" I asked.

The wraith boy gasped and fell silent again, but a bubble of tension formed around him, an almost physical force.

Six paces.

The wraith boy's knuckles were white at his sides. Tendons stuck out along his hands and wrists. He was a thing of tightening fury, growing denser before he exploded.

Two paces.

James signaled the soldiers to back away from the door, then glanced at me behind the wraith boy, his eyebrow lifted. I nodded, and he stayed put as I took the last step to the storage room.

It wasn't much of a space, just a narrow area that used to hold cleaning supplies or linens—something maids or servants might need to fetch quickly for the royal family.

"In you go." I lowered my dagger and touched one hand to the back of the wraith boy's jacket, not firmly. Still, the tension in the wraith boy's hands and shoulders unwound, and he stepped into the room without protest.

He stayed right by the door, just on the other side of the threshold, and didn't move.

"You can take off the sack. Leave your clothes on."

He reached around and up and plucked the sack off his head, then held it at arm's length as though it were a filthy thing. The canvas sloughed on the floor where he dropped it.

"You are to remain in this room. If you leave, there will be consequences."

"There are already consequences." The wraith boy pulled forward like a cat exploring a new territory: cautious but confident.

"Do you need to eat?"

"My nourishment comes from your affection, my queen." He knelt at the back of the room, his face just a breath away from the wall. "I found a secret. Oh, I like it."

What?

No, maybe not knowing was better. As long as he was happy. "There will be guards outside your door. They won't bother you, but if you yell or bang on the walls or do anything

I won't like, I'll tie up your hands and put the sack on you, and *order* you to stillness and silence. Understand?"

The wraith boy looked over his shoulder and smiled. "I understand, my queen. I'll see you soon."

I moved out of the way as James shut the door. As soon as it latched and he turned the key to lock it, the anxious air whooshed out of the hall, as though a door and lock could keep the wraith boy contained.

James handed the key to me. "I have a spare, but I don't anticipate wanting to use it much."

I put the key in my pocket.

While James dismissed the guards, I strode toward my quarters once again, keeping my shoulders thrown back and my chin high. Sergeant Ferris followed in my wake.

"He didn't do anything yesterday in His Highness's parlor. Or on the way to your apartments." Ferris's voice was soft under the hum of men talking and moving about, relief in their stances, as though they'd just dodged a hurricane. "Why the fuss?"

"Were you present when all the wraith in the city came together and formed him?"

"No."

"Or when he grew larger and leapt across the courtyards onto the crown prince's balcony?"

"No."

I opened the door to my room. "He's not a tame animal, Sergeant Ferris."

"Indeed he's not." James hurried up. "Sorry, my lady. My chance to see your famous pen at work will have to wait."

"Is something wrong?"

He shook his head. "I'm being called away for coronation security. Many of our allies are coming to attend the memorial and coronation following. I have to ensure their safety. But I should have some free time tomorrow morning if you'd like to visit my new office."

"New office?"

"It came with the promotion." James grinned.

"Have a big stack of paper waiting. But let's make it afternoon. I plan on sleeping late." I inclined my head toward the bag of Black Knife supplies, which still rested on the table in my sitting room.

"I should have guessed." James gave a deep sigh. "Afternoon it is. But what I said earlier: you shouldn't."

We both knew I would.

I spent the rest of the day with the Ospreys.

Their suite was as grand as I'd expected. Four individual bedrooms, all with fireplaces, fully stocked bookcases, and even a sculpture of an osprey made of Aecorian sandstone.

"Wil!" Carl looked up from inspecting a crystal vase. "Have you *seen* what they just leave lying around here?"

"Mind your manners." I grinned when he put the vase back on the large central table. "If you're going to steal, take something that's *not* in your room. You don't want to incriminate yourself, do you?"

"At least wait until we leave the palace before looting it." Theresa stepped forward, shaking her head. "Show them a few shiny things and they turn into ferrets."

"Hey, Rees." I hugged Theresa, relieved to see that she—and

the others—had bathed and eaten; the plates and trays on the table were licked clean. All of their scrapes and cuts had been treated, and they wore clothes that looked as though they'd been borrowed or handed down from other young nobles—a little worn, but still finer than anything they'd had in the last ten years.

"Come to check on us?" Kevin asked, towering over the two younger boys. In the months since Melanie and I had come here, Kevin had grown taller, and now he was all knees and elbows.

"That's part of it." I motioned at Carl again as he slipped a fork into his pocket. "Did you not hear what I just said?"

He hung his head and unloaded his pockets onto the table. Silverware, crystals pried from a candlestick, and a jar of ink with gold flecks in it. "That one was for you." He tapped on the lid.

My heart melted a little. "Actually, I have a job for all of you." When they took seats at the table, I began. "Crown Prince Tobiah is going to ask me to sign the Wraith Alliance."

Connor pulled in his shoulders, making himself smaller.

I leaned onto the table, my weight on my palms. "I don't know why my parents wouldn't sign, or my grandparents. Even if there's anyone left in Sandcliff Castle who might know, how could I trust them to be honest or objective?"

"What will you do?" Theresa asked.

I took a steadying breath. "I'm going to sign the Wraith Alliance, but first, we're going to make some changes."

"What kind of changes?" Kevin asked.

I drew a folded paper from my pocket and slid it toward him. "These, for now. But I'm sure I will need more than this."

He snatched the paper and skimmed the list. "So you want us to study the treaty and look for other changes you might need?"

"Exactly." I'd have to get them a copy, but that wouldn't be difficult. "Read it. Study it. Ask questions. I want you to become more knowledgeable about the treaty than anyone else in the world."

Theresa grimaced. "So no big demands, then. Do you want us to run laps around the city wall while carrying packs of rocks?"

I flicked a crumb of bread at her. Carl caught it midair and ate it.

"I'm going to do everything in my power to negotiate for control of Aecor. Tobiah is agreeable, but his uncle is not. Obviously, he doesn't want to let it go."

"When will you start?" Kevin stood, my list of treaty amendments in hand as he began to pace. "Now?"

"Our presence here is the start." I forced encouragement into my voice. "But formal negotiations will begin after Tobiah's coronation. That's fine. He'll have more power when he's king. And we'll need it." I hesitated. "There are some who will try to delay negotiations longer. We must practice patience."

Carl shook his head. "I hate patience."

"That seems foolish," Kevin muttered. "Delaying truce negotiations. Patrick's going to start a revolution in Aecor."

"It is, but Skyvale and Aecor are far apart. It's not as much of a concern for most people here. And in spite of the Inundation, the Indigo Kingdom is still in a much stronger position than Aecor. Whatever troops Patrick manages to mount will be nothing compared to the might of the Indigo Army."

Theresa bit her lip. "You make Aecorian independence sound impossible. Was there ever any hope?"

"I don't know." I sighed. "Patrick made it sound inevitable. But he has that inevitability about him, doesn't he?"

"I miss it," she said. "That certainty of knowing we were right and we would take back our kingdom because of our rightness—that was comforting. Now everything seems so gray."

"It's awful." I forced a minuscule smile. "I'm going to hire a tutor for the four of you. They should be able to help you understand any confusing parts of the document, in addition to instilling some courtly manners into you barbarians. Maybe help with the grayness of everything, too."

"A tutor." Carl made a face.

Kevin looked up from his pacing, and the list he'd been studying. "The crown prince will allow for magical experimentation to help solve the wraith crisis?"

"He's desperate. The Liadian refugees have left Skyvale, probably heading for Aecor. Already the southwestern edges of the Indigo Kingdom have fallen to the wraith. Soon, everyone will begin looking east."

"Who will be using magic? All the flashers in Skyvale get captured. Or—" Kevin cocked his head. "Are the rumors about you true?"

A sinking feeling washed over me. I'd intended to tell them, but his tone of betrayal was cutting. "Some of the rumors are true."

"What do you mean?" Connor whispered.

"I am a flasher. I've always been, but I've kept it hidden. I try not to use my power."

All around the sitting room, jaws dropped as I told them about the locust attack in the wraithland, what I'd done there, and how the wraith became a boy.

Theresa covered her frown with a fist. "I'm not sure where to start asking questions."

"I know." I sank back into a chair and sighed. "There's a lot to take in."

"Will we get to meet the wraith boy?" Carl asked.

"You don't want to." If I could, I'd keep him locked in his room forever. "I just wanted you to know the truth—from me, not from rumors."

"That's why Tobiah is willing to amend the Wraith Alliance." Kevin dropped to a chair again, knees banging the table. "Because even if it's just rumors, your power is public now, and if he wants you as an ally, he has to justify it by making sure magic is allowed under special circumstances."

"Can it work?" Connor asked. "Could your magic help stop the wraith?"

I rubbed a spot of tension from my neck. "Maybe. I don't know. What I did before—it was messy. Uncontrolled. I had no idea what I was doing because it was too big. And while I could try it again, I don't know if I *should*. How much more wraith did I create by doing that?"

Of course, they had no answers.

I spent the rest of the afternoon with them, showing them around the public areas of the palace, warning them of who to avoid angering. Sergeant Ferris and another guard trailed after us, not quite invisible as I familiarized my friends with the library, ballrooms, and training rooms.

A copy of the Wraith Alliance had already been delivered by the time we returned to their suite, so I bade them good evening and happy studying. Only Kevin looked truly chipper at that.

At the door, I turned back to the small group and forced cheer into my voice. "Remember, we're here as ourselves—*not* to steal valuables—but be guarded, too. Secrets remain secrets."

They all nodded.

"Remember your lessons."

"Our lessons on eating the fastest?" Kevin asked.

"Or picking pockets without being detected?" Theresa offered a sly smile.

"Or," Carl mused, "do you mean the lesson we all learned when you and Mel threw knives at us and we had to be faster?"

"They were wooden knives. They wouldn't have hurt you. Much." But I smiled, just a little, even though Melanie's name hurt. "Your lessons on *manners*." With an utterly false grin, I left the suite and hurried back to my own quarters, Sergeant Ferris close on my heels.

Maybe Tobiah and his mother had been right: I should have gone after Patrick when I had the chance.

In my bedroom, I tore open the bag of Black Knife supplies. The clothes and boots were my size, the latter with black ospreys embroidered around the top, invisible except to those looking closely. The belt—black, obviously—accommodated several weapons and tools, including *my* daggers that had been taken, my grappling hook and line, and a pouch with coiled silk cords. There was also a tiny handheld crossbow and a black-handled sword, meant to fit in a baldric strapped across my back.

Though several of my own tools were included—I recognized the worn parts on my lock picks—everything else was just like Black Knife's, the size adjusted to fit me.

"And to think," I muttered at the array of darkness on my bed, "I really just wanted pants."

There wasn't a note, but I knew where everything had come from. Tobiah must have worked for weeks to put together this bag.

By the time the Hawksbill clock tower chimed twenty, four hours before midnight, I was ready. All in black, my braid shoved down the back of my shirt, I armed myself and stepped onto the balcony.

I pushed up to my toes; the boots were stiff with newness, and felt strange around my calves, but the treads were deep and strong. I could climb.

Scanning the darkness for guards, I hooked my grapple to the rail, near where it met the palace wall, and rappelled to the ground. My toes touched with barely a sound, and I coiled the line to stow it on my belt. There was a place for everything. Beautiful.

Soft voices carried on the breeze, coming from the far end of the palace. There'd be more nearby. In the forest. In the ruins of the outbuildings. I avoided them all as I moved toward Greenstone.

Usually this area was quiet after dark, when most of the workers returned to their homes, but now, a soft rumble of life swirled up to my perch on the Hawksbill wall. Voices skittered from inside doorways and alleyways where people huddled under threadbare blankets and in patched caps and jackets.

Heart sinking, I sidled along the wall to plan my path through the district. I shouldn't have been surprised to find dozens—maybe hundreds—of displaced people hiding here, and I couldn't begrudge them the meager warmth they found in the lee of wide buildings. But their presence was going to make my investigation more difficult. Greenstone roofs were harder to navigate than those in Thornton and the Flags. Here, the buildings were spaced to allow for large carts. Railroad tracks sliced through a few streets, though in the century since trains had been decommissioned, much of the iron had been stripped to put to better use.

"Hush," someone hissed.

The hum of voices was silenced immediately, replaced by the *thud thud* of boots on pavement. I pressed myself flat on top of the wall and watched over the slight lip in the stone.

Lanterns held aloft, police poured through the streets. "This is a restricted area!" one called. "No one is permitted to be here after dark. If you leave now, you'll receive no punishment. But if we have to remove you by force, you'll be taken out of the city and not permitted inside again."

No one moved. The police formed lines down the center of the streets, peering into the shadows, though with those lanterns their night vision must have been shot. "We know you're here. You have two minutes."

I held my breath, waiting to see if anyone would follow orders, but the homeless pressed tighter into hiding places, and shadows shifted in the grime-smeared windows of abandoned buildings.

The first minute slipped by.

"Just step into the light," one of the officers shouted. "This area is dangerous. You can't stay here. But there are shelters in the Flags."

Another officer spoke directly to a doorway where I'd seen a family huddled. "Greenstone was hit hardest during the Inundation. It hasn't been fully secured—"

"Nowhere has been secured but the palace!" a man shouted. "Even the shelters are dangerous! We live in terror while nobles plan more parties!"

Chaos exploded in the street. Homeless scattered in all directions, some toward the police, who lifted their batons to defend themselves, but most just ran away. Shoes—even bare feet—pounded the paving stones as people began grabbing their belongings, lifting children, and vanishing around buildings.

Icy wind breathed in from the west; I shivered on the top of the wall, watching as lantern-wielding police officers took off after the homeless. Screams and cries sounded as people were captured. Officers cuffed some to poles, and cuffed others to them, creating a chain of prisoners guarded by a few officers while the others chased down those who'd escaped.

After the initial frenzy, the roads below me grew quiet, with only the occasional sob and cough to break the long note of wind cutting around corners.

I peered down to count how many the police had arrested.

There were several groups of people huddling together—families, some with small children—and many who looked like strays caught when their friends or relatives took off.

There were just over a hundred people, plus others the police were dragging back. Only three or four police stood guard.

A handful of officers was no problem, but even a hundred frightened people could turn into a mob. I'd seen people react to Black Knife's presence before; often it was friendlier than I wanted to risk. Anyway, I doubted Black Knife being revealed as Princess Wilhelmina would win me favors. But what could I do? I was just one person, and wasn't finding Patrick more important?

Shame welled up inside me. Allowing the police to force these people out of the city was as good as giving my approval.

Cold air seared the back of my throat as I felt my hip for the small crossbow. Just because I couldn't risk going down there didn't mean I couldn't give the prisoners a chance to escape.

I cocked the string and loaded a small bolt into the slot, then adjusted my position and took aim.

The bolt struck home in an officer's leg, and a new wave of panic erupted as prisoners screamed and struggled to free themselves. My next four shots went quickly, all but one finding their targets.

"Black Knife is here!" someone yelled, followed by, "Black Knife will save us!"

I pulled away from the edge of the wall. With any luck, the prisoners would simply steal the keys to their cuffs and leave.

Officers returned to help their injured comrades. I took a few more leg shots before springing up to run along the wall, away from the action.

Wind pushed at me, but I ran until the shouts and cries faded with distance. Only when I was alone again did I pause and crouch, and survey the northernmost edge of the district before me. My breath came in short gasps, mist on the winter air.

Had I done the right thing back there? Had I done enough?

There were so many people displaced because of the Inundation. Maybe Greenstone wasn't the safest district in the city, but surely it was safer than being forced outside the walls, or into crowded shelters in the Flags. With new refugees coming into the city, the shelters would only become more congested.

I shook away those worries. I'd done what I could.

Cautiously, I descended to the street and kept to the shadows, making a straight line for Fisher's Mouth. It felt good to stretch and push, to allow the night air to surround me. Everything in the palace seemed so far away now.

But the problems of Skyvale were more real than ever. Though the Inundation had lasted only a few hours, the effects were profound: ripples of stone cascaded down a warehouse, as though the building had been momentarily molten; squirrels that had been darting over buildings were now petrified, caught mid-crouch forever; and pipes meant for plumbing had partially phased through the factory where they were manufactured, giving the huge building a weirdly skeletal look.

This was the beginnings of the wraithland.

I hurried on.

Fisher's Mouth was on the far side of the district, where the river coursed under the city wall. During the day, fishermen ran nets across the water. They could usually be persuaded to part with some of their catch in trade for items pinched from the more wealthy areas of Skyvale.

Tonight, the fishery was empty, save the sounds of a handful of people downstream. A child shrieked at the chill spray of water while adults scolded the girl. *"Be quiet,"* they said. *"Police will find us."*

I slipped along the river, wrinkling my nose against the pungent odor of fish. It was hard to believe no one had come to steal a few meals, given the dozen barrels ready to be transported into the building.

One look into the barrels told me why. Brown-striped bass and red-bellied sunfish lay dead, but where the fins had been, now were hands. Tiny and brown, with webbed fingers. Their dead-eyed stares were strange, too. They looked human. Some had lips.

Bile raced up the back of my throat, and I turned away.

I had brought this here. My magic. My wraith boy.

Wary, I crept into the building, hands on my daggers. Heavy, wet darkness wrapped around me like a cloak, and I paused to let my eyes adjust.

A feral cat yowled. A deeper growl followed, coming from somewhere behind crates of packaged fish, which rose along the walls. The damp storage area and the crash of the river rushing at my back absorbed the sound.

I checked behind every crate and barrel, but found no sign of Ospreys. The small office had been raided for its supplies.

In the distance, the clock tower struck twenty-three. I needed to get back soon. Thanks to the additional patrols, I'd have to give myself plenty of time to sneak back through Hawksbill. Rushing had gotten me caught before.

Halfway out the door, I stopped. A creamy white paper fluttered in a draft, caught against the wall. Even dirt streaked and crumpled, it was easy to see the paper was too fine for a fishery.

I smothered a laugh as I rescued the palace stationery from the wall. The list was in Melanie's handwriting, as familiar to me as her face and voice.

Locations, numbers: I knew this list. These were the resistance groups in Aecor, the list we'd copied during our infiltration of Skyvale Palace, though in a different order than the one I recalled.

"Oh, Melanie." I folded the paper and tucked it into a pocket. "You are so clever."

I could almost hear her reply: *"Say it again."*

Melanie *hadn't* turned. She hadn't. Patrick must have wanted to move on as soon as she'd returned, so she'd left something she knew I'd be sure to spot.

Outside, I started for Hawksbill, but a scream downriver cut the silence.

My heart thundered as I hurtled myself toward the shrieks and adults' shouts for the girl to move away from the water. Someone called for the police to help.

I sprinted along the riverside, the churning waters inky at my right. In the high moonlight, spray glittered as a creature lurched from the depths. It was all sinuous scales and snapping jaws, some terrible fusion between lizard and snake, and as big as a hunting hound. Enormous fangs dripped black fluid as it plodded toward a group of six or seven people, including the girl who stood just ahead of the others. Carefully, she backed away, one long slow step at a time. The whites of her eyes shone wide.

"Come on," urged the adults. "Just a little farther."

The girl whimpered, making the wraith beast leap forward—

"Hey!" I jumped out from the shadow of a melting wall,

sword sliding out of its sheath without a sound.

The wraith beast whipped around in a flurry of claws and fangs and scales, wraith-white eyes trained on me. The girl spun and ran for her family; they caught her with reaching arms and dragged her from the beast's sight.

It slithered toward me, four stubby legs pumping to keep up with the rest of its body. Wraith had not been kind to this creature.

My sword shone between the beast and me, an unfamiliar stretch of steel. I'd wielded swords before, but not this one, and never one so fine. The hilt fit my hand perfectly, though; like the rest of my gear, it had been made to suit me.

I held my ground until the beast reached me, and then sliced my blade through the air. The creature leapt back, a tangle of long body and tail, but righted itself quickly. The milky eyes fell back on me as it came around to my left side. I brought my sword inward, but the blade connected with a fang and slid down the length with a *shing*. The black liquid dripped from the tip of the fang, catching on the edge of my blade. Metal sizzled as the venom dribbled down the steel.

Swearing, I thrust my sword at the creature, catching its nostril. It shrieked and pulled back, almost as though reconsidering its chosen prey.

"You ruined my new sword," I grumbled, turning slightly to dip the sizzling metal into the dark river to neutralize the venom.

The snake-lizard hissed and struck; I barely had time to lift my sword in defense as the fangs crashed toward me. Water droplets glittered as the blade arced through the air and caught the creature's mouth, cutting a long gash across its face. The creature made a sound between a scream and hiss before it whipped around me, toward the water.

I couldn't let it escape. It would just find someone else to attack, and I could only imagine the kind of damage it would do if left unchecked.

I lunged for the beast, driving my blade deep into its side. Too deep. As I tried to pull it out, the snake-lizard swung around and the hilt slipped from my hand. My sword went skittering across the paving stones and the creature crouched as though to leap onto me.

My hands found my daggers, but I was too slow. The wraith beast's front feet hit my shoulders and I dropped backward, trapped under the weight of the beast. Venom glistened on the fangs—

I jerked up my daggers and thrust both blades into its throat at the same time as I brought up my knees and shoved it off me.

The beast rolled away, blood pouring from its wound. It didn't attack again, but its chest still moved with breath.

One eye on the creature, I bent to rinse my daggers in the river, then find my sword.

"Black Knife," someone breathed.

I spun to find the family still huddled in the entrance to the street, away from the fighting, but close enough to watch.

Without a word, I snatched my sword and dragged the good edge along the snake-lizard's neck once more, just to be sure. White mist poured upward; I moved out of the way.

"Thank you, Black Knife!" one of the women called. "Thank you for saving my daughter!"

"Don't." It was my fault the wraith had come. My fault Skyvale had been transformed into this nightmare. My fault it would only get worse.

EIGHT

THE NEW PATROLS were such that climbing up the front of the palace would be asking to get caught. That made my placement at the back of the Dragon Wing convenient for sneaking in and out.

When I climbed to my balcony and hopped over the rail, my landing was silent.

A light shone in my sitting room.

I'd left the suite dark, but obviously *someone* was there now. A maid might have come looking for me. Sergeant Ferris, maybe. Still, I made sure my daggers were loose in their sheathes, ready to draw, and I slipped into my bedroom.

The room was dark. Quiet. I stepped deeper into shadows as I pulled the door closed behind me.

Light flared: the gas lamps in my bedroom hissed to life, and a portly man appeared next to the door.

Prince Colin Pierce. *Overlord* of Aecor Territory.

My daggers were in my grasp before my eyes finished adjusting to the blaze of light, but Prince Colin held up a hand. "Better not, Princess. There are those who aren't certain you weren't the one to assassinate my brother."

"You know I didn't touch King Terrell."

"Do I?" He motioned toward my weapons. "Seems to me you're capable of reaching well-guarded locations *and* using those weapons. You are Black Knife, after all. Suppose I was to tell someone I saw you creep back into your quarters like a thief, after you were forbidden to leave the palace? What would everyone say?"

"Suppose you did. Oh, how awkward the questions would be for you. Why were you sneaking into a young lady's bedchambers? What were you planning on doing to her?" My pulse thrummed in my throat; that was a *good* question.

He narrowed his eyes. "Oh, dear Wilhelmina. All I'd have to say is that I was invited here. You want Aecor, after all. Everyone knows what you are: Black Knife, identity thief, flasher, wraith animator. You can claim you're trying to apprehend your friend Patrick Lien as much as the rest of us, but for all I know, you were out there warning him of our plans and tactics."

Blood pounded through my ears. He was *threatening* me. "What do you want?"

His smile crept up like a spider. "What do you think I want?"

"Aecor. You want me to give up my kingdom." And if I resisted . . . then what? He'd instigate an investigation? Happen upon proof I'd gone out as Black Knife?

"I want you to give up everything." His gaze slid down my body, as heavy as a touch. An awful crawling sensation made my breath hitch and my body shudder. Phantom hands slithered across my skin, bruising, and a desperate part of me wanted to rush forward and drive my daggers into his chest.

With a sharp smile, Prince Colin's attention lingered on my legs. "Sleep well, Your Highness. I know I will." He bowed and left the room.

Head spinning, I took two deep breaths and listened to the sound of his footfalls through my sitting room. In *my* space.

Rage fogged my vision as I darted after him, my blades ready. But he was already halfway through the door as I approached, and he shot me a chastising look, as though reminding me how utterly stupid it would be to kill him.

"By the way, I heard an interesting rumor about my nephew. He was near death when I visited, but he seems quite recovered now. Interesting that you were present for both his miraculous healing, and that of his bodyguard."

With that, he strode down the hall, leaving me to stand in the empty doorway with my daggers clutched in my fists.

No one was standing guard. Where—?

Prince Colin. Of course.

He could threaten all he wanted, but he couldn't keep my kingdom.

And I'd kill him before he touched me.

I was out my door before dawn.

Sergeant Ferris stood there with his arms across his chest, his brow drawn inward. "What happened to Chris?"

"Who?" I scanned the hall, but other than the pair of guards at the wraith boy's storage room, it was empty. There wasn't even anyone standing outside Tobiah's suite, though perhaps he was not as opposed to having them stationed inside.

"Your overnight guard. And while I'm at it, where were your wraith monster's guards?"

"Ask them." I brushed past him, focusing on keeping a neutral face as I strode down the hall.

Sergeant Ferris followed. Of course. "Where can I take you?"

As if he was the one doing the leading.

"I have an appointment with Captain Rayner."

"This afternoon."

"He'll see me this morning."

Further questions were met with silence, and only the dagger I'd strapped around my leg—hidden beneath my ocean-colored gown—helped the anxiety building in the back of my thoughts.

The wood-paneled walls of James's new office were bare except for a small plaque with the Rayner family crest engraved in brass, and a line of bookcases along the interior wall. They were filled with histories and tactical studies and atlases.

"Your Highness." James stood, his tone formal when I entered the room. "Please, come in and sit. Excuse the mess. I haven't had much time to set up in here." He motioned at the papers and books strewn across the desk. And in spite of his invitation, the chair on my side of the desk bore a tray piled with empty teacups and caddies.

"Captain, a moment?" Sergeant Ferris lingered in the hall.

James picked up the tea tray and took it with him. The door shut, muffling their voices, but they spoke only a moment before James returned. "Sorry. I got shoved in here yesterday afternoon.

It's an upgrade from my previous office; this one has a window."

"Nothing to be sorry for. You've had a lot to do since you awakened." It was hard to believe that had only been two days ago.

James's eyes lowered and he nodded. "Yet I feel the same as ever. You're *sure* you didn't have anything to do with my awakening?"

"Absolutely sure." It had to be a coincidence that he'd opened his eyes just as I touched his hand. "Have you made any progress finding Patrick?"

"We know where he *isn't*." James sat behind his desk and cleared a small canyon between us.

Melanie's list hissed against the desk as I slid it toward James. "I found this last night."

His face was dark as he tilted the paper toward him. "Where did you get this?"

"Fisher's Mouth."

He released a long sigh. "All right. What is it?"

"It's a list of Aecorian resistance groups. It's rearranged, and I think the new order indicates where Patrick is going first."

"Can we trust this?" He tapped the first location. "We need to be sure before sending people there."

"I trust Melanie." I pulled out the letter she'd left in the Peacock Inn. I'd read it a hundred times already; most of it was what we'd covered when we met. "The list was her second attempt to leave information for me. She was delivering this when we bumped into each other outside the inn."

He skimmed the letter. "The Red Militia?"

"That's what he's calling his army."

"Your army, he hopes." James folded the letter. "You can't give in to his demand. If you declare yourself queen, you'll provoke Prince Colin. And then Patrick gets what he wants."

"But if I don't declare myself queen, Patrick marches against the Indigo Kingdom."

James narrowed his eyes. "Are you planning to—"

"No." I sucked in a breath. "Not right now. It just seems like I can't win, no matter what I do. Prince Colin won't give up Aecor, and Patrick won't wait for me to claim it myself. Unless Patrick is arrested, there's going to be a war, and I don't know what side I'm supposed to be on."

James rubbed his temples and nodded. "All right. I'm sorry. I wasn't thinking about how this puts you in just as bad a position as the rest of us." He placed the list of resistance groups on top of a pile of papers. "I'll have people sent to these locations, though even Melanie says Lien doesn't trust her. If he told her this was the order, it could be more false information to lead us into a trap."

Better than anyone, I knew about lying on paper. "I understand. But meanwhile, I can't sit around and do nothing."

"I wouldn't call your nightly excursions 'nothing.'" He shook his head, but at least he wasn't giving me a hard time about it. "What of the letter to Aecor?"

"I've been making notes."

"Good." James glanced at the small clock on a mostly empty bookcase. "I have some time now, if you want to get started. There are writing supplies here somewhere."

He gave me the comfortable seat behind the desk while he leaned on the edge, keeping out of my light.

"Tobiah would be better at helping you with this, but he's still trapped in his quarters. His guards are already asking questions, but they know better than to voice their misgivings to anyone."

"What about the messenger? Alain?"

"I had him followed. He eventually ended up with Prince Colin, but if they've done anything with that information, I haven't heard about it yet."

When I closed my eyes, I saw Prince Colin in my quarters last night. His sneer. His satisfaction. The memory made me shudder.

James didn't notice my discomfort. "Anyway, I've sat in enough meetings to be able to assist you with this."

"And I've forged enough official documents—"

"*Really?*" He looked incredulous. "Do I even want to know?"

I smirked. "No, actually, I haven't. Nothing like this, anyway. But I know the tone and language, more or less. Still, it might be wise to have someone look over it before copies are made. I'd hate for anyone to think I didn't know how to be a proper princess."

James rolled his eyes. "I can't imagine there's any question about what kind of princess you are, Your Highness. Now, let's get this finished. I have both a memorial and coronation to coordinate security for, you know."

I flapped my hands at the other chair. "Sit down and try not to drool on the paper."

Once James was settled beside me, I arranged my writing supplies around a sheet of creamy, white paper. It was smooth, without blemishes or watermarks, and unlined. While the palace had plenty of fine paper, sending a letter like this on paper with an Indigo Kingdom crest on top might not be the best idea.

With a ruler, I began measuring line widths and making guide marks. Once the sheet was covered with pale hashes, I adjusted the ruler and traced faint lines.

Usually, the necessary carefulness of lining pages calmed me, but now my tired mind wandered toward the reason for this work. What would the people of Aecor think when they realized I was alive? Would they feel betrayed, like I'd purposefully neglected them all these years?

More importantly: what would Patrick tell them when my letters arrived? How would he twist my words until people believed what he needed them to believe?

No doubt he'd win them over just as he'd won the Ospreys. And while his goals were noble, his method for achieving them—

At what point had he become a *murderer*?

Betrayal burned through me as I shoved my pen into the ink. The words I'd rehearsed flew out in a flurry of anger.

This is an official statement . . .

I, Princess Wilhelmina Korte, daughter of King Phillip and Queen Angela Korte, and rightful heir to the vermilion throne at Sandcliff Castle . . .

Crown Prince Tobiah Pierce, House of the Dragon, son of the late King Terrell the Fourth, was previously unaware of my survival. Now he wishes to help me set matters right between Aecor and the Indigo Kingdom, and we will begin discussion with his uncle, Prince

Colin Pierce, House of the Dragon, Overlord of Aecor Territory . . .

Patrick Lien, son of the former general Brendon Lien of the Aecor Army, has acted without my consent. He is to be taken into custody and held until my arrival, at which point I will conduct a trial and determine how he can begin atoning for his crimes . . .

The Red Militia is an unsanctioned force . . .

I wrote, furious scrawls and flourishes and scratches across the page. The scrape of my pen against paper was an awful, unlovely sound, and I couldn't remember why I usually liked it. Why it usually grounded me and brought me peace.

Giving in to Patrick's demands was out of the question; it would only give him more power. But I wanted to take back my kingdom with that kind of directness. Trying to persuade Prince Colin to let it go peacefully was never going to work. He'd already said he wouldn't give up Aecor.

And that he would retaliate if I insisted on claiming it.

My hand cramped around the pen, and my wrist throbbed from holding it too stiffly as I added the final lines of my letter.

I stopped short of signing my name.

I couldn't make my hand shape the W. What did my signature even look like? Small? Clipped? Wild? Was it legible, or a scrawling mess of ink?

And the letter itself . . .

The letter was like the storied monster of many parts, with my handwriting fading from tidy to flourishing, from flowing to scratching where I let the ink run out. Teardrops marred the words, darkening the paper, carrying the ink in translucent blots across the grains. There were at least seven different hands.

"You didn't sign your name." James spoke softly.

"I haven't signed my name to anything since I was a child." My fingers shook as I lowered my pen, ink still pooled in the nib. "Patrick never let me; he never even told any of our tutors or trainers my true identity. I was a secret."

James rested his forearms on the desk as he leaned toward me. "You aren't a secret anymore. You can sign if you want." He glanced at the monster of a letter, his unspoken words plain in his expression: I could try again.

"I don't know what my signature looks like," I whispered. "I know priests', generals', merchants'. Even yours and Tobiah's. But not my own."

"And your handwriting?" He studied the letter, tracing a wild flourish with the tip of his finger. Ink smudged onto his skin. "After you were taken to prison that night, I said I'd found samples of handwritings. I asked which was yours."

"None of them." They'd all been practice, and because sometimes I simply needed to feel a pen in my hand, and the glide of tines on paper.

James's smile was faint but encouraging as he took my abandoned pen and cleaned off the drying ink, leaving black smears across the cloth. He offered the pen to me, handle first, as though it were a knife or dagger. "What does your writing look like, Wilhelmina?"

"I don't know." The pen fit in my hand, but it felt like a new and unfamiliar thing now. I didn't know what to do with it. "I've spent so long writing as everyone else, I've never learned my own handwriting. Even as a child, before all this, I mimicked my tutor's hand."

Was I really that pathetic?

"I don't even know my own handwriting." The mess of paper filled my vision, blurring as I blinked back tears.

"Maybe it's time you learn."

"It's such a stupid thing to worry about." I placed the pen on the table. "I've gone my whole life without thinking about it. Why should it bother me now, when there are so many other things—more important things—going on?"

James shook his head and slid my writing supplies to the other side of the desk. "I don't know you very well. Like Tobiah, there's a lot that you keep hidden. But I consider myself intelligent and observant, which means I've been able to determine a few things about you over the weeks you've been at the palace—in your various disguises."

I waited.

"You take pressure very well. Now that I know your identity, I can only imagine what a trial it must have been sharing a meal with military men, or meeting Prince Colin. Or even just coming here, knowing Tobiah might recognize you from the One-Night War. I've seen you improvise. I've seen you fight. And you've endured Lady Chey's best efforts to force you to leave." He dragged in a breath. "But not even the strongest can defend against *everything*. Not forever.

"You have a million different things trying to stop you, Wilhelmina. A million different things chipping away at your armor. I don't know this Patrick of yours, and I'm in no position to help you win back your kingdom. Your romantic entanglements are your own business, and I don't know *what* to do about your pale friend down the hall. In truth, I'm allowed to take very little action, except what my cousin commands, or when his life is in danger. I'm of limited use to you, but there may be one thing I can help you with."

It seemed to me he sold himself short. But I leaned forward. "I don't need to be rescued, James. I can do this on my own."

"Yes." He smiled gently. "I've heard that about you. And I don't want to rescue you. I want to give you an option."

"For what?"

"Tell me what happened on the balcony the other morning, when my people tried to take you to safety."

My jaw clenched. "I didn't want to be taken anywhere. I had to help."

"Wilhelmina." My name came out a sigh. "You froze. You panicked. Your wraith boy came to kill anyone who touched you because you were so afraid."

Was that what had happened? The wraith boy had been chasing Patrick until the guard had grabbed me.

"I've never seen you panic, not once."

I studied the grains on the desk. Of course he hadn't seen me panic. I'd been in the wraithland alone. Only the wraith boy had seen what I'd done, how weak I'd been when the locusts arrived.

"Was it because—" James hesitated. "After you were captured in Hawksbill, when the men searched you?"

I didn't say anything.

"I heard you throw up in your cell after I'd walked away. I know about the bruises." He glanced at my arm, healed now.

"The other morning, the guards grabbing you reminded you of"—he hesitated—"a situation that made you feel violated."

My jaw hurt from gritting my teeth.

Even more gently, he said, "It took away your sense of control."

"They took advantage of my incapacitation." The words came out like venom.

"I understand."

But he couldn't. Not unless he'd ever been groped between the legs and his assailant justified it by insisting there could be a hidden weapon there. Not unless he'd ever been surrounded by frightened people who mistook his identity, and wanted to touch him for hope or luck or curiosity. Not unless someone had crept into his bedroom at night, threatening him.

"It's all right that you feel this way. It's all right if you hate the people who did this to you."

Did I hate them? Besides Prince Colin, I didn't even know their names.

"I remember who was there," he said. "I'll have them released from the Indigo Army and Order."

And Prince Colin? Could anything be done about him?

My list of allies was frighteningly small, and my list of enemies was already full; I didn't have room for bitter, dishonored soldiers.

"Don't. Just leave them." I didn't want to see them again, but I wasn't sure I'd recognize faces from that day. Anyway, the safety of our world was more important than my discomfort. "I appreciate the gesture."

James shook his head. "It's not a gesture. The security of this palace and its inhabitants is in my hands. I'm sworn to protect Tobiah, primarily, but my duties go beyond that. You're not only a current resident of this palace, but foreign royalty. In protecting you, I am protecting Tobiah and the castle. I'm also your friend, Wil. At least I hope so. I'll do everything in my power to make sure you feel safe."

I would never feel safe. Not here.

"What happened to your guard last night?"

I lifted my chin. "Ask him."

"I intend to. But I'd rather you tell me."

"He was dismissed, I assume." I was glad it hadn't been Ferris. I didn't care for him, but James appeared to trust him, so at least that wouldn't change.

"By whom?"

I shrugged. "How should I know?"

"Prince Colin."

I forced the edge of panic out of my voice. "What makes you say that?"

"Because there are very few people my men will take orders from, and even fewer people who could rattle you. You look like you haven't slept in a week. What happened?"

"Well, he wasn't visiting for tea. But I've dealt with it."

"I have no doubt."

"He knows Tobiah is recovered."

James let out a long sigh. "And *I* will deal with that." Then he removed the mess of papers from the desk and slid a ruler onto the next fresh sheet. "Now, I know you enjoy my company more than anything else in the world, but we've both got a lot of work to do. And since you've never been one to refuse show-ing off your skills, let's see the famous pen at work. This time in your handwriting. And if you don't know what it looks like, maybe it's time for you to learn."

NINE

JAMES, THE OSPREYS, and interviewing tutors kept me busy the rest of the day. As soon as I found someone who wasn't terrified of them—a young woman named Alana Todd—I made introductions and left her to the demanding task of taming Aecor's high nobility.

My rooms were quiet when I returned from a long dinner with the Goldberg family, only the faint hum of gas greeting me as I turned on the lights. I was alone.

A knot in my chest eased. I had to trust James and Ferris, and whoever they assigned to guard my apartments at night. Someone different this time, I hoped.

The clock in my sitting room struck twenty-two. Outside, the sky was dark and wind battered the balcony door with its near-winter chill.

As I pushed aside the curtains, an envelope slipped to the

floor. A W shone gold against the black paper.

My heart thundered as I took the letter to my room and pulled the flap free. The letter itself was regular white paper with black ink, but the packaging was so very . . . Black Knife.

Wil,

After your quick exit yesterday morning, I found the letter you left in my room. I decided to reply in kind, and leave it in a place you're sure to find it. My next delivery won't be so obvious.

Regarding my first letter to you: I'm glad you understand. I knew you would. With or without your kingdom, you are a queen; you understand what it means to take risks and make sacrifices for the good of your people.

I also wanted to say: thank you for the risks you took for me. You don't even like me—Tobiah me—but I know what you did during the shooting and after. (James told me.) Everything about our relationship is complicated right now, you suddenly the lost princess of Aecor, and me . . . you know. After the way I treated you, in all regards, I didn't deserve anything you did for me.

Wilhelmina, while going after Patrick might have been the more logical choice, you had no reason to believe he would elude the Indigo Order so quickly. Had our positions been reversed, I'd have done the same as you.

In complete understanding,
Tobiah

I reread the letter a few times before I wrote a response, changed clothes, and went out the balcony door.

Chill night pressed around me as I weighed my options. Go down and around and back up, a sure way to get caught, or go over.

Over it was.

Senses straining to hear any sound beyond the groaning wind, I tossed my grappling hook and climbed the wall. At the top, I threw an ankle over the roof and rolled up and onto the slate tiles.

With my line and hook secure at my hip, I belly crawled up to the peak, using chimneys to give me boosts and resting places so I could listen for patrols.

The other side of the roof was more dangerous, with bits of glass sticking up from between the tiles like traps. Moonlight caught the larger shards, but others were hidden. I took care as I crept down, my feet first. The sword on my back limited my movement, but I could compensate.

I sidled along the edge of the roof until I sat above the balcony I wanted. There were no guards stationed there; the thud of boots was far off. Wind blew in cold and sharp. I pushed off the roof.

I landed in a crouch, gloved fingertips brushing the stone. Hardly a sound.

There was no trace of blood on the balcony; some poor maid had already scrubbed and rinsed the stone. Nevertheless, the place where Tobiah had fallen drew my eyes and held me captive. We'd almost lost him.

The balcony door was locked, but the mechanism was easy to pick. It took only half a minute to open the door and slip through the curtains that caught the breeze. Quietly, I latched the door behind me.

Something spun me and slammed me against the glass. A flash of gold hovered above, and a blur before me resolved into an ashen face.

Tobiah's palm pressed against my breastbone, and he had his antique spyglass raised like a weapon. His eyes were wide, a little wild, until he recognized my mask, and we both glanced down to find my daggers out of their sheaths, pointed at his stomach.

The blades dropped to the rug with soft thumps. I hadn't even realized I'd drawn them.

He heaved a breath and tossed the spyglass onto his bed. "Wil." Then his arms were around me, strong and solid as he buried his face against my neck. "You shouldn't be here."

And he shouldn't be holding me like this, not when he wore nothing but a loose nightshirt and trousers, and his hair was messy from sleep. Still, my heart galloped as our bodies pressed close together, and my fingertips explored the ridges of his spine. He fit me.

"What are you doing here?" he whispered. "Never mind. Don't answer. Just don't be a dream."

"Would dream-me threaten to split you from stomach to sternum only a day after healing you from a similar injury?"

He gave a soft snort. "Yes. Absolutely."

So he dreamed about me? Often?

I closed my eyes, indulging in the feel of his body pressing on mine for only a moment more before I whispered, "We can't do this."

He groaned, like reality returning, and stepped back. "I'm sorry." His eyes followed me as I knelt and retrieved my daggers. "I wasn't thinking."

Forgive me.

He'd probably just been relieved I wasn't Patrick, creeping in to finish the job. But word was that Patrick had been spotted in one of the piedmont villages across the mountains. He was far from here.

I slid my daggers into their sheathes and took the folded note from my belt. After a second's hesitation, I offered it to him. "I thought if you were going to sneak letters into my room, I should get to have fun, too."

"And you had to dress as Black Knife to do it?" He took the letter, holding it like it might bite.

"Do you know how hard it is to climb over the roof while wearing a gown?"

A sly smile welled up in the corner of his mouth. "None of the court ladies will loan me a gown to try."

"Well that's just rude of them." I started a slow circle around him, making a show of inspecting the way his nightclothes hung over his lean frame. If he wore a bandage anymore, I couldn't see it beneath the dark blue silk. "I have a dress you could borrow, but your hips are all wrong for it."

He offered a playful frown. "Now who's rude? You'll have to learn to be more diplomatic if you're going to be queen, Wilhelmina." He moved to a bookcase, struck a match, and lit a candle. Soft firelight glowed across the angles of his face, revealing the tension that still hung about his jaw and neck and shoulders; this teasing was a desperate attempt for normalcy, though between Tobiah and me, or Black Knife and me, I couldn't tell. He looked like one and acted like the other, and wasn't truly either.

Why couldn't they have been separate boys?

"Now tell me the truth." His tone was somewhere between the prince who always got what he wanted and the vigilante who was never denied. "James already warned me that you asked for clothes and weapons, and while I'm flattered you wanted to deliver your letter personally, in the middle of the night, and looking like you're ready to do battle . . ."

My fingers trailed along the balcony curtain, making shadows ripple. "It's no trouble. I was going out anyway."

This scowl was real, and fully the disapproving prince. "Don't."

I crossed my arms and thrust back my shoulders. "You can't stop me."

He slammed the letter onto his bookcase and stalked toward me. "What are you going to do? Steal a horse and ride to Aecor after him? He's *gone*, Wilhelmina."

"He tried to kill you!"

Tobiah pressed his fingers against my mouth, just thin silk between us as he tilted his head toward the bedroom door. "There are guards." His voice was low, but demanding. "Let the Indigo Army and Order handle Lien. It's their job."

I wrenched myself away from him. "You really think your men will find him?"

He gave a deep nod; his expression betrayed only weariness. "I must believe it."

"How well do you trust them? Do you know all your soldiers personally? The police?" Images of police marching through Skyvale wormed into my mind: the lights in the street, the homeless hiding in shadows, the children shivering in the cold night.

"Of course I trust them. I don't know them all personally, but I know their superiors, and they know their men."

I shook my head.

"What's this about, Wil? What's going on?"

"It's nothing." If he'd ordered the mandatory evacuation of Greenstone, he wouldn't appreciate what I'd done last night. "Ask your police what's going on."

"Ah. What did you see?" When I didn't respond, his tone shifted toward practiced patience, the same as a prince would use to handle a hysterical subject. "I've seen police abuse power, and I've always made sure they're removed from their duties. That's one of the reasons I kept on as Black Knife. I wanted to help people."

"And then you came back here to your palace and safety. You haven't lived with that fear. Not really. Last night, I saved a girl from a fused wraith monster—both a lizard and a snake— and if I hadn't been there, she would have died. There are people squatting in Greenstone, hungry and more afraid than ever, and the police won't let them stay."

He opened his mouth to deny it, thought better of his words, and bowed his head. "I will investigate. Although when I do, I expect to see a report saying Black Knife made an appearance?"

"No one saw me directly. It'll be rumor only."

"I'll deal with it." Tobiah closed his eyes and blew out a sigh. "Teach me about this life, the one you say I don't understand. I care about my people and I want the best for them, if it's in my power to give it to them."

"Of course it's in your power."

"If only that were true." He took my shoulders, gentle but firm. "I'll learn, but you need to learn, too. You're going to be queen one day, and you'll crash straight into the limits of your power if you're not careful. I put on the mask because of those limits, and I can see you doing the same thing right now."

"I need this mask. *They* need it, too."

His voice turned kind, cautious. Not the prince, but not the vigilante, either. "Where is it coming from? This anger."

"Everywhere."

"It will cripple you, Wil." He let his hands slide off my shoulders. Down my arms. "Trust me."

Trust me. Forgive me. He needed so much from me, and what could it accomplish except my broken heart?

"Promise me you won't go into the city tonight."

"I can't make promises for anything that far in advance."

"That's five minutes from now."

"I don't know how I'll be feeling in five minutes."

He closed his eyes and seemed resigned. "I suppose I wouldn't act any differently."

"I have to do *something*. I feel disconnected staying here. Restless. Useless." How could I explain it? "He almost ruined *everything* for us—our kingdoms, our ideals, our lives." I whispered, "He tried to kill you."

He swallowed hard, fingers unconsciously brushing his

stomach. Ghosts of pain fluttered across his face. "Take off your mask."

I shook my head.

"Please. I want to see your face."

"And I don't want you to." Beneath the mask, my skin felt hot and sticky and damp.

Tobiah caressed my cheek. "Letting other people do their jobs doesn't mean you're doing nothing. You have people here who need you, Wilhelmina. Your Ospreys, for example. And if you want Aecor, you're going to need to fight for it in a new way. My uncle won't give it up easily."

No. Prince Colin wouldn't. He'd been controlling Aecor for almost ten years, doing whatever he wanted with it. He'd even sent Aecorians to fight the wraith beasts and glowmen at the edge of the wraithland—farmers and fishers and people who had no idea how to defend themselves from monsters.

How would I persuade anyone the kingdom was mine? Let alone someone who'd gotten used to controlling it?

I'd wanted to negotiate peacefully for my kingdom, but I didn't even know how to begin. What use was I in the palace? In the city, I could do good. In the city, I could help people.

"You're going to be a queen," said Tobiah. "At some point, you'll have to accept that you can't personally take charge of everything. You'll have to trust people to work for you."

"I trusted Patrick."

"A difficult lesson. You'll be more careful next time."

"My Ospreys are looking into changes for the Wraith Alliance, and Melanie is spying on Patrick for me."

He offered a faint smile. "That's a good start, Wilhelmina."

With a deep sigh, he stepped away from me, like distance could snap our tense connection. "Why don't you sit? You can be comfortable and surly at the same time." He dragged out his desk chair to face me.

"And you'll be in your nightclothes for our whole argument?"

"I'd protect my modesty, but I'm afraid you'd flee while I was indecent in the dressing room."

There would be no imagining Tobiah indecent in the dressing room. Not from me. "I don't flee. I evade."

"Call it what you want."

"Thank you for the invitation to argue, but your diversionary tactics won't work on me. Patrick or no, there's work for Black Knife in the city."

There was no denying that.

"You could come with me," I said. "Unless— Does it still hurt?"

Eyebrows drawn inward, he pressed his palm to his stomach. "It feels like it should hurt."

I stopped myself before reaching to press my palm atop his.

"I need to prepare for the memorial and coronation. But I will join you sometime. I promise." His eyes locked with mine. "I miss Black Knife."

"Me too."

TEN

PRIOR TO KING Terrell's memorial, Theresa arrived at my quarters to prepare for the ceremony. I donned one of the splendid gowns the late king had commissioned for me. It had been part of his plan to marry Melanie and me to some lucky noblemen from the Indigo Kingdom and fulfill his obligation as our guardian. He'd done his best, truly.

The entry hall was packed with people waiting for their carriages. A few people glanced my way as Theresa and I arrived, with Sergeant Ferris in tow.

The other Ospreys hovered around the far edges of the hall, shifting uncomfortably in their suits. When Connor spotted me, he straightened and nudged the others, and all three boys grinned as they moved to join us. "Wil! Rees!" As if they hadn't seen us in weeks, rather than hours.

The display drew curious looks, which none of them noticed.

"Took you long enough to get ready." Carl's pockets hung

heavily at his hips. Later, I'd have to find the owners of whatever he'd stolen, and have everything returned discreetly.

"This way, Your Highness." A footman signaled our carriage's arrival, and I pulled my lacy shawl tight as our group snaked through the room.

Our carriage was white with red trim, and spread-winged ospreys painted across the top. Tobiah's doing, no doubt.

The interior was crowded, but the journey was mostly pleasant, with the boys admiring a clock installed in one of the doors. Carl and Kevin held a whispered debate over what was worth more: the gold clock hands, or the gear mechanisms in the back.

I reached across them and drew the curtains over the windows. Although it was unlikely we'd be threatened during the journey through Hawksbill, I didn't want my rowdy companions to draw too much attention. The bright birds on the carriage already singled us out.

If Melanie had been here, she'd have filled the ride with polite talk and charm. As it was, Kevin asked questions about which nobles lived in which mansions, and Sergeant Ferris—perhaps unwisely—told him about fortunes made by inheritance, entrepreneurship, and scandal.

The sun touched the horizon just as we reached the Cathedral of the Solemn Hour, an immense pre-wraith building of sparkling white stone. It boasted three square towers, innumerable arches, and hollow places where there used to be windows. Those had been blown out the night of the Inundation, and not yet repaired with emergency shipments of glass from nearby towns and cities, like the palace and several Hawksbill homes.

Now the empty frames looked like eye sockets. Blind, but always watching.

Our carriage pulled up the long drive, past gardens and statues and fountains. An enormous line of people waited at one side of the drive, some standing, but most sitting. Police officers paced the line, keeping people from spilling into the carriages' path, but as we rolled by, voices lifted. Just before the curtains fell shut, I caught glimpses of people pointing at us.

"They'll be admitted later," said Ferris. "Once all the nobility is seated."

"They look like they've been there all day." Connor slumped in his seat. No one needed to confirm it.

The carriage halted and the door was opened. Sergeant Ferris climbed out first, wearing a hard scowl as he touched the sword at his hip. He gave a wary look around, then motioned for the others to emerge. Connor, Carl, Kevin, and Theresa. Once they were out, I scooted toward the door.

The thunder of voices crescendoed as the line of people waiting to enter the cathedral watched me emerge from the carriage. Their cries slowly shifted into a recognizable chant.

"Wraith queen! Flasher queen! Wraith queen!"

A few chanted "Black Knife!" instead, but they were the minority. Most shoved their fists into the air.

The Ospreys surrounded me, while Sergeant Ferris took the rear as we walked up the steps, past the first groups of people. Their chanting continued, and several reached out as though to touch me.

My heart thrummed and my hands slipped to my hips for daggers, but all I felt was silk and wool. I breathed through a surge of panic. Even unarmed, I could defend myself. There was nothing to be afraid of.

The police inserted themselves between the crowd and me, brandishing short swords and batons. It killed me not to look over my shoulder as I ascended the wide staircase, but I forced myself to remain tall and face forward, as though I trusted the police to protect me.

"Wow." Connor brushed my hand as we climbed the last stairs. "They really don't like you."

"They're punishing me for the Inundation."

"But you didn't want anyone to get hurt."

I squeezed his hand. "My intentions of learning about Mirror Lake were noble, but my choices in the wraithland were unwise. My choices led to the Inundation. I didn't want people to get hurt, but they did anyway."

And now the wraith was closer than ever. Already in the Indigo Kingdom.

"You could tell them what happened?"

"I think that would make it worse." I shushed more questions. This wasn't the time.

Though the cathedral was massive, there was but one door in the front, and it was tall and narrow—so narrow we had to enter in single file. Every sound from the outside became muffled as soon as I crossed the threshold. The entrance hall was just as majestic as the exterior, with gilt friezes and marble statues of unnaturally tall saints; they rose up the walls, praying over the people passing beneath them.

Small alcoves and drops of shadow hung to the sides, but a silver light shone ahead, keeping my attention as I led the others.

The Ospreys' gasps and exclamations of awe were music nipping at my heels.

At the end of the hall, a white-robed figure ushered us around a corner, where others waited to direct us into the sanctuary in the center of the building.

An immense chamber opened before me, lit by great chandeliers. Hundreds of benches sat in rows on the main floor, with thousands more in tiers along the sides and on balconies. Columns created aisles down several series of steps with long landings, all leading to a dais in the center. There was nothing on it but a shallow pool guarded by a low, gold rail.

The benches in the front were already filled with the king's family and closest companions. The queen stood near the dais, statuesque in her floor-length gown. Nearby, Tobiah held his hands behind his back and his shoulders squared. Dark hair hid his downturned eyes as he spoke with Lady Meredith, though whatever they said was too soft and obscured to hear over the echoing footfalls and other voices.

She reached for his hands in a comforting gesture that seemed to have little effect. The king was dead. His father was dead. And tonight there would be no forgetting it.

I was halfway down the stairs when Tobiah glanced up and found me watching him. Even from this distance I couldn't miss the naked ache in his gaze. Not a crown prince. Not a vigilante. Just a boy who'd lost his father and might face the rest of his life in a spiral of questions: What if he'd been there? What if they hadn't argued that night? What if . . .

Our gazes held for another moment before Meredith twisted

in her seat to see what had distracted him. My name took shape on her lips.

Another face turned up, this one with a scowl. Lady Chey said something, drawing Tobiah's and Meredith's attention.

Theresa leaned close and kept her voice low as we continued down the stairs. "What was that?"

"You know all about Chey," I said, but we both knew she hadn't meant Chey. People didn't share long looks with princes they'd written—at length—about hating.

A minute later, I took my seat in the second row, right behind the duchess and countess. Chey turned her head just enough to show me her profile as she muttered to Meredith, "Don't you think it odd they were invited here, considering it was an Aecorian under Wilhelmina's command behind King Terrell's murder?"

Meredith pulled back and scowled. "That's inappropriate, Chey."

Whether she meant the comment in general, or specifically saying it at the memorial, I couldn't tell. I just glared at the back of Chey's head as Meredith shot me an apologetic glance.

"After the wedding," Chey added, "you'll have more influence over who he invites to important events."

"Chey!" Meredith's tone turned warning.

"Speaking of your wedding, we should discuss your dress and all the arrangements soon. Winter solstice isn't very far, and there's a lot of planning that must be done."

"This isn't the time to speak of such things." But Meredith glanced toward Tobiah, her expression warming.

Quiet mutters echoed in the chamber as everyone arrived. Skyvale nobility, those from other cities in the kingdom, and even foreign. There was a duchess from Laurel-by-the-Sea, followed by nobility from kingdoms farther to the north. Gowns and suits rustled in the echoing quiet.

The late king's brothers were already here, sitting in the first row with other family members. Prince Colin was too deep in conversation with Prince Herman to notice my arrival, thank saints. No, tonight their eyes moved toward Tobiah, who stood stiffly, but with far more ease than anyone who'd been shot just days prior should.

What had the messenger told them? How much did they know?

Theresa nudged me and jerked her chin toward Connor, on the other side of her. He pointed upward.

I lifted my face just slightly, my gaze traveling along a column across the dais. The marble split into several sections at the top, splaying like finger bones as the column flared and held the roof. It looked like a great forearm and hand; they all did.

And the ceiling itself—

I bit back a gasp as chandelier light caught veins of gold laid into the white stone. The ceiling was covered in angles and swirls that shimmered in strange patterns. But when I blinked and my eyes refocused, the gold lines resolved into constellations.

Astronomy lessons fluttered in the back of my mind. Five stars connected into the rood, and a nearby woman dipped water from a well. As the chamber grew warm with the heat of bodies, I let my thoughts wander to an overlook on Sandcliff Castle where my father taught me star stories. Radiants' Walk was what he called it. It had been cold that first night, with the breeze coming off the Red Bay. He'd bundled me in his own cloak and stayed by my side as I peered through the pre-wraith telescope.

I'd forgotten about that. But now, more than ten years later, the memory surfaced with the salty scent of the ocean and the cries of gulls as they found their nests. I could almost hear my father's voice in my ear as he showed me how to find the boat and the cup.

I missed him. Those moments. That innocence. The security of my father's arms around me.

Now Tobiah's father was gone, too.

I dropped my attention back to the dais where Tobiah was speaking to his mother, urging her to sit and rest until the memorial began. But even as she started to acquiesce, a hidden piano struck a chord, and other instruments joined a moment later. Strings, winds, and bass.

As one, the audience stood.

As the priests came down the aisles, the thousands of attendees sang a remembrance hymn. Our voices swelled through the chamber, crashing and crushing like waves. I shivered with chills; on the dais, Tobiah looked just as haunted.

By the end of the song, a handful of priests stood on the dais with the queen and crown prince. They dipped their hands into the pool of water and began a prayer. Everyone sat as the memorial began with an account of Terrell's life and his honors.

A few times I had to shush Carl and Connor, while our neighbors flashed glares, but the chamber was noisy with the movement and breath of thousands of others. My mind wandered to the city rooftops, the open sky, and pure, uncomplicated vigilantism.

The cathedral was silent as one speaker stepped down and another stepped up. But before he could begin, water erupted up from the pool and the entire building trembled. Gas lamps shuddered and flickered, and droplets of water sprayed over us.

Screams sounded from all around the cathedral, echoing in the huge chamber. Guards surged to their feet, swords drawn as they moved toward their charges.

"Under the bench!" I pushed Theresa to the floor. Just as I was reaching for Connor, shouting the same instructions, a booming voice came from above.

"Wilhelmina!"

I knew that voice.

"You cannot hide from me!"

Dread seeped into every piece of me as I stepped backward, away from Theresa and the others, into an aisle—and into enormous white hands.

A sharp crack ripped through the chamber, and everyone looked up as the golden heavens split in two.

ELEVEN

I WRENCHED MYSELF away from the wraith boy just as the first pieces of stone fell. "Everyone get out!"

My cry was lost in the cacophony of screams and collapsing stone. The whole cathedral was cracking open like an egg. Chunks of gold and marble plummeted to the dais, landing in the empty pool with a deafening crash and shudder. Frigid night wind blew in, and the whole space stank of wraith.

Priests fled, their robes fluttering. James dove for Tobiah, who was reaching for his mother. The three of them, along with another handful of guards, made their way into the aisle. More stones from the roof crashed down, spraying white dust like snow. Their clothes were coated with it.

On the stairs above, people packed so tightly there was no way to get out.

"Wil!" Connor screamed for me as Sergeant Ferris heaved him into Kevin's arms. Half covered in white rubble, my bodyguard picked his way toward me, drawing his sword as though he could do anything against the wraith boy. It was too late.

There was no way we could escape before the building came down on us.

I spun and grabbed the wraith boy's forearms, giant and straining against the clothes I'd given him. "Stop it."

"I can't." He grinned down at me, too wide, too wild. A fist-sized stone dropped overhead, but he batted it away before I had the chance to move. "There's no way to stop it."

Streams of people poured up the aisles. The gap overhead widened as the building shuddered again, shaking loose a chandelier. The fixture smashed into the bench where Tobiah and his family had been; I couldn't see them anymore, not through the debris and a fire that raged upward. Heat blasted through the cathedral.

"Stop the building from collapsing." I gripped the wraith boy's wrists. "Put out the fire."

"That's not within my power."

Thousands of people were going to die because of him—because of me.

Unless I did something.

People trampled one another in their efforts to reach the stairs. Real starlight shone through the gap in the roof, faraway points that lined up exactly with the gold constellations.

My Ospreys were leaping across the benches, heading toward the exit. I couldn't find the royal family, but several more chunks of the roof had fallen in. Another crashed downward, crushing nearby benches. The floor shook, but I stayed on my feet because of my grip on the wraith boy, who wasn't bothered by the chaos he'd caused. He calmly stepped sideways as a head-sized chunk of roof broke off and flew at me; he blocked it with his own body.

I had to stop this.

I dropped to the floor and pressed my hands against the stone. "*Wake up*," I said, and immediately, my breath grew short. My vision turned to fog. "*Stay together. Do not break. Do not fall. Do not shake.*"

One last stone thudded to the floor, creating a new plume of dust, but the building stopped moving. The constant low rumble ceased. Wind sucked the smoke and dust from the upper reaches of the sanctuary, revealing the impossible.

Great hunks of marble clung to the jagged crack in the ceiling. Chandeliers clutched the golden constellations like iron spiders. The splayed-finger tops of the columns crept out and linked with one another, as though in prayer.

My heartbeat was hummingbird quick in my ears, but the cathedral had animated. It had done as I'd commanded.

Slowly, bracing myself against a bench, I stood and whispered, "*Now smother the fire.*"

Debris slithered across the floor and rained from the ceiling, focusing on the burning chandelier. The air began to clear as dust settled. The intense heat faded as flames died.

"*Get off any people trapped. Make a path so everyone can escape.*"

There were voices all around, people sobbing and screaming, but they were distant now—or maybe it was just me. Black shapes dotted the edges of my vision with that last command,

and all I could see was the wraith boy's enormous grin as he looked around the chamber.

My arm trembled as I sucked in deep breaths, but my head wouldn't clear. It was too much, bringing the entire building to life, commanding it again and again. I had to get out. I had to put the cathedral to sleep.

I groped for the next bench, ready to drag myself out.

White hands fell on my shoulders, and I jerked away. My elbow caught a stair as I landed and glared up. "Don't touch me. *You* did this, so don't touch me. Go back to your closet."

The wraith boy scowled but vanished, leaving me to regret the command. Now I was alone, on the floor, and unsure whether I could actually get up on my own.

The building groaned with the strain of keeping itself together. I groaned, too, as I turned over and began crawling up the stairs. Masses of bodies writhed up and ahead, people escaping the doomed cathedral, but they were just blurs of color against the white. They were all so intent on escape that no one would look back. No one would notice I wasn't with them.

Or if they did, they were grateful. The wraith boy had brought down the cathedral because of me.

I dragged myself up, using a bench arm to steady myself. My gown tangled in my legs as I staggered and caught myself on the next bench, and then the next and the next. Dizziness spiraled around me, and my limbs were all cold. Numb. My knees wouldn't straighten.

"Wil!" The voice seemed to come from far away. I lifted my eyes, but everything was dim.

Warm arms wrapped around me. "Hurry."

"Rees?" I dug my fingers into her shoulder. Another familiar figure hefted me up on the other side. "Kevin?" My Ospreys had come back for me.

Step by slow step, they helped me climb the stairs. When the lights flickered out—someone had turned off the gas—and everything went dark, Theresa yelped in surprise, but her grip remained strong.

We reached the hall where the crowd caught and slowed in the narrow space, but now that the building had stopped shaking and everyone thought they were out of immediate danger, the pace was steady. There was less trampling.

"Does she need help?" That was Connor's voice. Thank saints, he was safe.

"I'm fine." My words didn't come out any stronger than a mumble, but I could still speak.

Swimming in and out of consciousness, I let the others help me through the hot, noisy halls. It seemed like forever, but finally cold air hit my face as we reached the exit.

But for the moon and stars and lanterns that dotted the huge crowd below, the cathedral yard was dark. Even so, and in spite of my tunneled vision, I could see the legions of police and guards in Indigo Order uniforms. Officers on horseback rode through the crowd, iron shoes striking the cobblestones with mind-jarring rings. They urged the crowd back, farther from the building frozen mid-collapse.

I was the last one out. Those ahead surged down the staircase, throwing themselves into the safety of the crowd.

"Go," I rasped, drawing myself out of Kevin's and Theresa's arms. Connor and Carl stopped on the stairs and turned around, their eyes big. "I need to finish this."

They left me standing in the narrow doorway of the living cathedral; only when everyone was a good distance away did I press my palms against the stone. I spoke with every drop of authority I possessed.

"Go back to sleep."

The cathedral sighed and sloughed inward.

Blackness thundered through me, dropped me, and my body—limp and useless—rolled down the stairs, too fast for anyone to catch me.

I opened my eyes and rolled to my back—and dropped another stair before I realized I shouldn't move. The impact forced the breath from my lungs. I blinked and breathed until my vision focused, only to find a dark figure standing over me.

"Princess Wilhelmina Korte, you are under arrest for the destruction of the Cathedral of the Solemn Hour. Do not resist or we will be forced to use drastic measures." The voice was too familiar. After Prince Colin's invasion of my rooms, I would always recognize his voice, his stance, and the slimy way he said my name.

I managed to lift one hand and show him my little finger.

People crowded around us, protesting my arrest. The Ospreys' voices, plus others I didn't know. "She needs medical attention," said Sergeant Ferris.

"She needs to be contained!" Prince Colin's voice went ragged. "Look what she did here!"

"Yes." Tobiah's voice carried across the yard. "Look what she did here."

My heart sank. Him too?

I pushed myself up so that I was sitting, more or less. I was still light-headed and my body ached with incipient bruises, but if I was going to have to explain myself, I should try to be upright for it.

Connor took my shoulders to stabilize me, question in his eyes, but I shook my head. I didn't need healing, and the *last* thing I wanted was for him to demonstrate his ability in front of all these people.

The crown prince strode up, James and a handful of guards behind him, and lifted his gaze to the destruction behind me.

"Look at what she did here." The prince swept one hand toward the cathedral. His movements were intentionally stiff as though still recovering, but he commanded attention with the way he held himself and lifted his voice. "How many people were nearly crushed to death? How many were nearly consumed by the fire? How many were nearly trampled?"

The crowd seemed to hold its breath.

"And how many of us were saved because of her quick action?" Dust covered and sweating, the prince climbed the last few stairs and shouldered aside his uncle. He offered one hand to me.

I wasn't ready to stand—not at all—but I placed my hand in his and let him take most of my weight as I lurched to my feet. My stomach flipped and I started to sway, but Tobiah planted his free palm flat on my back, steadying me.

"Are you all right, my lady?" His words were soft, for me only, but everyone was watching and listening. The police held up their arms, creating a human barrier.

I met the prince's eyes and squashed the quiver in my voice. "Thank you, I'm fine."

"Relieved to hear it." The way his fingers closed over the cloth on my back said he knew I was lying.

Prince Colin pushed forward again. "The wraith creature was here for her," he said. "And she used magic. *Magic*. This flasher will draw more wraith to us."

Tobiah raised his voice again. "Princess Wilhelmina saved countless lives. While the wraith boy was indeed seeking her, she cannot control all of his actions. We all know how unpredictable wraith is. It wasn't her fault the wraith boy came to find her any more than it's a farmer's fault when his cattle stampede." Tobiah motioned for a decorated police officer to approach. "Chief Tegen, question everyone and find out whether there's anyone missing. Get everyone's names and addresses, and should any-one *dare* insist my dear friend Princess Wilhelmina is responsible for what happened here, you are to correct them."

I cleared my throat.

Both men glanced at me; Tobiah's expression softened.

"You're right, of course." He looked back to Chief Tegen. "Forget I said that last part. Find out what they believe hap-pened tonight. But if anyone makes any sort of threat against Wilhelmina's life, you will alert me immediately."

"Of course, Your Highness." Chief Tegen bowed and departed.

"Where's the carriage?" Tobiah asked James.

"It should be here momentarily."

"Very good."

"Nephew—"

Tobiah faced his uncle, his arm still around me. "Thank you for your concern, but I have everything under control." His tone grew bored. "You're free to return to the palace."

Prince Colin narrowed his eyes at me, the crown prince's arm around me, and the close way we stood. But he left, a handful of guards in his wake.

It seemed like ages before the carriage arrived, clattering down the cathedral drive. It was a small vehicle, meant to quickly slip through narrow streets.

"This way." Tobiah guided me down the stairs, and when I stumbled, he dug his fingers into my side and took all my weight. I hoped no one else could see how weak I was, but I was too exhausted to do much about it, or protest that the prince was still recovering.

Tobiah escorted me down the last set of stairs only after the police had pushed back the crowd. My knee gave out as I climbed onto the velvet-covered bench, but his support never flagged. One hand curled around my shoulder. The other kept tight around my fingers. He held me steady.

When I was seated, I looked over his shoulder to see what remained of the cathedral.

Most of the building had collapsed, with only a few walls reaching up like teeth of a mutilated lower jaw. Rubble pattered down the stairs, and dust blew in a pale column over the destruction.

Two centuries of service as a religious sanctuary, built using pre-wraith methods we'd never again be able to replicate, and one of the most iconic buildings of Skyvale: gone. Destroyed in less than a quarter hour.

"I'm sorry," I whispered.

"Don't apologize. You saved everyone from being caught in that." Tobiah angled himself toward the others. "Sergeant Ferris, please escort Her Highness back to the palace. Her companions will take the next carriage."

Theresa stepped forward. "I'd like to remain with Wilhelmina." Her gaze darted to my hand, still in Tobiah's.

"I'm sure that would be a comfort to both of you. Please." Tobiah moved aside, releasing my hand as he helped Theresa into the carriage. Sergeant Ferris took the seat next to Theresa. Tobiah addressed him. "Place extra guards on both Aecorian suites tonight. Hallways and balconies. If anyone abandons their posts tonight, they will be dishonorably discharged from the Order and their families disgraced. Understood?"

"Yes, Your Highness."

Tobiah offered me a curt nod, and then shut the door. "James!" he called, voice muffled now. "Come with me. We need to—"

Whatever he said was cut off by the *clip-clop* of horse hooves on cobblestone as our carriage jerked into motion. Lights blurred past as we drove through Hawksbill. I closed my eyes.

My bedroom was dim and quiet when I sat up, covers puddling at my waist. "Rees?"

The door opened and her silhouette filled the space. "I'm here."

"I need something to wear." My body was stiff and bruised from the fall, but I pushed myself up and began rolling my shoulders, ignoring the stabs of pain that flared across my body.

"You need rest."

I shook my head and winced. "No, I need to yell at the wraith boy."

She searched my wardrobe and found a plain blue dress. "The prince stopped in, but you were sleeping. Sergeant Ferris had to carry you into the washroom, and then put you in bed after the maid and I cleaned you and changed your clothes."

I glanced at the nightgown and robe I was wearing. Other people had changed my clothes while I'd been unconscious. Theresa was one thing, but the maid? I didn't even know the maid's *name*. Maybe I was less terrifying to her now that I'd proven myself mortal, at least.

"How long was I out?"

"Several hours." She hung the walking dress over her forearm as she elbowed the door open wider to reveal the clock in the parlor. "Five, it looks like."

"Ugh." Stiffly, I switched dresses, then allowed her to brush and braid my hair.

"This pain isn't all from the fall. Does magic usually affect you like this?"

"No." I rubbed my temples. "Never, except in the wraithland. But I don't usually awaken large things. It's mostly been small items. Candles. Toys, when I was a child. The Hawksbill wall was difficult, but nothing like this." My hands fell to my sides. "When I awakened the wraith, I immediately passed out for hours. Or a day. I don't know."

"There has to be a better way to recover than unconsciousness."

"One would think. Perhaps it's simply another muscle, one

131

that requires regular exercise to build up to larger feats." At least I could see straight now. And walk, even if I was unsteady. "Perhaps the effects would have been less dramatic if I'd practiced more growing up, or if I wasn't also keeping that awful wraith boy animated." I shrugged and checked my reflection in a cracked hand mirror. Bruises and scrapes marked my face, but I looked presentable otherwise. "Stay here. The supply room isn't far. Ferris can escort me."

"Are you sure?"

No. "Yes. I don't want you or the others anywhere near him, if we can help it." I shoved the mirror into my pocket, glass side down.

"Will you tell him to"—she frowned—"go back to sleep? Would that kill him?"

Could one *kill* something like that? Did it count as murder?

"Not here. He'd turn back into wraith and we'd have another Inundation. I'd have to take him back to the wraithland, but I don't know what would happen then. Wraith is already infecting the Indigo Kingdom."

She dropped her eyes.

"Other things I bring to life, like a match, aren't really *alive*." I hoped. "They just do what I command. But he—he's alive. Aware. Sentient."

"So what will you do?"

"For now? Yell."

TWELVE

SERGEANT FERRIS AND the other guards jumped out of the way as I burst from my suite and into the hall. My whole body ached, but I wouldn't show it—not right now—so I kept my strides long and even, my chin tilted up. Heavy footfalls sounded behind me.

"Your Highness?" Sergeant Ferris caught up easily.

"Just stay out of my way, Sergeant."

I slammed into the wraith boy's room, adrenaline buzzing through my system as the door clapped against the wall and came bouncing back. I turned on the light, illumination flaring over the small space.

"You!" My voice was ragged. I hoped I looked stronger than I felt.

The wraith boy was curled up in an empty corner of the room, so small that the clothes swallowed his gaunt arms and body. His feet were bare, and he shivered as though cold.

"Wake up!" I snatched a discarded shoe and hurled it toward him, aiming just above his sleeping form. It hit the wall with a *bang*, and the wraith boy peered out from under his arm.

"Hello, my queen. I'm pleased you've come to see me."

"Get up."

He rose to his feet, unnaturally graceful and deft in his motions. He was too flexible, too inhuman.

Glancing at me, he straightened his clothes and adjusted his size so he filled them out better. The seams bore signs of strain from earlier.

Strange, though. The fuzz of hair on his head had grown, and the wraith-white skin had darkened into a more natural hue of soft brown around his eyes and mouth and ears.

I made my words hard, like steel. "Give me one reason why I shouldn't send you to the bottom of the ocean to rot for the next hundred years."

He unleashed one of those strange smiles that didn't fit right on his face. "You won't do that. You won't send me away, or kill me, or order me to chase the boy who will not be caught. You will keep me here with you. And now you will give me your attention." He closed his hands together, a small hollow between them as though he held a mouse or sparrow. As though my attention were a mouse or sparrow to be trapped there.

I stalked forward, drawing the cracked mirror from my pocket. My reflection flashed at me, hard and bruised. "Is *this* the kind of attention you want from me?" I turned the mirror toward him.

As quick as lightning, the wraith boy threw himself into the corner, shrinking as he covered his face with the top of his shirt. "Stop! Please!"

I pressed the mirror against my thigh. "Tell me what you did earlier."

He peeked out from inside his shirt. "I came to find you."

"Why?"

"Every night you leave the palace, always without me." He straightened, his clothes falling back to normal. "I want your attention. But not"—he held up his hands—"with that mirror."

What *I* wanted now was to smash the mirror in his face, but my hands shook so badly I could barely hold on to it. "So you decided to destroy the cathedral with thousands of people inside?" My mouth curled into a snarl.

"I wouldn't have let you get hurt."

I hurled the mirror at him. "That's not the point!" He ducked aside and the mirror hit the far wall with a loud *crack*. When it landed faceup, the wraith boy jumped away, as though I'd thrown poison or swords.

"What should I have done?"

"You should have stayed here. Or trusted that I would have returned. Or—I don't know. Not risked thousands of lives."

"Yours is the only life I care about."

"Theirs are no less important." I moved forward and grabbed the mirror, its glass shattered even further after the impact. "Do you understand that?"

"I wanted you to notice me."

"Well I didn't want to notice you, and what I want is the only thing that matters." A note of hysteria edged my tone. "*Do you understand?*" I asked again.

He hesitated, and then nodded. "What you want is all that matters."

"There will be no more attempts to get my attention like that. You will not endanger lives for mere *attention* again."

"Yes, my queen." He knelt and made himself small, not a threat at all. "I will remember what you have said."

"Good." I bit down the urge to yell. He wasn't human. I had no idea how he'd respond to continued assaults, and already my head thrummed with pain and rage and a hundred other things.

I stumbled for the door and grabbed onto the latch to steady myself.

"Why didn't you catch Patrick when I sent you after him?" I asked, my back still to the wraith boy.

"I don't know. He was good at hiding."

The pressure in my head was overwhelming, pulsing around my eyes as I slowly turned around. "You need to answer honestly or I don't know what will happen with this mirror." I waved it around for effect, but the motion just felt crazed.

"You don't need to threaten me, my queen." The wraith boy looked up through white eyelashes; he hadn't had any before. "I'll tell you the truth. I don't know why I couldn't catch Patrick. He was fast. Good at hiding. I tried."

Then it would be pointless to send him again—especially not knowing what kind of destruction he might cause in the effort. Sending him before had been reckless.

As we stood there, watching each other, his skin rippled and it was as though ink ran down his face and throat. The flesh darkened all at once, and his hair grew past his ears: a warm shade of golden brown, darker at the roots. When he blinked, his eyes shifted from blue to brown. His face, too, had slimmed at some point, though who could say if it would stay like that?

"What's happening to you?" I whispered. There was something unnervingly familiar about his appearance.

"I am changing. It's what I am. I am a changing creature, made from the changing lands."

"Chrysalis," I murmured. This room was his chrysalis.

The wraith boy straightened, a hound catching scent of his quarry. "You've named me?"

What? "No."

"You said Chrysalis." He wrapped his hands in the bottom of his shirt, stretching the fabric taut against his knuckles. "It sounds like a name."

"It isn't."

He leaned forward, eyes wide and eager. "Please name me Chrysalis. I like"—he cocked his head—"the way it sounds. The way it fits on me. Like a skin."

"And why should I give you anything that you *like*?"

"Because I want to give you what you like."

"I like answers."

He clasped his hands together. "If I give you answers, will you give me the name?"

The last thing I wanted to do was bargain with him, but I'd take what I could get. "Why do mirrors frighten you?" As though it were a weapon, I flicked the cracked hand mirror so it reflected the ceiling.

The wraith boy skittered away, though the glass hadn't been aimed at him. "Careful! Careful!" His chest heaved as he peeled himself off the far wall.

"Tell me why you don't like mirrors."

The wraith boy touched his face, as though memorizing his own features. "There's something about them, isn't there? Don't you feel it when you look in the mirror?"

"What do you mean?"

"Mirrors." The wraith boy's voice dropped lower as he slinked around the room, watching the hand mirror as though it might leap at him. "Mirrors are both truth-speakers and liars: a contradiction made of glass and shiny backing. Don't you know anyone who's hated their own reflection? Haven't you ever seen something you wouldn't have without a mirror?"

I'd have never seen my own *face* without a mirror.

"I know people who've been disappointed by their reflections. And—" A memory moved in the back of my thoughts, one of leaping across rooftops and catching a figure in one of the city's mirrors. It was how I'd caught Black Knife while he'd been following me one night.

The wraith boy nodded. "There's this truth about mirrors. It's inescapable. But they can lie, too. They can distort the truth, even hide the truth. They create illusion."

Like the glow of starlight all across Skyvale, or the way afternoons were so bright as the sun fell toward the horizon, shining in the mirrors.

"I see."

"Do you?" He crept around my mirror, careful to keep out of its reflection.

"You don't like mirrors because you see them as unpredictable. Unreliable. You never know what you'll get from them, or how they might turn against you, even though they're inanimate objects. You don't like mirrors because they're just like you."

He bristled and shot a dark frown. "We are *not* the same."

I gripped the handle of my mirror. "These don't frighten me. I'm not afraid of the truth."

"There are tales of losing oneself in reflections, or the essence of self being drawn out . . ." He went on, but I'd lifted the mirror to look into the biggest of the glass shards. My breath caught, and the wraith boy paused. "Do you see?"

His face was my face.

Not *exactly*, but the similarities were undeniable. His jaw tapered to a point, same as mine. The shade of his roots was the exact color of my hair. Even his eyes had changed to match mine.

Looking at him was like looking at the brother I'd never had. Anyone who saw us would have insisted we were siblings.

"My queen?" He spoke softly. Cautiously. "Do you want help? Are you trapped?"

I slammed the mirror glass-down against my thigh, making him leap back. "No. I don't want your help. I want you to tell me what you're doing. Why do you look like me?"

"Does it offend you? Frighten you? Do you not like what you see?" He drew himself up tall, shaking off the illusion of a scared boy. With his hands behind his back and his shoulders straight, he revealed shades of Patrick Lien, who he'd followed for days.

"You are a mirror."

"No more a mirror than you, my queen. No more a mirror than anyone else who unconsciously shifts to reflect those around them. But"—again he touched his face—"some of my changes are more physical and I find I cannot transform as I once did."

Was that good? Or a problem? I couldn't even tell anymore.

"If you'd let me be around other people, I think my face would hold echoes of theirs as well. But yours is the face that matters the most. So yours is the one I wear. My unconscious reflection of you."

"I don't want you to look anything like me."

"It is too late to stop it. If you let me see others, maybe—" He shook his head. "But you will not. You want to keep me locked in here where you don't have to think about me. With walls between us, you can focus on everything you think is more important." He settled into a neutral stance, his arms at his sides and his face clean of any expression. "Don't worry."

That was like a hailstorm telling crops not to worry.

"You created more wraith tonight," he said, "when you awakened the cathedral. But that amount was so insignificant to the enormity of what is coming."

"I know." I swallowed hard. "Will it be able to break mirrors, too? Like you did?"

"I broke the mirrors because you made me strong. They scared me—and I still don't like them—but I was strong enough to break them because of you. Because I wanted to be with you." His gaze flicked up to meet mine. "This other wrath? I don't know. It's not alive. It's not like me. It doesn't have you to make it strong enough to fight the mirrors. But there's a lot of it."

Another non-answer. "The wraith was slowing not long ago, but now it's touching the Indigo Kingdom."

He tilted his head and dared step closer. "Explosions do not extend infinitely. The progress slowed because it was time for it to slow. But soon this land will change, too. Everything will."

"What can I do? How long do we have?"

"I don't know. Soon, I think." He slinked closer. "Time for you is different. Or, it means something different. For me, it's not as important. But the change will come on this land like an ocean pouring over the mountains. It will be fierce and fast."

"That sounds like a prediction for something that's supposed to be unpredictable."

He bowed. "I tell you only the truth, my queen. Not because I don't want to be trapped in your mirror, but because you are my queen and I will always do what I can to help you."

As though we were friends. As though he cared about me beyond the control I exerted over him.

"It doesn't matter why you answer me, or tell me the truth. Only that you do." I spun and left the room, and when the door fell shut behind me, I slumped against it and sucked in a heavy breath.

"Your Highness?" Sergeant Ferris approached, cautiously. "What happened?"

"Call an emergency meeting of the wraith mitigation committee. When is the soonest I can address them?"

"First thing in the morning, Your Highness."

I hated waiting even that long, but the delay would give me time to figure out what I intended to say.

"What shall I tell them the meeting is concerning?" Sergeant Ferris glanced at the door beyond me. "Him?"

"We need mirrors." I lifted my eyes to his, and offered the hand mirror to him. A tin-backed shard of glass dropped to the floor. "It won't be enough, but it's the only chance we have."

"For what?"

"To stop the wraith."

PART TWO

THE DRAGON CROWN

THIRTEEN

AN ICY BREEZE fluttered through my bedroom as the clock tower struck four.

Darkness moved on darkness, and I was out of bed with my daggers drawn, every piece of my body groaning in protest. "Announce yourself or I'll kill you."

"I'm sorry." It was Black Knife. The prince. "I didn't mean to startle you."

Everything startled me now, but I didn't want to tell him so. I just sheathed my daggers and dragged a blanket from the bed to wrap around my shoulders like a cape. My nightgown afforded little in the way of modesty. "I should be apologizing to you."

In the far corner of the room, the prince was a motionless black shape. Only the glint of moonlight on polished leather boots and the slither of silk on silk gave him away. He'd dressed as Black Knife to come sneaking over the rooftop, just as I'd done. My heart squeezed.

"But I don't think there's any way to properly convey my regrets." I glanced toward the light switch, but this was better in the dark. It was easier to think of him as Black Knife and not the prince. "I'm afraid of the wraith boy. I don't know what he is, or how to stop him, and I'm terrified of what he'll do next."

Black Knife crossed the room, a shifting heat and presence. A gloved palm cupped my cheek, hesitantly. "I don't blame you for what happened."

"You're the only one." It took everything in me not to lean into his touch; he was warm and solid, and like this he was my friend. But he was also Tobiah, and meant for someone else. I pulled back, and he let his hand drop to his side. "What about the memorial?" I asked. "Will it affect your ability to take the throne tomorrow?"

"I had the memorial completed in the palace chapel last night. It was small. Private."

"That's for the best."

"There was no choice. My enemies would have protested my enthronement otherwise."

Another apology sat on my tongue, but I couldn't make it emerge. I'd almost cost Tobiah his crown. "Do you have many enemies?"

"Everyone here has their share. Worry about yours, not mine." He spoke kindly, though he shifted away from me. "Tell me why you want a mitigation committee meeting called."

I pulled my blanket tighter around my shoulders. "The

wraith boy thinks we have no time at all before the wraith floods the Indigo Kingdom, and because right now, after the Inundation and the cathedral collapse, the committee will need to listen and explore every option available."

"Then let's do this right. List every point you want to discuss. Give me warning so that I can help." He sounded like the prince, but nothing could break the spell of this boy in those clothes. The way he moved, and the way he wanted to do what was right: those were qualities I'd grown to admire in Black Knife. "I think you'd go rushing into this with your convictions and good intentions, but one of the more difficult lessons I've learned about politics is patience, and planning, and knowing that no matter how good you are at both of those, there's always someone who's better and willing to go further. Unfortunately, my uncle is very good at it."

"I don't need to be rescued from Prince Colin—"

"I'm not trying to rescue you, but I am trying to help you succeed. There's a difference." He moved to the balcony window. "You have a hundred enemies, Wilhelmina. Thanks to your magic, the wraith boy, your various identities, and your connection with Patrick Lien, there's a lot going against you."

Did I have anything going *for* me?

"Let me help you, Wil. You don't have to do this alone." With that, he was out the window, a black blur on the balcony, and then gone.

He was right. I did need to plan the committee meeting, just as I'd have planned anything with the Ospreys. I needed to understand what actions would get me the results I wanted, take all variables into consideration, plan for possible counteractions. I needed to strategize.

Perhaps politics was not so different from revolution after all.

By design, I was last to the meeting.

Theresa was at my heels, still looking like a refugee who'd stolen a noblewoman's burgundy gown. No matter how she lifted her chin and straightened her shoulders, she never quite managed the mask of confidence she needed. But she'd been in the palace only a few days, and already everything had gone wrong.

Having Theresa here wasn't the same as having Melanie, but it was better than being alone.

Sergeant Ferris opened the committee chamber door, and when I strode inside, the buzz of conversation fell away. Every face turned toward me, most with crafted neutrality, others with open dislike.

Theresa paused just behind my shoulder, and Sergeant Ferris let the door fall shut as he took his place with the legion of body-guards along the wall.

"Your Highness. Welcome." Tobiah offered a small, polite bow from where he stood at the head of the table. He was the prince today, with that dry, dull tone I'd disliked so much, but now that I knew to look for it, I could see the fraying seams of that mask. In his eyes, in the jump in his throat, and even in the way his frown softened when our eyes met. "Lady Theresa, please take a seat."

"What is the meaning of this?" Prince Colin pushed himself up, leaning heavily on the table. "What are *those* two doing here? It's one thing for the queen regent and your fiancée to join us, but them? Aecorian thieves?"

There were a few muffled agreements around the table, coming from behind fist-covered mouths and down-drooped mustaches. I knew Captain Chuter, Generals Frederick and Adam Goldberg, Francesca, and Meredith, of course, but there were several new faces.

"This *is* most irregular," offered one of the strangers. "What with His Highness's coronation this evening. There's so much to do today. . . ."

Tobiah stood with his hands behind his back and addressed his council. "Princess Wilhelmina is the reason we're here today. I called this meeting on Her Highness's behalf."

"What an outrage!" Prince Colin strode around the table, toward Tobiah. "Her participation was not appropriate when she was masquerading as Duchess Julianna of Liadia, and it is even less appropriate now."

"I believe," I said, "this is Crown Prince Tobiah's committee. It is for him to decide whose presence is appropriate."

Someone in the back gasped. Meredith's eyes were wide and bright, while Theresa smirked. Even Queen Francesca looked pleased.

Tobiah stood straighter and glared back at his uncle. "When Her Highness was here as Julianna, I acquiesced to the demands that she be excluded from the meetings. I did not know who she was, or whether anything she said about the wraithland was true. But now we do know her identity, and I do know that she has been to the wraithland." He glanced at me and nodded.

I pulled a pair of Liadian barrier scales from a pouch at my hip, and tossed them onto the center of the table. Everyone in the room gasped.

"As for the coronation this evening, you're correct, Lord Craft. This is irregular, but important. And since we all have a lot to do today, I suggest everyone sit down and listen to what Princess Wilhelmina has to say." His gaze cut around the room. "If anyone is opposed to listening to Her Highness speak, they can leave now."

No one moved, except Prince Colin, who went back to his seat, and gradually, my heart migrated out of my throat and back to my chest. This boy was meant to be king.

"Very good." Tobiah moved to help Theresa into her chair near Francesca and Meredith. The queen regent offered a delicate nod, while Meredith touched Theresa's arm in a comforting gesture.

Theresa relaxed, and gratitude filled me. After everything, Meredith still treated us with kindness.

Tobiah guided me to the head of the table. "I'll make quick introductions to the members you haven't met, and then we'll begin."

I nodded.

"Lord John Price, House of the Sun; Lord Samuel Craft, House of the Unicorn; and Count Alexander Davis, House of the Sea. They are the official representatives of the other three Houses. My uncle is here as the representative of Dragon."

Ah. Now that he'd said their names, I recognized them by reputation. They were all minor lords, no one important.

Tobiah turned toward me. "Let's begin with your time in the wraithland."

"Can we surmise this will be a different tale than the last we heard?" Clint's words were harsh, but his tone was not cruel.

"Quite." I pulled out my notes, each point written in a different hand and color of ink to help organize my thoughts. "There are a number of topics I'd like to discuss, beginning with my journey to the wraithland, and why I decided to go there in the first place.

"Until I attended my first meeting of this committee, I had no intention of ever venturing into the wraithland. To me, the wraith was a distant threat, not as pressing as my desire to ensure Aecorians' safety, and reclaim my kingdom." I avoided looking in Prince Colin's direction. "It was my experience with this council that made me realize the wraith was not as far away as I'd always felt, and that *something* must be done. And when I saw this map"—I gestured toward the wall—"everything changed."

The guards in front of the wall map shuffled aside to reveal the inked planes and mountains and valleys, and the bands of color that represented the wraith's approach each month.

"Those two words—*debated* and *confidential*—inspired me to search for the truth about whatever this committee had been hiding about Mirror Lake." Choosing my words carefully, I told the group about chasing rumors, joining the merchant caravan, and stealing into the wraithland on a borrowed horse. I told them how I'd fought glowmen, learned to sleep only a few hours at a time, and ventured deeper into the wraith than anyone had in decades.

I pulled a section of papers from my stack and handed them to the queen regent. "Please take one." As the papers went around the table, I said, "These are copies of the notes I took during my journey. I wanted to be thorough, so you'll find details about the weather, vegetation, and wildlife." Nothing personal, though. There were too many things I didn't want to share with this group. "Especially important are my notes on Mirror Lake."

Tobiah lifted an eyebrow. "When did you make all these copies?"

"This morning. I couldn't sleep."

Smiling faintly, he shook his head. "Please continue."

So I did. I told them about the locust swarm, what I'd done to save myself, and how the wraith boy had been created. "My power isn't supposed to do that. I temporarily animate objects, but I never give real life. I haven't yet figured out what was different this time."

"Is it something you could do again?" asked John Price. "If you brought the wraith to life and we just explained to it—"

"Don't be stupid." Adam Goldberg banged a fist on the table. "You saw the creature last night. If Princess Wilhelmina hadn't been there to stop it, we'd all have died."

"If Princess Wilhelmina hadn't been there," corrected Prince Colin, "the wraith boy wouldn't have been, either."

That was true.

"We're getting off topic." Tobiah held up a warning hand. "At any rate, that was one of my first questions, and the answer is no. Animating that much wraith could kill Wilhelmina."

"And before anyone suggests my life is worth sacrificing for this, keep in mind that I don't know what will happen if I die while in control of something, especially something as unpredictable as the wraith." I glanced at Prince Colin, whose eyes

152

were narrowed and flinty. "My mother was an animator, too, and her mother. I've heard stories of animated knitting or pens that fell lifeless once more when the flasher died. If that happened while the wraith boy, or any other animated wraith, were here in Skyvale . . ."

I gave them a moment to recall the Inundation: the chaos and screams and *crack* of shattering glass.

"At any rate," added Meredith, "what would it say about us as a people if we were to sacrifice someone like that?"

The queen lifted an eyebrow. "The saints died for our salvation."

"Yet Princess Wilhelmina is not a saint." Meredith pressed her hands to her mouth. "That was rude. I'm sorry."

I shrugged off the comment. Of course I wasn't a saint.

We needed to get back on topic. I glanced at my notes and cleared my throat. "With what I learned in the wraithland, and what I learned about the wraith boy last night—"

"When last night?" Prince Colin's eyes narrowed. "As he was bringing down one of our most iconic and beloved buildings, risking thousands of lives?"

Several people frowned. Theresa glared like she'd murder him. "The only person who endured true harm last night was Princess Wilhelmina. She's the one who acted quickly enough to ensure we all survived."

"One cannot hold Her Highness responsible for every action taken by others." Meredith folded her hands over the papers in front of her.

Their defense of me was nice, but unnecessary. "I spoke to the wraith boy once I awakened."

Captain Chuter leaned forward, a pen poised over paper. The sharp, straight lines of his handwriting drew my gaze for a second. "What did you learn?"

"He is terrified of mirrors." I glanced at Tobiah. "That is to our advantage."

"All the mirrors in Skyvale are broken," said another. "How does that help us?"

"After the Inundation, Skyvale is filled with people who need work. Create jobs by opening the factories to produce as many mirrors as possible. Pay people to gather the biggest shards from the streets, and have them pieced together. Then you'll need people to hang the mirrors, and have them transported all along the western border of the Indigo Kingdom."

"That's your solution?" General Adam Goldberg shook his head. "That is not enough, Your Highness."

"It's not a solution," I said, "but a mitigation effort. Something this council should be very familiar with." That brought a few snorts of repressed laughter, and even the queen regent looked amused. "Not only that, this is something we can do *right now*. It will help the city recover from the tragedy of the Inundation."

"And the city does need help," said Tobiah. "We must do what we can to protect it." The crown prince heaved a long sigh. "We also must prepare evacuation routes, to be safe. Parts of the Indigo Kingdom are already suffering the wraith's effects."

Mutters of unease rustled around the room.

"Discussing evacuation routes is bad for morale, I know. Nevertheless, pragmatism is necessary." He left no room for argument. "Moving along: Princess Wilhelmina, there's one more item on your list." Tobiah lifted his dark eyes to mine.

"Yes. Thank you." I took a sip from my wineglass. "I think we should turn the committee's attention to the Liadian barrier once more. I'm not suggesting sending anyone else out there; I hope the information I collected will be enough, once paired with the official reports from Liadia."

"What are you suggesting?" Clint asked.

"Mirror Lake was completely normal: the life inside it and above it. And when the locusts swarmed, I observed several dying as they flew over the lake, like the wraith had been removed from them all at once."

The chamber was quiet, save the scratch of pens on paper, and someone's rattling breath.

"My parents—and monarchs before them—refused to sign the Wraith Alliance, a stance that has baffled the allied kingdoms for a hundred years."

No one spoke.

"The rulers of Aecor wouldn't sign something they had no intention of obeying, and they didn't want to be prevented from finding answers in unlikely places. Like magic."

Clint shook his head. "Magic *causes* wraith. How will it stop it?"

"I'm not sure," I said. "But my parents firmly believed there was a way. So did Liadia; they broke the Wraith Alliance to build the barrier, and for a little while, they succeeded. They held back the wraith for a year." I gestured toward the barrier scales still sitting in the middle of the table. "And a lake now littered with pieces of that barrier is a more formidable ward against the wraith than I've ever seen."

Protest erupted across the room. Someone pounded on the table with each inarticulate point he made. Around the perimeter of the room, bodyguards looked to their charges, a few masks of professionalism slipping at the display. James caught my gaze, offering a slight roll of his eyes.

The outrage continued for a full minute before Tobiah rose and stood at my side. "Silence!"

Everyone turned to look at him.

"You can't be serious about allowing this kind of talk." Prince Colin's glare cut to me. "It was only a month ago that you were certain *not* using magic at all would stop the wraith."

"A month ago, I did believe we could stop the wraith by ceasing all magic use. I believed because that was what I was taught, as were all of you. Since then, however, the Inundation has come, and it was Wilhelmina who stopped it from completely destroying the city—by using her magic."

"It was also Wilhelmina who *caused* the Inundation," muttered someone down the table, and no one argued.

"Regardless," I said, "wraith is already in the Indigo Kingdom. This is no longer tomorrow's problem. It is today's."

"I don't see how we can trust *Her Highness*'s intelligence on anything, given her history." That came from a man sitting close to Prince Colin.

"You don't have to trust her. Trust me, because today I am your crown prince and tonight I will become your king, and I trust Wilhelmina." Tobiah shifted his weight toward me; his elbow brushed mine. "Now, if you're all finished yelling . . ."

Eyes turned toward him again.

"Here's what we know about the Liadian barrier: every

flasher in the kingdom was forced to pour their magic into it, presumably while the metal was still molten, before they were shaped into scales and pieced together. We have details on the construction of their barrier, though it doesn't list *magic* as one of the ingredients."

Of course it didn't.

"I'm open to discussion of creating a barrier of our own. It could hold back the wraith an extra year, giving us a chance to find a more permanent solution."

"We'd still need flashers," said Clint. "Unless you plan to use only Princess Wilhelmina. And given the punishment for using magic in the Indigo Kingdom, I can't imagine others stepping forward."

Certainly I wouldn't volunteer Connor's magic.

Tobiah shook his head. "The barrier was a kingdom-wide effort—"

"Which," Lord Craft added, "they hid from the rest of the allied kingdoms, going so far as to send a false report. We should ban the remaining Liadian refugees from the Indigo Kingdom. They should all be arrested and forced to leave."

"And where would they go?" asked Meredith. "Our world grows smaller every day."

Lord Craft's tone was dark. "Send them back to the wraith-land they helped create."

"No." I curled my hands into fists. "That's a death sentence."

"Well," Prince Colin muttered, "they certainly aren't going to Aecor Territory."

I turned to him, keeping my voice deep and even. "Aecor is my kingdom, and when I am in control of it, it will be a safe haven for flashers and refugees alike. Should the wraith one day overtake Skyvale, even you will not be refused shelter in Aecor."

Meredith shot a tiny smile of support, but the rest of the room fell into death-like silence as Prince Colin stood and strode around the table, and finally stopped in front of me. He was taller, and broader, and so close I could feel his breath stir the air between us.

For a heartbeat, I was back in my room the other night when he'd been there. In the dark. Waiting for me.

My whole body shuddered with the memory as Prince Colin smirked down at me, a silent reminder of his threats.

"You don't intimidate me," I hissed.

Without a word, he turned and left the room. A pair of bodyguards went after him.

A quiet murmur filled the room, and it took everything in me not to slump with relief.

"I suppose the meeting is adjourned," said Tobiah. "We will reconvene tomorrow to further discuss our own barrier. But effective immediately, I want those evacuation routes planned, and I want mirrors covering Skyvale once more. There will be no more removal of the homeless from the city. Everyone—foreign and domestic refugees alike—will be invited into the city and given jobs. We need those mirrors."

The council members stood and offered their farewells, and soon began to trickle from the room. Francesca and Meredith were among the first to go, their heads bent together in soft discussion. "Over lunch, let's discuss how we'll decorate for your wedding ball. Your parents *are* meeting us at noon, correct?" The rest of the conversation fell under the buzz of other voices.

Tobiah warmed my side, barely a respectable distance between us. "You did very well today."

My smile was shaky, but he pretended not to notice. "I'll bring it up tomorrow, but I had an idea about where to get magic to fuel a barrier."

Tobiah's eyebrows raised. "Don't keep me in suspense."

"Perhaps you've heard that when wraith beasts die, a white mist flows out of them."

"Yes." Of course he knew. It was with Black Knife I'd first seen this phenomenon. "It's wraith, isn't it?"

"Perhaps. Or perhaps it's something a little closer to magic. On my way to West Pass Watch, we fought a giant scorpion." He'd been there, of course, but I couldn't chance anyone knowing that. "When it died, the mist split and went into certain people—flashers in hiding, if I had to guess."

Tobiah's lips parted as he put all that together. He'd seen the mist go into me the night we fought a wraith cat together, but he'd had no way to know that wasn't normal. It was unlikely he'd ever killed a wraith beast in anyone's presence before. "I see," he said at last. "You think we could harvest the necessary magic from wraith beasts."

"I think it's worth investigating, and perhaps offering a sizable reward for either the captured mist or live creature."

"That would be dangerous, holding the creatures in the city."

I nodded. "Perhaps a facility outside the city."

"Indeed." A faraway look fell over his eyes: he was already forming a plan. "I'll have someone look into it."

There was no doubt: Tobiah Pierce was meant to be king.

Unfortunate aspects of his princely mask aside, he knew how to behave and make decisions. He knew how to reward people who earned it, and scold those who deserved it.

He would be a good king.

I offered a faint curtsy. "I'll see you at this evening's coronation."

FOURTEEN

AFTER MEETING WITH the seamstresses for our coronation gowns, Theresa and I made our way to the Ospreys' suite,
Sergeant Ferris following at a respectful distance.

"It's going to rain tonight." Theresa's announcement came
out of nowhere. "I saw clouds when I looked out the window.
Dark clouds."

"The coronation is inside. Rain won't matter."

She lowered her voice. "Do you think it means anything? A
big storm on coronation night?"

I shook my head and smiled. "You sound like Connor, all
signs and superstitions. Are you keeping a mirror in your pocket,
too?"

"The mirror thing turned out to be real."

She had a point.

In the Ospreys' suite, Kevin was pacing again. "We should
be preparing for *your* coronation, Wil."

I gave him a sharp look. "Don't say anything like that tonight. Show respect to Prince Tobiah."

"But you hate him."

"After tonight, he'll be the king granting us sanctuary. It doesn't matter how I feel about him; he's taking care of the people *I* care about, and that earns my respect."

"Fine." Kevin slumped onto the sofa between Carl and Connor. His limbs splayed out everywhere, forcing the younger boys to dodge flying elbows. "This is boring. When can we go into the city again?"

"Never." That came out too harshly. I softened my tone. "Not for a while. It's not safe."

"The city is never safe."

Theresa flicked her little finger at him. "Oh, stop your whining. There are so many worse problems out there than your boredom." She stomped toward the balcony door and vanished outside. A ribbon of cold wind cut through the room, and was sliced off by the slamming door.

Carl crossed his arms. "What's *her* problem?"

"Maybe you should ask her yourself." Not that I was sure what was bothering her, either. "Do you like your new tutor?" I perched on the corner of the table.

"She's fine," said Connor.

"Fine." Carl shrugged.

"Really pretty." Kevin shot a rueful grin. "Smart, I mean. She knows a lot about the Indigo Kingdom. Even Aecor. This morning we went over how to behave at the coronation."

"Do you think you can manage?" I asked.

"Give us some credit. We managed the memorial last night.

You were the troublemaker."

I scratched my chin with my little finger.

"We had a vote." Carl leaned forward. "We don't like your wraith friend. We think he's a bad influence. And messy."

"He *is* messy. And definitely has worse behavior than any of you." My smile was faint. "What about the Wraith Alliance? Have you made any progress on that?"

"We're still working on it," Kevin said. "You only asked us to look at it the other day."

I pushed a note of impatience out of my tone. "All right. Be quick, but thorough. The sooner I sign it, the better leverage we have getting Aecor from Prince Colin."

"If Patrick doesn't get it first." Connor folded his hands in his lap. "What if the Indigo Army finds him? *He* should be in trouble, but what about Melanie and Paige? Ronald and Oscar?"

"Melanie is on our side, and the other three didn't kill King Terrell. They didn't try to kill Prince Tobiah. The Indigo Kingdom wants them, but not as badly as they want Patrick. That will be taken into account."

Connor nodded thoughtfully. "And what about us? Do we get to punish him, too, when he's caught?" His tone was careful and even, betrayed only by the white of his knuckles and tightness of his jaw.

"When Patrick is caught, he'll be tried for all his crimes, including sending Quinn and Ezra on the mission that killed them. And all those who came before them. We'll build memorials in their honor, right?"

All three boys agreed, solemn now.

I stood and smoothed my dress. "I'm going to check on Rees. Make yourselves useful. And be nice to her when she gets back in."

On my way out, I grabbed a blanket to ward off the cold.

Theresa was leaning on the rail, staring east over the woods. Gold and red leaves of late autumn rained like drops of colored ink, breathtakingly beautiful in the gloaming.

"Is it possible to be homesick for a place you can't remember?" Her voice was soft, caught up and carried away by a gust of icy wind.

"I think so." Next to her, I put the blanket around both of us, and she rested her cheek on my shoulder. "We'll go back home one day. Soon. And we'll make new memories there."

"I wonder what Patrick and the others are doing now—if they're thinking about your coronation, too. He always intended for you to take it back on the anniversary. That's only a few months off." The clock tower chimed fifteen, and a cloud-shrouded full moon started to rise over the horizon. The early moon, the storm-darkened sky, and the frigid wind made the afternoon feel like evening.

The acrid scent of wraith rode on the air, but it was faint. For now.

"I don't want to talk about Patrick and the others." I pulled her toward the door again. "Come on."

Just as we started to move, voices below caught me.

"Let's speak out here, Your Grace." Prince Colin strode into the garden below our balcony, just beyond the rail.

I crouched, waving Theresa to follow so he wouldn't look

up and see us. We crept forward and watched the pair from between the balcony rails.

"I'm in a hurry, Your Highness." Annoyance colored Lady Meredith's tone, but she appeared in the garden, cloaked and hooded.

"Certainly." Prince Colin spoke too sweetly. "I only wanted to say how glad I am that Tobiah recovered so quickly from his injury. It's such a relief he'll be able to take his place as Sovereign of the Indigo Kingdom, at last."

Meredith dipped into a slight curtsy. "Indeed. I am grateful for his recovery, too."

"Just like his cousin, James Rayner."

I imagined Meredith's thin smile at that; her tone reflected one. "Yes. They do have access to the best physicians, though."

"I think it's more than luck or physicians." Prince Colin began to circle her. "*What* could have happened? How is Francesca's side of the family so blessed, I wonder?"

Theresa adjusted the blanket over us, making the wool rustle, but the pair below was too engaged to hear.

"I'm sure you know better than I do, Your Highness, though given how many terrible things have happened to them lately, I'd hesitate to say they are blessed."

"Hmm. I do have a hypothesis." Prince Colin pressed his hands behind his back, his chest puffed out.

Part of me wanted to rescue her, but if she needed it, she didn't show it at all. Meredith hadn't moved, her cloak spread out around her like a shadow. She was a statue.

"I think it's that foreign princess. Wilhelmina. She and he

165

are so close. Always sharing some secret. Don't you think?"

Meredith tilted her head, just a shift in the shadow of her sculpted regality. "I was under the impression they weren't fond of each other."

Beneath the blanket, Theresa nudged me, but I didn't tear my gaze from the two below.

Prince Colin strode deeper into the gardens. "I simply do not trust the princess." He said it as an announcement. As though anyone would be shocked. "She paraded around in another woman's identity for months."

Meredith remained silent.

"She's lived on the streets for years. What does that do to a young lady? Let alone a princess." He allowed that to sink in a moment. "It was her man who killed King Terrell. She was responsible for the Inundation, leading the wraith here. And now she keeps that creature she created—with her magic—as a pet. Tell me, why hasn't she sent it away? Why does she insist on keeping it in the palace?"

"I cannot tell you." Meredith's tone was mild, and vaguely annoyed. "And while those things may be true, and those questions are important to ask, none of it signals a dangerous closeness between Princess Wilhelmina and Crown Prince Tobiah. Why would you think they have any kind of relationship?"

There it was. A shred of uncertainty edged the last question.

Prince Colin heard it, too, because he turned and appeared to study her. "This morning. Did you see the looks they exchanged?"

Again, silence from the duchess.

"It's worth noting, too, that her response to his injury was rather . . . dramatic. Wasn't it?"

Was it? I closed my eyes for a heartbeat, remembering the attack. Remembering the way I'd felt everything inside of me burst when Tobiah dropped with that bolt inside him.

I shuddered, and Theresa touched my hand.

"I wasn't there to witness it," Meredith said. "I saw a commotion too quick to immediately understand, and then the guards were dragging me inside, along with Her Majesty."

"I see. Then you'll have to take my word for it."

Meredith could probably count on one hand the times someone said she'd *have* to do something.

If I were her, I'd be remembering the morning of Tobiah's awakening, when she and the queen had walked in to find me already there. And the look Tobiah and I had shared as I descended the steps in the cathedral. And, if she'd seen it, the way he stood close last night, holding me upright after I'd put the building back to sleep.

"More importantly, don't you think it's interesting that the same man responsible for the king's assassination is also responsible for two attempts on your fiancé's life? And that the assassin works for Wilhelmina?"

He made such compelling arguments. I wouldn't trust me, either.

"I worry," Prince Colin continued, "what her influence on Tobiah will be. The grief of losing his father, the near loss of his closest friend and bodyguard, the attack on him, and now the collapse of the cathedral on top of everything?" Prince Colin shook his head, as though honestly uncertain, and honestly concerned.

"Your points are all valid, certainly, but I am not worried about Tobiah's faithfulness. He is honorable."

"But she may not be. I can only pray Tobiah resists her, but if he changes at all—if the stress of what he's been through begins to affect his duties as a king—please know that I want only what is best for the Indigo Kingdom. That, above all, is my priority, as I'm sure it is yours as well."

He was telling her to spy for him. To keep watch over Tobiah's activities and report to him. He'd already planted the seeds of doubt in her mind, though they must have been there already. She knew what I was. What I'd done. But still she'd made overtures of friendship. She'd shown me support and kindness in spite of the way I'd hurt her best friend.

Meredith had trusted Tobiah all these months, and he had betrayed her. In the breezeway. With me. He was honorable, but he wasn't infallible.

We'd both betrayed her.

"The Indigo Kingdom is in a state of flux," added Prince Colin. "I worry constantly for my nephew's life, and his ability to rule the kingdom when those to whom he gives his trust are not trustworthy. I *pray* that he recovers from all of these traumatic events and proves himself a strong sovereign."

"Crown Prince Tobiah is strong."

"I agree. As proven by his swift recovery." He paused. "And now it's being said the injury wasn't as great as we first thought, but saints, I saw the wound myself. It's a miracle he lived. Truly a miracle."

Meredith regarded him with a steady gaze.

"Though I certainly want my nephew to be king, more than

anything else in this world, I hope no one else questions this miracle. Or . . . whatever it might have been. The law is clear, though. About magic. If someone were to contest his ascension to the throne—"

"Who would do that?" Meredith lifted her chin.

"No one, I'm sure. But I am so aware that I am next in the line of succession. When Tobiah becomes king this evening, I will become the crown prince. Heir to the throne."

The duchess remained motionless, but it was a different kind of stillness, now. One filled with doubt and contemplation and unease. For a thundering heartbeat, I wondered if she'd give in and accept his not-so-subtle threats.

She could spy for him and be cared for when Colin made some kind of move against Tobiah.

Or she could go down with him.

Instead, she simply curtsied and said, "Excuse me, Your Highness. I must prepare for my fiancé's coronation."

"Of course. I'm sorry to have detained you. Please remember what we've discussed."

"I don't see how I could forget." Before he could reply, Meredith turned and vanished from my sight. A door slammed, and Prince Colin glared after her for a breath. But then he clasped his hands behind his back, making a small noise of satisfaction.

Only after he went inside did I allow myself to move. My limbs groaned in protest, having stiffened from the cold. Theresa used the rail to help herself up. "I—"

The balcony door opened and Connor peeked out. "Wil? Rees?"

Theresa and I scrambled to our feet, the wool blanket falling to the balcony floor. Streaks of dirt smeared across the fronts of our dresses, and a few drops of rain dotted our faces.

"Oh." His eyes widened. "What were you doing on the ground?"

"Eavesdropping. And it's very rude, so you shouldn't ever do it." I bent to seize the fallen blanket. "Get ready for the coronation, Connor. We have to prepare as well."

We waved to the boys on our way out.

Sergeant Ferris waited in the hall, as always. The pair of guards looking over the Ospreys stood with him. "Back to your quarters, Your Highness?"

"Yes. And I need Captain Rayner to meet us there."

"I'm afraid he's very busy today."

I pulled myself tall and regal, like Meredith in the courtyard. "Send for him, Sergeant."

Ferris's gaze was long and steady, but at last he nodded to one of the other guards. "You. Fetch the captain to Her Highness's sitting room. Be quick."

James was already there when we returned, clad in his finest Indigo Order uniform. His sword hung at his side and he perched on the arm of the sofa, gloved hands on his knees.

"Pretty dress." He inclined his head toward tonight's gown hanging from a peg.

"Thank you." The gown was a glorious creation of lavender silk and wool, with flowers and vines embroidered across the shoulders and down the sleeves. A thick sash of white crossed the ribs, and the front split revealed a layer of cream fabric. "I didn't ask you here to discuss ladies' fashion."

"Maybe next time. You have so many more options and I admit I'm jealous." He grinned and picked invisible lint off his sleeve. "How can I help you, Wil?"

"Prince Colin wants to keep Tobiah from becoming king."

Every muscle in him tensed, and his eyes grew hard. "Start from the beginning. Tell me everything."

With Theresa's help, I recounted the conversation between Prince Colin and Meredith, even the accusations against me.

James's expression grew darker as I finished the story. "But he didn't say when he was going to do anything?"

"No, but the threat was clear. He'll reveal the use of magic when it suits him."

James nodded. "I believe you. I doubt anything will happen today. It's too late for him to take any kind of action against the coronation—"

And *I* doubted *that*.

"—but I will post extra guards and ensure Prince Colin is being monitored at all times. Would that help alleviate your worry?"

"Some." But not enough.

James pushed himself up, straightening his jacket. "Wil, Tobiah and I were taking care of each other long before you arrived. I don't say that to diminish anything that you've done for him, because I know your entire future is riding on his taking the throne tonight."

There was a pause that seemed to last eternity, but the clock ticked only a few times and I added nothing to his reasoning. It wasn't my place.

"Believe me," James said. "It's important to us all that

Tobiah take the throne. The last thing I want is for someone like Prince Colin to have control over the Indigo Kingdom—and it must kill you that he has control over *your* kingdom. But I cannot simply arrest him, no matter the pleasure that would bring me. He's done nothing besides talk, and unless Lady Meredith speaks up, it's your word against his. And your word isn't the best, all things considered."

I closed my eyes and dragged in a heavy breath. "Very well."

He stepped forward and held out his hands, and when I took them, he squeezed. "Thank you, though. For telling me. For trusting me. I understand that you'd rather do things on your own."

"Don't imagine I was asking for help." I pulled away and strode toward the door. "It's only that I want to be able to brag I'd warned you after Prince Colin does something awful."

James smirked, but gave a small, respectful bow. "I'll see you at the coronation." Then he was gone.

"That's it?" Theresa pulled a tie from her braid and began untangling her wind-mussed hair.

"That's all we can do." I glared at the door for a moment before peeling off my day dress. The maid would come soon, and she didn't need to see what I'd done to it.

Theresa sighed. "I don't like that man. Colin."

"No one likes him."

"Is what he said true? Any of it about you and Tobiah?"

"We've learned to overcome our differences, more or less."

More when he'd dressed as Black Knife and I hadn't known his true identity. Less when he resembled a prince.

She frowned. "You have a look. Your feelings toward him

really have changed, haven't they?"

"It doesn't matter. He's getting married and I can continue to be a terrible influence without compromising his honor." Further compromising, that was. "There's only one thing you should have taken from that conversation, Rees, and if you think my *feelings* have anything to do with it, you're wrong.

"The most important thing we just learned was that Prince Colin is willing to take the throne by slandering Tobiah. And if Tobiah isn't king, we will never reclaim Aecor."

FIFTEEN

ONCE, WHEN I was very young, I'd attended a coronation in the kingdom just north of Aecor. The old ruler of Laurel-by-the-Sea had died, leaving his middle-aged son to inherit the small kingdom known mostly for its seafood and salt exports.

My memories of that event were faded, now only glossy impressions of a banquet and soft dresses and my father tucking me against his side as I began to droop halfway through the ball. The briny scent of the sea sharpened the glittering chamber, replaced by a floral perfume as I'd shifted to press my face into my mother's gown. She'd held me, swaying with the music as though we were dancing, and I'd drifted off to sleep.

I hadn't understood the Wraith Alliance then, so I'd never questioned why we'd been invited in spite of my parents' refusal to sign the agreement. Perhaps it had been a polite gesture, or happened during some other diplomatic visit. Whatever the circumstances, it had been one of the last adventures with my parents before their murder and the One-Night War.

Everything about the Indigo Kingdom coronation ceremony was different.

First, it was raining.

The storm had swept in just as I finished dressing, heralded by the odors of winter and wraith. Clouds crashed over the mountains like waves, and the palace sounds were muted under the constant *tap tap tap*.

It was a heavier atmosphere. More somber. After all, King Terrell hadn't died quietly in his sleep from old age. He'd been murdered, and everything since then had been horrible event after horrible event. It didn't seem as though the situation would improve. A new king might help, but real hope seemed impossible.

In spite of the Inundation and cathedral collapse, the throne room was resplendent. Silver dragons perched on chandeliers, and were etched into the glass shields of sconces. Cresting waves, unicorns, and suns with radiating lines peeked from ornaments and shimmered on banners above. Though they tried to hide it, the Ospreys gaped as we filed into the chamber and took our places. Conner and Carl nudged each other, sharing subtle glances toward crystals and other small pieces of finery.

I bumped Connor's elbow and shook my head, just slightly. He offered a small, good-natured sigh, but nodded and kept his hands at his sides. The others noticed, and clasped their hands behind their backs one at a time, secret smiles pulling at the corners of their mouths.

On a balcony, a small orchestra was playing, and slowly the chamber began to fill with nobility from all across the Indigo

Kingdom, a few from the surrounding kingdoms, and the wealthy merchant class from here in Skyvale. The throne room grew hot, even with the upper windows open to let in a near-winter breeze. Lady Meredith and her parents glowed where they stood in the front with their heads high. Next to them, Princes Colin and Herman wore blank expressions. Another woman stood with them: Kathleen Rayner, if I had to guess. James's mother. She looked like her sister Francesca, tall and thin, with dark brown hair.

Prince Colin leaned toward her and whispered something, but I caught only the shape of Tobiah's name.

Queen Regent Francesca sat on her throne, looking contemplative and regal. Her sharp features were knives in the slanted golden light that fell from the gas lamps. A priest and the major-domo of Skyvale Palace stood in close attendance. Sweat dripped from their hairlines and the priest kept stealing glances at me, possibly remembering last night at the cathedral.

There was barely standing room by the time the music shifted and began to play a piece at a faster tempo: the Indigo Kingdom Royal March.

Though I'd meant to watch Prince Colin to make sure he didn't do anything untoward, when Tobiah stepped through the double doors at the far end of the throne room, flanked by his guards, I couldn't make myself look anywhere else.

His jacket was the darkest hue of indigo wool, with gold embroidery at the hems and around his collar. An ankle-length cape flowed from his shoulders, trimmed with the sigils of all four Houses. His boots, gloves, and shirt were spotless. He strode forward, immaculate with those strong features and dark eyes.

Exhaustion left his skin pale and darkened the spaces below his eyes. Every step was steady, controlled, and though he held his head straight and high, I caught furtive glances until he found me.

Flutters rippled down my middle.

Whispers fell from the crowd: "The heir to four Houses," and "The Mirror King has risen." Prophecies. Predictions. *Hope* that Tobiah would save the Indigo Kingdom from the wraith.

The procession seemed to take forever, but his eyes remained locked on mine. These were the last moments of Tobiah as the Crown Prince of the Indigo Kingdom, the last moments of him as the boy I'd met ten years ago.

Within weeks, he'd be married and burdened by responsibilities.

He wasn't for me.

As his mother stood, a slim figure in the corner of my vision, I dropped my eyes. An ache stirred inside me as Tobiah's expression slipped and straightened. As though I'd hurt him.

He finished walking to the dais and empty throne next to his mother. The queen regent offered her hands to her son in greeting. Then, Tobiah knelt and the others began their parts.

I waited, watching Prince Colin for any sort of threat, but he just smiled and pretended to be happy, and somehow that made everything worse.

Within the hour, Tobiah was king.

A celebratory ball followed the coronation. The room was filled with glittering people dancing and laughing as though there were no problems outside this room. Gowns flared and ladies swirled. Men congratulated one another on their suits, or the women on their arms.

I spent the majority of it performing my duties of dancing with every high-ranking official who asked. Several tried to weasel into my good graces by offering support for my return to Aecor. A few were drunk already, and offered to be my king. Although I didn't have a chance to dance with Tobiah or James, I kept them in the corner of my vision, along with Prince Colin. The longer he went without making a move, the more nervous I got.

Toward the middle of the evening, while I was talking with the Ospreys between dances, Lady Meredith approached, her chin lifted and her jaw tight.

"Princess Wilhelmina, may I speak with you a moment?" A thread of nervousness wove through her voice.

Memory of her conversation with Prince Colin seeped up like oil. "Is something wrong? Is there something I can help you with?" I wasn't sure there was anything I could really do besides urge her to speak with James, but maybe that was all she needed: a nudge.

She glanced around the ballroom. "Would you mind stepping outside?"

"Of course not."

Outside, rain pattered on the terrace and thrummed on the canvas awning above. Water leaked across the stone in shimmering streams that smelled faintly of wraith. The air was sharp and cold, making both of us shiver, but Meredith looked determined.

"I'm going to speak plainly," she said.

"Go on."

"When you first came here, disguised as Julianna Whitman, I was under the impression you didn't care for Prin—King Tobiah very much. Now that your true identity is revealed, your attitude toward him seems to have shifted and I find myself uncertain whether your previous disdain was part of your act, or true dislike. But either way, I'm aware that *something* has changed."

I clenched my jaw. This wasn't a plea for help; this was a confrontation.

"Perhaps it is that *he* has changed, too. He's less severe. More open. He smiles now, in spite of everything." She hesitated and dropped her voice. "He smiles at you."

I said nothing, but my stomach tied itself into knots and that terrible yearning washed over me.

She shifted her weight to one hip. "Your Highness. I won't pretend I know you well, but my fiancé seems to see something worthwhile in you. Since he does not trust easily, I must assume you've somehow earned it, and proven yourself honorable in his eyes."

If only I'd managed that. I couldn't imagine what Tobiah saw in me. Perhaps he'd admired me when we were children—I'd saved him—but now, with all he knew about me, I knew better than to think he believed I was *honorable*.

She continued. "His Majesty and I have been engaged since long before you arrived in Skyvale Palace. I do not suppose His Majesty *loves* me. I know why he's marrying me. But I do love him, and this kingdom, and you should know that I intend to take my place as queen."

"I have no intentions of coming between the two of you."

The duchess softened a touch. "We haven't spent much time together, but I've enjoyed your company when we've had the chance. I believe you genuine in your desire to better Skyvale, especially if you truly are Black Knife."

The clatter of rain filled a pause, both of us perhaps remembering her discussion about Black Knife with the ladies in the solar. She hadn't liked the vigilante then, and it was impossible to tell what she thought of him now. Her tone was completely neutral.

"I want us to be friends. I hope you know I am sincere when I make that offer."

She was everything King Terrell had believed her to be: kind, generous, and graceful. "I do know," I said. "And I hope you know that I have no intentions of interfering with your relationship with King Tobiah. I dislike him less now, but I never wanted him like that."

Never the prince. Only the vigilante.

Meredith smiled, tension rolling from her shoulders. "I believe you. Now, shall we dance? We have a lot to look forward to. The restoration of mirrors, Skyvale pulling itself back together, and I can even teach you how to spin yarn if you like. . . ."

Arm in arm, we turned to go back inside, just in time to see a curtain swish back into place and Prince Colin's shape sliding away from the window. Meredith's hand tightened on my arm.

He'd been watching us.

SIXTEEN

I MISSED MELANIE more than ever.

Meredith was not my best friend, not even close. After we talked a few minutes, smiling at each other in plain view of the guests, she went off to visit with Lady Chey and Lady Margot.

I wandered the fringes, spotting Kevin trailing after his tutor like he was trying to work up the courage to speak with her. He was too slow, though; Alana accepted another man's offer to dance. Meanwhile, Theresa flirted with a young man from the Indigo Order. Karl and Connor were drooping, having eaten half the buffet table by themselves; I sent them to their quarters to sleep it off.

I spotted Tobiah and James not quite concealed by a hanging banner, and made my way toward them. "This isn't the time." The king's voice was low. Anxious.

"Then when? I realize it's not a priority, but I want to investigate what happened." James's hand breezed over his stomach.

"I'm not sure." Tobiah drew him toward the public again. "After all of this is done with . . ."

"Dance, Your Highness?" Prince Colin stood directly behind me. The swelling music did nothing to conceal the dislike in his voice.

I spun to find him wearing his typical sneer. He held out a hand, mocking me.

If I declined, what would he do? What kind of show would he make? I was trying to give the impression I was cooperating with the Indigo Kingdom. But if I accepted and later it came out that he'd been in my room the other night, what would people assume?

Did it even matter? What would Melanie suggest?

"I have a proposition for you," he said. "I'm willing to give you Aecor."

I didn't move. "You're lying."

"Very well. I'll just stand here and let everyone see you snub me."

"I'm sure no one will blame me." I started to turn away, but he grabbed my arm and yanked me back.

"It's a good offer, Your Highness."

I pitched my voice low and dangerous. "If you do not remove your hand from me, I will remove it from you."

A smile sliced across his face. "Wouldn't that bring talk?"

People around us were beginning to notice our exchange. A few lifted eyebrows. Kevin paused his pursuit of Alana Todd.

"Dance with me, Your Highness, or I promise you will never retake your kingdom."

My stomach turned over, but everyone was watching now. I

caught James take a step forward, and Tobiah motion him back.

"Very well." Because I wouldn't let them see me weak. "One dance. Make your proposal quick. And do not touch me again."

Prince Colin pulled away and bowed, and on the dance floor, he placed his hands behind his back.

I buried my fists in my skirts and tried to ignore the stares of surrounding nobility. "Well? You have until the end of this dance." The waltz was halfway through, thank saints. And while it was awkward, uncomfortable even, to dance with our hands down, I would not let him get closer than a low speaking voice would carry.

"You want Aecor Territory returned."

"You know I do."

"And I would be happy to return it to you—in exchange for a piece of information."

The room suddenly seemed too cold, but I kept my tone mild. "I doubt I'll be able to help you."

"Oh, I'm sure you can. It has to do with my nephew and his miraculous recovery. I'm so pleased, you understand. I was afraid I might lose a nephew in addition to a brother, but by Terrell's memorial, he seemed quite well."

"We're all fortunate His Majesty's injuries were not as dire as announced. Unfortunately we weren't able to flush out Patrick Lien, but he's no longer in the city, and no longer a threat to King Tobiah's life."

"I wouldn't say that, Your Highness. My people in Aecor Territory inform me that Lien is *not* heading for the locations presumed by Captain Rayner's, ah, intelligence."

The list of resistance groups Melanie had left flitted through

my mind. Had she been wrong? Had Patrick caught her? Or . . .
No, I couldn't believe she would play both sides. Not after everything we'd been through.

Prince Colin could be lying.

"Lien remains a threat," said Prince Colin. "And I think we both know what he wants. What you want, too."

To declare myself queen.

"I'm willing to give you that opportunity. Save your kingdom the war. Save the Indigo Kingdom from fighting both the wraith and your people."

Loathing surged through me. This was a man with no shame, and no sympathy for the people in either kingdom. Not for the soldiers who'd be fighting the war, and certainly not for the civilians who'd be caught in the middle. "If you're so concerned, why angle for an exchange? Why not just acknowledge my birthright?"

"It's never wise to give away something valuable." He glanced toward Tobiah and Francesca. "Not without certainty of receiving something more valuable in return."

"And that would be?"

"My prize is none of your concern." He stopped moving as the music ended. "I suppose we're out of time."

"What exactly do you want to know?" My heart pounded as we stepped off the dance floor. The hum of conversation kept us from being overheard, but still I caught questions in the eyes of my friends.

"My man saw you the morning after the shooting. He said you nearly killed him." Prince Colin smiled again. "He saw my nephew standing when, hours before, I'd seen a hole in my nephew's stomach. I want to know what happened."

"Nothing happened." Lying, at least, had always come easy. I gave away nothing.

"I know you have no love for my nephew, Princess. It's such a small thing to trade for your kingdom."

Meaning if I told him what Connor had done, he'd use the information to malign Tobiah and take the Indigo Kingdom—a much better prize than Aecor, at least until the wraith arrived.

But if I didn't, he'd believe it confirmation of what he hinted to Meredith earlier.

Meredith, who hadn't budged when he'd approached her. She was stronger than I'd realized.

When Prince Colin saw us together tonight, having gotten nothing out of her earlier, he'd decided to change tactics with his other target: offer me the thing I wanted most, rather than try to frighten me from it.

"What you saw the night of the shooting was your nephew feigning sleep, and covered with cosmetics," I said. "It was an illusion meant to fool everyone. We hoped news of his condition would put Patrick at ease, making him easier to capture."

The music began for another dance, and couples moved toward the floor again.

"I see." Prince Colin smoothed the sleeves of his jacket. "That's not what I was expecting to hear, but if you decide to change your answer, the offer stands until"—he seemed to think—"winter solstice eve."

The day before Tobiah and Meredith got married.

"Good evening, Your Highness." With that, he slithered off to harass someone else.

* * *

Manners dictated I stay until the twenty-third hour, so I dodged questioning glances and spent time with the buffet, which would never be the same after Carl and Connor. But as soon as the clock struck, I found Tobiah—who was speaking with his mother, Meredith, and her parents—and offered my congratulations before I left. And because he was already engaged in conversation, he could not pursue me.

Sergeant Ferris, of course, strode only two paces behind me. "Your Highness, it's not my place to ask—"

"Then don't ask."

He was silent the rest of the way to my door, and there he bade me good night.

It was there, on the interior side of my door, that I found a black envelope pinned to the wood. It was thick with paper: a long reply to my last note to him.

A bubble of laughter formed in my chest as I freed the letter and found a chair by a light.

> *Wilhelmina,*
>
> *James is always telling secrets about me, isn't he? Though some truly are lies. You've seen me fight with a sword. And have you ever seen me chew with my mouth open? No, not once. What a horrible gossip James is. Why are we friends? I'll have to begin searching for a new best friend. If you're interested in applying for the position, I'll need your referrals and a testimony of your honesty—*
>
> *Never mind. You would simply forge yours, if indeed you could even be bothered to apply. I suppose I will have*

to continue as I have been, suffering James's company.

In spite of his history of scandalous lies, he was correct about my interest in magic.

Until I met you—in Skyvale, not as children—my stance was unwavering, as you know. But my stance did not diminish my interest in the subject, though I was forced to hide my fascination with such an unsavory topic.

Once, the world existed on magic. Factories employed appropriately skilled radiants to produce clothes or furniture or building supplies. Farms hired them to plant crops or encourage growth, and then assist with the harvest and distribution. Shops kept employees who could spot the dishonest to prevent thievery. It seems to me that relatively not long ago—for history is long—radiants were coveted people and those who didn't possess magic were mere second class. What a sight it must have been two hundred years ago, when radiants built Skyvale Palace and shaped the foundations of the city with just waves of their hands. The legacy of magic is feats we may never again accomplish without its aid.

Plumbing and lighting originally installed in the palace and mansions all over the Indigo Kingdom have been made useful once again, with new technology that doesn't require magic. That is an impressive feat of its own, and one I don't want to diminish, but how can it compare to what once was?

Even further, while those major magical accomplishments are certainly something to admire— under the light of the past, rather than today's nonmagical standards—I am even more impressed when I imagine the smaller ways the lives of our ancestors were affected by magic. Imagine: pens that didn't need to be re-inked, paper that absorbed the likeness of a person as though a master artist had painted their portrait, lights that illuminated the moment someone walked into a room. Imagine a blade that never dulled, a mask that never slipped, or a device that distorted one's voice just enough to disguise it without making it sound unnatural.

That world of magic and convenience is fascinating to me.

Perhaps I was born in the wrong time. Two hundred years ago, my interests would not have been so forbidden. Indeed, I would have been able to study openly, without embarrassment. I'm not embarrassed that you know—I'm glad James told you—but I wish I'd been able to tell you myself.

I wonder what you would have used your magic for if you'd lived two hundred years ago, too. In those days, Aecor and the Indigo Kingdom were on much more friendly terms, so no doubt we would have grown up as companions.

With deep affection,
Tobiah

I moved to my desk to write back, taking my time as I selected smooth paper and glossy ink. My choice for nib was easier: I took a pointy, flexible nib that would give me wide swells on the downstrokes, and fine hairlines on the upstrokes.

James had tasked me with continuing my search for my own handwriting, and I intended to practice until I was satisfied. Writing calmed me, and by the time the maid arrived to help me out of my gown—and tut over the ink smears on my fingers—I felt almost at ease.

When the maid left, I changed into my Black Knife clothes and went out the window, over the roof, and onto Tobiah's balcony.

The lock was easy enough to pick again, and I slipped inside the dark room without resistance, pausing only a moment to let my eyes adjust. The shapes and shadows were the same as the last time I'd been here, except now there was a framed drawing of Black Knife on one wall. How scandalous.

I slipped my letter in the corner of the frame just as the dressing room door opened. A banner of light shone over the far wall as I ducked into the shadow of a bookcase. The gas lamps flickered on, dazzling me.

"Well," said Tobiah, "you're later than I expected."

I leaned on the wall and let my head drop back. "Someone couldn't just get crowned king and be done with it. I had to stay for almost the whole party after."

He laughed as he stepped around the bookcase, clad in a loose shirt and trousers. Black, predictably.

"Dressed for bed already?" I lifted my hand to my sword hilt. "I thought you might want to get some air."

He wrinkled his nose. "I was crowned king today and held a party that went on too long. Isn't that enough for you?"

"Being king has changed you. You never want to have fun

anymore." With a fake pout, I slipped around him and unhooked my baldric. "But I suppose I can see why you might need to rest after dealing with all those people."

"Speaking of all those people, what did my uncle say?"

I stopped short of laying the baldric and sheathed sword on his desk. "Nothing interesting." My things dropped to the desk with a heavy *thunk*.

"Unfortunately, my uncle is rarely *uninteresting*."

I shrugged and made sure my mask was on straight. "He made a request, but it doesn't matter. I've already decided what to do about it."

"And?"

"I'm going to do the worst thing one can to a man like him: ignore him. Show him that he's nothing." Even if I thought he'd actually release Aecor to me, betrayal was yet another method I wouldn't use to take it back. I needed to do it honestly. "What about you? I heard a tense discussion with James. Are you all right?"

"Eavesdropping is rude."

"And yet it's a way of life for some of us."

He gave an exasperated smile. "James wants to know how he healed. I'm looking into it, but mostly I'm grateful he's still with us. Losing him would break me."

"I feel the same about Melanie." I shifted my weight toward him and put on my best mock-serious tone. "Did you know snake-lizard venom eats the edges of swords?"

"Wil!" He threw his hands in the air. "Consider that my final gift to you. You haven't even had it a week and you've already ruined it."

"You must have a low opinion of me, Your Majesty. I took very good care of the gown."

"The gown?"

"Silver, with ospreys clutching swords embroidered across the bodice. They looked just like these boots, so I know you're responsible for it." I propped my foot up on the edge of the desk chair. Black ospreys soared around my calf, just below my knee. "Tell me, Your Highness, do you embroider?"

"Ah, *that* gown." His smile faltered and memory fogged across his eyes. "The one you wore to my father's . . ."

My breath hitched. His father's birthday ball, when he'd argued with King Terrell about marrying Meredith, and later we'd kissed in the breezeway, maybe at the same moment Patrick was sneaking into the king's sleeping chambers.

Tobiah slumped toward the edge of his bed and sat. His fingers clutched vaguely at his heart, as though he could rip out the pain. But it wouldn't go away. Not ever.

"I'm sorry," I said. "I didn't mean to bring that up." I was thoughtless.

He lifted his eyes to me. "No, it's part of my life now." Understandably, he'd think of his father now, when only hours ago he'd taken his father's place. "I didn't accept your help after the Inundation. It was foolish. I'd like to accept your help now, if you're still offering," he said.

"Of course." Haltingly, I crossed the room and stood before him. "Of course I'm still offering."

He reached for me, arms lifted up like hope, and suddenly we were holding each other so tight. His fingertips dug into my shoulder blades. I hated myself for ever thinking he was spoiled, having ten extra years with his father. It hurt fiercely, no matter when it happened, and there was no pain compared to that of seeing one's father die, or finding his body.

"I'm so sorry," I whispered into his hair. Neither of us could have prevented our parents' murders, but the pain and what-if were undeniable.

I'd been a child when it happened. Innocent. Terrified. Forever changed because of what I'd seen.

He was older. Less innocent, but still terrified, because he was expected to be a king now.

Get married. Win a war. Stop the wraith from destroying everything.

He spent so much time being everything for everyone else: a son, a prince, a hero.

"I should have protected him," he whispered, drawing back. He looked so devastated. "I should have spent more time with him and been there when Patrick came. I thought the city needed me, but it was my family I'd neglected all along."

"You were doing something good. Your father would have been proud if he'd known." I bit my lip and met his eyes. "I didn't get to know him well."

"I know."

"During the breakfast I shared with him, he only wanted to talk about you. His regrets. But I think he would have been proud that you'd taken the initiative to venture into the city, how you fought to help your people in a way most kings or princes would never dream. The night of his birthday ball, he said he hadn't put his family first. It was always his kingdom that got his attention. That might be the price of ruling. That was a lesson you learned from him, and one you put into action when you put on your mask. So yes, I think he'd be proud of you for becoming the king he'd trained you to be."

"Yet I still disappointed him. The last words we exchanged were in anger."

I touched his face, my gloves ink against the parchment of his skin. "That would never stop him from loving you. You're his son."

He tilted his face so the curve of his cheek fit in the cup of my palm. His hair tangled around the tips of my fingers and his breath warmed a sliver of skin showing between my glove and sleeve. "You are a mystery, Wilhelmina. You won't accept anything that even resembles assistance or comfort, but you offer both so freely."

The mask hid my tired smile.

Cautiously, like I might run, he leaned forward and kissed me. Silk clung between our lips for a heartbeat, and he pulled back to search my eyes. Only the mask prevented more, and his expression was a question of hope and yearning.

My heart thundered as I shifted toward him, chin tilted upward.

His fingers slid beneath the mask, cool against my throat. Slowly, the silk slipped up and off my mouth and nose and eyes, then dropped to the bed as Tobiah moved close. There was a long, hesitating moment with fire surging through me. All the places we touched were bright and sharp and sensitive. More than anything, I wanted this part to linger—this aching and wanting, with his fingertips glancing off my jaw, when anything was possible. We might still make the right choice.

But what was one more mistake?

A soft groan escaped as I pushed toward him, and he pulled me in, and then I sat astride his lap, kissing him. Our mouths, touching. Our breaths, gasping. Our hands, grasping. The silk of his shirt slid across his skin where I caressed. His shoulders and arms were strong and toned, and the muscles flexed when he pulled the tie off the end of my braid and combed his fingers through my hair. His palm pressed flat against my spine and lit fires at the small of my back. His free hand rested on my hip, holding me in place.

He whispered my name between kisses, moving from my lips to my cheeks to my jaw to my throat. He made me feel alive.

This *felt* right. It felt like being back in the breezeway with the night around us, and our bodies pressed close together. When I'd explored his face with my fingers, not knowing his true identity. I'd never wanted someone like that. *Loved* someone like that.

Reluctantly, I pulled away, pieces of me at a time. My arms from around his shoulders. My chest from his chest. My legs from his lap.

"Wilhelmina." His eyes were still closed. Time stretched like distance between us, and finally he looked at me. "I'm sorry. I shouldn't have—"

"It's my fault, too." My eyes cut to the balcony where I should have gone as soon as he'd declined to go out tonight. "And I'm sorry."

He pushed up from his bed and took my mask. "I wish we didn't have to say that." He ran the mask between his fingers for a moment, expression unreadable when he looked at it. Then he handed it to me and nodded toward the frame. "Thank you for the letter."

A strange sort of tension formed between us, palpable and ugly. Once, we'd known each other as enemies, and now I could still feel the shape of him in my arms. Now we were our own enemies. "I'd better go."

On the balcony, wind picked at my loose hair, but I pulled on my mask and turned my eyes to the diamond-dark sky, listening for the cadence of patrol footfalls and voices.

Through the chilly night, I ran as far and fast from Tobiah as I could.

SEVENTEEN

THE FOLLOWING DAY, an invitation card arrived:

> *Princess Wilhelmina,*
> *Please join me in the ladies' solar at ten. I have been*
> *throughout the palace collecting donations for the poor,*
> *but I need assistance sorting. Bring your friends. All*
> *hands are helpful hands.*
> *Very best,*
> *Meredith Corcoran*

The reverse had a gold unicorn embossed on the heavy paper.

I shouldn't have been surprised it was Meredith who stepped forward to help. She'd also been the one to initiate sewing time in the ladies' solar, creating works of art to send to soldiers.

Groggily, I found blankets and clothes from the suite to add to the boxes, and then fetched the Ospreys.

When we arrived in the solar, the duchess was surrounded by baskets and crates overflowing with donations.

"Oh, thank saints!" she cried. "I'm so glad you're here."

It wasn't the usual reaction to my arrival, but I hazarded a smile. "We brought a few items." Which was silly, perhaps. All these things had been given to us by King Terrell or Tobiah. None of it was ours to give.

But if we didn't want it or need it and there was a better use . . .

"How kind of you." Meredith cleared a place on the floor for our boxes. She flitted about the room, placing large, empty crates along one wall. "We'll fill these for shelters in the Flags. Try to put an even number of every type of item in each crate. There are lists for which shelters are requesting specific items; some we might be able to accommodate, but most are requesting *everything*."

"Sounds simple." I waved for Theresa and the boys to begin. They rushed through the room, each of them taking charge of a group of crates.

"I'm so glad you came," Meredith repeated, watching the Ospreys work. "I invited a dozen ladies. I don't know why they aren't here. They all said they wanted to help."

"Did they know I'd be here?"

She hesitated, almost like she wanted to lie, but she was incapable of dishonesty. Her shoulders dropped. "I mentioned I'd sent you an invitation."

"We don't have to stay if it will affect your time with your friends."

Meredith waved that away. "It was their decision to put

their personal feelings above the needs of our people. I would like you to stay."

I eyed her askance, searching for hidden agendas, but she appeared genuine.

"It is human nature to avoid what makes us uncomfortable." Meredith took a pair of slightly worn dancing slippers and placed them in a nearby crate, though what use those would be in the Flags, I wasn't sure.

"And Chey?" I asked. "What about her?"

Meredith pressed her mouth into a line, thoughtful. "Her absence isn't surprising, and not entirely without justification. You gave her hope that her friend was alive. You attempted to deceive her, along with the rest of palace society. But she wasn't honorable, either. She should have confronted you directly, rather than allow the deception to continue. She shouldn't have tried to humiliate you."

I'd probably have done the same thing in Chey's place.

"The others likely followed her lead. That's something she and I and the others will work on later. For now, we have boxes to fill."

King Terrell had been correct: Meredith was exactly what this kingdom needed.

Heart heavy with guilt, I worked with her for three hours, taking only a short break for lunch.

Carl and Connor held an eating race, both trying to impress Meredith by how quickly they could shovel food down their throats without chewing. Theresa tried to hide a vaguely sick, embarrassed look, and Kevin made fun of the younger boys in a way designed to make Meredith laugh. Of course, she didn't.

"Where will your wedding be held?" Theresa asked as we finished with the last of the day's work. "Since the cathedral is"—she glanced at me—"gone."

I pushed away the memory of last night: Tobiah's hands on my back, his mouth on mine. . . .

That couldn't happen again.

"The palace has a lovely chapel." Meredith didn't miss a beat as she pulled a lid onto a full crate. "We'll use that. I prefer a smaller, more intimate wedding anyway. My parents are paying for much of the ceremony, feast, and ball, but with the kingdom in such a state, I don't think an extravagant wedding would be appropriate."

"Oh, of course not." Theresa shot me a look asking how *that* wasn't extravagant.

The clock chimed thirteen, and Meredith turned to me. "His Majesty's first audience is going to start soon. I thought we should be there to offer a pair of friendly faces."

"Good idea." I turned to Theresa and the boys. "Lessons or audience? It's your choice."

"Lessons." Kevin had the gleam of infatuation in his eyes. "Audience will be boring. Just a lot of problems and people talking."

Grudgingly, Carl and Connor agreed, and I sent the three of them back to their apartments with a guard.

"I hope you don't mind me coming with you," Theresa said. "Their company gets exhausting sometimes."

"Saints, I'm sure." Meredith hooked her arm with Theresa's. "I've never seen sweeter, more hardworking boys, but they do require constant supervision, don't they?"

We walked to the throne room, Theresa and Meredith chatting the whole way.

The chamber was already full when we arrived, but there was space at the front reserved for Meredith and me. We squeezed Theresa in between us. Several of Meredith's friends—Chey, Margot, and the others who frequented the solar for needlework—cast frowns our way, but if Meredith noticed them, she didn't comment.

Theresa gazed at the dragon art filling the room, awestruck as if she hadn't spent last evening here, too. "Imagine the redecorating if another House were to take the throne one day."

"It's said if another House took the throne, the kingdom would fall apart." Meredith smiled indulgently. "But that's just a story House of the Dragon made up centuries ago. The Gearys were Dragon, too, you know."

"King Tobiah is Dragon, but what's this 'heir to four Houses' I keep hearing?" Theresa frowned at a dragon sculpture. "Doesn't that count as another House taking the throne?"

"Oh no." Meredith leaned close and lowered her voice. "It's another wishful tale, but it is true that King Tobiah's parents are from two different Houses, and his grandparents cover the other two. Hence the four Houses."

"That sounds like everyone making themselves feel better by assigning significance to nothing special."

"Some people appease their fears by idolizing their king." Meredith nodded thoughtfully. "But that's what people do sometimes, and there is a little specialness in being a direct descendant of four Houses. It's unusual."

The general hum of voices lowered as Tobiah emerged from

a group of men he'd been talking with. He took his throne, and his mother took the smaller one next to him. Both were formally dressed; Tobiah wore a gleaming crown.

His eyes scanned the audience, settling on Meredith and me. The prince mask returned. King mask, now.

One of the attendants called the audience to order. "Presenting His Majesty King Tobiah Pierce, House of the Dragon, and Sovereign of the Indigo Kingdom."

Applause exploded over the throne room, and the king mask fell away to reveal a smile that shone with something between pride and grief. He was king, as he was meant to be, but he was king *now* for only one reason.

As the cheering died, Tobiah lifted his voice so it rang across the chamber. "My father was known for being a fair and generous man during his audiences. That's something I always admired. I want to be known for the same strong qualities. I'm afraid our current wraith situation will make that even more of a challenge, but even more necessary, too. Already Skyvale is receiving refugees from the southern reaches of the land. Every decision I make from this moment forward must be colored by that knowledge.

"To that effect, I would like to announce that I am making a number of immediate changes. First: all refugees, regardless of their homeland, will be welcomed into Skyvale."

A few people clapped, Meredith and Theresa among them.

"This brings me to the second point: those same refugees, along with anyone else in the city, will be given jobs. In addition to restoring normalcy to Skyvale, I intend to restore the mirrors that were shattered during the Inundation. As well, I want mirrors all along the western border of the Indigo Kingdom."

That announcement was met with a mixture of alarm, confusion, and hope.

Behind me, someone whispered, "We need *food*, not refugees and mirrors."

"Finally, I am finished relying on passive measures to resist the wraith. This morning, I sent orders to build a facility south of the city. Plans are already being drawn up, and construction will begin by the end of the week."

People in the front rows shifted uncertainly.

"The Liadian barrier held off the wraith for a year. We are going to build one as well, with an eye toward improving the longevity. Our barrier will be created in the new facility. Additionally, there will be a holding area for wraith creatures, and rewards for those brave enough to capture them alive, and bring them to the facility."

Murmurs erupted across the throne room: the new king was mad, or wraith-touched, or the Aecorian princess was too much an influence.

Tobiah lifted a hand, and the whispering stopped. "I know this sounds alarming and outrageous to a lot of you, but our kingdom is in danger. We are desperate." His dark eyes found mine, making my stomach drop. "My wraith mitigation committee is hard at work, and from now on, we will not simply try to *mitigate* the wraith's effects, but *prevent* it from further entering the Indigo Kingdom."

Meredith, Theresa, and I clapped, and gradually others joined in. A slight lowering of his shoulders was the only indication of relief Tobiah showed.

When Tobiah indicated, the audience began, first with petitions for food or financial aid disguised as praises of his generosity. He sat through all of these, granting some requests, but denying others.

"Why is he saying no to some?" Theresa whispered. "Those people need help."

Meredith kept her voice soft. "Some are testing him, hoping to get favors they don't need. This one, for example, says he needs shipments of grain, but the land he controls around Hawes has plenty of unused fields. They're not starving, and they're certainly not affected by the wraith."

"Ah. So if he wants more grain, he should plant it, rather than take it from areas that actually need it."

"Right. And His Majesty knows that. He studied with his father for years to gain this kind of knowledge."

Theresa nodded toward the next petitioner. "What about this one?"

They continued on for a while, Theresa asking questions and Meredith giving opinions on why Tobiah made certain decisions. I listened, but found myself studying the others in attendance. Most were leaning toward one another in conversation, while a few looked ready to sneak out.

And who could blame them? None of the petitioners were particularly interesting, but everyone stayed because this was the *first* audience, and no one wanted to be remembered for leaving early.

The audience continued for three hours. Everyone wanted to see the new king, it seemed. But at last Tobiah said no more, and those closest to the doors began to slink out. But before the exodus could begin, a man crashed into the chamber, not waiting to be announced.

"Your Majesty—" He bent over his knees to catch his breath. Damp, too-long curls covered his face, and torn, ragged clothes hung off his wiry frame. Through the layers of mud and smears of grass, hints of indigo shone: he was a soldier in the Indigo Army.

Tobiah either knew the man or recognized the tattered uniform, because he surged up from his throne and met the man in the aisle. The crowd pushed close around them, held back by the Indigo Order. "What is it?"

My heart pounded. It had to be the wraith. Another town had fallen. It was happening again.

The man coughed and cleared his throat. "Aecor," he said. "I've just ridden from Aecor."

The throne room was silent.

"What about it?" The new king's voice was firm and gentle as he helped the man stand upright. "What about Aecor?" I could almost feel the effort it took for him to not look for me in the crowd. Several others did, though. Theresa, too.

"Patrick Lien has taken the Aecorian city of Northland."

More eyes darted toward me.

"When did this happen?" asked Tobiah.

"Yesterday. The Red Militia is only a small army, but they were devious and the city—they *fought with him*. It had been quiet for so long, but they knew he was coming. We were overwhelmed within hours. My captain sent me to warn you immediately. I rode all night. All day."

Tobiah's jaw clenched. "I see." He motioned for one of the

servants standing by. "Prepare a room and meal for him." He made his voice soft as he spoke to the soldier again. "Rest. I'll speak with you further this evening."

"Thank you, Your Majesty."

The man bowed and left, and Tobiah stood in the aisle, arms hanging at his sides, his head dipped in thought.

Everyone just waited.

Tobiah's chest expanded with a sigh. "General Goldberg. Is he here?"

"No, Sire." Captain Chuter stepped forward. "But what can I do?"

"Alert the forces in Aecor. Send food and supplies. We need to move swiftly, before Lien's control moves south to Aecor City."

"And reinforcements?"

"I'll do what I can."

My breath came in shallow gasps as horror tore through me. Oh, Patrick. Paige. Ronald and Oscar. Melanie.

It was too soon. Why hadn't Melanie stopped this?

After another long pause, Tobiah said, "I regret to inform the court that we are now at war."

EIGHTEEN

I SPENT THE evening pacing in my suite, mind whirling with the thought of war. My kingdom. Tobiah's kingdom. At arms.

For almost ten years, Patrick and I had been working toward war. And now . . .

Dinner arrived. I ate. And when night fell, I busied myself with my writing desk, arranging papers and pens and other tools, only to find myself unsatisfied and rearrange everything again.

At last, I pulled on my leather and silk, and just as I strapped my sword to my back, a tap came on the balcony door. I pushed aside the curtain.

Black Knife watched me, his head tilted, one gloved palm pressed to the glass. Heart pounding, I lifted a hand and laid it flat against his. Only the cool glass stood between us, and the faint light of my bedroom made me cast a reflection over him.

We stood there a moment, Black Knife and me, and then he

touched the door handle, his movements like a question.

Cold wind gusted when I opened the door and stepped outside.

"I thought you'd like to take a walk." He strode to the edge of the balcony, looking over the woods.

The rail was solid against my hips as I leaned on it, next to Black Knife. "What happened this afternoon—it's all I can think about."

"Me too. And it's the last thing I want to discuss right now. I want to go back to how it was before, even if it's just for a few hours."

His arm was only a hair's breadth from mine. If I shifted my weight just so, we'd be touching. "I want that, too."

"I don't want to talk about the war, or what happened last night, or Meredith, either." His shoulders hunched as he leaned forward onto the rail. "I know you've been spending time with her. That's probably good."

"Probably." I started toward the exterior wall where I could easily rappel down the side of the palace.

"I lied." Black Knife faced me, his mask hiding his expression. "I want to say one thing. Meredith is a wonderful and kind person. She's beautiful, smart, generous, and everything a king should want in a queen. But I've always felt"—he touched his mask, as though to reassure himself it was there—"a little like a monster. There are parts of me that I hate, and I face them every day. I'm not good enough for her."

Oh, how I knew that feeling. Easily, I recalled standing in the breezeway, Black Knife saying we were the same, but I hadn't been able to believe it. He was just so *good*, while I'd spent most of my life as a criminal. "What about me?" The question was out before I could stop it.

His regard was thoughtful, searching, and a triplet of heavy moments passed between us before his posture shifted. Shoulders down, chest angled away from me: he'd discarded whatever he'd been about to say. "Sorry, nameless girl. I don't think you're good enough for her, either."

"Obviously." I rolled my eyes, and a few minutes later we were on the ground and racing through the King's Seat and Hawksbill.

Black Knife and I avoided guard patrols and climbed the Hawksbill wall, both of us scanning the city for a direction.

"Flags?" he asked, crouching low. "Or Greenstone?"

I dropped next to him, scowling at the dark city. After years of getting used to the mirrors, it would never look right without them. "Some of the shelter areas need help. The Nightmare gang was harassing one in White Flag last night. I stopped them, but they'll be back."

"Then let's start there."

"She isn't perfect, you know," I said before he could stand. "No one is perfect, and imagining that she's an exception is just setting her up to disappoint you."

"Are you cataloging her faults?"

"No. She *is* all those things you said: kind and generous and smart. But for all those wonderful qualities, she isn't perfect. She loves King Tobiah. She doesn't love Black Knife. She couldn't accept this part of you."

"I'm not supposed to be Black Knife anyway."

"But Black Knife is who you are." I shook my head. "She

might be everything a queen should be . . . for a different king. The way you see her isn't fair to either of you. She'll never live up to the image you've painted, and you can't live your life thinking you're not good enough."

His breath puffed out his mask.

"You're not a monster. You never were."

He stood and offered his hand to help me up. "Let's go. We have work to do."

I didn't take his hand, but I did follow him deeper into the city.

I felt whole. Alive.

Over the next several nights, we hunted glowmen, wraith beasts, thugs, and those who used this strange, transitional time to exploit others. We followed the requests for aid painted onto walls and fences, and located missing friends or family.

It was helping. New shelters sprang up in the Flags and Greenstone, most with reputations of being friendlier toward families than the original ones.

Communities formed, with people cleaning the neighborhood, others guarding, and even more gathering food and caring for their groups.

Even the police seemed more inclined to help the homeless, rather than hunt them. They protected people. The first time we saw it, I looked at Black Knife in shock, and he just smiled beneath his mask.

"I do pay attention to what you say." He bumped his shoulder against mine and nodded toward a glimmer in the west. "Look there."

The glimmer resolved into a glass pane hanging on one of the western guard towers. A mirror. A bubble of laughter gathered in my throat and escaped. "You know what they're going to call you now, right?"

"What?"

I shook my head and jumped to another roof. It was time to find our next request for help. "You're a smart boy. You'll figure it out."

He leapt after me, silent and graceful with every movement. "Just tell me."

"Come on, Black Knife. Your people need us."

Today was a historic day.

The air in the throne room was sharp with anticipation and uncertainty. Nobility from all over the kingdom crowded in, though not as tightly as on the evening of the coronation, or the king's first audience. Also in attendance were the foreign royalty and dignitaries who'd traveled here for the memorial and coronation.

A hush fell as Tobiah strode down the aisle and stopped before a large table set in front of the thrones. His gaze swept over the paper, ink, and pens before he turned to address the assembly.

"There have been several more reports of the Red Militia's movement across Aecor," said King Tobiah. "It's only a matter of time before Lien marches on Aecor City, so the Indigo Army is mobilizing troops."

Soon the Indigo Army would march on Aecor City again. The image made me shudder.

"Because of this," Tobiah said, "we are being forced to move ahead on several items sooner than expected. The first of these is, of course, the Wraith Alliance." He motioned me forward, along with the dignitaries from Laurel-by-the-Sea and the other nearby kingdoms not yet flooded with wraith.

We approached the table, dressed in our best as though we were going to do something grander than sign a piece of paper. My silk gown was vermilion with gold embroidery along the hems. It was a beautiful creation that looked like dripping blood when hanging in my wardrobe.

I stood at the end of the line, next to the king from Laurel-by-the-Sea. When I faced the audience, lines of people stared back at me. There were the friendly faces of my Ospreys, who'd worked so hard to ensure we hadn't missed anything. There was Meredith, tucked in with her group of friends. Chey didn't look angry at me, for once.

Tobiah raised his voice. "Today, a hundred years after the first Wraith Alliance was signed in this very room, we are gathered to sign the agreement once more. The absence of those we've lost is keenly felt, and it is for them, and those who come after us, that the Wraith Alliance has been revised in order to begin a new effort to stop the wraith."

Polite applause sounded through the room, but frowns deepened.

"For a century, we have believed that ceasing all magic use would put a stop to the wraith. For a century, we have been proven wrong. New findings show us that there may be a better way of protecting our kingdoms, and in light of that, the treaty will be revised to allow the use of magic in highly regulated experiments to halt the wraith's approach."

So many people gasped at once, it was a miracle there was any air left in the room.

"While this will likely be the most criticized revision, it means two things: a plan to prevent the wraith from further inundating the kingdom is already in effect, and magic users are invited to join in our effort."

I doubted many flashers would walk up to the palace and offer their services, but at least they'd no longer be sent to the wraithland as punishment for having magic. What *would* happen to people illegally using magic—that was still under debate, but it wasn't part of the Wraith Alliance, so we'd moved on.

"Previously, allies were obligated to shelter only nobility from wraith-fallen kingdoms, leaving thousands of people to suffer in refugee camps, or worse."

Like being forced to remain in the wraithland.

"Under the revised Wraith Alliance, allied kingdoms guarantee entry into their lands to all citizens of wraith-fallen kingdoms. Our world is so small now. We must *protect* those who survive."

That brought a more enthusiastic applause.

"Finally," he said, "the exchange of information regarding the wraith will remain the same. Allied kingdoms will continue sharing, though emissaries will be sent into all kingdoms to ensure there are no omissions."

For example, an entire kingdom's worth of flashers pouring their magic into a barrier.

I hadn't cared as much about that point, but when representatives from other kingdoms heard what happened with Liadia, the debate had lasted hours.

With the revised points out of the way, Tobiah gestured toward the audience. "You, my friends, are here today to witness this historic moment. Today, the new Wraith Alliance is born."

He inked a pen and signed the bottom of the paper. The next man signed, and then the next.

When at last I stood in front of the document, the signatures of those before me already drying, I took the pen and drew a breath. I had no right to sign this. But I'd sworn I'd add my name, and so I would.

But first: "While I'm not yet Queen of Aecor, I sign the Wraith Alliance as a promise. For a century, my ancestors refused this agreement, a stance which has been a source of contention between Aecor and its neighbors. But today, I let go of the past. If there is to be a better world, we must forge it now. Today, I look toward the future."

Light flared out the windows, chased by a long roll of thunder and the slap of rain on glass and stone. But the sound didn't fade. When I blinked, I realized it wasn't only thunder I'd heard, but the din of clapping, and cheering from the Ospreys—and even Meredith.

I'd expected surprise, maybe apathy, but never approval. Not like this. *Everyone* was clapping, both familiar faces and unfamiliar, as if they'd momentarily forgotten all the things I'd done.

Maybe this was as big for them as it was for me: a hundred years of unease was behind us. Signing the Wraith Alliance wasn't going to *fix* problems, but it was a start.

One face stood out from the others. Prince Colin was

smiling, but it was the curled smile of calculating his next move. If I signed this, he'd retaliate.

If I didn't sign it, I wasn't the queen my people needed.

I dipped my pen into the heavy black ink, and hesitated only a moment as I put together my signature in my mind. I'd practiced it since that day in James's office, but this wasn't practice. This was real.

I signed: *Wilhelmina Korte, Princess of Aecor.*

The applause lasted while I cleaned the nib and set aside the pen to join the others who'd signed.

As Tobiah took the center again, he sent a faint nod my way, and waited until the cheers died. "Today is indeed monumental. I only wish we could celebrate this signing properly."

I bit my tongue to contain a snort. That was a lie if I'd ever heard one. Tobiah was *notorious* for skipping social gatherings.

"There is one more event I'm pleased to say has been moved up." He lifted a hand toward Meredith. She glided forward, a smile playing at the corners of her mouth. "It's important to both Lady Meredith and me that all our guests join us on our wedding day. While we considered keeping our original date of the winter solstice, we know the uncertain climate here must make everyone eager to return home.

"As such, my fiancée and I have decided to move forward our wedding. The ceremony will be held in the palace chapel in two days, and will be immediately followed by Lady Meredith's coronation. In two days, the Indigo Kingdom will have its new queen."

NINETEEN

I HAD TO stop going to the throne room. Every time I did, Tobiah delivered bad news.

Though to be fair, the war situation was probably worse than the wedding being moved up.

But that evening, and the following, I went out earlier than usual so he wouldn't find me; the last thing I wanted was a couple of awkward nights of vigilantism, both of us avoiding saying what we were thinking. I needed time alone. And finally, as I dispatched the final glowman of the night and started toward the palace again, I knew what I had to do.

I had to go home.

The Wraith Alliance was signed, the barrier facility was under way, and mirrors gleamed along the western reaches of Skyvale. I'd done what I could here, and now it was time to find Patrick and stop him from destroying my kingdom with this war.

The decision soothed me as I sneaked back through Hawksbill. It didn't matter that what was coming would be incredibly difficult, or that I'd be fighting friends I'd trusted for years. What mattered was that I had a goal, even if I had to ride into Aecor, hunt down the Red Militia, and arrest Patrick myself.

Without thinking, I'd taken the usual route into the King's Seat, so I wasn't surprised when a black-jacketed figure peeled from the darkness around a statue of Terrell the First. "Avoiding me?" asked the shadow.

"Avoiding everyone."

"I see." His gaze stayed steady on mine. "Tonight was my last night."

Because tomorrow he'd be married. "I know." I hadn't thought about it, maybe, but of course it had to be over for him.

He started walking the path we normally took, motioning for me to follow. A few minutes later, we reached one of the outbuildings behind the palace.

"James and I used to practice in here," he said. "Before you came. Then we spent most of our free time trying to figure out why you and Melanie were impersonating Liadian nobility."

He closed the door and turned on the light, revealing a wide, empty floor of dusty hardwood. Crates had been shoved against the walls, while shelves sagged with molding table linens, place settings, and old lighting fixtures.

"This was a storage building until we took over." He tore off his mask and scowled around the room. "It still is, I guess."

I took off my mask, too. "This is the kind of place where the Ospreys trained. You were a prince. Wasn't there somewhere nicer? Actual practice rooms?"

"Sure," he said. "But there were always people watching me. Not just our trainers, but nobility, too. It was alarming how much they wanted to see whether James and I would cut each other, or watch our teachers smack us with the flat of their blades when our performance was unsatisfactory." He swept his hand around the room. "I needed this place where I could really practice, because in public, I had to give the illusion of being a mediocre swordsman."

Tobiah's past floated on the dust motes around us. If I closed my eyes, maybe I'd be able to hear echoes of his sword crashing against James's.

"You should use this room," he said, "unless you're planning on giving up this nocturnal habit."

"I still need it," I whispered, and drew my sword. The blade was clean, but the steel was melted and lumpy on one edge.

"That poor blade. Do you even feel bad?" He eyed it with a look of feigned disappointment.

"I blame the snake-lizard. And maybe this other person who called himself Black Knife. He promised lessons and never delivered, so I've had to use the one trick I know."

"And that is?"

"Putting the appropriate end in my opponent every time."

Tobiah drew his sword and allowed the light to glint off the flat of his blade. "Maybe he can make it up to you now."

"Don't be silly. You're not Black Knife. Everyone knows Princess Wilhelmina is that awful vigilante."

He lunged to attack; I lifted my blade to block. "Everyone doesn't know that. A lot of the city people believe you are"—his blade slid off mine with a *shing*—"but there's quite the rumor spreading that while Wilhelmina was in the wraithland, Black Knife was still in Skyvale."

"Outrageous! Untrue!" I twisted my sword down for a slice across his flank, but he pulled away.

"I've heard Black Knife isn't as good as he used to be." Tobiah aimed for my chest, forcing me back a step as I hurried to block. There was no time to flick my little finger at him, because he thrust toward my stomach; I dodged.

We traded blows, attacking and blocking slowly as we warmed up. The sound of our blades clashing filled the room.

"I really was looking for you tonight," he said between blows. "Patrick and the Red Militia—have taken Aecor City. Sandcliff Castle is his."

His.

No, Sandcliff Castle was meant to be mine. Gritting my teeth, I attacked Tobiah's side, breaking our rhythm. "What happens now?"

He blocked the stroke with ease. "My uncle rides for Aecor in three days."

"With an army?" I attacked his chest, but he parried and moved inside my guard.

"With an army." The point of his blade rested at my throat, and neither of us moved. "It's not ideal, but it's the decision I have to make as king, and the action he has to take as overlord."

"And what action do you suggest I take as the rightful heir to the vermilion throne?"

"I know what you are. *Everyone* knows." He lowered his sword and stepped close, so we were only a breath apart. "But the Indigo Kingdom conquered Aecor during the One-Night

War. It belongs to me, and to my uncle, and as much as I want you to have your kingdom, we both must wait."

"Until when? Until the barrier is built? Until the wraith has flooded the Indigo Valley? Until there's nowhere to go but Aecor? I imagine my kingdom will be very useful to you *then*." I clenched my jaw.

His tone softened. "You know that's not how our Wraith Alliance works."

"Then when?" I asked.

"When we are all ready."

"Your uncle will only relinquish the title of overlord when he's acquired the one he truly wants." The memory of our conversation at the coronation ball made me shudder.

"Did something happen?" He searched my eyes and read the truth. "He said something to you?"

"He doesn't need Aecor if he has the Indigo Kingdom, does he?" My grip on my sword tightened. "Not that he'd ever give up Aecor. If the barrier doesn't work, Aecor is too valuable."

"*What* did he say?"

"He offered Aecor for the truth of your recovery. To malign you."

In the long pause that followed, I waited for him to ask whether I'd taken the deal, but he just shook his head. "Then perhaps it's best he's going away."

Perhaps this was a bad time to tell him I was going away, too.

Tobiah sheathed his sword and rubbed his temples. "I wish you'd trusted me enough to tell me."

"I told you I was going to ignore him."

"That's not trust, Wilhelmina." He took a long breath. "If you think that trusting someone—allowing them to help you by performing their own duties honorably—somehow makes you *less*, then it might be time to reexamine yourself. Start asking why *you* need to do everything. How can you really be close to someone if you never let them in?"

"Forgive me if I find that difficult." My hand ached from gripping my sword hilt. "It isn't *easy* to trust or be close to someone when the person I love won't even follow his own heart."

Oh, saints. I'd said that out loud. And now the words hung between us, heavier than the dust motes of his past.

His expression stiffened into that proud, bored mask he'd worn as a prince, and he spun and strode toward the door.

For a stuttering heartbeat, I almost let him go.

But I took a step after him, and my fingertips brushed his sleeve. We both stopped moving. "I want to trust you. It's just that everyone I've ever trusted has betrayed me in some way. Even"—not *you*—"Black Knife."

He faced me, hair half hanging in his eyes, shadowing them. All the fire of his argument had drained away, and now he was just a boy who happened to be a king before he was ready.

"I'm sorry," he said. "I hadn't thought about it like that. It wasn't fair of me to judge you." He glanced at my hand still on his sleeve, and I jerked away. "I suppose I'm not as deserving of your trust as I thought."

Trust me. Forgive me. Tell me. How could he ask so much?

"I want to trust you."

"I want to deserve it." He shifted his weight toward me and drew his sword, letting a beam of light glance off the flat of the blade. "We have to work together. I know we can. That's why you're wearing those clothes. And why I'm still alive. We have the same goals, and if we work together, we can achieve them. Imagine what could happen if we stopped fighting each other and started fighting our enemies. You and me together."

My stomach flip-flopped. His sword loose in his grasp was such a familiar sight, the stance and grip and confidence. Only now, his face was uncovered and he was a king, and he'd be married in a few hours. He'd never be Black Knife again.

He sheathed his sword and sighed. "I know I promised a lesson, and kings should always keep their promises. But I don't think it would be appropriate . . ." His throat jumped when he swallowed. "Perhaps James would be a more suitable replacement."

My heart squeezed, but I pushed down the anguish and resentment and forced a note of aloofness into my voice. "I'm sure he would be."

His hand strayed near mine. "Wilhelmina, I *am* sorry."

I stepped backward. "You made a promise to your father. I know." I withdrew farther, deeper into the storage building. "I'm sure you have a lot to do to prepare for your wedding. Please don't let me take up any more of your time."

He drew himself straighter and vanished behind his kingly mask. "Good night, Wilhelmina."

When he was gone, the door secured behind him, I swung my sword around and caught a pile of folded tablecloths. Linen and lace flew into the air as I grabbed tarnished silver candlesticks and hurled them across the room. A pile of plates, a box of wineglasses, a huge serving platter: they all clattered and smashed against the far side of the floor.

A high keening tore from my throat as I ripped more and more *junk* off the shelves and from crates. I pushed over shelves and threw boxes across the room, filling the floor with everything that had been shoved aside.

My arms and legs were shaking by the time I was finished. The room was in ruins, with broken trash strewn across the now-dented floor. Tablecloths lay like shrouds.

"It helps, doesn't it? Breaking things." The wraith boy stood across the room, dark brown hair shading his eyes as he surveyed the wreckage. His skin was brown, and his features knifelike. It seemed his appearance had settled, and he looked too much like me for comfort.

How had he escaped his closet?

"Go away." My voice was hoarse from screaming.

"A man came to my door last night. He told me you're sad. Sad. Bad. Mad. How—"

"Leave!" I hurled a splintering crate at him. "Leave me alone."

"Very well." He sidestepped the crate and bowed low, his tattered clothes fluttering. "What you want is the only thing that matters."

Then he vanished, leaving nothing but the odor of wraith and the awful feeling that he'd known I was upset, and had come to help.

Wraith help. That was one thing I didn't need.

TWENTY

THE BELLS BEGAN pealing at dawn.

Even in my chambers where I prepared for the wedding, I could almost hear the words that rode on the constant ringing. *King Tobiah will save us. The Mirror King will drive away the wraith. King Tobiah and Queen Meredith . . .*

I resisted the urge to cover my ears while a maid plaited my hair into an intricate knot, with tendrils softening the harsh lines of my face. She used cosmetics to conceal the circles under my eyes, and shadow the lids. When she used another powder to highlight my cheekbones she said something about me looking beautiful, but in the mirror, all I saw was my face. And the wraith boy's face.

Morning light shifted, and a small lunch was served.

"Aren't you hungry?" Theresa asked. Her plate was already clean.

I glanced at mine, still full, and slid it across the table to her.

With a suspicious frown, she cleaned my plate, too. I turned my attention out the window, toward the clear sky and the seemingly endless forest behind the palace. Evergreens twisted between the cold, bare trees. The mountains were deep blue, with wisps of clouds washing down between them.

"Try to have fun," Theresa said. "I wish the rest of us could go."

"I'd send you in my place, if I could." Since the cathedral was a pile of rubble, the wedding guest list had been slashed. I'd made the cut, but the rest of the Ospreys hadn't.

With Sergeant Ferris in close attendance, I made my way to the palace's glorious chapel. It had the typical dragon regalia, with unicorns added for Meredith. Blooms of blue and violet and ivory dripped from balconies and banisters, with verdant highlights. The scent of perfume and anticipation danced through the room as the guests were seated.

The memorial had been grand and stately and solemn; the wedding was smaller, but filled with life and hope for the future.

A footman guided me to a bench near the front. I waited as the chamber began to fill with rustling gowns and coats, and murmuring voices. Next to me, a foreign countess took her seat, keeping a large space between us. A string quartet played by the altar. A bubble of hushed voices formed around me.

"The wedding was meant to be held in the cathedral," someone whispered. "But you know what happened to *that*."

"I can't believe she was invited."

I kept my mouth in a line. What would I say to them? That I deserved to be here? That the cathedral collapse wasn't my fault?

The last thing I needed to do today was cause a scene.

"She's a curse on this kingdom," someone muttered. "And she'll curse this wedding."

"Don't say that!"

Surely they knew I could hear, even over the gentle strings playing nearby, which meant they *wanted* me to know what they said.

I glanced over. One of the speakers was Lady Chey, who wore a splendid red gown and a smug expression. A few other ladies I recognized from the solar sat near her, though most of them avoided meeting my eyes.

Tobiah's aunts and uncles and mother sat in the row in front of me. The queen mother held herself stiffly, and if she showed any emotion for her son's wedding day, I couldn't see it from here. Meredith's family sat in the opposite row, all of them with their fine blond hair and bright smiles, visible whenever they turned their faces toward the altar.

They were so happy. Happy for Meredith. Happy for their family. And if they were as nice as Meredith, they were happy for the kingdom as well.

I wanted to sink deeper into my seat. Vanish. Stop feeling at all. It would be easier to be numb than to think.

It wasn't long before priests flowed through the chapel, their robes fanning behind them. A handful of bodyguards moved toward the front of the chamber. James caught my eye and offered a pale smile, but it was only a moment before he resumed scanning the room for danger.

It seemed like the person James *should* be watching was me.

The music shifted, everyone stood, and Tobiah came forward, dark eyed and proud. He wore a suit of deep indigo with gold edging, and long tailcoats that fluttered with his every step down the aisle. Even his hair had been wrestled into submission. A small, plain crown rested on his head, golden contrast to the dark strands.

At the altar, he took his place and turned his attention down the aisle to wait for Meredith.

Instead, his eyes locked with mine.

My breath tripped and I was back in the moment we'd met in his father's office, when I'd come in wearing Lady Julianna's personality like a mask. Me, knowing him from the One-Night War. Him, knowing me from his nights as Black Knife. Neither of us saying anything for long heartbeats, waiting to see if the other recognized . . .

"Recognize this now," I wanted to say. *"Recognize that I love you and when you do this, there's a part of me that will never recover."*

He lowered his eyes as the music built, and a shower of ivory rose petals burst from the ceiling, making the small crowd gasp with awe.

The petals floated like snow, catching in hair and on gowns and in children's cupped palms. Another gasp rippled through the room as Meredith stepped down the aisle and everyone turned to look.

From my aisle seat in the front, my view was partially obstructed by those in the back who leaned outward, but I saw her soon enough.

Meredith was resplendent. Luminous. A glittering net of diamonds rested over her golden hair, while twists and curls spiraled down to her waist. She held her chin high, every part the duchess bride—soon to be queen.

The lengths and folds of her gown hugged her body in shimmering ivory silk, and lace across the bodice. Seed pearls and tiny diamonds had been stitched into outlines of unicorns all around the collar and shoulders, and around the hems of her open sleeves. When she walked, a short train rustled against the floor and the petals strewn there.

Never once did she look away from Tobiah, as if she didn't notice a young girl and boy tossing petals into the air, blowing them toward her. As if she didn't notice her mother and the queen mother clasping their hands to their hearts. As if she didn't notice the music soaring through the room like triumph.

Just Tobiah. Always Tobiah.

At last she took her place beside him, light to his shadow, and the priest began the first of nine saints' blessings. Everyone sat again.

While the priest spoke of love, then joy, then peace, Meredith gazed up at Tobiah, her face soft and lit with happiness. But he looked dull and bored. Cold and distant. What everyone expected him to be, even now.

A knot of agony built in my chest while the priest moved on to the patience blessing, then kindness. Watching Tobiah obey duty, not his heart—I couldn't breathe, and my eyes felt swollen with tears.

Finally, the priest reached the last of the blessings. I bit my cheeks and squeezed my hands together, as if that could hold back the expanding tangle of sorrow.

The words of Tobiah's first letter to me came rushing back as the priest completed the final blessing. *Please forgive me for*

what I'm about to do; know that it is duty and honor that com-
pel me to act against my true feelings.

This was what it had been like for Melanie with Patrick, the aching and longing to be close to someone you weren't supposed to have feelings for. This was why she'd sneaked around for weeks. This was what she'd felt when Patrick had announced his intention to marry me after we reclaimed Aecor.

I wished she were here so I could tell her I understood now, and I didn't blame her. I wished she were here because most of all, I needed my best friend.

At the altar, the priest joined Tobiah's and Meredith's hands, and people all around were crying with happiness. But anguish filled my chest and throat. I was going to explode with it.

Thunder clapped and a boy appeared at the back of the chapel. Everyone turned as he strode down the aisle with dark purpose. My hair, my face, my eyes—Patrick's movements.

The wraith boy.

It happened so quickly:

People yelped and rushed deeper into the seats.

Someone shouted my name.

The priest stopped mid-sentence and pressed his hands to his chest.

Tobiah stepped in front of Meredith.

Across the aisle, the queen mother reached for her son, even as a guard pulled her back. The duchess's mother and father struggled against their guards, too. Prince Herman seemed confused, while Crown Prince Colin wore a strange expression somewhere between horror and triumph.

And I—I was rooted in place.

The wraith boy reached the altar and shoved Tobiah aside. Everyone was shouting, rushing in, and guards moved to intercept the wraith boy, but they were too slow. He was too fast.

He yanked Meredith to him—her eyes went wide—and he snapped her neck.

She dropped to the floor, dead.

"What Queen Wilhelmina wants is the only thing that matters," he announced as the duchess's ivory gown settled around her, and her hair flowed over the floor like a river of gold. Then the wraith boy turned to me, lifted one hand toward Tobiah, and bowed low. "He is yours now, my queen."

TWENTY-ONE

THE SCREAMING STARTED immediately.

Guards threw themselves onto the wraith boy, tackling him to the floor. Others snatched Tobiah and the priest, dragging them from the chaos at the altar, but the king wrenched himself away and ran for Meredith.

The wraith boy threw off the guards. Bodies flew back, some caught by their comrades, while others slammed into benches or the altar. Another layer of guards hurled themselves onto the wraith boy, grabbing for his hands and feet and hair.

"Your Highness!"

I blinked away my stupor, finally registering that Sergeant Ferris was pushing his way between the benches to get to me. Like the wraith boy might attack me.

But he'd *killed* Meredith. For me. He'd *murdered* her.

I surged toward the altar, where the guards still struggled to subdue the wraith boy. He threw them off every time.

The corner of a bench caught my dress. I jerked it free, ripping the fabric. And like a ruined gown was the worst of my problems, the wraith boy shoved toward me. "My queen! Your dress!"

"Take it back!" I screamed. "Fix her!"

As guards moved to block the wraith boy's path to Tobiah, I caught sight of the broken duchess lying before the altar, her gown spread around her like ivory wings.

"Fix her," I rasped. "She can't be dead."

"But you wanted him." The wraith boy pointed at Tobiah, who was bent over his bride.

"No!" I gripped the nearest bench for balance. "I didn't want her to die. Now fix this. Take it back. Undo it."

He shook his head, not quite sadly. "I don't fix things; I break them."

My knees buckled.

James and a handful of other guards grabbed for Tobiah, but he shook them away. Tears streaked down his face as he touched Meredith's white skin. Her cheeks, her throat, her closed eyes. I couldn't hear him over the cacophony, but his mouth formed her name over and over.

"You have to bring her back." I couldn't look away from Meredith.

"This is what you wanted, my queen." The wraith boy smiled, a sly little thing like he believed that and thought I protested merely for the benefit of others.

The scent of crushed rose petals and the sound of stomping boots saturated the air as more guards poured into the chapel, and someone grabbed my shoulders from behind.

"No!" Tobiah lurched to his feet, reaching for me. "Stop!"

It was too late. The wraith boy was already ripping the guards away from me; bones snapped and men screamed. One landed against the altar and didn't move again.

"Stop!" My shout tore through the chapel. "Wraith boy—Chrysalis!"

The wraith boy halted just as he broke a guard's wrist. He let the guard fall to the floor, and turned toward me, awe spreading over his face. "You called me by my name."

Other guards moved in, but Tobiah held up a hand to halt them. James stuck by his cousin's side. Both of them watched me as the remaining guards fell back, dragging their injured with them.

My breath heaved in and out, too heavy. I turned my glare on the wraith boy. "Don't hurt anyone else."

"I was protecting you," the wraith boy whispered. "They were *touching* you."

A high, panicked laugh came out of me. "They were trying to protect me from you." True or not, that was what he needed to believe. "You just killed a woman and a handful of guards. They thought you were going to kill me, too."

His mouth fell open. "I would *never.*"

Meredith's body filled the corner of my vision. Then there was Tobiah, braced between James and a bench. Indigo-coated guards fanned around them. All eyes were on the wraith boy, waiting.

"All you do is break things," I said. "That's all you are. Destruction. Chaos."

"I wouldn't hurt *you,* my qu—"

"No!" I advanced on the wraith boy, as though I had any power to hurt him. "You said that what I want is the only thing that matters. How dare you presume to know what I want?"

"I felt what you wanted. On the balcony, when those men grabbed you, you were terrified." The wraith boy's eyes were wide and pleading. "You wanted to be safe, and I made sure they wouldn't hurt you. And now you want him"—he pointed at Tobiah—"and I thought it was my duty to make sure you could. You were sad, weren't you? Now you don't have to be. What you want is the only thing that matters to me, and you don't even have to tell me what it is, because I know, my queen. I already know."

"What do I want now?" I stopped only a pace away from him. He was exactly my height, and again I had the strange feeling of looking into a warped mirror.

"You want me to go back to my room." His voice was small.

"*Go*," I hissed. "Don't come out again unless I tell you."

He was gone a moment later, vanished, and the air in the chapel suddenly felt less dense. Less oppressive.

I stood alone in the middle of the aisle, not very far from the body of the duchess. Only vaguely was I aware of the dead guards around me, the wedding guests huddled at the door.

In a corner, Meredith's parents held each other, sobbing. The queen mother stood by them, her hands on their shoulders. Strands of hair escaped the diamond-studded pins, obscuring her face.

And from behind a wall of guards, Chey and the other young ladies of the solar huddled close to one another and wept. A few prayed.

I couldn't meet anyone's eyes.

As much as I wanted to deny it, I understood the wraith boy's decision to remove a problem in the most direct way possible. He didn't know. . . . He couldn't understand what this would do.

Tobiah pulled himself straight, and everyone looked at him. His crown was on the floor, forgotten, and his clothes were torn and askew. His hair, tame just minutes ago, was a disaster. He couldn't seem to pull his gaze from Meredith.

"Your Majesty?" someone whispered. "What do we do?"

The whole chapel held its breath as the king turned toward me, jaw clenched and eyes hard. Tears shone on his face. "Just go, Wilhelmina."

I didn't need to be told again. With a pair of guards trailing me, I left the chapel and went back to my apartments.

For five hours, I listened to the clock ticking like a heartbeat.

Tick tick tick.

Footsteps outside my door.

Tick tick tick.

Protesters screaming my name from the opposite side of the palace.

Tick tick tick.

Memory of the deafening *snap* of Meredith's neck, and *thud* of her body hitting the floor.

Connor and the Gray brothers had once told me that people rarely died right away from broken necks. It was the suffocation. The restricted blood flow.

Meredith could have been alive and aware for several

seconds, listening to the chaos around her. Alive but unconscious for entire minutes. Maybe she could have been saved, if
I'd thought about it, and done away with the wraith boy more
quickly, sent for Connor to rescue her.

Tick tick tick.

A knock sounded on the door, and Tobiah and James entered
the sitting room without waiting for me to answer.

Tobiah's voice was rough, barely recognizable as he glanced
down at my dress. "You haven't changed."

I hadn't *moved* since I dropped into a chair at the table in
the sitting room. What would I have done anyway? Tidied my
quarters? Written a letter? I should have at least lit a fire; now
all the rooms were cold.

"Did the injured guards"—I swallowed hard—"did they
make it?"

"Connor helped the ones who wouldn't have otherwise."
Tobiah stood by the door, unmoving, while James prowled the
perimeter, checking inside the other rooms. For intruders? For
the wraith boy? Finally, he lit a fire, filling the room with the
rush and crackle of flame, and then took up a post by the music
room door. "A few protested because they wouldn't be saved by
a flasher whose kind had created that *thing*, but I insisted. I told
them it wouldn't make a difference anymore. Not at this point."

"I'm glad they're going to live." The words were thoughtless.
Glad was an emotion I couldn't remember anymore, like relief
or hope. It was as though that knot of agony watching Tobiah's
wedding had exploded, and now every feeling I'd ever felt lay
flat and dead at the soles of my feet. Useless, except to weigh me
down. "Prince Colin will use that decision against you, though."

"He doesn't know about it."

Which meant Tobiah's recovery was still safe. And James's? Secret because no one had a clue what happened to him.

"There's been a rider from West Pass Watch." Tobiah stared westward, as though he could see the wraithland from here. "The wraith is flooding across the mountains, and only a few hours away from West Pass Watch by horse. And in the south, another village has been swallowed."

I closed my eyes and exhaled. I'd known this was inevitable. "He said it would come faster."

"He said a lot of things." Tobiah stepped closer to the table, to me, as though approaching a wild animal. "He said there would be consequences. This was one of those consequences, wasn't it?" He almost sounded gentle, but a bitter note grew. "Meredith didn't deserve this. She was a good woman. Kind. Generous. Forgiving." He choked on the last word.

"I know." She'd been my friend. Or could have, if I'd let her.

I dropped my gaze to the table again; my eyes were too dry and swollen, and I didn't want to meet Tobiah's. I didn't want to see the disgust. The disappointment. The hatred.

"She liked you. She told me several times." He drew a ragged breath. "Saints, Wilhelmina. I wish you had sent him back to the wraithland as soon as he became solid." As though there were a way to go back in time and change everything.

"I thought we might need him," I whispered. Heat from the fire pressed at me, suffocating. "I thought we could learn from him. And I felt . . . obligated to him. My magic did something unexpected when it brought him to life, and how could I dismiss him so easily? He was my responsibility."

Even Meredith would have insisted.

"But you can't just bring things to life, Wilhelmina. There are always consequences."

"I didn't expect it would be this." My throat constricted and the words came strangled. "I didn't think he would go this far."

"Didn't you?" He dropped to the chair next to me, voice low and urgent. "Don't tell me you weren't dreading today. I know you were, because I was, too. But you can't allow your pet wraith to kill people because you don't like what they're doing."

"I didn't want him to kill her. I didn't want him to do *anything*."

"But he did! And he did it for you. Didn't you hear? He said that I'm yours now, like I'm a prize to be claimed."

I shook my head. "No, I—"

"You didn't want her to be killed. I know. Just like you didn't want my father to be killed, but Patrick did it anyway. For you. For your kingdom. For your revenge."

"No!" I slammed my fists on the table. "I didn't want either of them to kill in my name."

"But they did. Whether or not you asked, they did it for you, and you let them."

"I didn't *let* them do anything."

"Then how did this happen? Twice!"

Tears burned my eyes. "I can't help what other people decide to do; if I could, you'd have followed your heart, rather than married someone because you were told."

He hesitated.

"It wasn't as if you didn't already know how I felt. You knew before I did." My eyes throbbed with grief, and I blinked back more tears. "It wouldn't have mattered. You'd already agreed to it, and I was merely a distraction. I knew that. I accepted that."

"Marrying her was the last thing my father ever asked me to do. Surely you remember; you were eavesdropping."

"You didn't *always* do what your father asked. You didn't *behave* like he wanted you to. Instead you wore that mask as a prince so you could be yourself as Black Knife, because that was more important to you than how other people perceived you."

His voice shifted low and controlled. Deadly. "You should know better than anyone that promises grow heavier when the person you made them to dies. You become obligated. Surely you know that. How many years did you spend training and arming yourself to take back Aecor because you thought that's what your parents would want? How many children died for that cause? How many friends? And now, another man has taken Sandcliff Castle in your name. He's killed hundreds of our soldiers.

"People—things—keep acting in your name, attempting to accomplish your goals no matter the collateral damage. And you keep letting them."

"I didn't let them!" I shoved myself up, hunched over the table. At my outburst, James stepped forward, but that was all. A warning. I dropped my voice to a growl. "You have no idea what it's like when people are willing to go to frightening lengths for you. When you can't predict their actions. You have no idea what a terrifying burden that is."

"Believe me, I do. I've seen enough well-meaning and untrained people pretend to be Black Knife because they wanted to help. But I stopped them, because I couldn't allow them to get hurt—or anyone else they came in contact with." He balled his fists and leaned forward, so close I could feel the heat of him. "You have to *stop* those people from making mistakes, especially the ones that hurt innocents like Meredith. How will you be a strong queen if you can't trust your people to make wise decisions?"

Chills crawled over my body. I sat back down and whispered, "I don't know."

"You need to figure it out, Wilhelmina. What kind of queen will you be? The kind who allows others to murder in her name, or the kind who makes decisions her conscience can agree with? You might have spent the last nine years as a criminal, doing what you thought was necessary for survival, but you aren't that girl anymore."

"Aren't I?" I fought to keep my voice level. "I'm still a criminal. I'm a flasher. I've forged dozens of official documents. Being a princess doesn't cancel the fact that I impersonated a duchess for weeks. I am *still* that girl."

The room was silent.

"But maybe you're right. Maybe I'm not that girl anymore: maybe I'm worse. You don't know what I am, anymore. You cannot fathom what I've endured. Don't imagine you've tamed me."

Tobiah stood, disgust written on his face. "Here's what I know. You want your kingdom back. My uncle is less inclined than ever to enter negotiations, and most everyone thinks you should be in prison. I must do something, though I disagree prison is the answer. Your wraith pet could see it as a threat against you. Or you could just call him to you—or turn him against the city."

He might as well have punched me. "If you think I'd even consider that, you really don't know me at all."

"Maybe I don't. As you've reminded me." He strode toward the door, James at his heels. When he faced me again, his expression was stiff. Resolved. "I've arranged for a house in Hawksbill. You will move in tonight, the rest of the Ospreys with you. And in case you think I'm simply allowing my people to be in danger, rather than myself, the house will be guarded at every opening. Doors. Windows. Even fireplaces. Mirrors are being installed on the ceiling of every room. Your wraith boy, if you will not send him away for good, will be confined to a wardrobe with mirrors surrounding it. If he tries to leave—"

"Will we *all* be confined to the house?" I asked.

"Everything you need will be provided. The tutor you hired will go to the house for lessons and training. When your presence is required here, you will be escorted. You will have no other reason to leave."

My stomach knotted. "So we will be prisoners."

"I cannot prevent you from seeing yourself that way." His expression hardened. "Your wraith killed my fiancée. Not to mention several guards of the Indigo Order."

"I wonder if others in the Indigo Order will be satisfied with that arrangement." I cocked my head, as though honestly curious. "I wonder if they'll see their new assignments as opportunities for revenge."

"This isn't the first time you've questioned my people's honor," Tobiah said, "and I know you struggle with trusting anyone in a position of authority. But I'll tell you this one more time: you can trust that *I* trust them."

"You want to keep me prisoner. Tell me why I should trust you."

He jammed his fingers through his hair. "I must do something to show I am not complicit, nor do I approve of what was done today, regardless of your instructions—or lack of—to the wraith boy. There was a murder. Further lives were lost in the fight. Your wraith boy cannot understand the consequences of today, but surely you must see that being relocated to a comfortable house in Hawksbill is a punishment offered only to queens."

I glanced at James, and he shifted closer to Tobiah. "Don't punish the rest of the Ospreys."

"They're already on their way to the house." He pulled open the door. "Your maid will be up to help you pack the necessities. The black bag isn't one of them. And when it's time to move your friend, a box will be provided."

"I have another idea."

Tobiah waited.

"You said Prince Colin would leave for Aecor—" After the wedding. After the disaster. "You said Prince Colin wanted to quell Patrick's rebellion and retake Aecor City."

"Yes."

"I will go with him." I lifted my chin. "You say I'm not your hostage or prisoner. Let me prove it to my people. In the meantime, it will get me out of Skyvale. No one wants me here."

Muscles around Tobiah's jaw flexed. "There's war in Aecor City. You'd be walking straight into danger."

"If I don't take that risk, I have no business being queen."

For the first time since the wedding, he locked eyes with me. But there was no warmth. No worry. Nothing but assessment and barely contained grief. "Fine. But you'll go without the other Ospreys, and you'll be closely guarded. You will be under Indigo Kingdom authority, with none of your own. You are still a ward of the Indigo Kingdom and subject to all that entails."

"I understand."

When both boys left the room, I began to pack.

TWENTY-TWO

"HOW LONG DO we have to stay here?" Connor asked.

"Until King Tobiah gives you permission to leave."

By Hawksbill standards, the house was small, but it had plenty of space for us. Several rooms had a private washroom attached, so no one would have to share. The kitchen pantry was fully stocked, and Carl had already declared his intentions to learn to cook. Four small desks had been moved into the library for their sessions with Alana Todd. Mirrors on every wall and ceiling made the house a fortress against the wraith boy, who was locked in a wardrobe, which was tucked into a broom closet.

In spite of the generous accommodations, to the Ospreys, moving from the palace to the house was not much different from being transferred from one prison to another.

"I don't want to stay here." Carl picked up a silver box of mints and started to put it in his pocket, but laid it down instead. He didn't even want to steal anymore.

I paced the length of the parlor, the plush carpet softening my footfalls. "You'll follow the king's orders, attend your lessons, and behave exactly as you would for me."

Theresa cocked an eyebrow.

"*Better* than you would for me," I amended. "Behave as if you actually know what it means to be nobility and future leaders in Aecor."

"Shouldn't we go with you?" Kevin asked. "There's only a few months until the anniversary, and if we're supposed to meet that deadline . . ."

The other Ospreys nodded in agreement.

"None of you are coming with me." I held up a hand to forestall Theresa, who perched on the arm of a chair, tracing the fleur-de-lis pattern in the upholstery. "No, not even you."

She scowled and slumped back. "What will people say, you going to Aecor without a female companion?"

"What does that matter, compared to what they already say? I can silence entire rooms by walking through a door." It had been two days since the wedding and I'd been back and forth from the palace seven times to sign things, answer questions, and mostly just be inconvenienced. As though forcing me to make the short trip so often were anywhere close to the punishment I deserved.

But I was a princess—a future queen: nothing they were permitted to do would ever come close to making reparation.

"I don't like you going alone," muttered Kevin.

"I'll be traveling with Crown Prince Colin," I said, "and heading toward Patrick. I won't drag any of you into a war."

"How will we know you're safe, though?" Connor turned

his silver mirror in his hands, faster and faster. "I don't want you to get hurt."

"The wraith boy will be with me." I glanced at his broom closet. "He won't let anyone hurt me."

The room went silent while everyone took that in.

"What is your plan?" Kevin asked. "You'll be traveling with enemies, and the wraith boy isn't exactly trustworthy. And in Aecor . . ."

There'd be Patrick and the Ospreys who'd followed him, and the resistance groups who'd united to fight in my name. The Red Militia. Not to mention the other dangers present in a city whose leadership was in flux. Crime. Violence. Desperate people doing desperate things.

"Will you declare yourself queen?" Carl asked. "That's what Patrick wants you to do. And what everyone will expect."

The others all nodded, their message clear: *they'd* like me to declare myself queen, too. They viewed it as a solution to all our problems.

If I declared myself queen, *I'd* start a war against the Indigo Kingdom.

"I can't." I looked them all in the eye, one at a time. "Not yet. Our relationship with the Indigo Kingdom is already fragile. Even more now that Meredith—" Her name caught in my throat. I took a steadying breath and tried again. "I'm not sure we'll ever be able to fully recover from what happened at the wedding."

"But it wasn't your fault!" Connor pressed his mirror against his knees. "You didn't tell the wraith boy to kill her. You didn't want any of that to happen."

"You're right." I fought to keep my voice even, but it was too late: the cracks were showing. "I didn't want that to happen, but it did, and because the wraith boy is supposed to be under my control, I need to accept responsibility. That's part of what it means to be a queen."

Connor and Theresa both stared down at their knees. Carl and Kevin glared toward the closet containing the wraith boy.

"If I declare myself queen now, it will mean I've sided with Patrick, and that Aecor is truly at war with the Indigo Kingdom. It won't be just the Red Militia rising against Indigo Kingdom rule. I don't like Prince Colin controlling my kingdom any more than the rest of you, but for now I must help him calm the rebellion growing in the capital. I must announce directly to the people that the letters I sent were genuine, and that I'm working with the Indigo Kingdom to peacefully reclaim the vermillion throne."

"You think that will be it?" Kevin asked. "That you'll just go in and everything will be fine once you explain?"

"And you'll accept Prince Colin's authority?" Theresa shuddered.

"No, I don't anticipate it will be that simple, but I hope that the reappearance of their long-lost princess will force people to listen. The wraith is already close. I need to stop the war so we can focus on bigger problems."

"Patrick will find some way to turn this all against you." Kevin drummed his fingers on his knee. "He's wanted this war for years."

"He has." I paused next to a bookcase, the gold-foil titles gleaming in the lamplight: *A History of Mirrors, The Flora of* the *Indigo Valley*, and *The One-Night War: An Indigo Kingdom Victory*. "Nevertheless, I'm going to do everything in my power."

"I don't think this is safe," Connor said.

It wasn't safe. Not here. Not there. The only safe place in the world was Mirror Lake. "I know."

"How will we communicate?" Connor asked again.

"By courier, I assume. Unless you know of a better way."

"Magic?" His voice was small. "I just want to know you're safe. You'll be all alone."

I ran my fingers across the spine of *The World Poison: Magic* and sighed. "I have an idea." I headed into the study, where I found a pair of white notebooks, blank on every page. *"Wake up,"* I whispered. *"Be the same. What is written in one will be written in the other—at the same time and in the same hand—no matter the distance."*

A wave of dizziness surged through my head, and I gripped the desk to steady myself. When it passed, I took the notebooks out to the parlor again to explain how they'd work.

I emerged from the house as cold dawn glowed over the valley. The mountains were dark with winter, and as familiar as the Ospreys' faces. For years we'd lived in the old palace in those mountains. Now I'd be going through them, down the piedmont, and beyond. . . .

"This way, Your Highness." Sergeant Ferris ushered me toward the carriage that would take me to Prince Colin's convoy. The driver sat on the front seat, glaring at the pair of bay horses. "Your belongings are already stowed in the convoy wagon."

"The wraith boy?" I was stalling. I knew his wardrobe had been taken to the convoy because I'd ordered him to cooperate—to simply accept any bruises gathered while the wardrobe shifted around him, and not react to any jeers or insults given through the crack in the door.

Sergeant Ferris motioned at the carriage. "Your Highness—"

The front door opened again and Connor threw himself outside, clad only in his bedclothes and a too-big coat. No shoes. "Wil! I caught you!" He hugged me so tightly I nearly fell over.

"Barely." I glanced at the carriage, as though irritated and pressed for time. "I was about to leave."

Sergeant Ferris's disapproving frown shifted into the palest of smiles.

"I wanted to give you this." Connor thrust his small silver mirror into my hands. "In case he turns on you."

I gripped the tarnished piece of metal and studied his thin, earnest face. "Won't you need it?" It was his prized possession, with stylized birds stamped into the border.

"You'll need it more." He offered an awkward, sideways hug.

I forced a smile. "Thank you."

Before I could say anything else, he was back inside.

"That was a sweet gesture."

Inside the carriage, I spread my gray travel dress over my legs and tucked the silver mirror into a pocket in my bag. "Connor is the younger brother I always wanted." My chest felt heavy as I glanced at the house once more, and found four faces peering out of the second-story bedroom overlooking the road. I snapped and thumped my chest, but the carriage jerked into motion before I had a chance to see if they'd noticed the salute.

"You've known him a long time."

"After the One-Night War, a handful of toddlers were taken to the orphanage. Connor and Carl. The third, Ezra, died a few months ago during a mission Patrick sent him on. His older sister was killed, too." I squeezed the signet ring on a chain around my neck. "I hadn't wanted them to go. I thought it was too dangerous. But Patrick insisted."

"I'm sorry."

"I want him stopped, Sergeant. No matter what anyone thinks about me, I want Patrick Lien stopped."

As we drove through Hawksbill, I could almost pretend this was an official state visit and something good was about to happen. Not that this was a desperate ploy to halt a war. Not that I was fleeing the Indigo Kingdom where I was unanimously reviled.

At last, we stopped at the main avenue leading out of the district. This was where I'd been arrested after my Liadian residency papers had been discovered as forgeries, and where I'd been revealed as Princess Wilhelmina, thanks to the newly solid wraith boy.

The convoy was almost ready. Bridles clanked and men called orders. Maids scurried from place to place, carrying baskets and boxes. Soldiers checked wheels, hinges, and locks on supply wagons. Indigo banners snapped in the breeze, bearing family crests and House sigils. Hawksbill residents stared out from their windows or doors; some of the ladies gave silk scarves or lace shawls to the soldiers. For luck. For protection, as though they were going to fight the wraith.

"Where will I be?" I asked Sergeant Ferris.

He handed my bag to me, Connor's mirror peeking out from a pocket. A proper princess would have allowed him to carry it, but the idea of being separated from my emergency supplies—a change of clothes, weapons, rations—made me nauseous.

"The king ordered a wagon for you." He pointed toward a pale wagon with red trim and wheels, and a flock of ospreys painted under the eaves.

"What a good target it will make when someone wonders if it would be easier to set me on fire than endure my presence on the way to Aecor."

"Ever the pessimist." Tobiah's voice made my stomach drop, and I spun around.

"Your Majesty." I dipped into a polite curtsy as Tobiah and James emerged from the crowd of nobles saying good-bye. "Come to see off your uncle?"

He glanced toward the fore of the convoy. "Yes, of course. But there was something I needed to discuss with you."

I straightened my shoulders and lifted my chin. "Yes?"

"Walk with me to your wagon." He gestured forward, and James and Sergeant Ferris took up their places behind us. "There are two things. First, I'm sending James with you."

I turned my head so sharply my neck stung. "James?"

Tobiah gave a stiff nod. "Sergeant Ferris will stay here with the Aecorian nobles. He will be their guard."

I hated when plans changed at the last minute.

As we strode down the avenue, soldiers and maids hurried out of our way. A few bowed or curtsied, but toward Tobiah, who wore a mourning gray suit and nothing to denote his rank. They simply *knew.*

Several rude looks and little fingers were aimed my way, but I ignored them.

"I have found Sergeant Ferris a more than adequate guard, and I'd hate to deprive you of your cousin," I said at last. I kept my tone even, but I knew why he'd switched my guard: both the captain and sergeant would spy on me for him, but this way he could keep the Ospreys feeling secure. By leaving them with someone they knew, they'd speak more freely. After all, he'd been *my* guard. He was a trusted figure, as far as members of the Indigo Order went.

Tobiah eyed me askance. "Captain Rayner is an officer in the Indigo Order. His duty is to go where he's needed."

"I appreciate the consideration. I know Captain Rayner is valuable to you." The question was, what was he looking for? What more did he think I would do, surrounded by enemies?

"In here, Your Highness." Tobiah opened the door to my wagon. "You'll find your belongings in order, I think."

I hesitated. "I was brought to the Indigo Kingdom imprisoned in a wagon. I wouldn't like to return to Aecor in the same manner, no matter how fine the accommodations."

"I thought you might feel that way." Tobiah waved to James, who vanished around the other side of the wagon. A moment later, he returned with a familiar chestnut horse, already saddled. "I had him brought in from West Pass Watch."

"Ferguson!"

"He was given a real name, you know." James tied the lead

to the wagon. "But I suppose you don't care."

"His name is Ferguson." I petted the gelding's forehead as he nosed my stomach in greeting. At least on a horse, I'd have freedom of movement in case of an attack. I turned to Tobiah. "Thank you again. Ferguson will be a welcome companion."

Tobiah offered a small bow. "I'd like to speak with you on the final matter in private. Inside your wagon?"

He'd said two things, so *now* what? "It won't be private. The wardrobe is inside."

"That's all right. It doesn't matter if he hears, as long as he doesn't tell anyone, and you can order that, correct?"

"I can." I checked the busy avenue, but if people were still watching us, they were doing a good job of hiding it.

The interior was set up like a bedroom, with a foldable partition to dress behind, and a second wardrobe with mirrors reflecting the doors. Most of my belongings—well, the things the Indigo Kingdom had given to me—were in crates pushed against the back wall. Another large mirror was propped against those.

They didn't want to take chances. Good.

I dropped my pack on the small bed and knocked on the side of the wardrobe.

"My queen!" The wraith boy's voice was muffled through the heavy wood. "I'm glad you're here."

"Cover your ears and hum. I don't want you to overhear what anyone is saying."

Immediately, a deep humming came from within the wardrobe, followed by a double *thud* as his elbows hit the wood.

I turned to Tobiah just as James closed the door, cutting off the flow of cold air. They'd left Sergeant Ferris outside. Interesting. "What is it you wanted to speak about?" Even though the wraith boy wouldn't hear us, I kept my voice low.

Tobiah pulled a pair of notebooks from his jacket, not the ones I'd taken for the Ospreys and myself. These were pale blue, with silver foil mountains stamped into the leather. Flat braids decorated the edges, and silk bookmarks peeked out from the pages. They were identical. Pre-wraith, definitely.

"Thank you?" I lifted an eyebrow and didn't touch them. Considering what I'd done last night, this couldn't be a coincidence.

"I know about your entangled notebooks." He offered these to me. "Perform the same magic on these two."

"Why?"

When I didn't take the notebooks, he placed them on the small writing desk at the foot of my bed. "You're going into Aecor with my uncle. He's threatened you. You've made it clear that you will not give up Aecor, so who knows what he'll do? And Lien is there, waiting. What does he have in mind for your return? Not to mention that." He motioned at the wardrobe. "Why do you think I'm sending James? Ferris is a good man. James is better. But I still need a way to communicate with him, quickly and securely. Only you have the power to offer that."

So he hadn't meant the second notebook for me. The realization fell halfway between relief and disappointment. "How did you know about the ones I animated for the Ospreys?"

Tobiah shifted his weight, uncomfortable at last. "Connor told me. He sent an urgent note to meet me in the gardens at the first hour. He sneaked past all the guards at the house, and went all the way to the King's Seat."

I frowned. *Connor* had sneaked out? And no one had known? *I* hadn't known?

Tobiah blew out a breath. "I don't know why he insisted on meeting in secret. I'd have gone to him, or had him brought somewhere warmer than the gardens. Guess it's the Osprey paranoia."

I crossed my arms and waited for the rest of the story.

"He was hoping there might be a way for you and me to mend our relationship—to keep you from going to Aecor. He's worried. Terrified, though he did a good job of hiding it. But what happened at the wedding—that's not the only reason you're returning to Aecor."

"It's time for me to go."

"That's what I said to him, and he replied he was just relieved you'd still be able to write to him. The notebook magic was a slip."

Sure it had been. Connor wasn't normally what I'd call *calculating*. Maybe it was time to revise my view of him. But I said, "I see."

"I'd be grateful for a way to communicate with my cousin while he's away, though I understand if you refuse. I know your feelings on magic use have become more complicated lately." He nodded toward the wardrobe where the wraith boy still hummed.

If I refused, I'd insult him yet again. And while annoying Tobiah didn't usually bother me, maybe I owed him a favor.

"As long as you know what you're asking." I slipped around Tobiah to the desk and touched the smooth covers. He shifted his weight as though to look around me and watch, but I shot a scowl and he moved back without a word. "*Wake up,*" I whispered. "*Be the same. What is written in one will be written in the other—at the same time and in the same hand—no matter the distance.*"

Dizziness washed through me. Gasping, sweating, I swayed as blankness swarmed at the edges of my vision.

"Princess?" James's voice was distant, but his hand on my shoulder was solid.

"I'm fine." I'd leaned onto the desk, both palms digging against the wood. As my vision and stability returned, I breathed through the remaining light-headedness and stood, waving James off. "Thank you."

He withdrew.

Magic this small didn't usually hit so hard. But I hadn't ever animated multiple things at once, and *kept* them animated. Add the wraith boy to that, and it was a wonder I was still standing.

I'd need to avoid using magic for a while.

"Your half," I said, handing one notebook to Tobiah. "And your half." I gave the second to James.

"Thank you."

There was a hard look on the king's face as he ran a finger down the notebook's spine, as though feeling for the magic. "You can't know what this means to me."

Except I did, because I knew the bond he and James shared. I'd have given anything to be able to communicate with Melanie now.

Saints, I hoped she was well. Safe. Waiting for me in Sandcliff Castle.

Outside, a whistle blew, signaling the convoy's imminent

departure. "You should see your uncle before we're off," I said.

Tobiah swallowed hard and met my eyes for a long moment. "Farewell, Wilhelmina."

That was all.

TWENTY-THREE

THE CONVOY LEFT Skyvale with much more pomp and celebration than it was really warranted. The cheers and bells followed us out of Hawksbill and on through Thornton, almost making me wish I'd stayed in my wagon, hidden and warm. But what I'd told Tobiah had been the truth.

I'd come to the Indigo Kingdom as a prisoner of war. I refused to leave in the same manner.

Through the crowded streets of White Flag, I was grateful for my hood, pulled low to hide my face, and my long cloak that concealed the fine cut and cloth of my dress. Ferguson plodded along near my wagon, but not so close as to give away my identity. James rode nearby, straight and tall on his own gelding.

At last, the city gate closed behind us, and the convoy began the long trek up the mountains, made difficult by the wagons and number of people. There had to be thousands of us.

"Are you doing well, Your Highness?" James asked as we

pulled farther from the city. Bare trees shivered around us. A cold wind gusted through the woods, and the sky turned silver and sharp with the scent of a coming storm.

"I'm fine."

"How does it feel to go home for the first time in almost ten years?"

"I don't want to talk about it."

James drew his horse alongside Ferguson so he didn't have to lift his voice. "I think I'd be nervous. It's your home, but so many things have changed since you were last there. *You've* changed."

"I said—"

"I know, but you're not talking. I am."

"So King Tobiah sent you to annoy me."

"That's one of the reasons." He lifted his face to the sky, drawing in a long, deep breath. "Another is that I asked to come."

I pulled my hood lower over my brow and glanced at the wagons rumbling and the soldiers calling and the horses snorting. A few flakes of snow escaped the clouds, drifting between the evergreen trees. "Did you want to see Aecor?"

James caught a snowflake in his gloved hand and held it while it melted. "I've been there before, with my mother when I was a small child. I don't remember it, though. I don't remember much from when I was young."

"Not everyone does." I relaxed my grip on Ferguson's reins. "And some people remember more than they want."

"You're thinking of the One-Night War." His eyes were gentle and understanding, and that was almost worse than the blankness in Tobiah's this morning. I didn't want James's pity.

"Do *you* remember the war?" I asked.

"Parts. I remember wanting to protect Tobiah when General Lien came for him. And I remember parts of the journey home."

"You weren't in Aecor that night." I leaned forward as Ferguson climbed a steep hill. The rest of the convoy slowed on the tracks as the horses strained. Men pushed against the backs of the wagons, chanting to keep in step with one another.

"No," James muttered. "I got hurt on the way there. The general left me to die, but the Indigo Army rescued me on the return trip." A frown creased between his eyes. "I barely remember it."

"The saints must be watching over you. Left for dead during the One-Night War, shot through the gut during the Inundation: you survived both."

"I pray to all nine saints every morning and night. I suppose it's working." His smile was strained, though. "Your Highness, about the wedding—"

"Add the wedding to the list of things we're not talking about." I kicked Ferguson into a trot the rest of the way up the mountain. James kept up, but he didn't push the conversation.

The convoy continued through lunch and the afternoon. I kept an eye on the soldiers and looked out for Prince Colin. But if he was riding, I couldn't spot him among the indigo-jacketed men. More likely, he'd stayed inside his wagon. He wasn't the type to suffer discomfort.

Snow came and went, but the air grew biting cold atop the mountains. By the time we passed the old palace—East Pass Watch—and I whispered good-bye to the place the Ospreys and

I had shared for so long, a film of snow covered the ground. At the foot of the mountains, the wide piedmont stretched white before us. The wagons continued over the tracks, steadier on the even ground. By the time the sun set and the convoy halted for the night, snow spat from the sky, stinging.

"I can take care of the horses and fetch dinner," James said.

"I don't need you to do my work for me." I dismounted Ferguson, relieved to stand on my own aching feet again, and motioned at his horse. "Just unsaddle Ferguson the Second—"

"His name is Bear." James loosened the saddle girth and unclipped the bridle.

"But he's a horse."

"Whose name is Bear." James lifted an eyebrow in my direction. "Do you have a problem with that?"

I shrugged and started unsaddling Ferguson. "He's your horse." We worked in silence. James put away the saddles and the rest of the tack, then laid out blankets to cover the horses for the night. While he went to find our dinner, I finished brushing the horses, then covered them both in heavy wool. The snow fell harder.

Just as I was about to climb into my wagon, Prince Colin walked up and leaned against the doorframe, making it impossible for me to go inside without brushing his shoulder. All levity from teasing James evaporated.

"Your Highness." My whole body felt heavy and stiff.

"I'm glad we're taking this journey together," he said. "I'm sure it will give us more time to get to know each other and discuss how best to proceed with such an interesting situation. The long-lost heir to the vermilion throne. And yet, I am the

Overlord of Aecor Territory."

My hands fell beneath my cloak, and I touched the daggers at my hips. Even through my gloves, I could feel the smooth hilts, worn with use.

He mused, "What *shall* I do with you once we reach Sandcliff Castle?" If he noticed my weapon-ward motions, he didn't show it.

"I know the castle well. I can think of several satisfactory arrangements." Prince Colin and Patrick in the dungeon, to start with.

"I'm certain you can." Prince Colin glanced downward, below my neckline. The crawling sensation fell over my skin, but it was only in my head. Not real. He hadn't touched me, not ever. Not like the soldiers the morning I was arrested, and not like the guards trying to drag me to safety when Tobiah had been shot.

Swallowing hard, I resisted the urge to look around for James. He'd return soon.

My heart thumped as I took a measured step back from Prince Colin. Not a retreat. Something that could simply be shifting my weight.

He advanced a step, fully blocking the door. "You must feel terrible about what happened at my nephew's wedding. That wraith creature, acting in your interests, but pulling you further from Tobiah. And even if he were to forgive you and take you as his wife instead, the people would never accept it. Meredith was well loved, like you will never be. That must be so frustrating for you."

"This discussion is inappropriate. Meredith was killed only

days ago. And she was my friend, too." I gripped the daggers at my hips and struggled to keep my expression impassive. He would *not* see the despair that hung below every word. Every breath. Every night, I dreamed of the wraith boy striding down the aisle, grabbing her, snapping her neck. I dreamed of her body, still and broken. I dreamed of his voice, so like mine, as he said, "He is yours now, my queen."

No. Tobiah would never be mine.

"I was wondering." Prince Colin rested his hand on the doorknob. "If your wraith can cause so much destruction in the Cathedral of the Solemn Hour, and the swift death of Lady Meredith, what kind of damage can he do to crush the rebellion in Aecor Territory? Lien wouldn't stand a chance if you loosed that creature on the Red Militia."

My heart thundered in my ears. "The wraith boy is not a weapon."

"That's all he is, Your Highness. A weapon. Why keep him if you will not use him?"

Snow stung my face. Soldiers hurried to their wagons, a few with their shoulders hunched against the cold wind. None of them looked at me, or noticed the way Prince Colin stood, possessive and predatory. I could take out my daggers and shove the blades deep into the crown prince's stomach. I could slice so that his entrails fell to my feet. At this point, only dishonorable actions were expected of me anyway.

Or I could have the wraith boy kill him for me. Chrysalis could slaughter my enemies, just as Prince Colin wanted.

"He's open to suggestion," said Prince Colin. "Just hint to him that you wish Lien weren't a problem anymore. That you'd be happy if Lien were gone. The wraith boy wants you to be happy, after all."

The wraith boy's words from the other night came back to me: *A man came to my door. He said you were sad.*

"Did you say something to him about Meredith?" My words were a breath.

"I never said anything about poor Meredith to your wraith creature."

Maybe that was true. Maybe he'd said only that I was sad, and the wraith boy filled in the rest; he *was* frighteningly attuned to me. But what if Prince Colin's words had inspired the wraith boy to act? He could be partially responsible for Meredith's murder.

Not that anyone would believe the testimony of a boy made of wraith.

The sun fell below the horizon, silhouetting the mountains far behind the convoy. In the pale caravan lights, Prince Colin's smile was all sinister shadows. "Well. I'll let you consider the options. It'd be best if we took care of Lien quickly. I know you have friends you care about back in Skyvale. I do, too." A sharp gleam edged his smile. "Good night, Your Highness." He stepped around me, his shoulder brushing mine.

My stomach turned at the contact; even through all the layers of clothes between us, he made me feel disgusting.

"Wil?" James's voice was gentle as he approached with a large tray. He glanced beyond me, after Prince Colin. "What did he want?"

"Nothing." I opened the wagon door and let James inside first. The interior wasn't warm, exactly, but we were out of the wind and a handful of lanterns cast a pale heat.

The wraith boy was still humming in his wardrobe.

"Are you going to tell him to be quiet now?" James asked.

"No." I pulled down a polished oak board from the wall. The hinges creaked as I leaned some of my weight on it, testing its strength, and backed off to allow James to place our dinner tray on it.

"So you'll just listen to him all night?"

"The rest of the journey, as long as humming keeps him occupied." I lingered near one of the lanterns, warming my face and hands while James finished setting the table.

"I'm not here to spy on you, Wil, though I can understand why you might believe that." He pulled out the desk chair and sat at the table. "But I do plan on telling Tobiah that you and Prince Colin had a conversation that left you shaking and cagier than normal."

"That sounds like spying to me." I perched on the bottom corner of the bed, close enough to the table. A cloud of spicy steam enveloped me, making my stomach rumble. "And I wasn't shaking because of my talk with Prince Colin, unless you want to blame the extra time he kept me outside. It's quite frigid. I'll probably come down with a chill, thanks to him."

James sighed and—once he'd muttered a quiet blessing over his meal—began to eat. "I miss the days when you were honest with me."

"Oh, you mean never ago." I poked my spoon through the soup, finding vegetables, chunks of meat, and spices. The thick broth warmed me from the inside out. James had also laid out generous slices of bread and cheese, and glasses of wine. "Yes,

I'm sure you are nostalgic for the weeks you and Tobiah knew I was a girl from the streets pretending to be Liadian nobility. Back when you didn't know my real name, let alone anything about my magic. I was much nicer to you then."

"Indeed. Much less sarcastic."

"And Prince Colin resented me only because I was a lady who'd come to the wraith mitigation meeting, not a rival to his rulership of Aecor."

"Is that what he was asking you about?" James was already halfway finished with his meal; he would have made a good Osprey.

I shook my head and finished my dinner.

"Well, I can't force you to talk to me." James drank the last of his wine and leaned back. The blue notebook came out of his jacket pocket, and he opened to the first page. "Tobiah says hello."

I rolled my eyes and put my dishes into a neat stack.

"No, he did. Look." James placed the notebook in front of me, and as promised, there was a note from Tobiah, which did include greetings to me.

> James,
> I hope all is well. Everything is different without you as my constant shadow.
> Life is proceeding as expected. Uncle Herman has gone back to West Pass Watch, along with another regiment of soldiers. Reports from the west have not been good. I don't want to fight two wars, but I'm afraid that may happen if Lien can't be contained. I don't know

what the answer is, though. I don't trust my uncle. I don't trust Wilhelmina right now, either, as grateful as I am for this way to communicate. The wraith boy . . . I don't know. Something must be done.

Please write daily. I hope to hear from you soon. Give Wilhelmina my best.

Tobiah

I handed the notebook back to James. None of it was a surprise.

"There's something I wanted to tell you." James piled all our dishes onto the tray and set it by the door. "Earlier I said I asked to come along. There's a reason."

"Spying," I reminded him.

"Besides that." He flashed a smile. "After I was shot the night of the Inundation, I healed. I don't even have a scar. Your friend Connor wasn't responsible for it."

"No." I stood and folded the table back into the wall, and fastened it shut with a small hook. "I told you what happened. Tobiah said you were well, just not awake. He called me in to use my magic on you, even though it doesn't work that way—"

He nodded toward the wraith boy's wardrobe. "It doesn't work *that* way, either."

"You're right. But he is made of wraith. You're just a man."

"Am I?" James squeezed the notebook. "Normal men don't heal like that. And he"—James pointed at the wardrobe—"keeps whispering that I'm not real."

"I'd ask him what he means by it, but he specializes in non-answers."

"I don't recall ever being hurt after the One-Night War, either." James was quiet for a few minutes, building up to whatever he needed to say. "I don't understand what's wrong with me. When I asked Tobiah about it, he swore we'd investigate, but every time I try, he puts off even beginning the investigation."

How surprising: Tobiah was hiding something.

"We fought about it last night." He sat tall and proud, hiding his anxiety. But I remembered his conversation with Tobiah during the coronation ball, the ghosts of uncertainty that stole over him any time someone brought up his healing.

"Was it a bad fight?"

"Aren't all fights with your best friend awful?"

"They are." At least with the entangled notebooks, the boys could discuss the issue from a safe distance. "To you, there's no one more important than him. And to him, there's no one more important than you. You'll work it out."

"And so will you and Melanie."

"I know we will." That was the only good thing about all of this: seeing Melanie again. Already, I could feel our connection pulling tighter as I drew closer to her. I wondered if she could feel it, too. "You and I can look into the mystery of your healing. If you want."

"Thanks," he said, "but I only told you that to help with my spying efforts. Did it make you want to tell me what you and Colin were discussing?"

"You're shameless." I touched my own notebook, the one connected to the Ospreys. "Prince Colin threatened my friends. Theresa and the boys. They're all competent fighters, and very clever, but there are only four of them."

"What did he want?"

"He wanted me to use him"—I inclined my head toward the wardrobe—"as a weapon against Patrick."

"Would that be terrible? You did send him after Lien to begin with."

"It wouldn't be just Patrick. It would be the people who are fighting under him, in my name, because they believe I'm a hostage. It would be hundreds—maybe thousands—of innocent people. And you saw what happens. He's chaotic. I can't unleash him against my own people. Not even to get at Patrick."

James closed his eyes and sighed. "You might not have a choice. Prince Colin might not leave you with one. I *will* warn Tobiah to put extra security on the Ospreys, and you can alert them, too. But the crown prince has many resources. After the wedding, he no doubt has people in the Order who'd be willing to risk their careers."

"That's what I'm afraid of." I hugged the notebook to my chest. "The Ospreys are everything to me."

"I know. I'll do everything I can to help you keep them safe." James bent to pick up our dinner tray. "Is there anything else you need before I go?"

"Where are you going after you return that?"

"There's a wagon for officers. I have a bunk there."

"I want you to stay here instead." It wasn't asking for help if I made it a royal order.

He glanced at the door and shook his head. "That would be inappropriate. If this is because of Prince Colin, I could have one of the night guards stationed outside your wagon."

"And put my life into a stranger's hands?" I deepened my

voice. "I need someone I can trust to keep me alive. They won't feel guilty if something happens to me. They'd look the other way." Not that I'd blame them. The cathedral was one thing, but the wedding was an entirely different matter.

"I'll come back, then. If anyone asks, I'm guarding you from him." He pointed an elbow at the wardrobe. "I answer directly to King Tobiah. Why would I entrust another to guard your door? Imagine the consequences I'd face if foreign royalty were harmed under my watch!"

The hardness in my neck and shoulders eased. "Thank you."

When he left, I changed into loose trousers and a soft shirt, and pulled a heavy wool dressing gown over everything. As I slid my travel boots under the bed, the toes hit something. I knelt and reached under the bed, and out came the bag of Black Knife clothes and weapons.

I pushed it back under.

Only two people might have put the bag there, and I doubted James would act without Tobiah's permission. But what did that mean? I wasn't ready to guess.

I kept my daggers within reach as I sat at the desk to read the Ospreys' letters in my notebook.

They hadn't managed to get into trouble—yet—but it was only a matter of time before Carl's pockets were heavy with other people's valuables, and Connor was nursing stray kittens back to health, and Theresa and Kevin were caught eavesdropping on important political discussions.

The letters made me smile, and it was late when I finished reading—and I was tired—but I took my time choosing a handwriting and ink. Not that there was much ink to choose from on this journey, but I wanted to feel normal for once, even when I was warning my friends to keep their eyes open.

James came back into the wagon with a bedroll under one arm, and took the desk when I was finished. One at a time, I doused all the lanterns but the one above where he wrote to Tobiah, and then I climbed into bed. A few minutes later, he spread out his roll in front of the door, and we both fell asleep to the sound of the wraith boy humming.

TWENTY-FOUR

THE CONVOY TRAVELED southeast across the Indigo Kingdom, away from the piedmont and closer to the sea. Soldiers had to ride ahead and melt the icy layers covering the tracks. Even so, I could sometimes feel the wheels slip and the horses stumble with the shifting load.

The weather meant James and I stayed in the wagon most of the time, reading, writing, and listening to the wraith boy hum new and haunting tunes.

"I want to tell you something." I closed my diary, my hand resting on the worn black cover. It was nearly full, and ragged after years of use. The letters Tobiah had written to me were folded neatly in the back, held in with a silk band.

"That would be nice." James wrote one last line in his book to Tobiah and faced me, an odd mix of tension and ease in his expression and posture. News from Skyvale was never good anymore. "What is it?"

"I've been reading through this today." I tapped my notebook against my knees. "I started keeping it when I was nine, and I'd just agreed with Patrick that we should reclaim Aecor. That I should take the vermilion throne when we were old enough to make a stand."

James just nodded.

"I've spent every day since then trying to make that girl's dream a reality. She wanted to do what she thought her parents would want: retake the kingdom. But they're gone now, and I'll never know more about them than what I remember. The truth is, I don't know what they'd have wanted for me."

"Maybe their belongings are still in the castle. Diaries? Records? Letters?"

"I doubt Prince Colin would have left those around during his years as overlord. No, I'm certain all their records are gone. And that's all right." I held up my journal. "What I'm saying is, I don't know if this girl exists anymore. Her world was red against blue. Us against you. But so much has changed."

James leaned forward.

"Everything I've done has been to get back my kingdom. It was all accomplished Patrick's way, though. Since parting with him, I've tried to change and take actions that would have made my parents truly proud. But what good is going to war with the Indigo Kingdom, or fighting with Prince Colin to reclaim it? The wraith is so close. There are only a handful of kingdoms left."

"What are you saying?"

"I'm not the girl who started this diary anymore. What if Tobiah was right? What if I wouldn't be a good queen?"

"Did he tell you that you would be a poor queen?" James's eyebrows pulled in with a frown.

"He may as well have." I placed my notebook on the bed and stood, stretching my legs.

James gave me a moment. "Do you *want* to be queen?"

I stood before the mirror. In the week following the wedding, my cheeks had hollowed and circles darkened the spaces under my eyes. I didn't look very much like the queen Meredith would have been: strong, kind, lovely. "It doesn't matter what I want anymore. What I want only gets me into trouble."

Was it possible to stop desiring?

From the wardrobe, the wraith boy chuckled.

I spun and ripped open the doors. A different, darker reflection stared back at me. Then he drew back, pressing himself against the side wall. His chest heaved, like he'd nearly been trapped in the glass forever.

"What?" I growled.

"Do you hear that sound?" Still flat against the side wall, he twisted his head to look westward. "There are drums. Shouts. They came across the sea."

I glanced at James. "The wagon has stopped moving." Without precautions, that was dangerous in this weather. The wheels could freeze to the tracks.

He was already standing, strapping his sword around his waist. "Stay inside."

"Where are you going?" My heart thundered with anticipation.

"To look." He tossed on his coat, not bothering to button it or find a hat. "I'll be back in a moment. Close that wardrobe." He was out the door and into thigh-high snowdrifts within seconds.

I slammed the wardrobe door—the wraith boy let out a small *meep!*—and found my own weapons. Daggers. Sword from the Black Knife bag. I slung my cloak over my shoulders, and just as I was about to move outside, James returned.

"Wil, I told you to stay here." His eyes were wide, and his clothes covered in snow.

"You're my guard, not my king. You can't order me around." I tied my cloak tight and pushed past him, but he caught my arm and spun me back to face him. Our noses almost touched.

"I do order you around when your life is in danger. Patrick brought an army. There are at least three thousand men on this side of the bridge already, with more on the way. We walked into an ambush. We're outnumbered. If the Red Militia knew you were here—"

"They'd stop fighting. Now let go of me." I wrenched myself away, and he backed off. He didn't try to stop me as I raced out the door, where a drift of snow and ice crumbled under my feet, causing a tiny avalanche to collapse beneath the wagon.

I grabbed the doorframe as I sank into the snow, then heaved myself to my feet and found the trail he'd made, though it wasn't much easier to walk through.

The sky was thick with stars, and the air sharp with snow and sea salt. The land was flat, flat, flat, nothing but frozen trees and marsh all around.

A dozen soldiers stood watch atop wagons and from horse-back, while most of the fighting was closer to the bridge and water. For a half second, I considered trying to jump wagon to wagon, but I'd never make it. Not with the horses and the spaces between, and definitely not in my travel dress and cloak.

I shoved through the heavy snow, keeping to James's path. Even so, my steps were all *whoosh-crunch* and sluggish, especially as the cold pressed through my clothes, numbing my legs. My face stung at the icy air, and my breath heaved out in bursts of steam.

"Wil!" James's voice carried across the space between us. "Wait!"

He'd catch up. I had to keep following the indigo-coated soldiers. The shore was lit with torches and lanterns. Though it wasn't far off, snow muted the shouts and clash of blades.

"Your Highness!" The cry came from a guard standing on top of a nearby wagon. "It's not safe out here."

That was exactly why I'd come. I pushed forward, half swimming through the snow.

"My queen." A palm landed on my shoulder, and I pivoted, dagger up, to find my wraith creation right behind me. He wore the same clothes as always, torn and hanging, and if the cold affected him, he didn't show it. "I'm here to help you."

"I don't want your help. Why are you out of your wardrobe?" Snow pressed around me, sharp and stinging against my legs. If I didn't keep moving, my muscles would stiffen and cramp, and then I'd never be able to find Patrick.

"James said you would need my assistance. He even moved the mirrors out of my way." The wraith boy reached ahead of me and brushed aside a layer of snow.

Heavy white powder and slush thundered away from us, leaving a shallower stretch across the next few paces.

James walked up behind me. "I'm not sorry," he said. "If

you won't be sensible, I won't, either. Neither of us will allow you to be harmed."

"You *know* what he did to Meredith. And those guards. And the cathedral." I squeezed my dagger hilt, desperate to keep circulation in my fingers. "Saints, James. You *know* what he is."

His hard expression never shifted. "Is this the time to argue? There are people dying on the shore—people from both sides. Do you want to stop it or not?" He eyed the wraith boy askance. "This is the only way you go."

"Very well. Clear a path, Chrysalis. Don't hurt anyone, or mirrors will be the very least of your problems." I sheathed my dagger and held my cloak tight over my chest.

"I will do only as you order, my queen." He bowed his head and shuffled in front of me to begin his work.

He would obey, but for how long? I glanced at James, keeping my voice low. "If he harms someone, that's on you."

Shouts came from atop the wagons, ordering us to put the wraith boy back inside, and for James to keep me from doing anything stupid. A soldier on horseback started toward us, but with Chrysalis heaving snow, we moved swiftly along the line of wagons.

"I outrank them," James said, as though I were worried they'd report him. "What are you going to do? Stand on a wagon and announce your presence?"

"I'll find Patrick and make him listen to me. That might involve standing on a wagon. I haven't decided yet."

"Decide soon. You don't have much time." Men were spilling from the fringes of the fighting just ahead. Red and blue uniforms shone with snow and blood. Swords flashed in the flickering lights.

We ran on, the wraith boy pushing ahead of us. I kept my eyes on the bridge arching above the bay as we dodged smaller fights that had splintered away from the main forces.

There were a lot more men in red than in blue.

James grabbed my arm and we tumbled into the snow just as a flaming arrow struck the place I'd been standing.

"Are you all right?" James climbed to his feet and scanned the area for the shooter, but the arrow could have come from anyone. Everyone moved so quickly.

"Fine." I stood and adjusted my sword at my hip, resolving to keep a better eye on my surroundings. "And thanks."

"That's why I'm here."

"Shall I find the shooter, my queen?" The wraith boy faced me, a shoulder-high wall of snow growing behind him, shielding the three of us. "I can find whoever tried to assassinate you and—"

I held up a hand. "I don't want anyone on either side to die."

"Too late for that." James glanced over his shoulder where bodies had already fallen. "But he's right. If you go into the fighting, you will get hurt. Maybe killed. And I promised Tobiah I would keep you alive."

I turned to the wraith boy. "We need to reach Patrick. I need you to help me get there safely."

A sinister smile spread across the wraith boy's face. "Oh yes. The mountain lion man. I remember him."

"Do not kill him—or anyone else, for that matter."

He lifted an eyebrow. "If we're attacked?"

"You know my orders, Chrysalis. Don't try to get around them. Don't do anything you *think* I want. If you do, I will take away your name."

His expression turned blank. "I understand."

"He could be anywhere," James said. "He might not even be here."

"No. He's here." I gazed over the distance, the blades and bodies everywhere. The stench of salt and blood filled the air, with a slight edge of wraith coming from Chrysalis.

"Where?"

"Where he can see everything." I pointed to the immense bridge, where the railroad tracks crossed the water.

Snowhaven Bridge was pre-wraith, all sea-battered steel that shimmered in the frantic light. The cables shone like silk strands, and the towers stabbed into the water, going farther than I could see. A pair of hulking guard stations stood at each side of the entrance, with an armored passageway stretching through the sky between them.

"That's where Patrick will be."

TWENTY-FIVE

JAMES AND THE wraith boy followed my gaze to the bridge that spanned the entire bay. "What if he's not there?"

"Then we stand in the center and draw his attention." A dozen flags snapped in the cold wind, and four indigo banners hung from the parapets, emblazoned with House crests. Gas lamps shone down on the battlefield, hot white lights above the flames.

"How will you get there?" James gestured to the fighting masses between us and our destination.

"You will help me reach it safely."

James heaved out a breath. "All right. Let's go. But we're doing this my way. We're going *around* the fighting, not through the worst of it."

"I can fight."

"It's not your duty to fight this time. It's your duty to stay alive."

Even so, I drew my sword in one hand and a dagger in the other. With the boys flanking me, we slipped around the edge of the battle. It took more time, but when combatants spilled into our path, James or the wraith boy pushed them out of the way. Only twice did I have to remind the wraith boy not to hurt people.

At last, we came to the shore; Tangler Bay surged below a small cliff. My homeland was still too far to see the lights of the city, but the bridge's towers and cables were lit with gas lamps.

My heart thrummed as James and the wraith boy carved a path to the guard station. The sound of the sea swelled within me. I was so close.

A blue-coated body dropped at my feet. James staggered and breathed a name, but we moved over the soldier and found ourselves at the main door. The guards wore indigo, but they were engaged with Aecorian rebels, and no one noticed us as James heaved open the door and ushered me into an antechamber, its walls covered with yet more indigo flags and signs.

With my dagger hand, I grabbed the metal-reinforced door handle to the main chamber and my shoulder almost came out of place as I heaved the unmoving door.

"What's wrong?" James asked.

"Locked. I can pick it." There was always magic, but considering how dizzy just animating notebooks made me, I shouldn't. Not now, when I needed to face Patrick.

"Let me." The wraith boy took the handle and gave it a sharp tug, and the entire door came off its hinges with a deafening *crack*. He staggered back against the size, but held the door's weight without a problem. "What should I do with it?"

"Just put it against the wall." I stepped clear of the door and into the main chamber filled with desks and bookcases. Hallways branched off, and a series of doors ran along the back wall. "Who was that outside, James?"

The body, I meant, but I didn't want to say it out loud.

"Someone I knew from school. A friend." His face was hard as he scanned the room and pointed his sword toward one of the hallways on the far side of the room. "There."

I flexed my fingers around the hilts of my weapons as we walked.

"Footsteps," whispered the wraith boy. "Someone's following."

We started to run as a handful of red-coated soldiers thundered after us, their blades drawn.

"Stop there!" The feminine voice was as familiar as my own.

I skidded and spun, my cloak flaring. On either side of me, the wraith boy lifted his hands like claws, and James melted into a guarded stance, but I sheathed both of my weapons. A true smile—the first in what felt like forever—slipped out. "Melanie."

"Wil!" She motioned for her five soldiers to stay their weapons, and a moment later, we stood between our groups, embracing.

A hard knot inside me loosened at last. "I missed you so much," I whispered.

"Me too." Her voice hitched. "It feels like forever."

There was so much to talk about. So much to do. But I wanted to stay like this. Magic, wraith, war: What were those things to true friendship? We could fight—with each other and on opposite sides of a battlefield—but our bond ran stronger than any of that.

"Wil," said James. "I know the feeling, but there's no time."

Melanie and I stepped back from each other, and she reached as though to move a strand of hair from her eyes, but she'd cut it. The black locks that had once fallen to the middle of her back were gone, leaving choppy sections that framed her face. It made her look older. More mature.

"Where is Patrick?"

Her gaze shifted upward. "Here. We learned Prince Colin was returning to Aecor. We've been waiting for his convoy to arrive. This side of the bay has been ours for almost a week— and the soldiers stationed here didn't even realize."

"Good work." The praise came automatically, making James give me a sharp look. "I mean, I'm impressed, but I've come here to stop the fighting. I won't allow Patrick to destroy the peace I've been working to build."

"Some peace, if what I heard is true." Her eyes cut to the wraith boy, then to James. "Captain Rayner. Lovely to see you again."

"This is taking too long," he said. "If you're on Wil's side, take us to Patrick."

She'd take me to Patrick, regardless.

Melanie gestured to three of her men. "Fix the door. Make sure no one follows us. And you two"—she turned to the others— "come with me."

The six of us moved through the room, into the hall and a dark staircase that switched back several times. We passed doors to other levels of the guard station, and to the interior of the passageway that stretched over the bridge entrance. Finally, we came to the top.

"You know what he's going to tell you to do," Melanie said as the guards hauled open the door. "You know what he wants."

"Patrick no longer gets to make demands of me."

Icy wind blasted through the doorway, tearing at my cloak. Lights shone in from atop the passageway, blinding as I stepped outside to find Patrick exactly where I'd expected. He'd torn down the Indigo Kingdom flags, and was releasing them one by one into the sea. The House banners hanging over the parapets were likely next, but he saw me first.

"Wilhelmina." The last indigo flag whipped toward the ocean.

James's whole body tensed, but he didn't stray from my side.

Patrick didn't move; he waited for us to come closer as he took in the group surrounding me: Melanie, two of his own men, a boy who looked like me, and the new king's cousin. He placed his hands behind his back. "The convoy is overwhelmed. Casualties on both sides will be heavy."

"Call them off. If you do, James can stop the Indigo Army. We will discuss everything peacefully, once we reach Sandcliff Castle."

Patrick shook his head. "It's not going to work like that. Colin will never give up Aecor, not willingly. There's only one way to get it back, and that is to take it. Our people don't want to be under Indigo rule. They want their queen. They want *you*."

"And you told them I've been a hostage in Skyvale."

"Haven't you? The Wilhelmina I know would never have

sent letters like the ones I intercepted, claiming to be from you."

"That just proves how little you know me."

"The letters weren't even in your handwriting."

I clenched my jaw. "Call off your soldiers, Patrick." Wind tugged at my clothes again, and flecks of snow from drifts stung my face.

"I will not. This is an important battle for our people. They'll see we *can* beat the enemy." Patrick glanced at the door opposite the one we'd come from, but the way was dark. "I won't stop you from doing whatever you came to do, though. You are still my princess, after all."

I turned to the wraith boy. "Chrysalis, I need to be heard."

A smile sliced across his face, and he leaned over the edge of the passageway. "People of Aecor. People of the Indigo Kingdom." The wraith boy's voice boomed across the area, thunder in my ears. "Stop what you are doing."

The sharp, ozone scent of wraith flooded the battlefield, but still the fighting continued.

The wraith boy looked at me, as though for permission.

"Don't *hurt* anyone," I warned. I touched Connor's mirror in my pocket.

James was already standing close to me. Melanie moved near Patrick, their red-coated guards in close attendance as they all watched, waiting to see what the wraith boy would do.

Chrysalis stretched out his hands and turned up his palms. A low rumble filled the area, making soldiers stagger to stay in combat, but when the snow began to draw away from the bulk of the battle, shooting between legs and away from the wagons, people halted and looked around. A few took the opportunity to run, and some finished the fights they'd been involved in, but most just stood and stared.

Someone pointed up. Toward me.

The snow pulled itself into a wall along the entrance to the bridge, covering the guard stations. It gathered higher and higher until the top of the mound touched the passageway. Shards of compacted snow jutted up, reflecting the light of gas lamps. Angles shifted and focused until the white light surrounded me.

Everyone saw me.

"Soldiers of Aecor," called the wraith boy, unnaturally loud in the sudden stillness below. "Your queen—"

"*Princess*," I hissed.

"Your princess is here. She wishes to address you."

I stepped onto the ledge. Behind me, Patrick and Melanie hadn't moved, and their guards were with them. I hated turning my back to Patrick, but I trusted Melanie. James hoisted himself up beside me, and together we gazed down the steep slope of glittering snow, where thousands of men waited at the base.

The angled planes of snow amplified my voice. "My name is Wilhelmina Korte. I've come to tell the people of Aecor the truth about my stay in Skyvale. King Tobiah Pierce has not held me as a hostage, nor has he forbidden me to reclaim Aecor. For the last several weeks, since I first revealed my identity, we have been in *peaceful* negotiations. Patrick Lien returned to Aecor without my blessing. He incited this resistance without my consent."

A blast of icy wind pushed at me, stealing my breath and whipping my cloak, but the wraith boy reached up and held me in place. James warmed my side: a steady, strong presence.

"I have with me Captain James Rayner, cousin to King

Tobiah. He is here as proof of our alliance, and our dedication to work together to resolve the conflicts between Aecor and the Indigo Kingdom."

"Very good," James muttered.

Below, people shifted. A low hum of voices came, but it was impossible to understand anything that was said.

"This fighting will cease immediately. When I reach Sandcliff Castle—"

At the far end of the passageway, a door slammed open. Ospreys Ronald and Oscar Gray strode out, and between them they dragged a limp and bloodied Prince Colin.

"Oh, by all the saints." James groaned.

Patrick beckoned the Gray brothers closer. There was no emotion on his face, just the same unwavering determination to do what he thought was necessary.

"I have what I came for." He didn't need to raise his voice, or even look at me. "This ambush was not to invade the Indigo Kingdom," he said, drawing a sword. The point touched the side of Prince Colin's neck, but the unconscious prince didn't move. "I simply want to take back Aecor. Terrell, the man who took it, is dead by my hand."

James stiffened beside me. I touched his forearm. "Don't move."

"Though my plans for the new king were thwarted, the message was delivered: Aecorians will fight for their home." When Prince Colin began to stir, Patrick edged the blade away. He wouldn't cut by accident; when he did, it would be with deliberate precision. "Now I have the *Overlord* of Aecor. He's raised incredible taxes on the people, forced them to the front lines of the wraithland, and has even had the audacity to live in Sand-cliff Castle—the home where the Kortes once resided. With his death, Aecor will be one step closer to reclaiming its independence."

"No." I drew my sword and dagger. "Drop your weapon, Patrick."

He met my eyes, only a flash of triumph in his expression before he said, "You know how to enforce that command."

Prince Colin blinked a few times and awakened. Blood dripped down his face as he scanned his surroundings, muttering curses under his breath. When he looked from Patrick to me, his eyes were filled with hate.

Patrick would kill Prince Colin. Just like he'd killed Terrell, and almost killed James and Tobiah. Just like the wraith boy had killed Meredith.

He'd kill Prince Colin for me. For my kingdom.

Tobiah's words haunted me: "*What kind of queen will you be? The kind who allows others to murder in her name, or the kind who stands up and makes decisions her conscience can agree with?*"

"Fine." The word was a breath. My heart sped faster, and the cold sapped at my strength, but I forced my voice to project. "I hereby declare myself Queen of Aecor."

PART THREE

THE
VERMILION
THRONE

TWENTY-SIX

THE EFFECT OF my words was immediate.

A great cry rose up behind me. The air shook with thousands of voices, some in protest, but many more in triumph.

Prince Colin glared at me with murder in his eyes, but Patrick simply nodded and took a slow, measured step away from the prince—but not before edging his blade a breath closer to Prince Colin's throat, leaving a long, thin cut. A reminder. A promise.

Then Patrick's blade hit the floor and he held out his arms in surrender.

"Arrest him," I told the red-coated guards.

They hesitated, looking between Patrick, Melanie, and me.

"Do it," Melanie said. "Wilhelmina is your queen. You answer to her, not to Patrick."

They obeyed without further question.

Within two hours, one of the wagons became a moving

prison, guards of both colors watching over Patrick. The soldiers stationed at Snowhaven Bridge were reinstated, and the wraith boy began to clear snow under my direction; I didn't trust him not to move it all into the bay and cause a flood.

"Prince Colin will not forgive this," James said as we walked back to my wagon where a dozen Aecorian guards waited.

"I did it to save his life."

"He won't see it that way."

"Unfortunately." Had I made things better or worse? It was impossible to know.

The night had deepened and grown colder. The snow Chrysalis had moved away from the caravan formed glistening walls to the north and south, stinking like the wraithland.

After that exertion, Chrysalis was paler, his movements sluggish, but I stopped myself before asking if he was all right. He was going straight back to his wardrobe. At least I didn't have to worry about him running away; he stuck to my side as surely as a puppy, desperate for attention.

"I should warn you." James kept his voice low. "Several Aecorians have named themselves part of your royal guard. You can accept or dismiss them as you wish, but you should make a decision soon. Some will want favors in the future. You should be mindful of who you owe."

"It doesn't matter. I don't want any of them. I already have you."

"Then you risk offending potential allies."

Not what I wanted to hear.

"At any rate, there will be new sleeping arrangements.

You're no longer incognito and I'm not willing to risk your reputation—"

"It's *my* reputation to ruin if I want, James."

"And I'm not willing to risk mine, either." He gave a smug grin and motioned to the wagon just ahead. "Lady Melanie will join you. I will station myself outside your wagon, along with any Aecorian soldiers of your choosing."

"Oscar and Ronald."

"The ones who brought Prince Colin to Lien?"

"They're Ospreys. They may have sided with him during the Inundation, but they won't allow any harm to come to me. The Gray brothers might have been born high noblemen, but they're clever and good with their weapons." I paused. "Besides, I don't know any other Aecorians."

James nodded. "Very well."

"As for the others who've named themselves my royal guards, I'll find out what Melanie, Ronald, and Oscar think of them before I accept any oaths. I'd like to know your opinions, too, if you happen to spend time with them."

"Of course." He wouldn't forget, either. That was one of James's best qualities: complete reliability. "As for the wraith boy, his wardrobe has been moved to the wagon following yours."

The wraith boy gasped. "No! I want to be close to my queen."

"It's only a wagon away." I leveled a glare on him, though the expression didn't feel as menacing as I intended; I was too exhausted. "That's close enough, and I will visit you in the morning."

The hardness of his face softened. "You trusted me tonight. I wanted to make you proud."

I forced my voice neutral and chose my words carefully. "You did well tonight. I was pleased with your work, and the way you obeyed my instructions."

A smile lit his face as we continued toward his wagon. The mirrors had been moved, too, though at the moment they were covered with sheets. He hesitated at a sliver of glass showing near the floor; I stepped in front of it.

"In you go."

His smile returned as he went inside his wardrobe. "Do I need to hum again?"

"Only if you want. Just behave. I'll see you in the morning."

"I cannot wait. Good night, my queen." He remained grinning even when I closed the doors and pulled the sheets off the mirrors. The glass reflected his wardrobe from every angle, making it impossible for him to escape.

How secure was it really, though? He avoided mirrors. He acted like they hurt him. But he'd destroyed the mirrors as wraith mist. Perhaps he couldn't anymore, now that he was a boy.

What about the rest of the wraith?

"Wil?" James touched my elbow.

I blinked and stepped back from the glass I'd been glaring into. My face was ashen with cold and exhaustion, and my eyes rimmed with red. "Sorry," I muttered. "I was thinking about mirrors again."

"It happens to all of us."

The wagon guards were eyeing me, too. I drew myself up and straightened my cloak. "Don't open the wardrobe doors for any reason. And don't taunt him."

Without another word, I swept out of the wagon, James at my heels.

"Do you think he can ever be useful?" James asked. "Can he learn to be more human?"

"Meredith thought so. And you saw what he did to her. There's nothing human about him." At James's flinch, I softened the edge in my tone. "He's just wraith and magic and destruction. A mistake I mean to correct. Tobiah said I can't just bring things to life without consequences, and he was right."

"Can you destroy them without consequences?" James shook his head as we approached my wagon. "Tobiah said that because he's made mistakes, too. And he's tried to correct them without thinking, and the results were even more undesirable than the original problem."

I lifted an eyebrow.

He shrugged. "It's not my story to tell. But I've said before that you two are a lot alike."

How strange that anyone besides an Osprey might know me well enough to make a statement like that.

Oscar and Ronald stood guard at my wagon door, their red jackets buttoned tight against the cold. Black caps hid their dark hair.

"Look, it's Wil," said Oscar, smiling.

"That's Queen Wil." Ronald elbowed his brother, but didn't smile. "There were about ten people here earlier. We told them to shove off for now."

"Thank you." Quickly, I gave them the same orders I had James, concerning a guard. "I need one of you to watch Patrick, too. I'm sure there are a lot of people loyal to him and I can't risk his escape. He needs to be tried for his crimes."

"I'll go." Ronald offered a quick bow before heading toward Patrick's wagon.

"He feels bad about Quinn and Ezra still," said Oscar, though I hadn't asked. "He's afraid you think it's his fault."

Their names stung. "It's Patrick's fault for sending them. Ronald did all he could."

Oscar nodded. "I'll tell him you said that." He opened the wagon door to let James and me inside. The lamps were already lit, and Melanie stood on the other side, near a small bedroll where the wraith boy's wardrobe used to be. She offered a quick greeting as James shut the door behind us.

"It's so unsettling to see you trusting anyone," James said.

"I've known them most of my life." I'd known Patrick most of my life, too.

He took the desk chair and pulled out the blue notebook he used to communicate with Tobiah. "I need to report what happened tonight. It will give him time to prepare for the official news."

Prince Colin's riders would be at least two days behind James's letter, more if snow impeded their travel.

"No doubt he'll appreciate the warning." I shed my cloak and hung it on a hook by the door. My hands drifted down the smooth fabric, cold and damp with bits of snow. "Tell him—"

James uncapped a jar of ink and waited.

I unhooked my sword and its sheath. My daggers. I placed all my weapons in a trunk and straightened. "Tell him I had no choice. That I haven't forgotten what he said about authority and my status, but I had to do something." Then, softer: "A declaration like that is hardly official. It doesn't make it real."

"It was real enough for Patrick," Melanie said. "After everything, you gave him exactly what he wanted."

"Doubtful he wanted to go to prison."

"Wanted? Probably not. Was willing? Definitely." She crossed the wagon and linked our arms together. "You know Patrick. Everything is part of some elaborate plan. I don't know how being arrested figures into it, but I'm not ready to say he's no longer a problem."

James opened his notebook to the first blank page and dipped his pen in ink. "You're sure you don't know his plans?"

Melanie shook her head. "He wanted to take Prince Colin prisoner and execute him in the courtyard." She squeezed my arm. "And on the off chance Prince Colin's forces overwhelmed us, Aecor City was prepared to resist. Known loyalists have been . . . dealt with."

"What does that mean?" I asked.

"Imprisoned until they're sufficiently encouraged to support you."

"We'll have to free them at once." *Saints*, the things Patrick had done—and was willing to do—in my name. "And whatever he gains by being in prison himself, we'll have to wait to find out. Prince Colin looks ready to murder me, and I don't think Tobiah will have a much more positive reaction."

"Oh, I can't imagine His Royal Sullenness being happy about anything." Melanie pulled away and sat on my bed. "Sorry,

James. I know you like him. For some reason."

James smirked and bent over his notebook. "Wilhelmina likes him, too."

"*Wil?*" Melanie lifted an eyebrow, but I was *not* going to get into that right now.

Time to change the subject. "Where is Paige?" She'd been the other Osprey to side with Patrick. So far I'd seen three out of four of them. "Is she—"

"She's fine. Waiting at the castle. We took it almost two weeks ago, while most of the regiment was still in Skyvale."

"And the soldiers who had to stay in Aecor?" I asked, though I could guess. A pit of dread pulled in my stomach.

"Dead. Or imprisoned, if they had military knowledge he wanted. Same conditions as the loyalists." Melanie sighed and ran her fingers through her short, choppy locks. "It's been hard. Ugly. I've seen more death than I ever thought I would. But we've held Aecor City, which is more than I thought would happen."

I tried to imagine Aecor City now. My memories of my childhood home were foggy with time, and charred black after watching the city burn during the One-Night War. I hardly knew it. Not like I knew Skyvale. Just closing my eyes, I could see the peaked roofs, the mirrors aglow in the light of the setting sun, and the blue mountains that surrounded everything.

But Aecor City as it stood now was a blank. Some queen I was.

Nevertheless, it was home. And it was right across the bay.

For a moment, we listened to the scratching sounds of James writing.

"Paige has made herself into quite the steward," Melanie

said. "Patrick told her to make the castle ready for your return. She'll be so panicked when she realizes you're here already."

"We've lived in poor conditions before. I'm sure everything is more than adequate." I pulled the tie off the end of my braid and threaded my fingers into my hair, unbraiding section by section. "Besides, Prince Colin and his regiment were living there, and the crown prince requires a certain level of luxury."

"That he does. He—" She hesitated and shook off whatever she'd been about to say. "We have a lot to discuss. I want to know all about the other Ospreys, and how you ended up traveling with Tobiah's bodyguard. And that boy who could be your brother."

"So much has changed. Including this." I touched her hair. "What happened?"

Her face darkened. "Oh—"

"Sorry to interrupt." James turned from his notebook. "Melanie, I need to ask you a few questions." He glanced at me. "Apparently he's awake. He keeps writing where I'm trying to write. He says congratulations."

"He doesn't mean it." I'd probably ruined a hundred of his plans I didn't even know about.

"What is this?" Melanie grabbed the notebook and turned it over and around. "Both of you write in here? How does it work?"

"Magic." I plucked the notebook from her hands. "I'll explain later."

More words appeared on the page—mostly questions with underlines and multiple pieces of punctuation—as I handed the notebook back to James.

"Thank you." He started writing on the next page, as Tobiah's questions continued appearing on the previous. "Let's start with the goal of the ambush. Patrick's force wasn't big enough to invade, though you said you managed to take and hold Snowhaven Bridge for a matter of days."

Melanie glanced at me, eyebrow raised.

"Answer all of his questions honestly."

She gave a quick nod and faced James. "That is correct. Patrick had no desire to invade the Indigo Kingdom. He wanted Aecor as it had been. The ambush was on the Indigo side of the bridge for two reasons: to prove to the Indigo Army that we were truly a force, and to keep them out of Aecor."

"I see." James's pen scraped paper. "And you took the bridge. How?"

While James and Melanie discussed, I slipped behind the partition and changed into my nightclothes. Once my dressing gown covered me, I stepped out to find James pushing back the desk chair.

"I've already sent a list of the Indigo Kingdom dead I know," he told me. "We'll have a more complete list once the dead are moved and on a wagon home."

"All right." For a moment, I wasn't sure why he was telling me that, but then I realized it was because I should have someone do the same thing for the Aecorians. See to the dead. Ensure the families were told. Figure out how to transport the bodies.

All things queens should remember to do on their own.

"In addition to my account of what happened tonight, Tobiah would like to hear it from you. He'd also like to know your plans for the prisoners in Aecor City and whether you plan to free them. What you intend to do with Prince Colin now. And the wraith boy . . . Well, you'll see the questions. I circled the ones you need to answer." James offered the pen to me.

"Thank you." So much for catching up with Melanie tonight, let alone getting any rest. Once James left, I dipped my pen into the ink and wrote.

Hello, Tobiah. It probably won't help to know that I didn't intend any of this. . . .

TWENTY-SEVEN

IN THE MORNING, I visited the wraith boy as promised, and then announced to James that we would be riding across the bridge.

"It's warm out," I said. A lie. The winter air was just as cold as it had been last night, but the sky was clear and bright.

And I was coming home a queen.

"Fine." The groggy cant of his voice indicated he'd slept as little as I had. "As long as you know I think it's unwise."

"Your protest is noted."

Ferguson was saddled for me—apparently queens didn't saddle their own horses—and I climbed atop, the Ospreys and James flanking me.

Night wind had swept clean Snowhaven Bridge, leaving patches of white in the frothing gray water below. As the first wagons rumbled onto the bridge ahead of us, horse hooves rang and gulls cried long and loud. The birds perched atop the passageway, and all along the bridge on posts. A few dove toward the convoy, looking for food.

Finally, we passed between the guard stations and stepped onto Snowhaven Bridge. For the first time since the war, I was off Indigo Kingdom land.

"Are you all right?" Melanie rode next to me, her eyebrows pushed together. Ronald and Oscar rode behind us, while James rode behind them; there wasn't enough room for all of us to ride abreast.

"My chest hurts." I glanced at Melanie. "My heart is pounding so hard."

Her look of concern melted into a smile. "I know. Mine did, too, when we crossed to Northland. It still does. We're going home, Wilhelmina."

I lifted my face toward the rising sun as the sea wind whipped around me. Home. At last.

"Don't get too eager," Oscar said. "It will take all day to cross the bay."

"All day?" I looked at him aghast. "I don't remember Snowhaven Bridge being so long." The only thing I could see ahead was the smooth line of stone and steel, a scattering of islands, and water all around. Patches of ice still glimmered on the bridge, evident where riders ahead slowed and directed their mounts around.

"All day," Melanie said.

"What I wonder," Ronald mused, "is how this thing was even built. It's amazing the ocean hasn't eaten it away by now."

"This water isn't as salty as the real ocean," I said. "The rivers that feed the bay are all fresh."

"Flashers built the bridge." Melanie glanced back. "Centuries ago, flashers—radiants, then—raised the support islands from the bottom of the bay. They struck the towers into the seabed, and caused the steel frame to snake across the span of the water. They made the stone unfurl, and the cables hold fast. This bridge has stood through hurricanes, battles, and things you and I can't even dream of. And it will stand for centuries more."

I lifted an eyebrow at Melanie. "Did you read a book about the bridge?"

She laughed and ducked her head. "Yes. The library in Sandcliff Castle has several. *Snowhaven Bridge: a Modern Wonder of Aecor* is the best, in case you were wondering. It was written four hundred years ago, so very modern indeed."

My heart warmed. Even during the chaos of war, Melanie had managed to sneak moments with books. That, I hoped, would never change.

"Seems incredible, given all the advantages flashers have offered, that the world turned against them." Oscar nodded toward me. "You, I hear."

"You've seen the wraith boy. You know about the wraithland." I clenched my jaw. "I hate what happened to flashers as much as anyone else, but I understand why the world reacted like that. It's fear."

"Fear doesn't excuse a hundred years of oppression and abuse," Oscar said.

"No. But I understand the fear." I reached forward to pet Ferguson's mane and neck. "When I saw the way wraith twisted everything, how it killed and *changed* the world, I was horrified by my own magic. I hadn't told the wraith to mutate the animals or give trees teeth, but I felt responsible. I didn't want to use my own magic ever again."

Though I had. Almost right away. And a dozen times since.

"But—"

I shook my head. "I don't want to talk about wraith and magic now. I'm going home. That's all I want to think about."

"Then you'll be thinking the same thoughts for a long time, Your Highness." Prince Colin's voice came from behind us. Everyone turned. "We won't reach Aecor City until tonight."

"So I've heard." I nudged Ferguson to one side as Prince Colin rode even with me. "And the proper honorific is *Your Majesty* now, in case you'd forgotten how to address a queen."

"That is actually what I wanted to speak to you about." He looked better than one might expect, given his brush with death just last night. His cheeks were flushed with cold, but he was as immaculately dressed as ever, his chin high. The cut Patrick left had been cleaned and stitched. "You have no idea what you did last night, do you?"

"Give me some credit, Your Highness." I forced my voice to stay calm, but tension knotted in my shoulders and neck. "I did what was necessary to stop the fighting and save lives."

"You told the Aecorian people that you're their queen. You undermined my authority as overlord, which I've worked to build for almost ten years. You acted rashly—"

I lifted a hand. "Patrick already undermined your authority." My throat was tight, roughening my words. "While you were in Skyvale, he led a revolution in Aecor. If I hadn't joined you on this journey, the Red Militia would have overwhelmed your forces, and you would have been brought to the courtyard in Sandcliff Castle to be executed. Even if your troops had managed to get through to Aecor City, the whole city would have fought your return, and they'd have won."

"No. They would not have. Aecor Territory is filled with my soldiers." Prince Colin thrust a finger at me. "This was you. You gave in to his demands and declared yourself queen. Maybe that was your intention all along."

I kept my voice low and cool. "I did it to save your life."

The crown prince leveled a long, threatening glare at me. But unlike in my bedroom and the other day by my wagon, this one didn't feel like a slimy touch and grope. This one felt . . . stronger. Deadlier. A hand around my throat, maybe.

"It seems, Your Highness," James said, "that you owe Queen Wilhelmina your life."

Prince Colin's face turned darker. "It seems so." He tore his eyes from me at last, looking back at James. "It would be wise for you to remember, Captain Rayner, that what Wilhelmina did last night might have appeased the peasants following the traitor, but it wasn't legal. She is still a ward of the Indigo Kingdom, and Aecor Territory is still a *territory*. It is mine."

"Not for long," I whispered. "They are my people. They always have been."

"Oh, we'll make a good show tonight." His eyes were back on me. "When we ride into the city, it will be as one. A united front. Overlord and queen. Two rulers who care deeply for the well-being of Aecor."

"You're afraid they will attack you."

"With you at my side, I have no need to fear an uprising." His smile curled up like drawing a knife from a sheath.

My fingers turned white around the reins. "Jump off the bridge and die, Colin."

He released a sharp laugh and rode ahead, followed by a half-dozen indigo-coated guards.

"I hate him," I muttered as Melanie returned to her position next to me.

"I don't know anyone who doesn't." She rolled her shoulders and readjusted her seat. "But there is good news: riders were sent ahead. There will be dinner and baths waiting for all of us."

"Sandcliff Castle has been updated with many of the same modern conveniences as Skyvale Palace," Ronald added. "Apparently, Prince Colin refused to live there until gas lamps had been installed in every room he might enter, and plumbing in *all* the kitchens and washrooms, not just in the royal wing."

I twisted in my saddle. "That castle is seven hundred years old! How could he rip it apart like that?"

The boys shook their heads. "It doesn't hold the same meaning to him," said Oscar. "But it doesn't look as bad as you're imagining."

Skyvale Palace was only two centuries old, and updated severely when magic was outlawed. Prince Colin had always had the comforts of gas lamps and hot, running water, as well as a hundred other minor conveniences because of his rank and place of birth. He'd never known an orphanage or run-down castle in the mountains. He'd never been truly hungry.

His privilege didn't excuse his behavior toward my ancestral home.

"Will you have the lights and pipes torn out?" Melanie asked.

"It's already done, and we have more important problems to address."

"Like what to do with Patrick." Her voice was almost lost under the cry of gulls and hum of wagon wheels on steel. "And what will happen when you return to Aecor City with a small army from the Indigo Kingdom at your back."

"I'll figure it out."

The marvel of being out of the Indigo Kingdom gave way to aching anticipation, and a melancholy note rang on the wind as we traveled the endless bridge.

Steel tower after steel tower plunged into the snow-streaked waves of the bay. At noon, we ate small lunches on our horses, and I listened to Melanie tell stories she'd learned from books in the Sandcliff Castle library, and the boys discuss how the battle had gone, and what certain people would think now that I was back and Patrick was going to prison.

Melanie pointed out Snowhaven Island, clustered in with a number of other islands filled with evergreen trees and water fowl. The bridge was anchored on the southern tip, and soon the convoy blocked my view, so the only thing to watch was the waves.

Finally, as the sun shifted behind us, I saw the pale scrape of land on the horizon, and the suggestion of towers in the south. My heart pounded as my homeland grew on the horizon, the cliffs becoming more solid and real. A lighthouse flashed and soon the end of the bridge was in sight. A pair of guard towers stood on the Aecor side, identical to the Indigo Kingdom side.

I kicked Ferguson into a trot, vaguely aware of James picking up his pace behind me as I maneuvered between riders. A few people shouted for me to slow down or watch out, but when people ahead realized I was coming, they moved out of my way.

Without my urging, Ferguson shifted into a gallop, his hooves ringing across the bridge. Gulls cried and waves crashed. Wind tore at my clothes and howled in my ears, but I was close. So close.

"Wil!" James's voice came from behind me. "It's not safe to go so quickly!"

I didn't care. Ferguson didn't care.

"We're almost home," I whispered. We passed wagon after wagon until we were ahead of the convoy. I could feel Ferguson's hooves slip on patches of ice, but he kept his footing. Then we were off the bridge.

Onto the dirt.

I reined him in and he slowed to a walk, snorting white clouds into the cold air. My heart thundered in my ears as I dismounted, legs wobbling with adrenaline and disbelief.

James caught up and leapt off his horse. "Wil, are you crazy?" He grabbed my shoulders. "You could have slipped right off the bridge!"

I laughed, high and giddy, and threw my arms around him. My eyes were heavy with tears from cold and wind and wild joy. "I'm home, James. I'm finally home."

TWENTY-EIGHT

THE BELLS BEGAN to ring as soon as the convoy started up the winding promontory.

Aecor City sat on a cliff side overlooking the Red Bay, where fishing boats were moored in the harbor. The rocky face glowed gold under the setting sun, crevices shadowed and fluttering with roosting eagles and gulls. Ospreys hunched in their stick nests, watching the noisy approach as the wagons were removed from the old iron tracks, their secondary wheels swung down.

I was home.

Peace had taken me home before war.

The thought swelled in my chest as we headed to the main city gates, carved from stone and reinforced with steel. The osprey sigil, framed by sharp ocean waves, shimmered in the setting sunlight. Enormous towers pierced the purpling sky, with vermilion banners hanging from the parapets. Trumpets sounded, and the gates cranked open.

Home, home, home: the word thrummed in my head like a second heartbeat, distracting. I glanced at James behind me.

"When people came here from across the sea, Aecor was flat. Like any place that's mostly coastal plains and marshes, it flooded. But the people loved the sea and couldn't bear to leave, so radiants raised a plateau on which to build the city. Sandcliff Castle is carved from the land below it. It was built of this land, with this land's magic, and for this land's people. The keep held my ancestors for nine generations."

Prince Colin's smirk slithered onto his face.

Finally, the main gates finished opening to reveal Castle Street, a wide avenue leading up the hill and to the main keep.

People crowded along the sides of the road, lifting small children onto shoulders, while others climbed onto buildings or statues—anything that might offer a good view. Others leaned out windows and filled balconies. Their shouts shook the entire city.

The most prestigious shops lined Castle Street. They were meant to entice and impress visitors. Even now, with the city packed onto the street, merchants waved packets of spicy-smelling food, trinkets, and lengths of cloth. Black-coated police wove between the people, but no one paid them mind.

My heart pounded in time with the rising cry of my name: Wilhelmina, Wil-hel-min-a. The roar made my head spin with giddiness, and not even the gloom of Prince Colin's stiff figure beside me could dim the fierce pride boiling in my heart.

Behind me, Melanie laughed and added her voice to the chorus calling my name. The Gray brothers roared.

We moved steadily up the road, our guards keeping the

people back. Their whoops and applause were thunder in my ears as evening faded into twilight.

Halfway to the castle, the crowd began to shift.

Little by little, they pressed closer. While the people at the gate had been eager to see us—me—I caught a group here shaking fists, and others with signs calling me an Indigo whore and traitor queen.

"What's happening?" Prince Colin shouted at his guards. "What are they doing?"

Suddenly Ronald and Oscar were flanking me, their horses pressed so close to mine our knees touched.

"We'll take you to the tunnels," Ronald said. "It will be safer."

"No!" I would not enter my family's castle like a thief, never mind my criminal history.

"Wil, it's not safe." James had kicked his horse ahead of ours, and one hand rested on his sword. "Look, it's getting worse."

People spilled into the streets. Police moved to corral them, but were largely ignored.

The jeers crescendoed, with people forcing their way to the front of the crowd. Some hefted clubs or wooden planks. A small, metal object flew through the air ahead of me: a chain link.

Melanie gasped.

"We can't make it to the tunnels anyway," I said. The crowd was so thick, impenetrable. People climbed onto the buildings lining the streets to shout from above.

One person threw himself toward the street, but fell short

and took down three protestors. The gap closed immediately, trampling the jumper and his victims.

"Saints," I breathed. My pulse raced as adrenaline spiked. This wasn't just a protest; this was a *mob*.

"At least put your head down." Ronald pressed his hand on my back, pushing me toward Ferguson's neck. Stiff mane hairs tickled my face. No matter how hard I resisted, Ronald wouldn't let me up. He leaned his weight onto me, and when I tried to twist my head, he called for his brother's help. Oscar's hand fell on the back of my head, heavy.

Cacophony sounded all around, people calling for Prince Colin's head and the Indigo Army's surrender. Thousands of voices filled the air, and with the brothers' hands holding me down, I couldn't even peek. The only thing I could see was a sliver of road where Ferguson and Ronald's horse didn't quite touch. Dirt, bits of metal, and debris were scattered across the paving stones. A patch of red-brown shimmered and splashed, and my small breathing space filled with the odor of blood.

Shouts roared. Our group jostled. Ronald's hand slipped while Oscar's fell away.

I pushed myself up to find lines of Indigo Kingdom and Aecorian soldiers surrounding us like a wall of bodies. Those in the front had created a wedge to drive apart the rioters who'd moved into the street. In the uncertain light, I caught glimpses of metal flashing: swords had been drawn.

The din was incredible, making the street tremble. Wood, stale food, and hunks of dirt zipped through the air. On rooftops and balconies, men and women drew bows and daggers.

They wanted to kill us.

The brothers jerked closer to me, and Ronald screamed. An arrow shaft protruded from one arm.

"No, no." This wasn't happening. Not here. Not at home. This should have been a celebration.

"Wil! Get down!" Melanie looked like she was about to climb onto Ferguson. If she lifted herself too high, she could be hurt. I started to duck again, but an explosion in the convoy— followed by an ear-piercing shriek—split the air.

"Wilhelmina."

It came from behind us, overpowering every other voice in the city.

The wraith boy. Chrysalis.

Then the screaming began. At first just one or two people. Then more. Cries for people to run, flee, the wraith queen was angry—

Questions formed on the Ospreys' faces.

"I need to get up," I shouted, but no one listened. They were distracted with protecting me.

Panic swelled in my chest, and the more I tried to push it away, the tighter it grew. How had the wraith boy escaped? Unless he'd broken the mirrors, I could think of only one way: he'd erupted through the back of the wardrobe and the side of the wagon. There were no mirrors there.

"Wilhelmina!" His voice was closer, but he'd been in the middle of the convoy. There were so many people between him and me. And he'd kill them. Without thought. Without remorse. He'd kill them and leave me to carry the burden of their deaths.

"Stop!" I screamed. "Everyone stop!" I pushed away from

the boys, struggling to unpin my legs from between the horses. "Let me up!"

They wouldn't listen. Even Ronald—with an arrow in his arm—tried to shove me back down and keep me from harm.

"I need to get up," I screamed. "He's coming. He'll kill everyone to get to me."

James would agree. He would help me. But I couldn't find him anywhere.

Another explosion shuddered through the street, and more of the angry screams shifted into terrified. Some of the horses spooked, but the mob wasn't as easily distracted. Arrows fell from some of the higher buildings, striking guards. Several dropped, making way for the stampede of rioters.

"Let me up!" I heaved away from the boys, away from Melanie, who was twisting to look over her shoulder.

Suddenly, I was on my feet, pushed and knocked around by the horses slowly marching down the street. Boots and knees struck me, but I shoved my way free of the line of horses—out from the protection of the guards.

"Chrysalis!" I couldn't see him from the middle of the mob, but he had to be close.

Someone grabbed me. I struck back with my elbow and spun to find a man cupping his now-bleeding nose. "She's here!" he cried, but the words were muffled and awkward. "The queen is here!"

Within moments, they surrounded me. Hands reached. Touched. Gripped my arms and ankles.

"Don't hurt her!" someone called. "He said not to hurt her."

Someone grabbed my hair.

I could draw my sword and fight them off, but then what? Kill my own people? Kill the very people I was trying to save from Chrysalis?

From the fore of the convoy, Melanie screamed my name. James did, too. But I couldn't see them through the crowd. I was trapped. Someone pulled out a rock and drew back to hit me.

My daggers were halfway from their sheaths—the only weapons I could draw in these close quarters—when the man with the rock flew away.

"My queen." Chrysalis took the man's place and shoved aside a handful of people who'd grabbed me. The crowd rippled backward, finally realizing who—what—had joined them.

"Wraith!" Screams erupted anew, but there was nowhere for people to go.

"I was coming to get you," I said to Chrysalis.

He knelt and offered a hand. "I will take you to safety."

By carrying me? Or . . .

Chrysalis tilted his head and straightened his shoulders. "They grow restless for you, my queen."

Heart pounding in my ears, I took the wraith boy's hand, used his forward knee as a stair, and stepped onto his shoulders. When I was faced forward, the skirt of my gown safely behind his head, he stood, one hand clasped around my ankle to steady me.

My cloak fluttered in the wind as I rose above the crowd. People gasped and drew back. They pointed and the panic began to ease.

"Say something," Chrysalis suggested. "You are their queen and they will never forget this moment, your triumphant return."

Melanie, James, and the Gray brothers were ahead. There was no sign of Prince Colin or his guards, but he couldn't have gotten very far in this madness.

And over everything, Sandcliff Castle rose against the darkening sky, interior lights dotting the windows like stars. Vermilion flags hung motionless as the wind died.

"So much has changed recently," I called as the last of the voices ceased, and everyone waited to hear what I would say. "There has been so much death and destruction. So many battles for control of this city.

"Not ten years ago, my parents ruled Aecor. Some of you remember them. Some of you are too young." I let my gaze travel over the sea of faces staring up. Men and women. Young and old. Angry and scared. "For nearly a decade, you were made to bow to a foreign king and his brother who called himself overlord. For nearly a decade you endured heightened taxes, drafts to the wraithland, and more.

"And then Patrick Lien returned, telling you I was a hostage in the Indigo Kingdom. There was fighting. Another shift in leadership. There was *fear* because of the unknown. But I am here to tell you not to fear. Because I am Wilhelmina Korte, rightful heir to the vermilion throne, and I have returned to Aecor.

"I was not a hostage in the Indigo Kingdom, but an honored guest as I negotiated for my return to power. As I negotiated for my return to you."

Someone was crying. Others pushed forward to hear better. Chrysalis's hand tightened around my ankle as he began to move toward the castle.

"I don't blame you for your reaction as I return with Prince Colin at my side. But know this: *I* am your queen. And *I* will care for you. I've come with representatives of the Indigo Kingdom— my friends and advisers—but Aecor will not be under Indigo Kingdom rule much longer. Nor will you live under Patrick Lien again, wondering if the frightening things he tells you are true, and if the terrifying things he does will affect you next.

"This morning you were ruled by a tyrant. Tonight, your rightful queen returns, and I promise you this: I will protect you."

A low cheer rolled through the crowd as Chrysalis and I reached the front of the convoy. Melanie and James hopped off their horses to make way for me, but it was unnecessary. No one wanted to get too close to the wraith boy. The threat was gone, for now.

Then, the chanting rose up again.

"Wilhelmina. Wilhelmina. Wil-hel-min-a."

I glanced over my shoulder. An ocean of eyes looked up at me, some with tears making them shine.

Our procession moved through the gates of the inner curtain and finally the castle rose above me, blocking out the sky.

Melanie and James helped me off the wraith boy's shoulders, and we all crossed the vast courtyard with wild, untended gardens, quiet fountains, and elegant but crumbling staircases that led to the main doors.

It was to the thunder of my name that I stepped back into Sandcliff Castle for the first time since the One-Night War.

The doors thudded closed behind me, muting the noise of my name. The Gray brothers were sitting on a nearby bench, with Paige standing over them. She wore a simple, smart dress with nothing to indicate rank; she should have been a duchess.

"Ronald," said Melanie, "get that arrow out of your arm."

"Cordelia is coming. She's our physician." Paige looked up at me, hopeful, but greeting her would have to wait a moment longer.

I faced the wraith boy. "How many people did you kill?"

"I didn't hurt anyone." Chrysalis tilted his head. "I was very careful, because that's what you wanted."

Relief poured through me. "Very good."

"Tonight's demonstration won't be the last." Patrick stood at the back of his cell, hands clasped behind him. His shoulders were straight, and his feet a hip's width apart. His eyes stayed level on me. "They will riot again, until you do something about Colin."

The riot was Patrick's doing. Of course. As punishment for us not returning in the way he'd wanted: with him as my general and future king.

James stepped forward as though to silence Patrick, but I held up a hand.

"Perhaps." I lowered my voice and glared through the bars. "But you won't be there to see it."

He was a statue; the flickering light of the oil lamp danced across his face, making his scar flash. "Even if you do send Colin back to the Indigo Kingdom, the people won't be happy. Not until you've sent away every one of the Indigo Kingdom's soldiers. Until you've exiled or executed every one of the loyalists."

"My friends from the Indigo Kingdom are here to help

maintain order. They're here to help me assert myself as queen."
A lie, maybe. The only one I might call a friend was James, and
he'd do whatever Tobiah ordered.

"The people will see through your deception." Patrick took
a measured step forward, putting his face in a banner of shadow
created by the bars. "You might think you have power. Control. But soon you will learn that it's an illusion. Real power
comes with willingness to obey necessity. You don't have that.
Not now. Not ever. But when you need it, before the anniversary
of the One-Night War, you will unlock those bars and together
we will take Aecor."

"Not now," I said. "Not ever." I turned and strode down
the hall, shoulders thrown back and chin high. Haughty. Like
a queen.

James stayed at my side. "Prison is too good for him, after
all he's done."

"I know." The cells we passed were crammed with blue-
jacketed soldiers and loyalists; most didn't look up as we passed,
but a few muttered insults.

"He acts like he's exactly where he wants to be," James said.

"Typical Patrick." I tightened my hand around the key to
his cell. "He always acts like that. Everything is part of his plan.
Maybe it is. Maybe he can plan for anything we'll do."

We stepped into the guard room and paused at a desk where
an Aecorian sergeant flipped through a stack of papers. Keys
rested at his elbow.

"Sergeant." James's voice came like steel. "You should rise
when your queen enters the room."

The young man scrambled up so quickly his chair fell

backward with a loud *clack*. He bowed. "Please forgive me, Your Majesty."

"What is your name?" I asked.

"Theodore Wallace, Your Majesty."

Wallace. That name was familiar. Merchants, perhaps, or— "Your family had a clothing shop. Your parents made suits and gowns."

His eyes widened. "Yes. My mother still does, though business has been limited during the occupation and revolution."

"And your father?"

"Died during the One-Night War." He lowered his eyes. "It's been hard without him. I was drafted and sent to the wraithland, but recalled a few months ago. When Patrick arrived, he said your group freed us. That's why I joined the Red Militia. To show my gratitude and help my mother."

James waved that away. "Queen Wilhelmina wrote the letter that freed you. Lady Melanie had it delivered. If you want to show your gratitude, serve your queen. You're out of the Red Militia."

"I will." Theodore stared at me. "I will serve you."

"Good. Until I've had time to meet and assess Aecorian officers, Captain Rayner is acting as head of castle security. You will answer directly to him. Understood?"

He nodded. "Yes, Your Majesty."

Keys jangled as I plucked them from the desk and handed them to the young sergeant. "We're no longer at war, Theodore. I want you to release the Indigo Kingdom soldiers, as well as the loyalists. A transport will be arranged so the soldiers can return to the Indigo Kingdom. Tomorrow."

His eyes widened. "And the loyalists?"

"Keep records of their names, but we're not holding them anymore."

"Of course, Your Majesty." He bowed again and headed for the cells. "With your permission. . . ."

I waved him on, and when James and I were alone in the guard room, I faced him and kept my voice low. "I want an Indigo Kingdom soldier watching Patrick at all times. Someone who will treat him with dignity, but feels no loyalty to him."

James nodded. "I'll choose someone myself."

"Thank you." I started out of the prison, James on my heels.

"At least he won't be a problem anymore."

"Just because he's in prison doesn't mean he's not a threat." I looked at James askance. "He has plans within plans. He might be in prison, but he's still one of the most dangerous people I know."

Whatever his intentions, I'd know by the anniversary. That much was clear.

TWENTY-NINE

I WASN'T TWO steps out of the dungeons before Paige found me, a sheet of paper clutched in her hands.

"What's that?" I dreaded the answer. I wanted to collapse into the nearest bed.

"People who want to meet with you, disputes that need your judgment, and documents that must be signed." Paige's eyes were wide as she walked backward so we could keep moving. "There are other things, too."

"I've been here less than an hour." I checked over my shoulder; Melanie and Oscar trailed behind James, all with hands on their weapons.

"Wait until it's been two hours," Paige said. "You'll have twice as many demands for your time."

"I can't wait." I slowed my walk as we returned to the main part of the keep, half strange and half familiar. The rugs and tapestries were the same, but faded now. Or maybe they always had been, but as a child I'd never noticed. Rather than oil lamps, gas lights filled the tarnished sconces. It was a steadier glow, but I could see the pipe running the length of the hall, and climbing up at every light. Skyvale Palace must have had pipes, too, but they'd been built inside the walls.

Paige was still on her list. "I think we could put off the meetings until tomorrow afternoon and the day following. I'll prioritize them, if you like."

"Very good. I'm not meeting anyone *now*."

She nodded, moving on to the next item. "I'll have these documents delivered to the queen's chambers—"

"My mother's rooms?" I stopped walking. "I'm not staying there."

Paige's mouth snapped shut and she glanced behind me, looking for help.

"Wil." Melanie hooked her arm with mine. "Where else would you sleep?"

"My old rooms." Obviously. "I'm not sleeping in my dead mother's chambers."

A pause fluttered over our group. Down the hall, someone else was approaching; a physician, by her robes.

"Wil," Melanie said again. "Are you the queen, or are you the same little girl you were ten years ago? What signal do you want to send?"

I twitched my little finger at her. "I'm the queen."

"Say it again." She released me and moved ahead to speak to the physician.

"All right." Paige jabbed a finger at the list, and we were moving again, now in the direction of the royal apartments. She kept up a stream of updates on the castle, the people working here, and a number of decisions I'd have to make about the staff.

I half listened, but the reality of walking these halls was too powerful. The last time I'd been here, I'd been a child. My kingdom had been minutes from annihilation.

There was my father's study, the last place I'd heard my parents' voices; they'd been fighting about Tobiah.

And there was General Lien's study, where I'd found the prince bound and beaten. We'd hidden on the ledge and watched my city burn until we were discovered. He was rescued. I was captured. Then my parents had been murdered and the rest was a nightmarish blur.

"Your chambers, Your Majesty." Paige handed me a key as I shook away the memories. "It's a little stuffy, but the previous steward did his best. I assigned Danie to be your maid, but if you don't like her I'll find someone else."

"I'm sure Danie is fine. What happened to the previous steward?" I stepped through the open door, into another tangle of memories. The parlor was just as I recalled, with wood panels along the bottom of the wall and ocean green paper on the upper half; it was bubbled in a few places, dirty and needing replacing. A portrait of my grandparents hung over the lit fireplace, and bookcases lined the walls. Only half the shelves were filled with books; the others held framed artwork, both in ink and paint.

I'd forgotten that she liked to draw.

"Prince Colin's steward was executed several days ago." Paige's tone was empty. "He instructed me as best he could in the time we had, but Patrick— You know Patrick. He didn't even trust an old man. He put me in charge of running the castle."

Yes, I knew Patrick. "Do you like it? Doing this?"

She nodded quickly. "I don't mind the assignment. It's better than what we had to do before we took the city."

Melanie and Oscar nodded, too.

"Very well. You'll keep this job until we hire someone who won't one day have to run her own estate." I glanced at Melanie and Oscar. "That goes for you two as well. We'll continue like this for now, but eventually you'll need to deal with your family inheritances, such as they are."

"I'll add that to the list for after your coronation," Paige said.

James muttered agreement, politely not reminding me to wait for a coronation if I wanted to keep peace with the Indigo Kingdom. "Best to keep people you trust close by for now. Take the rest as it comes." He placed his blue notebook on the writing desk. "There's a letter here for you."

My heart gave a painful lurch. I gave Paige a few more instructions regarding interviews and the upcoming days, and finally everyone began to make their exits. Paige pointed out my belongings, already delivered from the convoy, and Oscar announced he'd check to see who was guarding the wraith boy's new storage room before returning to take his post at my door.

"You don't have to stay there all night," I said.

He waved that away. "Someone does. You just released dozens of soldiers and people loyal to Prince Colin, and not to mention welcomed a thousand of his men into Aecor City. The Red Militia will keep an eye on them, but remember they're not happy with you, either. You've imprisoned Patrick and you're working with Prince Colin. That's why they instigated that riot when you arrived."

"Plus the people who aren't on either side, but are terrified you'll use the wraith boy against them," added Melanie.

"Fine." I dropped my shoulders as James, Oscar, and Paige headed out. "Everyone wants me dead. One day that will be out of fashion, I hope."

"You have me. I don't want you dead." Melanie started to hug me, but paused halfway there. "You also have a smell. I'll start your bath. We'll catch up after you've washed off the last week."

If only it were that easy.

When she disappeared to the washroom, I sat down at the writing desk and opened James's notebook to find the letter from Tobiah.

> *Wilhelmina,*
>
> *I must have read your account of the Snowhaven Bridge events a hundred times by now. I can't say I'm happy about what happened, but I think I understand. The decision to save my uncle, of all people, must have been a difficult one.*
>
> *Well, now that you have declared yourself queen, will you make it official with a coronation? You must be eager, but I am hoping you will wait, at least for now, while I try to sort this out with Uncle Colin. I expect to receive an angry letter from him any day now.*
>
> *Sincerely,*
> *Tobiah Pierce*

I let his note sit as I poked through the inks on my mother's desk. They were probably bad by now.

But when I opened a jar of sepia, there was no mold or anything else untoward. Paige—or her predecessor—must have replaced them. The nibs, too, looked shiny and new, not a speck of rust in sight.

> *Tobiah,*
>
> *I will wait for a coronation. There's enough to keep me busy even without making it official. My arrival— with your uncle at my side—triggered a Red Militia riot tonight. I'm still waiting for a report on how many were injured.*
>
> *Before, I wanted nothing more than to return to Aecor and become queen. But after spending time with you in Skyvale Palace, I've realized how unprepared I really am. I don't know what made me think I would be a good queen because I was born to it. Or because I ran off to the wraithland. Or because I was willing to do questionably moral things for my people.*
>
> *I'd even just told James I wasn't certain anymore . . . and then it was give in to Patrick's demands, or watch him kill your uncle.*
>
> *Immediately after, James warned me about new guards wanting favors, needing to write to the families of the dead—all things I would have gotten to . . . eventually. But as a queen, they should have been my first thoughts. My responsibility to my people.*

I'm not ready for this. Not like you are.

(And now the words are on paper and I can't take them back. Sometimes I hate ink. It's so permanent.)

Wil

I blew on the page, half thinking I should leave puddles of ink in a few strategic places, but Melanie returned just as I was ready to *accidentally* tip a jar of ink onto the entire notebook.

"Ready?" she asked.

For a bath? Yes. For whatever came next? Absolutely not.

I pushed myself up and started after her, but paused when I spotted a door. "That leads to the king's chambers?"

My father's chambers.

Melanie nodded. "There are two doors. Both are locked."

"Has anyone"—I couldn't bring myself to say his name—"been staying there?"

She tilted her head, studying me. "No. No one has used those chambers since the One-Night War. We can unlock the doors if you want the entire suite to yourself. I know this isn't what we had in Skyvale Palace."

It wasn't. And in spite of attempts to update, the royal chambers in Sandcliff Castle were simple by comparison: a parlor, a washroom, and a bedroom. The castle was old, built during a different time.

"Leave it locked. I don't want anyone in there. It already feels wrong enough taking my mother's chambers. But I might go in there sometime. To look."

Melanie smiled warmly. "I hope you do."

I spent the next day moving through Paige's lists, but by dinner-time I'd made barely a dent.

"Everything will still be there tomorrow," Melanie said as we headed up the spiral staircase to Radiants' Walk, the castle's main overlook. "If you try to do all of it at once, you'll just end up neglecting everything."

"And I'll make myself sick and be useless. I know. You told me." I cast her a quick smile as we passed through the arched door and emerged onto the wide, flat expanse of the overlook. "This looks just as I remember."

My parents had brought me here often. At night, my father and I looked at the stars, pointing out the bright one in the north that never strayed from its position, following with the others that wheeled through the sky. I'd learned all the constellations, though I couldn't recall half of them now. I'd kept the memories buried for so long.

Cold wind tugged at my clothes as I lifted my face to the sky, breathing in the sharp salt air and bite of winter. Birds called overhead, seagulls and ospreys and eagles, and waves crashed against the cliffs far below. When I was young, standing up here made me feel like I was walking on the sky.

"This way." Melanie motioned to the southern edge of the overlook where people—including Prince Colin and James—had gathered to watch the transport bearing former Indigo Kingdom prisoners move out. While I'd offered to let them stay another night, they were eager to leave.

Wagons and horses clattered, the sounds faint from up here.

"They don't know how lucky they are," muttered one of Prince Colin's guards.

"Oh, I think they know." Melanie's tone was dark. "They saw enough."

Not all the former prisoners of war were leaving. Some decided to stay and serve Prince Colin, protect him from this country of wild, rebellious people. But at least a hundred rode down Castle Street now.

James stood at my side. "Your first acts as queen are to stop the fighting and free prisoners. That's a good start."

Prince Colin glanced over, his eyes narrowed. "Remember that you're not truly the queen until you've been crowned."

"With you here to remind me constantly, Prince Colin, there's no chance I will ever forget."

He hmphed and moved away. Melanie, James, and a few others who'd been within earshot smirked.

"Tell me about your city," James said, probably to distract me.

But I went along with it. "It's smaller than Skyvale. It's limited to the solid foundation of cliffs that radiants built almost a thousand years ago."

"There's no room for growth?" he asked.

"That way." I pointed east, where the land sloped downhill into flat earth prone to floods. Several of the poorest neighborhoods stood on marshes, invisible in this darkness. "Nowhere you'd want to live."

We stared into the gloaming, silent for a moment.

"Factories and warehouses make a line between the poor and the slightly less poor. Most people work there. Or used to, at least." I motioned westward. "The neighborhoods grow gentler as you go uphill, until Castle Street. Everything there is very fine, but very expensive."

"Not too expensive for the queen, surely."

I snorted. James knew better than that. "Everything west of Castle Street is rich merchants and nobility. High nobles' mansions stand on the cliff." They were once-majestic buildings with glass windows and turrets and intricate ornamentation along the eaves. Now, they looked dark and dirty, neglected without their families. "Obviously, it's been a while since I've seen the city. Things have changed."

"I'll make sure you have time for a tour."

"Thanks." The wagons reached the city gates as light faded. Crowds were filling the streets, pushing in the wagons' wake. Some hefted torches into the air. Others had clubs or pipes—blunt weapons. "Look there." I pointed at the street.

Melanie leaned over the guardrail. "They're wearing red. The Militia. It's happening again, just like Patrick said."

"They're all beasts," said one of Prince Colin's guards.

Screams from below drowned anything else the guards might have said. Suddenly I couldn't see individuals, just masses of movement and shadows and pockets of red. People shoved and raised weapons.

A low cry rose up from the streets: "*No more Indigo!*"

"We have to stop this." I started for the stairs down, but James blocked my way.

"I don't want you anywhere near that mayhem." He took my elbow. "You were lucky yesterday. *Lucky*, that's all."

"Then what am I supposed to do?" The sun had fallen, but

the streets were bright with torches and lamps, and a fire in one of the shops. A column of smoke spiraled into the air.

It was hard to believe the uproar had escalated so quickly.

"Indigo must go! No more Indigo!" The cries were faint, barely perceptible.

My heart thrummed. Patrick had told them to let Indigo Kingdom soldiers *out*, but protest the ones who were still here. And now, as the former prisoners rolled down the cliff path toward the bridge, protesting was exactly what the Red Militia was doing.

No, not protesting. Rioting.

It was hard to see from this angle but there seemed to be people throwing themselves against the gate of the castle's inner wall. Or pushing others. Right now it was just a mass of bodies shoving and straining, but soon they'd move in time with one another. They'd get a battering ram.

"No more Indigo! Indigo must go!"

James shook my elbow. "This is my job," he said. "I'll stop this. Trust me to do my job."

"Fine. Go."

THIRTY

JAMES DISAPPEARED INTO the stairwell with a handful of guards, shouting orders as he went.

I turned my attention back to the riot, praying the violence would calm.

It grew worse. People banged on the wall with their clubs and pipes, chanting the same phrases. With the rush and roar of the fires, their words grew hard to hear, but I knew what they wanted.

We all knew.

Surrounded by his blue-clad guards, Prince Colin stood straight, his arms over his chest. A deep frown creased his face. "This is your fault." He didn't look at me, but there was no question where his comment was aimed. "They're doing this because you're here."

"They're doing this because you're here with me."

He moved away, along the edge of the overlook.

"What kind of queen hides in her castle while her people are in trouble?" I whispered to Melanie. James would be down the stairs by now. He'd tell his men where to go and what to do, and I'd watch all of it unfold from up here.

She pulled her cloak tight over her shoulders. "The kind who stays alive to help them on the other side of trouble. You can't personally handle every situation."

I could try. "I managed last night and the night before."

"You had the wraith boy. Do you really want to involve him again?"

The memory of the wedding welled up like beading blood from a cut. The king and duchess, on the verge of kissing. The wraith boy, striding down the aisle with terrifying intent in his eyes.

He was still a monster. And unless I wanted to bring the castle to life—and risk killing myself with the effort—I couldn't stop the fighting.

This was what Tobiah had meant the night I yelled about the Skyvale police: letting other people do their job didn't mean I did nothing. "Tell me about the Red Militia. Everything you know." Understanding the enemy was the first step to stopping it.

"It's complicated," she said after a minute. The wind and shrieks and thuds almost swallowed her voice, but she leaned close enough for me to hear. "The Red Militia is both an army and resistance. In addition to gathering a force large enough to move through Aecor, Patrick sent spies here to wait for his arrival."

"Patrick wanted people on the inside to fight, too."

She nodded. "Otherwise the Indigo regiment could keep the

city for weeks, and Patrick's army wouldn't be able to keep up a siege for that long."

"Everything happened so quickly." Patrick's plan—and mine, until a few months ago—had been to go to Aecor in the autumn and quietly raise our army until the spring, when we'd march on Aecor City and wrest it back. We'd wanted to make a statement by moving on the anniversary of the One-Night War. Instead Patrick had taken the city months early. "It's an amazing feat."

"You know Patrick," she murmured. "He always manages somehow."

I did.

"The majority of the Militia dispersed into the city once we took it. He kept enough people to move across Snowhaven Bridge, but most received orders to go into hiding until the goal was achieved."

"And that is?" Dread coiled like a snake inside me.

"You and Patrick running the kingdom together."

That plan hadn't changed, then. "So these"—I motioned below—"are the people he sent here early, or sent out when the city was his."

"That's right."

"Do you know any of them? From the march south?"

"Some. Patrick worked hard to keep everyone as separate as possible. I knew the people he kept close and the small group I led. No one else. It was an army of hundreds of tiny divisions, none permitted to interact with others."

That sounded like Patrick. He didn't care about unity—not at that scale, and not with plans as big and elaborate as his, with so many variables and contingencies. He'd always been paranoid; even with the Ospreys, he'd concealed the identities of his contacts in Aecor. He'd done his best to keep us isolated in the old palace.

"We're searching for the people we know. We are. But most are in hiding, and this is an old city with a lot of forgotten places. Our limited numbers won't make the search any easier."

"We must find them."

"We will. But it won't happen overnight." She pointed down. "Look."

Fires still blazed, but the crowd had thinned. There were fewer red jackets than moments before. Had James even had time to begin stopping the riot? My angle to see into the courtyard wasn't great, but it looked as though James's people were just now moving for the rampart.

Melanie shook her head. "He told them to incite a riot, then back off."

The fact that he was in the dungeon didn't make a difference. He'd have left orders that no one would disobey.

"He didn't tell me," she said. "He didn't trust me."

"He knew when I returned, you'd side with me."

We watched as James's teams sorted through the innocent people below, searching for the Red Militia that was long gone.

"I'll find the Red Militia for you," Melanie said as the crescent moon lifted into the sky. "You have my word."

The next day, I pushed through more of Paige's unending lists.

"When do queens sleep?" I yawned, but according to

Melanie, James, and Paige, all sitting lounging about my parlor, the day was far from over. Danie scurried about the bedroom, laying out a nightgown and lighting candles.

"Never, as far as I can tell." Melanie leaned back and propped her heels on my desk. "If it makes you feel better, the rest of us don't get to sleep much, either."

"Boots off the desk," I said, keeping my voice low. "I saw Danie scrubbing and polishing it this afternoon. I've never seen someone so serious about polish."

Melanie heaved a sigh and sat normally. Perfect timing, because a moment later, Danie emerged from my bedroom and whisper-asked if I needed anything else.

"That's all. Good night, Danie." I put on the same warm smile I'd have worn as Lady Julianna.

The maid curtsied and hurried from my chambers.

"That is certainly not fleeing." Melanie grinned at James, then me. "We have a bet going."

"That she runs to escape my room?" I had a flash of memory of my Skyvale Palace maid, who never stayed longer than absolutely necessary.

"Yes." James shrugged from his spot near the fireplace. "If you can get her to flee soon, I have plans for my winnings."

"James thinks it's inevitable," Melanie said. "I think Danie has incentive to stay right where she is. It means she works in the same building as Sergeant Wallace."

"They're together?" I hadn't seen them with each other, but I'd been here only a couple of days.

"Oh no." Melanie waved a hand. "She's far too shy to speak

to him. But I think she'll stick around so she can continue admiring him from afar."

"Meanwhile," James said, "I'm convinced of your ability to frighten even the most determined of maids."

I scowled. "I don't know whether to be flattered or insulted."

"Choose both." He winked.

"Oh for the love of every saint. Make an effort to be nice to the staff," Paige said, writing another item on one of her thousand lists. "I'll continue introducing you to everyone, but they need more than that. They need to love you, too, like they couldn't love Patrick."

That thought sobered me. How could I make a kingdom of angry, frightened people love me? "I'll do my best."

"No more betting, either." Paige shot glares at Melanie and James before she slid a paper toward me. "Now, about uniforms for the Queen's Guard."

Yes, after three long hours of interviews, I had a Queen's Guard. "Uniforms? Why is this my job?"

"Because you have to look at them every day." Paige smirked and tapped the page. "The treasury is one thing Prince Colin was careful to keep healthy. We can spare money for uniforms, especially since you refuse to hire more than just nine people."

"It's a lucky number." And it was the minimum number of guards James would permit.

"Uniforms will promote a sense of unity. We'll have a badge or pin commissioned, too. Rosanne Wallace would be a good choice for a seamstress—"

Outside, the screaming started.

339

"Indigo must go!"

I lurched up and stumbled toward the balcony.

"Wil, wait!" But James wasn't fast enough.

I threw open the balcony doors and stepped outside.

Icy wind blasted from the west as I approached the rail. Dread knotted in my gut as the same violence of last night came again. The screams, the cries, the flames licking the starry sky.

"Wil, get back inside." James pressed a hand on my shoulder. "Give me time to assess whether the balcony is safe. Remember what happened to Tobiah."

As if I could forget.

Already, I saw castle troops moving into the city, but the truth of these riots burrowed into me. "They're going to do this every night," I said, letting James draw me away from the edge. "They'll rush in and riot, then leave before you can catch them."

At the door, Melanie nodded. "Every night, until everyone from the Indigo Kingdom is gone and you are crowned queen, with Patrick as your king. I think that's why he took the city so early. You turned on him, and he needed to secure your dependence to him."

"By destroying the city from the inside out?" My whole body shook as I stepped inside and James locked the balcony door. "Only Patrick would think that was a reasonable option."

James dragged the curtain over the door. "We can't take much more of this, especially not over the winter. If they burn supplies . . ."

Then everyone would starve. Not to mention the morale. "What do you propose?"

He leaned on the table. "You won't like it, but I think a

citywide curfew is the place to start."

"Enacting a curfew doesn't send a good message," Melanie said. "Especially so early in her queenship. It says she can't protect people from the Red Militia."

"It says she's willing to take measures to protect them." James met my eyes. "They need to have confidence you'll do what's necessary."

Was a curfew necessary? Taverns and inns, which made their business off late-night customers, wouldn't be pleased. No one would.

But if there were no civilians on the streets, it might be easier to catch the Red Militia, and that was surely something we all wanted.

"Willingness to obey a curfew will only last so long," I said after a moment. "They'll need regular proof of our progress, as well as assurance that civilians won't be hurt or arrested for being out, just escorted to their homes."

James was nodding. Melanie was frowning.

"Only police will engage civilians. No military. We're not under martial law." Not that police were incapable of being cruel. I'd seen that much in Skyvale. "Anyone caught using violence will be brought to me."

"Fair conditions," James said.

The Red Militia here. The wraith in the west. Everything seemed eager to destroy my kingdom.

"If you're going to do this," Melanie said, "then you'll want to make a statement about the decision and how you hope it won't take long. Which means writing a speech. Tonight."

So much for sleeping. "Tomorrow I want to see the city."

"We'll see." James turned a chair out for me. "There's not much time for it, and the Queen's Guard is still untrained as a unit. Ensuring your safety on a visit to the city will take time and preparation."

Which meant I'd see only the elite parts of Aecor City, where everyone was cleaned up and wearing their best behavior. I wouldn't see the city as it truly was.

"Fine," I said. "Prepare a tour for me as soon as you can." It was certain to be a sterile, useless tour, but it might keep James from thinking too hard about the black bag under my bed.

But by the time everyone left my room, I had only four hours to sleep before I had to start another day as queen in name only.

Several more days proceeded in the same manner. I was over-protected and under-slept, and the castle walls seemed to grow closer every hour. But finally, I had a relatively early night, and a letter from Tobiah waiting in the blue notebook.

> Wilhelmina,
> Sorry it's taken a few days to reply.
> Here's the truth: I'm not ready, either.
> Power and responsibility don't wait for us to feel ready; they are thrust upon us, always too soon.
> Last week, I sent a contingent of soldiers to scout the wraithland border and bring back as many live beasts as possible for our barrier. The soldiers were on horseback, so it should have been a fast journey, especially now that the border is edging up into the mountains. It's close, Wilhelmina. It's so close.

Now I hear the soldiers are missing. Five hundred men. I made myself read their names again this morning, because I was the one who ordered a team to the wraithland. If they are dead, then the weight of their lives is on me.

My father often talked about this kind of responsibility, but I never understood it until now.

You're not ready. I'm not ready. How can anyone be ready to take responsibility for an entire kingdom's safety?

More than anything, I want to escape into the city and be Black Knife for a few hours. But I can't. Not anymore.

Tobiah

I closed the notebook without replying. There was nothing reassuring there. If he'd spent his life preparing for rulership and he wasn't ready, how could I be?

Well, visiting my city was a start. And not James's as-yet-unscheduled sanitized visit.

I hauled the Black Knife bag from its hiding place.

It was time to see my people.

THIRTY-ONE

IN SPITE OF the cold wind, it was embarrassingly easy to climb off my balcony.

The courtyard was quiet. Smooth, white flagstones glowed in the faint torchlight, but I kept to deep pockets of darkness as I crept toward the high rampart, which separated the main keep from the rest of the city.

I let my hands breeze over my tools and weapons. Sword, daggers, crossbow, grapple and line, and a dozen other small things I'd yet to find a need for—but Black Knife was always prepared. To an empty pouch I'd added Connor's small silver mirror, a reminder of my friends still far away.

Footfalls sounded, and I held my position in the shadows of a silent blacksmith shop.

A pair of guards marched their patrol route, holding a torch aloft. One wore red, and the other blue. That had been my idea, keeping Prince Colin's men and mine working together. Most merely tolerated the arrangement, but these two held a low, friendly conversation.

When they were gone, I hurried to the wall and tossed my hook over the ledge. The parapet made the throw tricky, but my aim was true. Climbing was easier; my boots gripped the stone securely.

At the top, I hopped the parapet and knelt to coil my line.

The city's gas lamps had been turned off for the night, leaving only the occasional torch on a wall or candle in a window for light. The streets were black rivers of silence. Faintly, I could hear water crashing on the cliffs, and birds roosting on the ledges. The keen of wind smothered everything else.

I swung my gaze to the lowcity: my destination tonight.

The faint *clink* of a hook hitting stone stilled me before I could stand. Someone else was climbing the rampart.

I drew a dagger and edged toward the newcomer, keeping my movements silent. The parapet hid me from view, even as I came upon the hook gripping the stone.

Relief shot through me as I glanced over.

Melanie.

I ripped off my mask and shoved it into my belt just as she finished the climb and swung herself onto the walkway.

"Out a bit late, aren't you?" I grinned and slipped my dagger back into its sheath.

"Wil!" Melanie's eyes widened as she took in my appearance. "What are you *wearing*?" Accusation filled her tone.

"Come on, before guards catch us."

She bit off further questions as we crept along the rampart, then descended. Brittle grass crunched under my boots as I headed for the shadow of the nearest structure: a three-story inn called Castleview. So close to the wall, guests would be lucky if they could see the tops of the towers from the third floor.

"What are we doing?" Melanie whispered as we moved away.

"Taking a tour James and the Grays won't allow." I motioned her faster. "I haven't left the castle since the day I arrived, and I need to *feel* the city."

She lifted her face to the sky. "It's not like when we were children."

The ride up Castle Street had made that clear. "It's darker. Sadder. But hopefully that will change after we root out the Red Militia."

"Maybe." Her mouth tightened. "Have you thought about giving in to their demands?"

"*No.*" I shivered off a gust of cold wind. "Well, yes, I've thought about it, but then we'd be at war with the Indigo Kingdom. Maybe Laurel-by-the-Sea and anyone else who cares. I can't do that to Aecor, and I can't let Patrick think he's won, even for one minute."

"Do you really think Tobiah would declare war?"

His name made my heart twist. "When we parted ways, it was under the worst possible circumstances. He's already deeply unhappy with me."

"You signed the Wraith Alliance, though. That should mean he wants you to have your kingdom back."

"He does." Or did. "But when you're king, nothing is as simple as you want. You learn the limits of your power so quickly."

I couldn't remember feeling as powerless as I did since returning to Aecor.

We held still as a pair of police strode past.

"So," I said when we were on our way again, "what were you doing before I roped you into my illicit adventure?"

"Following information on the Red Militia." She jutted her chin forward. "We're heading in the right direction."

"Update me."

"Well." She eyed me askance. "First, you should know that I'm the head of your secret intelligence. So secret, in fact, that I'm the only one who knew about it until just now."

"You can't appoint yourself head of secret intelligence."

"Then what's the point of it being secret?" Melanie flicked her little finger at me. "Anyway, you know now. And I'd have told you eventually, when I had solid leads to bring you."

"About the locations of the Red Militia?"

She nodded. "Patrick won't talk, but I've managed to wrest a couple of hideouts from those who've declared allegiance to you, like that Sergeant Wallace." Her voice dipped. "The ones who won't talk are scared of Patrick and his generals. I can't say I blame them, but I don't trust anyone who won't give up someone they claim to fight against. I'm having them watched."

We didn't have enough trustworthy people to have everyone else watched, but I didn't argue. "So the hideout?"

"There's an old factory in the lowcity. A handful of Red Militia live there. We hope."

We continued east, moving between low, rain-battered buildings. They were spaced close enough that roof hopping would be easy, but it was hard to say if they were sturdy. I doubted they'd hold our weight.

Building inspection and improvement: I added those to a long mental list of things Prince Colin had neglected and I needed to fix.

"So you decided to look into this hideout on your own? Without your best friend?" I allowed a note of suspicion into my tone.

"I'm head of secret intelligence." Melanie looked up at a sharp *bang*, but it was just a loose board in the wind. "This mission was a *secret*. I didn't want to involve James because I knew he wouldn't approve—"

"James never approves."

"And I don't trust anyone else not to leak what's happening. Patrick is the kind of man who will give seven people seven different stories so he can unearth a traitor. If I go to the factory and no one's there, I'll know it's just his paranoia, and I won't have betrayed my source's trust. Anyway, you're here now."

"You don't trust *anyone*? Even the other Ospreys?"

She shrugged. "I trust that they want what's best for you. Paige. The Grays. The others in Skyvale." Her voice hitched; we'd been separated so long now. "They wouldn't betray your confidence, but the fewer people who have all the facts, the less of a chance that anything gets back to Patrick or his people."

"Those sound like Patrick's words."

"I know." She stopped walking and crossed her arms. "When Patrick and I were together, it was exciting. Secret. I thought I could smooth out those pieces that made him harsh and reckless. I thought I could dig up his good parts and make them shine brighter."

"It's not your job to do that."

"I know that, too. Now. And I know he wasn't ever going to change, because he doesn't want to." She sucked in a deep breath. "But for all his faults, he does have virtues. He's an incredible strategist. He wins wars in spite of the odds. And he knows how to keep secrets."

"Oh, does he ever."

Her smile was faint, fleeting in the darkness. "I learned a lot of important lessons from Patrick, including how to be careful. And this situation with the Red Militia applies, particularly since I'm trying to use his own tricks against him."

"All right." I hugged her and kissed her cheek. "I understand why you went with him during the Inundation, but don't leave me again, Mel. I need you."

She put on a smirk. "Clearly. That wraith boy, Prince Colin, and now you're dressed as Black Knife." She swiped the mask from my belt. "The clothes definitely suit you, but this is unsettling. What's going on?"

"It's not just unsettling, but a long story, too."

"We have time."

"Not for the whole thing. Saints, I'm not even sure I should tell you the whole thing. There are too many secrets that aren't mine to tell."

A salty tang rode the breeze, chasing us as we moved deeper into the lowcity. Houses and shops and courtyards grew ever more shabby, some rotting away from the salt and marsh.

"All right," Melanie said at last. "Don't betray anyone's secrets. But tell me this: do we still hate him? Just a few months ago you were lecturing me on what a menace he is, and now you're wearing his uniform."

My memory conjured up the black-clad boy stopping me before I killed a thug, forgiving me my use of magic, following me out of the city because he was worried. And the way he'd trusted me not to look when we'd kissed.

That boy—I didn't hate him at all. "I miss him."

"Well. That's different." Her voice was soft, just under the howl of wind cutting around a corner.

"It is. Things I believed were straightforward aren't, really. Everything's so complicated."

She took my hand. Even through our gloves, her fingers warmed mine. "No matter what else changes, we won't. I still love you, even if you dress like a vigilante now."

"Really?"

"Well, I'm obligated to mock you for the rest of our lives."

I squeezed her hand. "Say it again."

Steering clear of police patrols, we hurried to the blocks of factories that hulked over the houses and shops, silhouetting starlight. As a child, I'd never been permitted east of Castle Street. Coming here now—even years older and having seen the worst parts of Skyvale—sent thrills of disobedience through me. "Which one is it?"

"Water processing and filtration. There." Melanie pointed to a large square building with pipes running along the roof and walls. Rusted metal gleamed with water droplets.

"Let's look around and meet on the far side in ten minutes."
She nodded.

The darkness was a curse and blessing. I crept around the north side of the building, feeling my way along the crumbling stone wall. I kept my steps silent on the gritty flagstones—heel, ball, toe—hyperaware of every scrape and hiss of gravel. Though I listened hard for voices or breathing, there was only me. The only scents were salt and water and waste.

At last I came to a metal door. In the darkness, I felt out the shapes of a lock and knob, but I didn't test them. I continued on, counting three more doors. There were no windows on the ground floor. No evidence of Red Militia occupation.

Melanie was already at our meeting place. "Anything?" she whispered.

I shook my head. "Doors. No guards."

"Same." Her frustrated sigh was barely perceptible. "No sign there's anyone here."

There might be footprints or scrapes on doors or walls, but those would be visible only during the day. And they wouldn't necessarily be from Red Militia.

"I saw a few windows up high, but Patrick would have warned them to stay out of view."

Definitely. If we couldn't hear voices conveniently plotting the next insurgency, that left one option.

"We go in." We had to be sure this was their hideout before we brought in police or soldiers, and alerted the Red Militia of information leaks.

She blew out a breath. "All right."

"Any idea of the layout?"

"Very little. I didn't spend much time away from Patrick." She jerked her chin to the south side of the building. "But I found what looks like a loading area. There *might* be people holed up near there, but I bet it gets drafty."

So they'd likely find an office or someplace closed off. I followed her around the corner.

Faint light glimmered as the moon began its descent; it was just enough for me to make out the paved drive wide enough for three wagons, and several sets of double doors. Definitely a loading area—and a well-maintained one, considering Aecor had stopped using industrialized magic a hundred years ago.

The trouble with using these doors was that they were *so* big. Wind would howl in and alert occupants to our presence.

Well, we didn't have much of a choice.

The second door we tried was unlocked. We slipped into a vast, echoing chamber, careful not to let the metal door slam behind us.

In the dim interior, I cocked an eyebrow at Melanie with a question. Had she noticed the silent way the door swung open and closed? Granted, we hadn't opened it very far, but it'd had the ease of movement that came with often-oiled hinges.

She tilted her head, and understanding dawned on her face.

Someone *very careful* had been here.

Melanie and I pressed our backs against the wall, taking in the expanse of the room.

Rows of cleaning stations filled the space, some so high they required two ladders to reach. When the factory had been functional, salty or marshy water was pumped into cisterns, which radiants cleaned and purified. Good water was pumped out, into the city for general use.

Dust and grime covered every surface, but not a hundred years' worth. Someone had been here. Maybe not now or yesterday or a year ago, but I'd lived in the old palace more than half my life. I knew what a century of neglect looked like, and this wasn't it.

Unease gnawed at me as I scanned the area, but I found no movement, no sign anyone had noticed our entrance. If there were occupants, they were beyond the double doors at the far side. A chair held one open, and yellow light fell across the stone floor in a narrow banner, angled away from us.

Definitely suspicious.

As Melanie and I made our way through the immense room, I imagined the noise of water rushing through the pipes, radiants working in unison, and supervisors' shoes tapping the stone floor as they marched through to keep everyone on task.

I forced my breath long and even as we approached the next set of doors and the lit room beyond them. Hopefully, we could get in, see any signs of Red Militia, and get out.

"I'll go first," I mouthed. Because she was my friend, but also one of my people. My heart beat hummingbird fast as I drew my sword and a dagger.

Melanie nodded and followed suit.

The chair was wedged into the door tightly enough that I could step onto the wooden seat, but I didn't want to risk it creaking. I went for the more awkward but quiet option: stepping over and around it.

Straddling the corner of the chair, I glanced into the room. Several oil lamps illuminated the space, but there were no signs of people. Only a smaller chamber with doors at intervals. Some had windows showing offices, though the glass had long since broken and been swept out.

I finished my gangly move over the chair and held my weapons in guard position while Melanie came after me.

We were two paces into the room when the lights went out, pitching the factory into blackness.

"The queen and Patrick's pet." The woman's voice came from just in front of us. "You're right on time."

THIRTY-TWO

A THOUSAND QUESTIONS raced through my mind, but only one mattered: How could I get out of this alive?

"If you know who we are," I said, "you know that we're more than able to take care of ourselves." I tightened my grip on my sword and dagger. The dark was disorienting, but Melanie and I had fought in all sorts of conditions. We knew how to maneuver and defend ourselves without risking the other.

"Certainly." The woman's voice was cool and smooth, higher than average.

"Claire." Melanie warmed my side and kept her voice steady. "Nice to hear you again. Please turn on the lights."

Melanie knew this woman, but it didn't sound like they were friends.

A snap echoed, and all the oil lamps flared to life, revealing a dozen men and women. All were armed, but none had their weapons drawn.

The speaker—Claire—had about ten or eleven years on us, but not height; she came up to my shoulder. Her black hair was pulled into a ponytail, and she stood with her arms crossed and one hip cocked. A smirk pulled at her mouth.

No, not a smirk. A short scar sliced the corner of her lips, giving her the look of perpetual attitude. Otherwise, her expression was blank, focused on assessing Melanie and me.

"You said you were expecting us." Melanie clenched her jaw.

Either Patrick or Claire had planted Melanie's sources to leak the information at the right time, or—

Claire had called Melanie "Patrick's pet."

No, Melanie wouldn't betray me. Even now, she stood ready to protect me from the small group of Red Militia. She hadn't even known I'd be out tonight.

"Yes," Claire said. "I have several ideas for entertaining you. My favorite is to hold Her Majesty here while you scurry back to your castle friends and tell them to send away the Indigos and release Patrick. Then they can have their queen returned."

A few others nodded.

"There's a flaw in your plan." I stepped forward to take eyes off Melanie, giving her a chance to find an escape, but the motion made everyone lift their hands to their weapons. Yet they didn't draw, supporting my next point. "Imagine how upset Patrick would be if he learned you held the queen *hostage*. What would that tell the people of Aecor? Patrick's goals would be derailed. No one would accept him as a leader of Aecor if he was involved with the people who held me hostage."

Claire shook her head. "You place so much of your safety in Patrick's hands, even while keeping him in your dungeon."

Unsaid was her counterargument: that Patrick would claim to break ties with the Red Militia, reminding everyone he was in prison while the riots and hostage holding were happening. And I'd come back with the point that Patrick was in prison for assassination and betraying me. And we'd go in circles about blame and who was at fault.

Melanie bumped my arm twice, the signal that she'd plotted an escape, but we'd have to fight for it.

No, I wouldn't fight. Not this time. As an Osprey, I'd have disabled them and left. Black Knife would have insisted we find police to help the wounded.

But as a queen, I had to behave differently. I couldn't jump to violence every time.

So what would Queen Wilhelmina do?

I sheathed my weapons. "Mel."

She wanted to resist—I could feel it in the way she tensed— but she didn't hesitate to slide her daggers back into her sheathes.

The Red Militia dropped their shoulders, hands falling away from weapons.

"Let's talk." I met Claire's eyes; hers were steel gray—an unusual color here.

"About what?"

"You lured us here, didn't you?"

"I sent information when I heard someone was looking." Her glare shifted to Melanie. "I wasn't sure who I'd catch, but I couldn't feel luckier."

"If my source is working for you," Melanie said, "he'll be in prison by dawn."

"Are you loyal to your queen?" Claire lifted an eyebrow and

inclined her head toward me.

"Of course."

"Then leave that boy where he is." Claire did smile this time. "Astor, find somewhere for us to have a nice conversation. Laura, take three and check if the building is secure. The rest of you find something useful to do."

They all snapped and thumped their chests, and moved to follow orders.

It was the same salute the Ospreys used. But they *weren't* Ospreys. We didn't incite riots. We didn't kill people.

A minute later, Melanie, Claire, and I were seated in one of the cramped offices. A desk dominated the room, papers and dirt and unidentifiable debris swept to one side; a sleeping pallet peeked out from behind. Astor arranged the chairs so that none of us had our backs to the door and the large, blown-out window on the interior wall.

Claire sat and threw one leg over the other, leaning back, her arms crossed. "Tell me what you hoped to find here."

"You, actually." I forced the shaking from my voice. Dawn was still hours off, so James wasn't likely to notice us missing for a while, but we'd need to get back to the castle without being spotted. Sleep wouldn't hurt, either. What had been a simple look-and-leave mission had grown to more than I was prepared to handle at this hour. "We wanted to see if there was anyone here. If the information was good."

"And that's it?"

"Then," Melanie said, "I was going to send in the military." She smirked and leaned back, one elbow resting on the desk. "But we can be persuaded otherwise."

Claire scowled and eyed the door. "I won't let you bully me."

For a moment I feared she'd close off, but Melanie knew Claire; she knew how to handle her, I hoped.

"Well, if you cooperate, I won't send the military in for a visit."

Claire narrowed her eyes. "What do you want?"

Melanie shifted her posture, signaling my turn.

"I'd rather talk than fight. Don't you agree?" I leaned forward, making myself open and approachable, but not too much. If she'd spent much time with Patrick, she would know our tricks. "How'd you end up here? In the factory. Or with Patrick."

Claire hesitated, but when she threw a glance toward the window to check on her people, there was real concern. She was hard, but not like Patrick.

"I want to help my kingdom," I said. "And that means learning about its people. You. Tell me how you got here."

Suspicion gleamed in her eyes, as though she was considering all the ways I could use the information to hurt her. But at last, she softened. "My parents worked in this factory when I was a child. When Colin took over, the factory was shut down and all the flashers arrested. I survived only because my neighbors claimed I was theirs, and I never saw my parents again." Claire's gaze leveled on me. "Does that surprise you? That this factory was still operating before the One-Night War?"

It did, but I wouldn't say so.

"This place provided clean water to most of the lowcity. The highcity and castle have other sources, but the lowcity relied on this factory not just for clean water, but to keep the marshes at bay. Perhaps you've seen the way it's eating at the houses there."

"Unfortunately, I haven't had a chance to tour the city because I've been busy trying to stop the riots." I pulled back and twisted my little finger at her.

"Watch it, Queen. I've been fighting for Aecor freedom while you were hiding in the Indigo Kingdom these last years."

As though I'd been lazing around Skyvale Palace this whole time, coddled and turned against my own kingdom. "I'm sorry about your parents. I lost mine, too, and I've been fighting. Just because you haven't seen it doesn't mean that isn't the truth."

"So I've been told. But you turned on Patrick." There was something about her tone, though. Something I couldn't quite interpret.

"I disagreed with his methods. He became an assassin for the cause. I won't. Nor will I allow assassins to rule in my kingdom."

"That's either very naive or hypocritical." Claire glanced at Melanie. "I suppose you two haven't had a chance to catch up, but I think maybe you should carve out some time. There's a lot you don't know about your friend, Queen."

Melanie scowled.

"It doesn't matter." I forced my tone even, but the thought of Melanie killing someone made my stomach roil. Maybe it wasn't true. "We have a problem that needs solving. That is, I'd rather not hurt any of you, and I don't think you'll risk hurting me, in spite of your threats."

Claire didn't respond.

I crossed my legs and angled toward her. "This is the truth, Claire. I came here because I want the riots to stop."

"Not until the demands are met."

"What, for the Indigo Kingdom people to leave?"

"That's right."

"With some exceptions, the Indigo Kingdom is supportive of my claim to the vermilion throne. I've signed the Wraith Alliance. King Tobiah is working to remove Prince Colin. I'm taking the kingdom *peacefully*." A moment stretched as she studied me. Evaluated. "Claire, you want to protect your people?"

She pressed her mouth into a line.

"I want to protect my people. From hunger, sickness, dehydration, wraith—and riots. I want to protect you and the Red Militia, too, but right now, you stand with Patrick. He and I are not on the same side."

"He wants you on the throne."

"I don't need him to put me there. I'm not a puppet. When the time is right, I will be crowned queen, but Patrick will have no place with me. Soon he'll be tried for his crimes, both here and in the Indigo Kingdom."

"And I can go with him, or with you?" Claire asked.

"More or less." I stood, and Melanie followed. Then Claire, her hands twitching toward weapons. "The riots must stop. There can be no negotiation on that. Nor the fact that my allies from the Indigo Kingdom will be welcome here. I told you I signed the Wraith Alliance. Do you know what that means?"

She sneered. "People like my parents are never seen again."

"Not anymore. People like your parents—and you and me—can volunteer to help fight our real enemy, the wraith. Using magic outside of that will still be illegal, but no more flashers will vanish from the streets. Not anymore."

"Say I believed you," Claire said. "Say I agreed and I'm

tired of watching my people get hurt every night for a man who allowed himself to be captured."

I'd been right. She'd lured us here hoping to negotiate.

"That doesn't change the fact that you signed the Wraith Alliance. That still means no magic, and places like the lowcity will continue rotting because they don't have this." She gestured around.

The factory. The water.

I'd always thought my ancestors had ceased industrialized magic a hundred years ago. Never had I imagined they might have kept such a scale of magic alive.

But it had been to help people. Everyone deserved clean water.

What a choice.

"I'll find a way," I said. "A nonmagical way to restore this factory." Skyvale Palace had been renovated after the Wraith Alliance. Why couldn't a factory?

"That's not a very firm promise."

"You haven't made any promises," I said. "Can you stop the riots?"

Her eyes were steady on mine. "I'll find a way."

"Then we can both get what we want." I smiled and offered my hand. "I don't suppose you'd be willing to share the names and locations of other Red Militia cells."

"Not a chance." Claire shook my hand, and escorted us to the exit.

"That was well done," Melanie said.

I hoped so. Part of me wanted to send a score of police to

apprehend everyone there, but I'd lose Claire's trust. If I let her be, she could help to pacify the Red Militia.

"Mel." I stopped at the rampart and placed a hand on her shoulder.

"Wil." She mimicked my stance.

Bitter wind cut around the wall, making me shiver. Dawn edged on the horizon and we needed to get inside, but I had to tell her first. "I'm not going to ask what Claire was talking about back there. Not because I don't care or want to know. I do. But you'll tell me when you're ready."

"Same as you'll tell me when you're ready to talk about Black Knife."

"It won't be long now, I think." I'd made decisions as a queen tonight. Not only an Osprey. Not only Black Knife. But Queen Wilhelmina, who was also an Osprey and Black Knife.

Being queen didn't prevent me from missing the way things used to be—simpler, though I hadn't realized it then—but what I'd done tonight shifted something inside me. There was a way to be true to myself and rule Aecor. I was unprepared, but I could learn. I *would*, just as I'd learned to fight and steal and survive after being a princess.

"It might be a long time for me." Melanie dragged her fingers through her short hair.

"It will take however long it takes." I pulled her into a tight hug. "But whenever you're ready, I'm here."

THIRTY-THREE

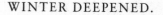

WINTER DEEPENED.

Icy gusts pushed through the castle. Even in my father's office—my office now—I shivered and pulled my cloak tighter. The fireplace was on the far side of the room from my desk.

Paige sat opposite me, sifting through lists and documents. "I've looked into clean water for the lowcity. There are several options, but developing the right system will take time."

"It's urgent. People there are dying." True to her word, Claire had made progress on the riots. There'd been no change the first night, but the following nights were quieter and quieter until last night when the streets around the castle seemed to hold their breath, waiting for a mob that never came.

This morning, I'd lifted the curfew. There'd been cheers in the streets; people thought the problem was solved.

Paige dipped her pen and wrote on clean paper. "We can pump some of our water to the lowcity—ration what the highcity and castle are allowed. People won't like it, but if everyone gives up a little, it will go a long way to helping those in need."

"Let's do it. Have one of your assistants figure out the details."

Paige glanced up after writing the final line. "I don't have assistants."

"You do all of this yourself?"

"Is that wrong?"

"No, it's just too much work for one person. Hire someone. Or two someones."

"I'll do that." She handed me the document she'd just written. "Please sign."

I took a steadying breath before committing my name to ink and paper, and then gave it back to her.

"Here's your order for mirrors." Paige flipped to another sheet. "The plans from the Indigo Kingdom arrived. They've sent as many supplies as they can spare, but it isn't much."

"It will be better than nothing if we can get the sandcliffs covered." That might protect Aecor City for a while, but most of Aecor was flat marsh, without natural places to put mirrors in the stretches without cities.

Updates I received from the Indigo Kingdom were not encouraging. More border villages had flooded with wraith. More refugees had moved into Skyvale.

Later in the afternoon, a knock sounded on the door, and James entered. "Wil, there's news. A letter from Tobiah." He handed his entangled notebook to me. "And refugees are crossing the bridge."

I held the notebook to my chest. "Refugees? Here?"

Paige's face was ashen as she looked between us. "Wraith refugees?"

"Yes." James's voice was heavy. "What should we do with them? The city isn't big enough to support the numbers arriving, and this is just the beginning."

"And we were just discussing water rationing," Paige added. "We don't have the resources. Not water, not food. Let alone the space to house many additional people."

I closed my eyes and dropped my head back. "Allow them entry. I signed the Wraith Alliance. I cannot turn them away."

"Correct," James said.

"Give them shelter. Make them welcome. Hopefully some brought food and other necessities."

"There are a lot of carts and wagons." James stood closer to the fire. "Livestock, too."

Finally, some good news. "Let them rest here—in empty factories, if we have nowhere else. Then send them farther into Aecor. Other cities will have to take them in, but create some kind of census that will allow friends and families to follow."

"Anything else?" he asked.

"Triple the police presence while the refugees are moving through. The Red Militia or malcontents might take action against them. But keep the police in small patrols. Nothing threatening."

"'Indigo must go,'" James muttered. "And the riots *just* stopped."

"Hopefully they won't start again, but we need to be careful."

He nodded. "I'll send soldiers—red and blue—to the bridge as well. They'll keep traffic moving and prevent bottlenecking."

"Good. Keep a lane clear so people can return to the Indigo Kingdom as well. They may go back for more people or belongings. Let them move freely. Have ships and ferries ready to take passengers, as well."

"It will be done." James shifted his weight. "When I'm finished, I'd like to request permission to return to the Indigo Kingdom."

My stomach dropped at the thought of losing James.

Of course he wanted to be with his cousin, his mother, and what was left of his family. I could never deny him that, but— "You're here by Tobiah's orders, not mine. Have you asked him?"

"No." James turned his eyes toward the curtained window. "I know what he'll say."

How difficult it must be, here because he wanted to be away from Tobiah—and because Tobiah had sent him away. There were too many questions and arguments gathering between them. But no matter their differences, they were like brothers. They needed to work this out.

"I'm sorry, James. I'll ask on your behalf."

He nodded and went out of the room.

Paige turned to me. "We're finished for now. Don't forget you have a meeting with Prince Colin before dinner, and you'll have guests from Northland arriving tonight. Jasper and Cora Calloway."

A count and countess, if I remembered. They—and other nobles responsible for various cities and towns across Aecor—had been in their homes during the One-Night War. It was only the high nobility in Aecor City who'd been slaughtered.

"Thank you, Paige."

She hesitated by the door. "Do you mind if I use the white notebook to write to Theresa?"

"It's in my quarters. Make sure everyone has a turn to write to the others." I took James's notebook to a chair by the fire as the door clicked shut.

> *Wilhelmina,*
>
> *I write with the worst kind of news: West Pass Watch has fallen. The western mountains are flooded with wraith mist. My uncle Herman is dead, along with over one thousand men who'd been stationed there.*
>
> *And now the west is gone. Only a narrow stretch of valley and Midvale Ridge stand between Skyvale and the wraithland. Wraith beasts wander everywhere; guards on the city walls see them roaming the forest. That means we have plenty of wraith beasts for the barrier, but I've heard the Flags are filled with signs begging for Black Knife to return. They're scared. Everyone is.*
>
> *Mirrors again cover every west-facing wall in the city, and all along the border, but they didn't save West Pass Watch. There's just so much wraith.*
>
> *The barrier is still under construction. It seems unlikely we'll complete it in time.*
>
> *Many families have already left Skyvale. The Chuters, Corcorans, and Davises. My mother and aunt have gone to Hawes. Others are packing, and I don't blame them. I worry for the ones who can't leave, like so*

many in the Flags. Lakeside—near Bracken Lake in the south—has already evacuated.

People are moving east. Advisers have suggested I should, too, but how can I leave Skyvale when there are still people here, and there's still a chance we can save it?

Tobiah

I trailed my fingers down the pages. No wonder James wanted to return.

Heart heavy, I went to my desk to respond with my condolences, as well as updates on the refugees moving into Aecor and the status of the kingdom. I also added James's request to return to the Indigo Kingdom.

Tobiah must have had the notebook open, because his writing began appearing on the next page.

Wil,

Thank you. Like no one else, you know the devastation of watching your home fall apart.

Please tell James I understand his desire to return, but I need him there.

Do you have time to write now? James and I have been drawing a line beneath our notes when we're finished so the other can begin.

Tobiah

My heart jumped into my throat as a black line spread across the page. We'd been writing every few days, but our letters were nothing that could be called a conversation. They'd been updates and advice, nothing more.

Now he wanted to talk.

And if I didn't respond quickly, he'd decide I wasn't here anymore and give up.

Letting him think I'd gone would be cowardly.

I'm here, I wrote.

For a moment, I sat with my pen hovering over the paper, wondering if I should say anything else. I drew a short, flourished line instead.

I'm glad.

Oh, this was awful. I should have shut the notebook and left it for James. How could anyone converse like this—when they couldn't hear the other's voice or tone, or see their face and mannerisms?

But I could imagine Tobiah in his office, or room maybe. In my mind, he was wearing his typical black clothes, with his hair mussed and hanging in his face. And he, too, watched the page with those dark eyes, waiting for me to respond.

I couldn't say what I wanted, though.

What did you need to talk about? I used my handwriting—still in development, and likely to change—adding a few flourishes to the ascenders and descenders. Maybe the question wouldn't sound rude.

A dot appeared on his line. Then another above it. As though he'd changed his mind about how to respond.

I think we should begin referring to magic users as radiants again, rather than flashers. The latter is rude, and if the barrier works, magic may be what saves us.

A smile escaped me. *That's thoughtful of you,* I wrote. *I'm inclined to agree. I'll take being called a radiant over flasher any day.*

I would, too. He switched to the line below, like a change of subject. *I want you to be crowned queen, Wilhelmina. My uncle won't easily let go of Aecor, but there's a plan already in motion.* There was a long pause, and finally, a line.

I wanted to ask what plan, but everything between us was so strained. I hadn't earned back his confidence.

Promise me something. I dipped my pen and shook off the excess ink. *If the wraith moves across the Midvale Ridge, you will abandon Skyvale and go east until you're safe.*

We'll never be safe, Wilhelmina. He started a line to signal my turn, but he stopped and added, *I must go. We'll talk again soon.*

THIRTY-FOUR

THE CLOCK ON the mantel showed half past the fourth hour.

I slipped out from under the covers and threw on my dress-ing gown. At the balcony door, I pulled aside the curtain and gazed at the night-black city, my bedroom faintly reflected.

My breath fogged the glass. From here, I could see a glow on the cliffs in the west: more mirrors were hung every day, though trying to protect Aecor *and* be mindful of the wildlife that lived there was a tricky balance.

I let the curtain fall as I moved away.

With a touch of the switch, the gas lamp hissed to life above my desk. Notebooks lay scattered across the surface. My diary, the two linked to the Ospreys and Tobiah, and a handful I'd pulled off bookshelves in this room and my father's.

I'd discovered their diaries weeks ago, but it had taken several days before I'd been brave enough to begin reading. But there'd been no comfort in my parents' words. They worried about the same things I did: feeding the people, ensuring their safety, and maintaining relationships with the surrounding kingdoms.

Absent from most of their entries: the wraith.

Meanwhile, I was reminded of the wraith each day when I visited the wraith boy. My dark mirror who spoke in riddles and warnings of the coming desolation.

I pushed my parents' journals aside and opened the entangled notebooks. Nothing from the Skyvale Ospreys. Nothing from Tobiah, either. Only my dozens of letters to him.

Some were short, simply queries about Tobiah and the Ospreys' safety, while many were longer updates about the city and kingdom and refugees building new villages off the main roads to other Aecorian cities.

Chest heavy with stress and grief and desperation, I reached for a pen and added another note. *Tobiah, it's been a month. I've sent riders to look for you in Skyvale. Please answer.*

I drew a line, signaling his turn, but his response never came. Winter's hold on Aecor eased over the next weeks.

In the very early morning, I sat down to write, even though I knew better. There'd been no replies for two months—not in the white notebook, nor the blue.

> *Tobiah,*
> *"Before the anniversary of the One-Night War, you will unlock those bars and together we will take Aecor."*
> *That's what Patrick said when I locked him in the dungeon.*
> *The anniversary is just days away. I've been looking*

forward to it for years. Before, because I thought it was the day I'd take back my kingdom. Now, it's a symbol of moving beyond that awful night. If Patrick thinks he can—

A knock sounded on my door. It wasn't Danie; she never knocked, just slipped in and out like a ghost.

"Enter!" I blew on the ink and shut the notebook.

Melanie peeked in. "One of the riders you sent to the Indigo Kingdom returned last night."

"Finally." I lurched to my feet, heart pounding in my throat. "What news?"

"I don't know. Prince Colin intercepted it first, and now he's summoning you."

I dressed quickly and followed Melanie, my mind boiling over with questions. But like Patrick, Prince Colin was the kind of man who enjoyed making announcements.

I'd been to the council room a hundred times since coming home, but the space always seemed smaller than I remembered. Still, it was gloomy, and thick with the ancient ghosts of Aecorian rulers.

An immense stone table stood in the center of the room, six thick legs carved into waterfalls. Age had darkened the crevices of the pale blue marble, adding to the illusion of rushing water. Ten matching chairs sat around the table, their cushions new and fat.

"Please have a seat." Crown Prince Colin Pierce, House of the Dragon, Overlord of Aecor Territory sat at the head of the table.

My father's seat.

I loomed in the doorway, staring at his relaxed posture. My jaw ached from clenching, and anticipation made my heart race. "Tell me the news."

Prince Colin stood, pressing his thumbs and fingertips against the table. "One of the riders from Skyvale has returned." His expression was oddly calm.

Only one rider? That did not bode well. "Tell me."

"Sit," he said. "Please."

I glanced at Melanie. James had approached behind us, and both wore masks of unease. Riders had left *weeks* ago. We'd been waiting every day for news.

"I'll stand." But I moved deeper into the room, careful to keep my expression neutral.

"Fine." He stepped away from his chair and crossed his arms. "The rider has already been sent to the hospital to be treated for the injuries the Red Militia inflicted."

My fists curled. Claire cooperated with me, but the entire Militia didn't. With Patrick in prison, the Red Militia seemed to have lost cohesion, which meant individuals and small groups tended to act in their own interests.

An odd note of sympathy entered Prince Colin's tone. "I wish you would sit."

I caught James's nod in the corner of my eye, and acquiesced. The captain pulled out the nearest chair for me, and then one for Melanie.

Prince Colin took his chair again. My father's chair. "Skyvale has fallen." His eyes moved from me to Melanie to James. "Skyvale, and the Indigo Valley, are part of the wraithland now."

My breath came in short gasps, and tears swelled in my eyes; I blinked them away. "And the people? Were they able to escape?" Please, saints.

"Some." He dropped his eyes. "Much of the Hawksbill nobility left the city as soon as West Pass Watch fell, but there were many who could not."

That much I knew from Tobiah's last letter. It was everything *after* that I needed to hear.

"My brother Herman is dead."

I'd known, but hadn't been able to tell Prince Colin without revealing the notebooks. "I'm sorry," I said. "He was a well-respected man, I know."

Prince Colin glanced toward the window and gathered himself. "The riders were delayed because they had to travel throughout the kingdom for information. The others were killed during their journey."

That thought chilled me. I'd sent those men to their deaths.

"Glowmen—bigger than any we've ever seen in the city—took out most of the Flags, while wraith beasts rampaged through Thornton and Greenstone. The Hawksbill wall held for a night, but eventually the beasts got through. Hawksbill and the King's Seat are gone."

"What about the evacuation routes?" My question sounded flat. Lifeless. Because I'd known, hadn't I? No word from Tobiah. No word from the Ospreys. And even if the king had often been slow to reply, Connor had written every day.

The first day I hadn't heard from Connor—that had been worrying. But the second. The third . . .

"Most of the routes were blocked," Prince Colin continued.

"Either filled with wraith and creatures, or the stampede of people escaping. Everyone looked for the king, but he wasn't at any of the evacuation points. His guards couldn't find him. Someone thought they saw him at the house where your Ospreys were living, but when they followed, it was empty. They're all presumed dead."

Numbly, I reached for Melanie's hand and squeezed. Connor. Carl. Theresa. Kevin.

James's hand fell on my shoulder, his fingers curled and white at the knuckles. His cousin. His best friend. His king.

Gone.

I placed my free hand on top of James's, and for a long moment sat connected with these two people: my best friend, and Tobiah's. The grief surged between us.

We'd all known, in a way. None of us had wanted to say anything, to be the one to voice the awful thought lest we be the one to make it come true.

Prince Colin glanced between us, his gaze settling on James. "Many people were sent to Hawes. Your mother, the king's mother. I've sent riders to investigate."

Then Hawes was still safe? "How far has the wraith come?" My voice sounded hollow.

"It's spilled out of the valley. We know that," Prince Colin said. "There isn't an accurate picture yet, but from what I gather, about half of the Indigo Kingdom is already under."

Half.

The wraith was coming so fast.

Because of me? Because of Chrysalis?

"I'll leave you alone for a while." Prince Colin stood. There was a soft, strange tilt to his tone. "I'm sorry."

"We don't need your pity," I whispered. "We don't need to hear how *sorry* you are. Everything you say is a lie."

He lifted an eyebrow. "I am not a monster, Wilhelmina. Skyvale was my home. Terrell and Herman were my brothers. Tobiah was my nephew. Francesca is my sister by marriage. I've known those families my entire life. If you think this news doesn't affect me, you are mistaken.

"And before you find some way to blame me, remember that *you* are the one who chose to leave your friends behind. You could have stayed with them and helped them survive the wraith, or you could have fought to bring them with you. But you did neither of those things. Instead, you followed me here because you wouldn't give up the kingdom you haven't seen in ten years."

I was on my feet before I realized, Melanie's and James's hands thrown off, and my fingertips brushed my daggers. "I chose my kingdom over my friends. It's what a good queen would do."

Something unidentifiable flared over his face. "And where is your kingdom without your friends, Your Majesty?"

He turned and left the room.

It was hard to believe the Indigo Kingdom was gone.

The timing was sadly appropriate. News of the Indigo Kingdom's destruction came just days before the ten-year anniversary of the One-Night War.

The Indigo Kingdom was gone, and half a year ago I would have celebrated. Now, all I felt was empty.

"We need to tell the others." I closed my eyes, but my mind conjured up memories from the wraithland: a vast, wasted world where trees had teeth and animals grew to terrible sizes. I remembered the white mist that glowed, obscuring everything, and the way it reeked acrid and burned my nose.

I shook away the images of Connor, Theresa, Carl, and Kevin struggling to survive in a place that looked familiar, but would eat them whole if they took one wrong step.

"If Skyvale is gone," I muttered in James's direction, "that means the barrier is gone."

He nodded and didn't say anything.

Two of the Queen's Guards waited at the door, Matthew and Cael, though I was unsure when they'd shown up or how much they'd witnessed. "Fetch Paige and the Grays. I need them immediately."

Both young men snapped and thumped their black-gloved fists to their chests. Their boots stamped on the thin rug as they disappeared down the hall.

"They're soldiers, not pages." James's reminder held no heat. He was lost in his own grief.

I sank into the chair Prince Colin had abandoned.

Pale sunlight angled through the windows as dawn broke. Dust motes drifted through the bands of light, and I mourned the lives my friends would never get to have.

Connor would never become the greatest healer the world had ever known.

Carl would never learn to use his incredible stealth for the good of the kingdom.

Theresa would never have the chance to show that behind

her quiet facade, there was a strong, compassionate leader ready to right injustices.

Kevin would never have a chance to put his sharp mind to use in a real council meeting.

The night Patrick announced Quinn and Ezra had died, I'd sworn to Connor and Theresa that we'd build memorials and hold days of remembrance. Not just for Quinn and Ezra, but for those who'd gone before.

They'd never know when I made good on those promises, or that the same would hold for them.

So many Ospreys had died in our struggle with the Indigo Kingdom. And now the wraith had taken more.

And wasn't it all because of the wraith to begin with?

"It's taken everything from us." My whisper drew Melanie's and James's eyes. "The war that took our families happened because of the wraith. Radiants became flashers because of the wraith. Our friends are dead because of the wraith. It will take Aecor, too, unless I stop it."

"How will you do that?" Melanie asked.

Paige, Oscar, and Ronald arrived, saving me from having to admit I didn't know. "Sit," I instructed, and they obeyed.

The boys had on their Queen's Guard uniforms, though they weren't on duty for another three hours. Later, I'd make a formal announcement for the city and kingdom. I'd write letters to the rulers of Laurel-by-the-Sea and the remaining Wraith Alliance kingdoms, though most seemed to have closed themselves off. But right now, my friends needed me to be strong. They needed not for me to make this right, but to make this make sense.

"The Indigo Kingdom has fallen. Our friends there are presumed dead."

Their expressions shifted from disbelief to horror to grief. Paige let out a small groan of despair, and Melanie moved to comfort her.

"Before I give you the few details I have, I want you to know this: I will do everything in my power to stop the wraith from taking any more of our friends."

THIRTY-FIVE

CHRYSALIS STOOD IN the doorway, shoulders hunched so his jacket hung awkwardly over his narrow frame. "You didn't come to see me this morning."

"Sorry." Not really. Sort of. "I've been busy all day." After meetings and announcements and attempting to comfort people when all I wanted to do was hide in my room, I was exhausted. My stomach ached with the hollow sensation of hunger; I'd skipped breakfast and lunch, but when I'd finally sat down to dinner, I couldn't force myself to eat more than a couple of bites.

Cold prickled over my skin, numbing me as night fell.

The wraith boy opened the door wider to let me into his storage room, and I motioned for James and Melanie to wait in the hall. They nodded and bowed their heads together to talk as the door swung shut behind me.

Hands clasped at his chest, the wraith boy gave me his most

imploring gaze. "It's not for you to apologize to me. Maybe I wasn't good enough—"

"Chrysalis." That sounded empty. I tried again. "Chrysalis. It wasn't you."

Not specifically. But he was wraith. His good behavior lately didn't negate his nature. He was destructive.

His small room challenged that assertion, though. Books in neat stacks lined the space, and his bed—a simple pallet of padding and blankets—was made up, with piles of folded clothes sitting on top. That part was easy, though, since he never slept, and he preferred the tattered clothes he'd worn since the beginning.

The space was stuffy and hot, but I wasn't ready to let the wraith boy out. I didn't want to remind anyone of his presence. People hadn't *forgotten* the night of my arrival here, or the battle on Snowhaven Bridge, but if he was out of sight, he was less of a liability.

"I need to ask you something," I said. "I need you to answer me honestly."

"Always." His eyes shone. "I'm so glad you have questions for me."

"Wraith has flooded the Indigo Valley. Skyvale is gone. The rest of the Indigo Kingdom won't be far behind. Maybe a few years. Maybe a few months."

His voice turned darker. "Maybe not even as long as that."

"Is there a way to stop the wraith from advancing?"

He shook his head. "There is no way to stop it forever. Your barrier might slow it for a time, but wraith doesn't like being contained."

Was he talking about wraith in general, or revealing his own unhappiness? What would he do if I never gave him more room to stretch? Maybe, eventually, he'd turn on me.

I took in his eager face, the set of his shoulders angled toward me, and the earnestness in his voice when he said, "I'll protect you when the wraith comes."

I let out a long breath. He was still on my side, but how long could I keep him caged? "It's not just me anymore, Chrysalis." I curled my fists into my dress. "It's the entire kingdom. I need to protect everyone here. Everyone who was born here, and all the people coming here looking for safety. Can you protect everyone?"

He chewed on his lip—a disarmingly human gesture. "I would try, if that's what you wanted."

"Would it hurt you?"

The wraith boy approached me with all the hesitancy of a kitten taking its first steps. "That's irrelevant," he said. "What my queen wants is the only thing that matters."

Darkness blanketed the castle by the time Melanie, James, and I returned to my rooms and dragged a trio of chairs closer to the fire.

A tray of tea and snacks waited for us. I poured while James pulled out a large map of Aecor and Melanie prowled the suite as though searching for someone hidden. When all was clear, I told them about my conversation with the wraith boy.

"He said he could protect you." James took his seat. Red rimmed his eyes, but if he'd cried over Tobiah's death, I hadn't seen. "Any idea how he'd do that?"

I shook my head. "Kill wraith beasts, maybe? I doubt even he knows. I get the feeling his actions are as much a surprise to him as they are to us. He never considers consequences. He just acts."

"He's like a wild animal." Melanie's gaze drifted toward the map sitting on a stand between her and James. "Trying to please, never getting it quite right."

"Usually never in the vicinity of right."

"Because you keep him caged, even when he behaves."

"My point is," I said, "Chrysalis may be willing to try to protect the entire kingdom, but there's no guarantee he'll be successful. He's too powerful to sacrifice without assurance of success."

"Plus, he's human now," Melanie said. "He's a person, not a tool."

"He murdered the last person who believed in him like that." James kept his tone even, but his eyes were hard. "He's *not* human. He's a human-shaped wraith creature, alive only because Wilhelmina commanded. So don't be so quick to defend him."

She frowned and went back to her study of the map of Aecor. "What of the barrier?"

"We must assume it's gone. Tobiah said—" James cleared his throat and touched the notebook he'd used to write to Tobiah. "He said they'd started to put up some of the barrier, but obviously it didn't hold."

"Maybe it wasn't big enough, or there wasn't enough magic.

Maybe the wraith beasts weren't enough, and it needed to be real, human magic." I sighed. "There are a hundred things we can't know."

"We have the construction plans, right?" Melanie tucked a strand of hair behind her ear. "What if we tried to make one? Aecor is smaller than the Indigo Kingdom. We could set up the barrier along the coast. Maybe ring the entire peninsula if it looks like it's going to work."

"What about Laurel-by-the-Sea?" I pointed at our northern neighbors. "James, do we know their status?"

He shook his head. "They've closed their borders. But a ringed barrier wouldn't prevent them from coming here if they didn't have defenses. How much of a population can Aecor support?"

I didn't know. "It might not matter. Chrysalis doesn't believe a barrier will do anything more than delay the inevitable. That was Liadia's experience, and what we were hoping for with Tobiah's"—I managed not to choke on his name—"committee. But we believed we'd have more time. Time to research, experiment, and build, and then the wraith would hit the barrier."

Then we'd have a year to live unless we miraculously found a solution.

Our parents and grandparents had left us this world that was spiraling out of control. All their efforts hadn't been enough to save it. How could we hope to make a difference?

"We don't have time to build a barrier," James said. "Even with the construction plans, we don't have the resources."

And even if we had enough flashers in Aecor to supply the magic, I doubted they would step forward. I wouldn't have.

"What do you propose?" Melanie asked.

"My king and cousin is dead." James's chest expanded with a ragged breath as he faced me, expression grave. "Two months ago, he forbade me from returning to the Indigo Kingdom, but now, Wilhelmina, you are my queen. Allow me to journey into the new wraithland with a team of volunteers and retrieve any parts of the barrier I can find. I'll bring it back to you."

"You'd be risking your life."

"It's nothing less than you or Tobiah would do. Besides, I have no intentions of dying. Best case, I return with barrier pieces to help protect Aecor for a time. Worst, I return with information about the wraithland and where the borders are."

"Worst case, I never see you again."

"I'm reasonably certain I can't die." James hazarded a smile, but we both knew he was thinking about the mystery of his healing. Now he'd never know what happened. "Maybe I can find refugees as well."

Maybe he could find his cousin, he meant.

I turned my eyes to the fire, watching flames jump up and around the blackening logs. "This is the only plan we have?"

"The only one that doesn't involve giving up." James leaned forward and touched my arm. "Let me do this. I know I can."

The idea of sending James into the wraithland was appalling, not just because the wraithland was a nightmare come to life, but because I needed him here. But he was the best choice for this mission, and if there was even the slimmest chance that Tobiah and the Ospreys had survived, James would be the one to find them.

"Prince Colin won't permit it."

"I know how we'll deal with Prince Colin."

I nodded. "I won't stop you, then. We need any parts of the barrier you can recover. In the morning, I'll work with Paige and her new assistants to see if there's any way to convert one of the unused factories into something like Tobiah's barrier facility. We may not be able to construct an entire barrier here, but we can do something."

We spent the remainder of the night discussing who would go with James, and what routes they'd take into Skyvale. When we'd finished our tea and they started for the door, I hugged both of them. Melanie for the friends we'd lost. And James for the hope he still carried.

"Remember, this won't be a rescue mission," I whispered. "I don't want you to stay in the wraithland any longer than it takes to fetch the barrier."

"I know," he said, and they left.

Alone, I opened the entangled notebook James had left on his chair.

Page by page, I read through the letters Tobiah and I had written each other, and the last string of notes and pleas I'd left.

I opened a jar of ink and dipped a pen.

How long have you been gone, Tobiah? Since we last talked? Was it that night? That hour?

I've only just had confirmation that Skyvale has fallen and even though part of me suspected this whole time, I hoped. I hoped. But if you'd survived an attack on Skyvale, you'd have reached me by now.

The last time we wrote, I wanted to tell you

something, but I didn't. Maybe there's no point anymore. But. But Tobiah, I miss you.

I miss you and I wish you were here.

Love,

Wilhelmina

Tears swam in my eyes as I cleaned the pen and then placed my hands on the notebook. *"Go to sleep,"* I whispered. *"Be a normal notebook again. Nothing more."*

THIRTY-SIX

MY EYES WERE gummy in the morning, aching with the loss of Tobiah and the Ospreys and an entire kingdom I'd been raised to hate, but grown to love.

In spite of the grief, there was work to do, and I needed to appear strong. Truly, I *was* stronger; keeping the notebooks active had been draining me, and without them I had a chance of enduring the day.

Today was an important day. Historic, maybe.

Tomorrow would be bigger.

I sat still as Danie smoothed powder under my eyes to conceal the evidence of my late, restless night. She found a soft, dove gray dress and waited while I changed behind the partition.

"Will there be anything else, Your Majesty?" she asked, once she'd finished braiding my hair.

"That's all." I smiled as warmly as possible. "When you admire Sergeant Wallace today, maybe you should try speaking to him, too."

Her throat and cheeks flushed. "Oh, I couldn't. He's much too good for me."

"Never say that." I stepped forward and squeezed her arm as I would have Melanie's or Paige's, and Danie tensed. Though she touched me all the time to do my hair or apply cosmetics or help me dress, she was always quick and efficient, never casual. I was a flasher queen, commander of the wraith boy: I was terrifying.

When I backed away, Danie forced her shoulders down. "Maybe I'll try. Good day, Your Majesty." She was out of the room in seconds. That probably counted as fleeing.

I grabbed my black notebook and papers, and headed out the door a moment later.

"What did you do to Danie?" Paige asked. "She looked somewhere between alarmed and ill when she came running out."

Behind us, Melanie fished a coin from her pocket and gave it to James; he'd won the bet.

I sighed as we headed to the council room. "I'm trying to be friendly to the staff. To show them I care."

Paige grimaced as I told her about my attempt to encourage Danie. "Just be nice. Let her do her job and be nice to her. Remember, you're not spying on the staff and you don't want to give that impression."

"I'll try." My heart pounded as we reached the council chamber.

Oscar and Ronald were already there, as well as a handful of nobles from other parts of the kingdom.

Everyone stood when I entered.

Jasper and Cora Calloway, the count and countess from Northland, had been kind to me, and supportive. Across from them were Harrison and Desiree Symonds from Trinity, the first destination for most refugees. They had twin daughters—Summer and Juniper—who raced through the halls of Sandcliff Castle, playing like the wraith didn't concern them.

Prince Colin was there, too, his arms pulled over his chest in a defensive posture.

Melanie took her place at the table while the rest of my guard watched from the wall. Red uniforms nearly outnumbered the blue here.

"Thank you for joining me this morning." I looked around the table, meeting everyone's eyes for a heartbeat. "We've always known the Indigo Kingdom couldn't stand between Aecor and the wraith forever. But none of us thought this day would come so soon."

There was nodding all around.

"After yesterday's devastating news, I promised a plan to keep Aecor safe. My closest advisers and I spent last night working out the details.

"We still think a barrier similar to the one Liadia constructed is our best chance. As such, Captain Rayner will lead a team into the wraithland to gather whatever remains of the barrier King Tobiah built. Meanwhile, we will build our own facility. Flashers who volunteer their magic for the new barrier will be compensated. I will be first to pour my magic into the barrier that will protect our kingdom. Paige, please see that the plans are drawn up."

She nodded and wrote a note to herself.

"A waste of resources," Harrison Symonds said.

I turned my glare on him. "The only other option is giving up, and I'm not willing to do that. Not when there's still hope."

"*Is* there still hope?" Lord Symonds rose and leaned forward, his hands flat on the table. His wife touched his arm and shook her head, but he ignored her. "Most of the continent has fallen to the wraith. A hundred years of wiser minds than yours have worked to contain or stop the wraith. The barrier in Liadia failed after only a year—"

"Then what do you propose?" My fingernails dug into my palms. "Should we sit here and wait to die? Tell thousands of people out there that we've given up? If you thought the riots were bad before—"

"I suppose you would know about the common people?"

"I know enough to tell you this: people are scared. In Skyvale, it was this constant, low-grade terror. Knowing the wraith was coming, knowing they could do nothing about it."

"They could have stopped using magic," Prince Colin said. "They could have turned in the flashers among them."

"Some did." My chest ached. "They told the police and left signals for Black Knife. But mostly, they wanted to be able to trust their king and queen. Their princes. They wanted to believe in the people whose responsibility it was to care for them. They wanted to trust that their leaders would find a way to keep them safe from the wraith. And now you want me to tell my people that we've given up."

"Just two men." Melanie's words jerked me back into the present. The Grays, the Calloways, Lady Symonds, and even the guards—they were all staring at Prince Colin, Harrison, and me. Melanie's tone remained level. "Not we."

I shook my head. "No matter what I said, it would be we. No one would care about the difference. Besides, if I allowed that kind of announcement to be made, it would mean I'd given up, too. And I won't do that."

"You don't have a choice." Prince Colin strode toward me, just a hair too close for politeness. "You're a queen in name only. I remain overlord."

I stood, tipping my chair back, and closed the gap between us, suddenly in his space. "Wrong again. As you said, the Indigo Kingdom is gone. Your king is dead. You're the heir to a falling kingdom, and your claim to the title of overlord is empty. That leaves you with two choices: leave Aecor, or admit you are now a refugee. In accordance with the Wraith Alliance, you are welcome to stay here as a ward of the independent kingdom of Aecor."

The council room was silent, save Lord Symonds's "I humbly respect my queen's wishes."

I wanted to see their faces, but there was no way I was turning away from Prince Colin. "Paige, prepare for my coronation. Tomorrow is the ten-year anniversary of the One-Night War, the anniversary of Aecor losing its king and queen. At noon, I will take the crown, and Aecor will have a queen once more."

"Yes, Your Majesty."

"No. This is outrageous." Prince Colin's neck turned red. "This isn't how the Wraith Alliance works."

"Actually, it is." James grabbed a folder from the center of the council table. "The Wraith Alliance states that if any kingdom and its sovereign should fall to the wraith, wards would be returned to their home kingdoms and be under rule of the rightful king or queen. The rightful Queen of Aecor is Wilhelmina." He pulled a stack of papers from the folder: the revised Wraith Alliance. "It's all here, if you'd like to refamiliarize yourself with it."

Prince Colin snatched the document and skimmed through to the parts concerning wardship. "This is outrageous. I have been ruling Aecor Territory for ten years. I am the overlord—"

"Not anymore." I made my words hard. "I won't continue this conversation. If you continue to resist, you will be in violation of the Wraith Alliance, which your king signed in good faith that all his subjects—you included—would obey."

From the corner of my eyes, I caught amused and amazed looks.

Prince Colin slammed the document on the table just as an explosion sounded in the northwest. Shocks rippled through the ground and floor of the castle.

People shouted, and guards rushed to protect their charges. I raced for the nearest window, ignoring James's orders for me to find safety, and threw open the shutters to let in a rush of early spring air.

A pillar of deep gray smoke rose above Snowhaven Bridge.

Others weren't far behind me. They gasped and swore. Someone started to pray.

"James, send rescue teams to the bridge. Everyone we can spare."

"Right away." His steps were clipped as he hurried from the

room, calling a handful of others to join him.

"Oh, saints." Melanie came to stand beside me, and together we watched the plume rise into the pale blue sky. "People are jumping."

Small, flailing bodies dropped into the water. Even from this distance, we could hear the shrieking of metal as suspension wires loosened and the bridge couldn't hold itself up. The deck was splitting apart, dripping toward the bay.

"They're trying to swim to shore." I leaned on the windowsill. "We need to get those people out of the water before the deck falls in. The suction will drown them. Boats. We need boats."

I started for the hall to tell James, but Melanie grabbed my arm, pulling me back. "Rescue boats are already on the way. Look." She turned her attention outside again. "James trained everyone well."

She was right: a dozen boats sliced through the water.

"Who would do this?" Desiree Symonds pressed a handkerchief to her mouth. "Saints help them."

"Lien. Of course it was Patrick Lien." Prince Colin was still in the room, witnessing the whole thing from my father's chair at the council table. "Who hates the Indigo Kingdom? Who resents their coming here? And who wants Wilhelmina to be queen?"

Melanie shifted her weight toward me. Her fingers grazed mine before she took my hand. "He said he had a plan to keep Indigo Kingdom refugees from crossing into Aecor, once you were safely home. But he didn't tell me how. Like I said, he was very careful about who knew what, and how much. He didn't want to have to change his plans if someone was captured."

I frowned and watched as the first boats reached the bridge.

Heavy cables dangled into the water, and the deck had slid down even farther, but the rescue was in progress. Horseback soldiers and medical wagons approached from the road.

"But I've been here over three months. Why would he wait until now?" What had changed between yesterday and today? "Skyvale."

Melanie nodded. "The city fell, and the Indigo Kingdom is in shambles. It's the Red Militia's way of shutting the door on their faces when they need us most."

"The Red Militia will pay for this." The former crown prince quit the room, leaving Melanie and me to watch the rescue for several more minutes. The deck finally slid into the water, creating a deep suction. Boats strained against it. People vanished beneath the waves and didn't surface again.

"All those people." I pressed my hands to my chest as bodies began washing to shore. Some were alive. Some were not. "Can we repair it? It's just one section." One section of an enormous, ancient bridge.

Melanie rubbed her temples. "I'm not sure. Maybe we can do something to get the rest of the refugees across, but it would be temporary."

"Once the injured are cleared and the dead removed, I want someone to ensure there are people working on the bridge. Get boats to the other side, with ropes and ladders—anything people can use to climb down. Their possessions might have to wait, but at least they'll have their lives."

"I'll assign someone immediately."

"Good." I faced my friend and lowered my voice, because beyond her, the rest of the nobles and their guards were staring out their own windows. "Once you have someone on that, I want you to come with me. We're going to visit Claire."

"Do you think she's responsible?"

"We're going to find out."

THIRTY-SEVEN

IT WAS THE middle of the day when I warned James that Melanie and I were going out. We disguised ourselves as boys, armed ourselves, and headed toward the lowcity.

News of my impending coronation had already spread outside the castle, along with gossip fueled by the bridge explosion. The subjects mixed together like spilled inks, darkening the rumors I'd have to address later.

"The queen will be crowned tomorrow, and her wraith boy collapsed the bridge to trap the Indigo Kingdom people here."

"No, the Red Militia did it because they don't want Wilhelmina to be queen."

"It was those Indigo people. They're protesting the coronation."

"But why would they collapse the bridge?"

"I don't know. . . ."

The rumors swirled on and on as Melanie and I slipped

through the crowds, the hoods of our cloaks drawn low to hide our faces. Midday heat pressed against the city like a solid force, though it was too early in the year for hints of summer.

Maybe it was an effect of the wraith on the way.

I shuddered as Melanie and I made our way to the water-processing factory. At the door, she knocked twice, waited a beat, and knocked three times—our code for Claire that we were about to enter.

She waited in the center of the room, her hands on her hips. "You're here about the bridge." There were rarely questions with her, just blunt, straight-to-the-point statements. "I didn't do it, and I don't know who did."

"Will you find out?"

"Why should I?" She strode toward us, her jaw tight and eyes hard. Her steps echoed and the whole place had a sense of emptiness about it. Though we rarely saw many of the others, there were often signs of their presence: whispering, clothing dropped in corners, and packages of food. But now, I sensed only stillness in the factory.

"Where is everyone?" I asked.

"Gone."

"Working?" Melanie didn't sound hopeful.

"Maybe." She gave a one-shouldered shrug and tilt of her head, trying to look casual, but red rimmed her eyes, and the skin underneath was swollen.

I made my voice gentle. "Claire, what happened?"

She shook her head and started to turn, but I grabbed her arm and drew her back. She pulled a knife and held the edge to my neck.

Melanie already had her daggers out, one on Claire's wrist and the other on her throat. I, too, had snatched a dagger with my free hand, and pressed it against Claire's stomach.

No one moved.

My heart sped in my throat, and carefully I relaxed my grip on Claire's arm. "My apologies for grabbing you."

Claire shook it off as she sheathed her knife. "No harm done."

"What happened to everyone? Where are they?"

She glared at a wall. "After Patrick was captured, the Red Militia fractured. When I stopped the riots, others began to question what we were doing or where orders were coming from. I could influence, but not control, what actions other sections took."

I nodded. Those were things we'd already discussed.

"But yesterday, my people began to disappear. Astor, Laura, Darcy. Adrian was here this morning, but I haven't seen him since the bridge explosion."

"You think they've found someone new to rally around?" Muscles around Melanie's jaw clenched.

"Not someone new." Claire locked eyes with Melanie. "Patrick. He's in control. He has been this entire time."

"From prison?" I hadn't been to see Patrick since the day we arrived, but I checked in with his guards frequently. James had selected them himself, so I'd trusted they were loyal to me.

But maybe not.

"The Red Militia is organizing again," Claire said. "Since your return, Patrick allowed them to run loose, causing chaos and hurting refugees, but nothing too big. Nothing you'd need to come down on too hard. But now the Indigo Kingdom is gone, and you're to be crowned queen. The anniversary is tomorrow."

I glanced at Melanie, and she nodded. Our next stop would be to Patrick's cell.

"You should return to the castle with us," I said. "There could be a place for you on the Queen's Guard."

"I'm hardly the type to serve."

"No, you're the type to fight for a cause."

"And that cause is you?"

"That cause is our kingdom's freedom from tyrants and overlords. That cause is food and water and safety for everyone. That cause is acceptance of our abilities while keeping the land clean of wraith." I shifted my weight to one hip. "I've had people working on the water problem. Within a few months, we'll be able to use this factory to clean water and pump it to the lowcity without using magic."

Claire released a smile. "Thank you."

"I promised I'd look for a solution." I glanced at Melanie. "We have to go."

Claire gave a small bow. "Tomorrow, after you're crowned, I'll be there to swear my fealty and accept the position. I'll fight for your causes."

I saluted, a snap and thump. "Until tomorrow, Claire."

Melanie and I were out the door and halfway back to the castle when she asked, "Are you sure you can trust her? She could be angling for a place closer to you to do more of Patrick's work."

"Am I sure? No." We dodged a cart and group of people selling raw fish. "The Grays can keep an eye on her, but she's risked her neck for me for months. I want to trust her. What do you think?"

"She was loyal to Patrick during the fighting, because she believed he'd make things right. If she truly believes you're on the same path, with less bloodshed, she'll be loyal to you."

"Well, then I just have to be sure I don't fail her." Or anyone else.

An entire kingdom was counting on me.

Paige walked with us on our way to the prison.

"I've been preparing the throne room for tomorrow's ceremony," she said. "And the ballroom for the celebratory ball."

The frivolous ball, but I didn't say it out loud. It was necessary to keep peace with certain traditions. "What's your progress?"

"Your mother's crown has already been removed from the vault and is being cleaned right now." Paige checked her list. "Oh, and Rosanne Wallace will fit you for the coronation and ball gowns the minute you can stand still."

"Will she have time to make them?"

"They're both already finished. They just need alterations. I hear Rosanne started working on the ball gown the day you arrived." Paige winked. "People have been waiting ten years for this. The anniversary, your coronation, Aecor's independence once more. Tomorrow will be glorious."

So much pressure on one day.

"You're doing a fine job. Let me know if there's anything else you need." I left Paige to her work and headed toward the prison with Melanie.

Sergeant Wallace was on duty in the guard room, along with a few other men in blue. They stood and bowed when I entered, and I took the time to meet their eyes and greet them by name.

Was one of these men the traitor? Or someone else?

"I need the visitor logs." I didn't move from my position, letting a guard named Jonah Hudson bring the current list to me.

"I'll fetch the older logs for you." He went to one of the filing cabinets and began pulling folders.

While I skimmed through the lists of names, looking for anyone who visited frequently or at odd times, Melanie moved around the room, scanning desks and shelves.

"Is there something I can help you find, Your Majesty?" Sergeant Wallace asked. Like the others, he stood at his desk, a hint of anxiety in his eyes and posture. That could be attributed to anything, though: my coronation, the bridge collapse, the fact that I was visiting the prison.

Or it could be guilt.

"No, Sergeant, thank you."

This uncertainty was awful. I should be able to trust the people under my command. It was one of the lessons Tobiah had been most insistent I learn. And I was *trying*, but if one of these people was a traitor . . .

When Sergeant Hudson brought another handful of folders to me, I flipped through and pulled out the ones dated since Patrick's incarceration. I gave the remaining folders back to him and turned to Melanie. "Ready?"

She gave a clipped nod, but her eyes spoke differently. Was anyone ever *ready* to interrogate someone like Patrick?

Not just someone like Patrick, but the man she'd been in love with? The man she'd thought she could redeem?

The man who turned out to be a murderer?

As we entered the cell block, I took her hand in mine. "I'm counting on you. You know him better than anyone."

"I'll do my best." She pulled back to straighten her clothes and run her fingers through her hair. Then we strode down the hall, between the cells holding almost a hundred Red Militia members.

Most of them ignored us, but a few jeered, some called me "Indigo whore," while others called out that Queen Wilhelmina was here, and everyone should behave. I didn't look directly at any of them, just kept my head high as Melanie and I made our way to Patrick's cell at the far end of the hall.

He was sitting, elbows on his knees and hands clasped before him. His short hair had grown a few finger lengths, and stubble covered his chin and throat, but when he looked up, his expression was as hard as ever.

"Wilhelmina." He didn't blink as he assessed my appearance. "You should get more sleep. You look exhausted."

"I've been too busy chasing your Red Militia."

"And after all that work seizing your kingdom for you." The words were flip, but there was no humor in his tone. "You should show some gratitude."

"There was an explosion on Snowhaven Bridge earlier. Did you organize that?"

He gestured around his cell. "I've been in here, Wilhelmina. Tell me how I could do anything."

"How are you communicating with the Red Militia?"

Silence.

"The Red Militia is coming together again. What is the purpose?"

Nothing.

"Who is your informant here?"

For an hour, I attacked from different angles, but he'd stopped talking whatsoever, and I had a flash of what it must have been like for James when he'd questioned me about King Terrell's murder.

Melanie waited at my side, her arms crossed and all her weight to one hip as she studied Patrick's manner. When I shot her a small, questioning look, she shook her head.

Even to the people who'd once believed they knew Patrick best, he was unreadable.

We pressed for another half hour before I backed off and ushered Melanie down the hall. "He's useless. Let's go."

Her face was tight; he hadn't even acknowledged her.

Just as we were out of his sight, Patrick cleared his throat.

I held a hand up for Melanie to stay, and then took a single step to see inside his cell.

He'd stood, hands behind his back and shoulders straight, and watched me with the same intense gaze he'd always worn: carefully crafted neutrality. He'd perfected it over the years. "Congratulations, Wilhelmina. You're really going to be queen tomorrow. It's just what I always wanted for you."

My own facade slipped. "How did you hear about that?"

"I hear everything." His eyes never left mine as a terrible, threatening smile formed. "Be mindful of Colin. No doubt you've made a real enemy out of him."

That was as much as I'd get.

* * *

"What do you think?" Melanie asked once we were on our way to my rooms.

I handed the visitor logs to her. "Perhaps we can find our traitor in here."

"Yes, hopefully our traitor is stupid enough to sign in under their real name." But she took the folders. Back in my rooms, we ordered dinner.

While we waited, we organized the logs and compared names and frequency of visits. A few people stood out for visiting every week, but were quickly explained. One had a cousin in prison, while another had an uncle. Of course, just because they said they were visiting relatives didn't mean they weren't actually visiting Patrick, but surely one of the guards would have noticed.

None of the listings specified they were visiting Patrick.

"Did any of the guards look suspicious to you?"

Melanie finished reading the last page of visitors and shook her head. "I'm the head of your secret intelligence. Everyone looks suspicious to me." She flashed a smile, but it didn't diminish the seriousness of her words. "I'd be shocked if it were any of the blues. It's possible, but unlikely. There are a number of reds who work in the prison, including Sergeant Wallace—"

The parlor door opened and Danie came in with a tray. Her cheeks were flushed. "Pardon," she whispered, and began to set up our dinner while we hurried to clear space on the table. "Do you need anything else, Your Majesty?"

I started to tell her no, but maybe there was something she could help with. "How much do you know about Sergeant Wallace?"

She blushed again, glancing from me to Melanie and—barely—to the pile of visitor logs on the table. "I haven't had the courage to talk to him yet, if that's what you mean."

"I don't want to pry into your personal life," I said. "Just . . . tell me what you know about him."

Her mouth formed an O as she finally understood the question. "He comes from a good family, Your Majesty. His mother is a magnificent seamstress. I never knew his father, but by all accounts he was a good, loyal man. Sergeant Wallace was gone for a while, first to the wraithland front, and then with the Red Militia. I'm sure it's been quite difficult for him. Some people think he's a Red Militia sympathizer, because he's kind to the prisoners, but I think it shows he has a good heart. He's loyal to you, Your Majesty. Very loyal."

"I'm sure he is." I smiled and reached for my silverware. "Thank you, Danie. That will be all for now."

She curtsied and left the room.

"You just let her go?" Melanie stared after her, expression like steel. "You know she's Patrick's source, right? You picked up on that?"

"Being queen hasn't made me stupid, Mel." I grabbed a buttered roll. "I noticed her in the visitor logs, and the way she made sure to throw suspicion on Wallace for being kind to prisoners."

"They could be working together," Melanie said.

"I don't think so. She wouldn't have tried to make him look guilty. No, she invented her affection to give her a reason to go to the prison. She could easily say she was looking in on someone for me, or plant a note on Patrick's meal tray. There may be more involved."

Melanie blew out a breath. "I'll alert James and have him look into it."

"It's a good disguise. Who would suspect the queen's own maid of treachery?"

"Not the queen."

I flicked my little finger at her. "And not the head of secret intelligence."

She smirked. "You're the worst best friend."

"I know. Just make sure James moves quickly on this. Whatever Patrick has planned, it will be big. The bridge was just a warning. The real event will happen tomorrow."

As tempting as it was to postpone the coronation and deal with the Red Militia first, that would send an undesirable message to the rest of my enemies, Prince Colin included.

"What can I do for you?" James asked when he arrived at our summons. His eyes cut to the notebooks on my desk, lifeless now.

"Do you have any proof?" he asked, after Melanie caught him up.

Melanie crossed her arms. "Isn't the queen's word enough?"

"No, James is right." I leaned back in my chair. "I won't be the sort of queen who makes arrests based on suspicion and fear. But I want her watched. I want to know where she goes, who she speaks with, and every detail about her history with the Red Militia."

"Do you want her replaced?" Melanie asked. "If she's a traitor and spy, you can do better for a maid."

"She is a good maid. Aside from possibly being a traitor and spy. She keeps my rooms immaculate." I did wonder if the frightened-maid act had been just that—an act. Or maybe she'd been afraid of being caught. "No, leave her until we know more. If she's working with other staff around the castle, I don't want to hire another spy."

"We must act quickly, though," Melanie said. "The anniversary and your coronation are tomorrow."

"As if I could forget." I stood and straightened my dress, breathing through the reminder of friends not here, and the king whose death meant I would be crowned queen. "There's another thing I need to do. I'm going to invite Chrysalis to the coronation."

Both their eyes went round. "Are you sure that's wise?" James asked.

After the memorial, when he'd collapsed the cathedral.

After the wedding, when he'd killed Meredith.

"No, I'm not sure. But he's had moments of usefulness. At the bridge, during the first Red Militia riot, and he's been quiet since. I've kept him in his room, and he's done nothing but obey. He isn't *safe*. He isn't to be *trusted*. But I can't keep him caged forever. He needs to be given some movement, and this will allow that."

James muttered he was going to triple security. As if tomorrow wasn't going to be stressful enough.

After they were gone, I headed for the wraith boy's room, a pair of silent guards trailing after me. They waited in the hall with the guards assigned to the storage room.

"I'm pleased you've come to see me." Chrysalis grinned as I drifted toward his sleeping pallet where piles of folded clothes waited.

"I need you to pick something nice to wear tomorrow."

His smile dropped. "I like this." He pinched a corner of his tattered, dirty blue jacket between his fingers, and held it up as though for me to see. "Can't I just wear this?"

I lifted an eyebrow. "Do you really not know?"

"Know about what?" He rubbed the dirty jacket between his fingers, still pouting.

I picked through the clothes for something both clean and acceptable, and pulled out a jacket and breeches, both white. "When you first transformed, you were completely white. Maybe these, to remind everyone how far you've come since then."

He shook his head, staring at the clothes in a forlorn way. "I'm definitely going to get those dirty."

"That would be very embarrassing for me." I dug out a pair of white stockings to match.

"Why? No one cares what I wear, or if I get it dirty."

"Not tomorrow." I folded my choices and separated them from the rest. Then I turned to meet his eyes—my mirror eyes. "Tomorrow, you'll be wearing these clothes to my coronation."

His jaw dropped. "I can go?"

I forced a smile. "If you dress properly and promise to behave, you're invited."

"I will do anything you want, my queen." Chrysalis knelt and lowered his head in genuflection. "Anything you want."

THIRTY-EIGHT

EARLY THE NEXT morning, the seamstress, Rosanne Wallace, came to my room with a long, paper-wrapped package.

"What is that?" I glanced at the clock; it wasn't even dawn.

"This was your mother's coronation gown." She turned on the light and hung the gown from the top of the wardrobe. Though there were likely several layers of paper for protection, the whole package seemed bigger than necessary. At least twice the size of any normal gown. "I thought you might wear it today. It was her mother's before her, too."

So it was old, out of fashion, and probably ready to fall apart. That seemed appropriate.

I rinsed my face and mouth before allowing her to measure me. She was quick and gentle, and muttered numbers to herself as she went. The whole time, the gown waited beneath its packaging, huge and mysterious.

"You're taller than your mother," said Rosanne. "And

skinnier. We can let out some of the hem and take in some of the seams, but you won't fill it out, I'm afraid."

"I'm used to it." I stepped off the measuring stool and started for the washroom again. The coronation was at noon, the ball in the evening, and then I'd be back to running the kingdom, this time with actual authority.

A terrifying thought.

"You'll look beautiful today, even if I lose a finger to this needle."

The corner of my mouth twitched up. "If you bleed on it, then I'll have the vermilion gown, not just the vermilion throne."

"There are a lot of us who've wanted you to take the throne these last months you've been here." She moved toward the dress hanging on the wardrobe.

"I've waited ten years for this day, and now that it's here, I can't stop thinking of everything it's cost." Deaths. Betrayals. The destruction of an entire kingdom. "Patrick always said today would be the day I'd take the crown. If I could have done it yesterday, I would have. Or tomorrow. The idea that I'm doing exactly what he wanted . . ."

I bit off my words. I barely knew this woman.

But she was warm and kind, and my mother had trusted her.

"It may be what he wanted, but it sounds like it's what you wanted, too." She smiled thoughtfully. "Your coronation couldn't fall on a more appropriate day. Today is the day the kingdom was lost—and the day it was reclaimed. Today will be remembered for the rest of time."

* * *

I'd been wrong about the gown: it was old, but it wasn't falling apart. It was a pre-wraith creation of scarlet wool and silk, with gold and silver embroidery over almost every surface. Swirls, angles, and intricate knots: the gown was an extraordinary creation.

The waist was lower than currently fashionable, settling snuggly around my hips and dipping into a knifepoint, but I liked the texture of the embroidery under my palms, and the way it fit flat against my stomach instead of looser like modern gowns. It felt old and regal, like a part of my family's history I'd never had a chance to learn about.

Radiants had crafted this gown, Rosanne told me while she worked. There was an entire book on the subject, filled with details about the type of fabric used, the embroidery thread, and the magic that repelled dirt and moths and rips. Alterations had to be made with special needles—illegal to make under the Wraith Alliance, but the Wallace family had some for emergencies.

Tobiah would have loved to hear about this, but he never would.

My coronation today was only because he was dead.

Tobiah. My Ospreys. Thousands of others.

Rosanne and Melanie swept my hair into a loose, low bun, and secured it with a delicate net of gold silk. They powdered my face, darkened my eyelids, and softened the circles under my eyes.

"Where's Danie?" Usually this was her job.

"Poor thing felt ill this morning, I heard." Rosanne frowned in sympathy. When her back was turned, Melanie lifted an eyebrow and shook her head. Danie was gone.

"That's such a shame," I said, and let them get back to work. So, Danie had run. Just one more thing to deal with today. *After* I had the vermilion throne.

When they put a mirror in front of me, I hardly recognized myself. I looked dramatic and otherworldly as they hefted a thick, red cape and fastened it to the gown's shoulders and sleeves.

"I suppose no one really likes being able to use their arms." I lifted my arms to the side and grimaced at the weight of embroidered wool.

"Try not to do that," Rosanne said. "Practice gliding instead of marching, and pulling the cape with your wrists as well as your shoulders to help distribute the weight. And try not to lift your arms until you sit, when attendants will unclip the cape. They'll fasten it again when you need to stand."

"My gown requires attendants." Unbelievable.

Rosanne nodded. "Many queens' clothing required either attendants or magic, pre-wraith. Fashion was forced to become simpler a hundred years ago."

The gown had a short train, and the cape yet another. "How am I supposed to sit with all this?"

But the clock on the mantel struck noon, and when Rosanne finished clasping my chain around my neck—my child-sized signet ring dangling from the end like a pendant—she hurried from the room.

"I'll fetch Chrysalis," Melanie said on her way out. "I'll keep him out of trouble and make sure he gets back to his room once the ceremony is finished."

"Thank you." I stepped out to find James in his dress uniform, waiting to escort me.

I gave him a moment to notice the gown, the sleeves, the enormous cape. A faint smirk appeared on his face.

"Say anything and I'll smother you with my cape."

"I was just going to suggest that red is your color."

With a weak smile, I practiced my glide on the way to the throne room, and James offered unnecessary reminders: when to move, when to sit, what to say before and after the crown went on, and how to respond to the endless line of people swearing fealty to me.

The throne room doors were closed, only a pair of guards outside to watch for our arrival. One in red, one in blue. Both bowed. A rumble of voices came from within.

James signaled to the guards, and they hauled open the doors with a creak muffled by the sound of voices.

A hush fell over the crowd and all eyes turned toward the open doors. Merchants, soldiers, and nobility from all over. I caught smiles from the Calloways and Gray brothers, and a sullen frown from Prince Colin near the front.

I held my place while James strode down the aisle, tailcoats fluttering behind him. When he stood at the dais where the vermilion throne waited, he faced the audience. "It's Aecorian tradition for visiting royalty to make a speech on coronation day. I regret that my cousin, King Tobiah, is no longer with us. Princess Wilhelmina has asked me to speak in his place. . . ."

There had to be a thousand people here. Everyone was crammed in close, and the stink of so many bodies wafted into the hall. But the tall, narrow windows on either side of the throne were wide open, which seemed rather unsafe, but this side of the castle overlooked a cliff and marsh and the wreckage of Snowhaven Bridge, rather than the city.

James had stopped talking.

Everyone was looking at me again.

I'd missed my cue, but the benefit of being queen was that people waited.

James stepped aside as I began what I hoped was a stately glide down the narrow aisle. As I passed, a couple of people reached out to brush their fingers against my sleeve, or touch the hem of my cape. Sometimes others shooed them away.

I clenched my jaw and kept my eyes on the throne, in silhouette earlier, but now that I was closer and the light had shifted, I could see that it was indeed carved from deep red wood, polished and gleaming, with a thin red cushion.

When I reached the dais, I climbed the steps and somehow—miraculously—managed to maneuver the dress and cape as I turned.

Standing before the crowd, my heart stumbling over itself, I wanted to pull back and slip into a persona. I wanted to wear the mask of a queen, something to hide behind so I didn't have to think about the enormity of what I was doing. Becoming *queen*.

But not now. Not this time. These people needed me, Wilhelmina, not my impersonation of what I thought a queen should be. So as I spoke the rehearsed words, I found Melanie in the front of the crowd, Chrysalis close to her side, and said it all to my best friend.

I'd fight for my people. I'd rule fairly. I'd always remember that I served them.

When I finished, she smiled and offered a slight nod, and

I performed the miracle of sitting while wearing an impossible gown. A pair of attendants sneaked up to unclip the cape from my sleeves.

A priest approached with a gold crown resting on a scarlet cushion.

Like my gown, the queen's crown was an intricate display of swirls and angles and knots, all twisted into a delicate dome. There were no gemstones or pearls on it, no bands of silk or pads to soften its weight.

When the priest said the Saints' Blessing over the crown, and then over me, my breath came in quiet gasps.

This was it. This was the day I'd waited over half my life for. I caught Melanie's eye just before the priest's sleeve swung in front of my face.

Then the weight began to settle. First in the front, around the sides of my head, and finally the back. It was forward heavy, but before I could reach up to straighten the crown myself, the priest nudged it back for me.

"Steady," he murmured. "Try not to move your head."

Glide. Don't move my arms. Don't move my head. Queens weren't allowed to do anything but sit in difficult dresses.

Someone cheered. Maybe Melanie, maybe the wraith boy, maybe someone else. But all at once, everyone was cheering. The sound shook the throne room, making the stone floor vibrate under my feet.

I was queen.

"Queen Wilhelmina! Queen Wilhelmina!"

Queen when I'd realized maybe I shouldn't be. Queen

because friends had died for it. Queen because there was no one else.

I'd been given more lines to say as people approached to swear their fealty. To some people, I agreed they would keep their lands and titles. To others, I granted what they'd lost during or since the One-Night War. To most, I simply accepted their offers of service.

I was partway finished when someone's attention strayed to the window beside the throne and they gasped. "The bridge!" Others shuffled closer to the windows to look.

"What?" I started to turn my head, but the crown slipped. I steadied it as I twisted to look out the window. "Oh, saints."

The bridge was whole. Debris floated in the water, and cleanup teams were hard at work, but the bridge was entire. The deck—a new one, perhaps—stretched across the gap, and scores of people were crossing. Running, like they were afraid this was temporary.

"Melanie?"

She was at my side in an instant. "I didn't have anything to do with this. How could I?"

"I was hoping you were just really good at your job."

"The only thing I've done in the last hour is take the wraith boy back to his room."

The answer was clear, though: a flasher was responsible.

A hum of anticipation filled the room as wagons and carts trundled across the bridge. People on horseback carried blue banners.

There were hundreds of new arrivals. Thousands, even.

419

After a while, the fealty oaths began again, but the distraction was obvious. Everyone from the Indigo Kingdom hoped one of their loved ones had crossed. But until the coronation was over, it would be insulting to leave, so everyone waited while we all tried to finish as quickly as possible.

An hour later, I'd accepted oaths from the remaining Aecorians, wondering if I should hold off on officially granting wardship to the Indigo Kingdom refugees until the rest arrived, when an attendant knelt and murmured, "Representatives from the Indigo Kingdom hope to greet you on your coronation day."

"Send them in." My head ached under the weight of the crown, and I was sweating under all the layers of clothes, but a good queen would greet them anyway.

The next part wasn't rehearsed, but I knew what to say.

I lifted my voice for the entire throne room. "Any remaining oaths of fealty will be taken tomorrow. People of the Indigo Kingdom, I know you must be eager to see who's arrived, so should you wish to become citizens of Aecor, that will happen tomorrow as well. Per the Wraith Alliance, titles of rank and nobility will remain, but will not hold any true authority unless specifically granted."

From near one of the windows, Prince Colin shot me a glare, but there was nothing he could say to contradict me.

The crowd shuffled and a few merchants and soldiers slipped out side doors to help make more room. People moved away from the center of the throne room, giving me a direct view of the representatives at the door.

They weren't just representatives, but people I knew: Queen Francesca and her sister, Kathleen Rayner. Chey, Margot, and

420

a few other familiar faces from the ladies' solar. And there was Sergeant Ferris and Captain Chuter, and—

A black-cloaked figure stepped ahead and pushed back his heavy hood and strands of unruly hair before he looked up.

King Tobiah Pierce.

PART FOUR

THE RADIANT HEIRS

THIRTY-NINE

THE THRONE ROOM was utterly silent as others recognized the new arrivals.

Four more people squeezed forward, eyes wide as they stared at the throne room, the inhabitants, and me.

Ospreys: Connor, Theresa, Carl, and Kevin.

They were alive.

As I leaned forward to stand, the attendants hurried to clip my cape into place. The heavy gown dragged at me, but I took to my feet and kept my neck stiff so the crown didn't slip as I descended the dais steps, almost dreamlike.

Everyone was watching, but there was only one pair of eyes that drew me in. Dark. Mysterious. Familiar. He was dirty, and exhaustion marked his face with lines around his mouth and hollows under his eyes. He was *alive*. He'd never been so beautiful.

"Tobiah Pierce." His name felt warm and sharp and hopeful. I stopped myself before repeating it, just to feel its shape again, but everything inside me felt like lightning. He was here. He was real. "I'd heard you were dead." Only years of practice kept emotion from cracking my voice now.

"I certainly hope I'm not." He was moving forward, too, striding toward me with the strangest half smile and heat in his eyes. The intensity, the honesty, was almost too much. It made the moments longer, like every step we took toward each other would be forever etched into my memory.

Others followed behind him. Some were quietly greeting friends, while others looked around with suspicion written on their faces. The Ospreys had already sneaked through the crowd and were hugging the Gray brothers, Paige, and Melanie.

Tobiah stopped just before me, tall, slender, and proud. When he reached from under his cloak to straighten my crown, I held so, so still. His fingers breezed through a strand of my hair; the near touch was electric. "You'll get used to wearing this," he whispered.

The crown. Yes. It was hard to think about the crown when he was here. He was alive. All the Skyvale Ospreys were, too. All the grief I'd trapped inside until I had a spare second to examine it and feel it—it surged through me now, transforming into relief.

I blinked away the tears blurring my vision. "You stopped writing. That was inconsiderate."

"Terribly rude, I know. But I brought you a gift. Maybe you'll find it in your heart to forgive me." He stepped aside and swept out one arm, cloak fluttering. A line of men pushing canvas-covered carts came through the door.

Five carts. Ten. A dozen.

Everyone in the throne room stared silently as the men ripped away the canvas to reveal hundreds of thousands of palm-sized mirrored scales.

The Indigo Kingdom barrier.

Whispers cascaded through the room as people realized what Tobiah had brought, and what it could mean for Aecor. A cheer erupted, clapping and weeping and thankful prayers to the saints.

"Queen Wilhelmina Korte." Tobiah dipped his eyes, a quick warning before he took my hand and lifted it to his chest.

Mine felt ready to explode, but I breathed through the sweeping elation of his life, our nearness, and the sound of his voice saying my name. I would be regal. I would be a queen.

"Wilhelmina," he said again, and brought my hand to his lips. He kissed my knuckles, his eyes closed and his fingers tightening around mine. It lasted a heartbeat too long for politeness, and not nearly long enough for my heart. His jaw tightened when he released my hand. "I'd like to congratulate you on your ascension to the vermilion throne, and formally request refuge in the kingdom of Aecor—both for myself, and for my people. The Indigo Kingdom is lost. You are our only hope."

It was a terrible, heavy burden.

Still, it was a burden I'd sworn to carry, so I pressed my hand to my heart and lifted my voice to be heard over the din. "King Tobiah Pierce, you and yours are welcome in Aecor for as long as you'd like. My home is your home."

The coronation ceremony ended there.

Tobiah and James embraced. James's mother found him and

427

kissed his forehead again and again, while his expression shifted from glad to embarrassed. Though I took a few minutes to greet the Ospreys and Indigo nobility, there wasn't time to enjoy this gift of their lives.

Paige hurried up to me, panic in her eyes. "Where will we *put* them? All the best rooms are already taken."

I resisted the urge to groan. "See if anyone is willing to cede their rooms to those with higher rank. Others will have to double up or go to inns, with apologies, but there's no other way."

She nodded and scanned the newcomers, already sorting them in her mind. "The rooms you had as a child haven't been taken. Would it cause offense if I offered them to the queen mother?"

"Probably, but they *are* rooms reserved for royalty. It may be helpful to remind her of that."

"I will. And shall I remove Prince Colin from his room for King Tobiah? I *know* that will cause problems, but Prince Colin may tolerate it for his nephew."

Problems indeed. I scanned for Prince Colin in the chaos. He was standing with his arms crossed and glaring around the throne room. Our eyes met, maybe for only a second, but it was more than enough time to communicate deep, boiling rage.

I turned back to Paige. "Put Tobiah in the king's chambers."

"Very good." She hurried off to set the room assignments in motion, and I moved to call a council meeting in one hour.

Quickly, my crown was taken back to its vault, not to be seen until the next event worthy of its attendance, and Melanie and Theresa joined me in the queen's chambers. I sent Theresa to the washroom to clean up; it'd be faster than waiting for her own rooms to become available.

Thumps and voices in the adjoining room indicated maids' presence—cleaning and dusting and preparing for King Tobiah's arrival.

"Tell me about Danie," I said.

Melanie stilled. "Danie and a handful of other castle staff are missing. A valet and two other maids. They've fled. Patrick is still where we left him, at least."

That was a relief.

"Whatever their plans are," she said, beginning to unclip the cape from the rest of my gown, "they don't want to interfere with your coronation."

"Patrick wouldn't."

A deep voice came from the next room, as familiar as the sound of my own breath. He thanked the maids and the door shut. Then, Tobiah and James began a low conversation, the captain no doubt apprising his king of everything that had happened.

Melanie drew my gaze from the doors between the king's and queen's chambers, both locked for propriety's sake. "That night at Snowhaven Bridge, James wasn't joking when he said you liked Tobiah." She gave me a long, appraising look.

"Was it obvious?"

She smirked and swept the cape away in a ripple of velvet and silk. "You two nearly started a fire in there. I thought the whole castle would combust when he took your hand."

"Scandalous lies."

"You put on that uniform every week and prowl the city like a vigilante queen. You said you *missed* that menace, and you had this look I've never seen on you before. And then when King Tobiah came in this afternoon . . ."

"Well, aren't you the head of secret intelligence?" I closed my eyes and exhaled, long and slow.

"Saints," she whispered. "I never imagined those two might be the same. Tobiah was Black Knife all along?"

"Until I took over." Cool air slithered against my skin as we began unbuttoning the heavy gown. "I never imagined either, though. I'd barely wondered who he was. Part of me didn't want to know."

"And now he's living in the next room." Melanie loosened the corset. "What are you going to do about it?"

"Nothing. Chrysalis killed Meredith. At the wedding. Just as the ceremony was almost finished. When he turned to me and said Tobiah was mine now, I knew he never would be."

He never had been mine.

"That's—" Melanie shook her head. "Awful. But now it makes sense. The rumors about what Chrysalis said. The way you choked on Tobiah's name, though I could tell you loved Black Knife."

"I didn't know how to talk about it. Or if I should. It would have meant admitting so many uncomfortable things about my time in Skyvale."

"You can tell me anything. Even if it's that two of the people we used to hate the most are actually the same person and you're in love with him." She tilted her head. "Or just one of them."

"It doesn't matter, thanks to the aforementioned murder." I stepped out of the gown, only a petticoat covering my skin.

"And right now we have more important issues to discuss. The council meeting begins soon."

The council chamber was full.

From my father's seat, I twisted to face Tobiah while he told everyone about the events in Skyvale.

"Once West Pass Watch fell, we realized the barrier wouldn't work—not for the whole kingdom. So we packed the pieces into crates and shipped them east."

"You shipped me east, too." Francesca feigned annoyance. "Many of the ladies and I went to Hawes at the same time, the barrier among our belongings. Tobiah was concerned that if people realized what was being transported, the pieces would be taken and improperly assembled. Wasted before we knew whether they worked."

"You guarded them well, Mother." He took her hand and smiled. "I tried to make those four"—he gestured at the Skyvale Ospreys—"leave for Hawes, too, but they insisted they could be useful. And they were. They were instrumental in getting people to evacuation routes, killing wraith beasts, and finding supplies for the journey. Without the Ospreys, we'd have lost thousands more."

The praise made Connor blush, while Carl and Kevin sat up a little taller. Theresa just stared at the table, her jaw clenched tight.

Later, I'd hug them and scold them for not writing to let me know they were alive, but for now I said, "I'm so proud of you. If I had medals to pin on you, I would."

"After we set up the barrier," said Carl. "I'm sure you'll

find something by then— Ow!" He glared at Connor. "If you're going to kick me, don't aim for the bruises."

"Let's talk about your award ceremonies another time." I turned back to Tobiah. "Please, tell us what happened when the wraith arrived."

He kept his posture solid and stiff, but I could see the urge to wilt at the reminder. "At first, it was as though the wraith splashed up against the eastern mountains and stayed contained in the valley. Many evacuees went straight east along the old rail lines, aimed here, but I went south to Two Rivers City, stopping in the towns and villages in between to make sure people were ready to leave."

"Were they?" Paige asked.

"Some." Tobiah's gaze strayed toward the window. "Others had never left their villages, and had no plans to leave now."

"Even if it meant—" Paige pressed her hands over her mouth. "Really?"

He nodded. "I spent a lot of time trying to persuade them before I realized they were more afraid of leaving than they were of the wraith."

How could someone be afraid to leave if it meant they'd live? But maybe there was no way I could understand.

Tobiah turned back to the council. "Most of Lakeside had already evacuated to Two Rivers City, so they were aware of the situation. Still, everyone thought they had several more months, maybe years. After all our projections and careful tracking, no one expected this."

All around the table, people lowered their eyes.

"From there," said the queen mother, "he came to Hawes,

where we continued preparing the kingdom for evacuation."

"Our riders never heard from you," I said to Tobiah. "After your communications ended, we sent people to search for you."

"I was forced to disguise my identity much of the time. Traveling as the king meant I was in constant danger from people who believed I could single-handedly stop the wraith." He turned his palms upward, as though wishing for that ability. "When the wraith began crossing the piedmont, I realized Hawes wouldn't be safe much longer, so we headed for Snowhaven Bridge—which was collapsed partway across, unfortunately."

"Then it was whole," said someone from the back of the room. "We all saw it from the throne room."

"Indeed." Tobiah gazed around the table until he met my eyes. "We took advantage of that and rode across as quickly as possible. Then we came here to find out I'd died and you'd become Queen of Aecor."

"I've never been gladder for false information." My knee touched his and I held there so he'd know . . . what? That I still loved him? Meredith was still between us, her death not that long ago—because of me.

"Me too." Tobiah pressed back, making my breath hitch. "We brought as many supplies as we could, including food, livestock, and building materials."

"Thank you. We can go over the specifics tomorrow, when you're recovered from your journey."

"I appreciate it."

"Perhaps we should hold off on tonight's ball so our guests can rest." We didn't really need a ball to celebrate my coronation.

If some believed building a barrier against the wraith was a waste of resources, surely a ball was completely useless.

"I think the ball should go as planned," Prince Colin said. "The preparations are already made. It would be awful to waste the food and hard work people have already put into it."

The food could be given to people in the city, but the hard work was already done.

"I think you should have it," murmured Tobiah. "We can rest tomorrow."

When I glanced around the table, the Ospreys all looked hopeful—for most, this would be their first ball, and Paige had put so much work into it—and even some of the Indigo Kingdom people appeared interested.

"All right."

"That said"—Prince Colin leaned forward—"we should consider what His Majesty's arrival means for Wilhelmina's queenship. As I recall, the Wraith Alliance granted Wilhelmina her queenship only because the sovereign of the Indigo Kingdom was dead. Much to my delight, my nephew is alive."

Silence fell around the table.

"Again, by some miracle." Prince Colin never looked away from Tobiah. "When Patrick Lien shot you, you recovered so quickly, just like your cousin."

Connor slouched into his chair, and James's jaw tightened.

"What are you implying?" A frown pulled at Tobiah's mouth—a reminder of his princely mask. "I've had a long journey and I'm not in the mood to untangle your paranoia."

Prince Colin's voice was steady. "I'm implying that it's convenient you were declared dead, Wilhelmina was crowned queen, and then you arrived immediately after."

Oh, saints. I opened my mouth to tell him to shut it, but Tobiah got there first.

"You think this was convenient?" Tobiah stood and looked down on his uncle. "You think I planned for the wraith to destroy my city? My home? Thousands of my people? You think I planned to have to abandon everything and trek across the wraith-flooded kingdom to seek refuge in the land I was kidnapped to as a child? You think I planned my numerous brushes with death, and having to persuade everyone that coming to Aecor was our only hope of survival? All so that Wilhelmina could be crowned queen?"

No one moved. Not even Prince Colin.

"Even if that had all been planned—which would make me both a mass murderer and capable of seeing into the future—do you think I'd have timed my arrival to look so suspicious? There is nothing convenient about today." Tobiah let that linger, and then he sat down again.

Well. Now that Tobiah had *that* out of the way. "Prince Colin," I said, "you are dismissed."

He shook his head. "I want to talk about the bridge."

I allowed my voice to dip lower, dangerous. "You are dismissed. James, please help Prince Colin to the door."

James stepped away from his place by the wall, but Prince Colin was already up and moving. He paused at the door, taking a heartbeat to glare at Tobiah, and then at me. "Isn't it alarming how quickly King Tobiah recovered from the death of his bride, and now he rises to support the queen who commands the creature that killed our dear Meredith?"

As members of the council glanced at one another, some with disgust or surprise, Prince Colin disappeared down the hall.

Tobiah motioned to one of his guards. "Watch him."

The man bowed and left the room.

"Now," I said, "there's a ball to prepare for. Everyone has one minute to leave the room."

As the council chamber emptied, leaving Tobiah, Melanie, James, and me alone, I drifted to the window from where Melanie and I had watched the bridge explode.

"He had a point about the bridge," Melanie said. "The Red Militia was thorough when they collapsed it. Forty-seven people died."

"I didn't think we'd see anyone else from the Indigo Kingdom. At least not for a long time." Outside, the bridge was jagged and broken once more. Gulls circled the dust plumes and remnants. "It was obviously a powerful flasher who made the bridge whole while you came across. All that magic contributed to the wraith, but there's a part of me that doesn't care. I'm just happy to see you again. All of you."

"Radiants," Tobiah said. "I thought we agreed radiants."

Through the notebook. "Yes. We did." I wanted to ask why he'd stopped writing and if he'd seen all the letters I sent after, but when I glanced at him, his eyes were still on the bridge. Muscles tensed in his jaw and neck and shoulders.

He'd survived war and loss and now the wraith.

This morning I'd believed he was dead. Now I faced days or months or years with only a door between us at night, but it might as well have been a kingdom. That door was Meredith and the wraith boy, and the never-fading memory of what he'd done to her.

I understood now what I hadn't before: Chrysalis wasn't good or bad; he was simply power. He wasn't human, but he was part of me, a reflection of my desperate wants.

Last autumn, Black Knife and I had talked about flashers and their magic, and why they might use it even knowing the wraith was coming. I'd said they were desperate, and their desperation made them dangerous.

Chrysalis was my desperate danger.

I'd created him. I was responsible for him. And though I hadn't wanted him to bring down the cathedral or kill Meredith, I'd wanted to be somewhere else and see the night sky, and I'd wanted Tobiah not to marry Meredith.

I understood, now, and how it might be unforgivable.

FORTY

THE BALLROOM WAS heavy with the beat of music, but the dancing hadn't yet begun.

I lingered on the threshold, watching everyone mingle. Though I recognized people from both kingdoms, they weren't as separated as I'd thought they'd be. Francesca spoke with Jasper and Cora Calloway. Lady Chey flirted with Kevin, who watched his tutor, Alana Todd, as she sipped from a glass of wine. Sergeant Ferris smiled at Paige.

The two kingdoms merged into one right before my eyes.

One figure stood apart. He wore solid black, with high, elegant boots and long tailcoats. The way he moved around the room was just like Black Knife: fluid and focused. When a soldier came up to him and spoke into his ear, he offered only a clipped nod and quick dismissal.

"Your Majesty?" The herald lifted an eyebrow, and I stepped forward. He turned to the ballroom to announce me: Her Royal

Majesty Queen Wilhelmina Ileen Elizabeth Korte.

I forced myself to smile as the music seemed to swell and every eye focused on me. I was impossible to miss, dressed in another gown of Aecorian red silk that glittered when I moved. The style was more modern than the coronation gown, but the designs across the bodice and sleeves were similar. This gown, too, boasted a useless cape, but it was shorter and lighter, made of a flowing layer of tiny-beaded silk.

Now that everyone was staring, I made myself look over the crowd appraisingly, as though I'd just arrived and hadn't been watching everyone for an entire minute. I met eyes, smiled warmly, and thanked people for coming tonight.

I said the things a queen would. I walked the way a queen should. As I greeted people by name, I ignored the discomfort knotting in the back of my thoughts. It was too late to change my mind. I'd gotten what I always wanted, and now I had to live with it.

A tall, dark figure stepped in front of me. "Dance?" Tobiah's tone was somewhere between exhausted and annoyed, but when I met his eyes there was something else. There was something desperate and starving in his gaze, and suddenly I couldn't *breathe* with the way he was looking at me.

He hadn't moved; he was a still shadow of a king, so striking and familiar, but foreign all the same. His face had barely shifted from the cool mask of a monarch, but I'd seen it. Like I'd learned to see behind the Black Knife mask, I could see through this one, too.

"I would love to dance." My heart pounded in my throat as I took his offered hand, and together we made our way to the center of the floor. The music shifted, and people cleared away.

The dance took us in measured steps around each other, like two predators circling. We couldn't speak about anything important, not with so many people watching us, but our eyes stayed locked.

To others, it must have looked fierce, like there was a battle between us, but the reality was deeper: I saw straight into his grief.

This was a king who'd lost everything. His father. His fiancée. His kingdom. His home. He'd been helpless to stop it; it was all so much bigger than him.

As the dance brought us closer, I whispered, "I understand."

The tension around his mouth relaxed as the music faded. "I knew you would," he murmured. "Better than anyone, I knew you would."

"You know me." My life, my secrets, my faults.

"I know you." A faint smile pulled at his lips. "Curtsy, Wilhelmina."

We'd stood a moment too long. I stepped back and dipped into a curtsy, while he bowed, and the guests applauded as though we'd saved the whole world from the wraith right there.

I held up a hand and the noise died. "I'm not going to make a speech tonight. I think we've had enough speeches for one day— for the year, perhaps—and we'd all like to see more *action*."

A few people cheered.

"Let's start with dancing and celebration. First thing tomorrow morning, we will face our problems: the Red Militia, the wraith, and the poverty our people have struggled under for so long. Tomorrow, we will begin the process of restoring Aecor."

More cheers rose up, and I had to call over them: "Thank you! Now please dance."

Tobiah walked me off the floor. "That was good."

"No one actually likes speeches." The music started up again, and everyone was talking and moving to take their positions. "They come for the gossip and food. And to show off their wealth. For me, it's about the food."

"Always food with you."

"Live on the streets a few years and life will be about your next meal, too." I hesitated when I saw the line of people near the chairs brought in for everyone with "Highness" or "Majesty" attached to their names. Flags were draped over the backs, and mine stood taller than the others, as though there might be confusion about who sat where.

"You're doing a good job at the showing-off-your-wealth part."

I frowned and slid the back of my hand along the edge of my cape. "I'm not even sure where these gowns are coming from."

"You look like a queen."

I forced a note of teasing into my voice. "And you look like a vigilante."

He looked at me with complete seriousness. "If that's what you want me to be."

Every possible response caught in my chest. Yes? No? I wanted Tobiah to be himself, with or without the mask. But I couldn't say that, not here, and not in front of all these people. Some conversations were best held in the dark.

I took my chair.

For an hour, we spoke to people, watched the dancing, and ate when food was brought our way. At last, people stopped creeping up to us with questions or requests, and I leaned on the arm of my chair, toward Tobiah.

"I wish I were in the city right now, as Black Knife."

He let out a soft snort. "Do you remember the night of my engagement ball?"

I remembered Meredith and how stunning she'd been that evening. I remembered the way she'd looked up at Tobiah, her happiness shining through.

Tobiah didn't comment on my sudden stillness. "Until I danced with you, all I could think about was Black Knife. And then you asked about him. Now I realize what a strange conversation that was. Me, knowing you as the nameless girl. You, knowing me from the One-Night War. Neither of us putting the final pieces together."

"Nothing has ever been simple between us, has it?"

"I don't think anything is simple. Ever." He stood and offered me a hand. "Is there somewhere we can talk?"

"They'll notice we're gone."

"We'll be just a few minutes."

I didn't take his hand, but stood up and led him to a nearby office. When I turned on the gas lamp, the flare of light revealed only an old desk, a couple of bookcases, and a faded painting of a long-dead king. I closed the door behind us, even though James and Oscar were the only ones standing outside.

"I don't remember Sandcliff Castle having so many gas lamps." Tobiah strode to the window and stared out toward the bridge.

"Your uncle had them installed."

"Ah." He glanced over his shoulder. "How does it feel to take your throne at last?"

I leaned a hip on the desk and sighed. "I'd like to say important and monumental, but that wouldn't be the truth."

"Since when does lying stop you from saying something?" His tone was all teasing.

"Never," I said. "But I will change. I want to be an honest and fair queen. I used to think my parents were."

"Perhaps you judge them too harshly? Perhaps they were doing their best."

"Perhaps." I pulled myself straight. "But they didn't even try to find an alternative way to provide the lowcity with clean water, or meet with the Wraith Alliance kingdoms. Perhaps they were doing the best they could, Tobiah, but I want to do better. I must do better."

"I believe you will." He faced me, his expression open and honest. "You have the advantage of empathy."

"What do you mean?"

"Those who crave power tend to be too selfish to have the empathy they need to be good leaders. But you care about your people as individuals, not some teeming mass to be reclaimed and ruled. Even before all of this started, you loved your Ospreys. They were never expendable to you."

No, they weren't. Not like they were to Patrick, just faces with sets of skills, ready to be deployed at his convenience.

My throat was tight. "You can't know how much it means for me to hear you say that."

"I'm not just saying it, Wilhelmina. I believe it." He walked toward me, his face shadowed as he turned from the light. "You will be a good queen, and I will gladly follow your lead now that I am a ward of Aecor."

Oh. He *was* a ward of the kingdom. Just like everyone else who'd crossed the bridge, the Wraith Alliance allowed him to retain his titles, but none of the power unless I granted otherwise.

Tobiah was a ruler in name only, as I'd been just yesterday.

He studied my face, and though I hadn't spoken or given any sort of reaction, he still read my thoughts in my eyes. "The Indigo Kingdom isn't all gone. Not yet. But the valley is. That was the heart of the kingdom. The rest will fall until there's nothing left. I can only hope that all my people find somewhere safe."

"There's nowhere safe," I reminded him.

"But there's still hope."

"Optimistic Knife strikes again."

"That menace." He dared a smile, but it was quickly put out. "My uncle is missing. After the meeting this afternoon, I had him followed."

"I remember."

"Well, they lost him. And now no one can find him. Nor can they find his supporters, the men who were stationed here under him, and even some of the loyalists you freed when you arrived." Tobiah leaned his weight on the desk, shoulders hunched and head bowed low. "It's about five thousand people, total. Nothing we can't defend against, but just the idea of my uncle marching through your city, tonight of all nights—"

"We can defend against it. Did you tell James? He's in charge of castle security, though I suppose you'll want him back."

"James knows." Tobiah closed his eyes, and his throat jumped. "He also told me about the Red Militia—your maid moving information between Patrick and the others, and this looming threat the Militia poses."

"Tonight," I whispered. "It will happen tonight. Patrick needs to make a statement."

Tobiah bowed his head. "That's why you didn't want the coronation ball. What would you be doing instead, though?"

"Denying a pleasure to my friends and guests so that I could indulge in worry and paranoia."

"Indeed. You already have police and military on duty. This is one of those times you need to let other people do their jobs, while you do yours. Right now, your job is to be the great queen people expect you to be."

I didn't feel like a great queen. Or a queen at all. Just a girl dressing up for yet another deception.

"After the wraith came though Skyvale, I felt so helpless. It made me think of you and the One-Night War, and the two of us watching my father's army burn through your city. I couldn't stop wondering if you felt the same hopelessness that night."

"Yes." I almost reached for his hand, but his face was dark and downcast.

"When I left Skyvale, I could have sent someone else for my mother in Hawes. I could have sent someone else to Two Rivers City." He pressed his mouth into a thin line. "But I'd never seen either city before, let alone any of the small towns and villages between. I wanted to go because I needed a memory of my kingdom before the wraith covered it."

"Are you glad you went?"

He opened his eyes and nodded. "The Indigo Kingdom is magnificent."

"Yes, it is." Easily, I could recall the rolling blue mountains, the Midvale Ridge, the glorious valley. It was a place I'd always denied was my home, but now that it was gone, I missed it. I didn't blame Tobiah for taking the time to create one last memory. But . . . "Why didn't you write back to me? Or James? What about the Ospreys? Did you lose the notebooks?"

"No," he said. "We had them. We never let them out of our sight."

"Then you know what you put us through."

"I know." Darkness passed over his eyes. "I had to make everyone believe I was dead. I traveled the Indigo Kingdom under disguise, revealing my identity to only those necessary."

"Why?"

"The Wraith Alliance. I knew James would make the argument for your coronation as soon as my death was presumed. I hoped it would be sooner, but I suppose people don't give up on kings easily."

"You could have waited until you were here. The Wraith Alliance holds even when you're alive."

He smiled faintly. "My uncle would have argued that if I were alive, I would still rule Aecor Territory. I had to leave no room for that. Your claim had to be irrefutable."

"Unfortunately, I think we've only angered him." I didn't like that he and his people were missing. Not at the same time large parts of the Red Militia were missing. Not tonight of all nights.

"I know."

A thread of silence pulled tight between us.

"Wil, I wanted to talk to you about Mere—" Someone

knocked on the door and Tobiah let out a breath of frustration. "Go away."

James poked his head into the room. "I'm sorry to interrupt, but people are looking for you."

"Wilhelmina and I are discussing important matters."

The last thing I wanted to do was discuss Meredith. "It can wait." I caught James's eye and motioned for him to enter. "You two had an argument before James followed me here. It's time to work that out."

Both boys shot frowns. "Are you sure this is the time?" James asked.

"You almost never had the chance to work this out. Don't waste more time."

James faced Tobiah; the two weren't mirror images, but could easily have been mistaken for brothers. Both were narrow faced and strong jawed, with piercing dark eyes. But where Tobiah stood with the lazy grace of disguise, James held himself tall and straight and just like a soldier. "I have to know something."

"All right."

James's expression pinched, as if questioning his king were physically painful. "I think there's something you're not telling me, and that's why you always put off investigating my healing."

Tobiah's expression flattened. "What do you mean?"

"I think you know."

As curious as I was, this was starting to sound like something I shouldn't witness. "I'll leave."

"No." James's eyes cut to me. "I'd like for you to stay."

Oh. Great. I glanced at Tobiah, but his face was hard and revealed nothing. "All right."

James squared his shoulders and seemed to gather his thoughts. "The night I got shot, after Wil created Chrysalis, I shouldn't have lived. I know my wound was as bad as yours. But I healed on my own. Mysteriously. Miraculously."

"It was a miracle."

"Wil said you called her to wake me. Her power doesn't work that way, though. It only awakens inanimate objects. But when she touched my hand—I awakened."

Tobiah's dark eyes darted toward me, like I'd promised to keep a secret and failed him.

"What's wrong with me?" A pleading note touched James's words, though he tried to hide it. "Why did you refuse to investigate?"

Tobiah's hard expression cracked. "Oh, James. Can this wait for another time?"

"No." I moved next to James. "He deserves to know."

James shot me a grateful look. I just hoped the answers were worth it.

"All right." Tobiah glanced at the desk, as though tempted to sink into the chair, but he remained standing. "I need a moment to figure out how to say this."

That sounded ominous.

The desktop clock ticked, and people in the hallway laughed as they walked by. Tobiah let out a long breath. "Maybe we should start with you telling me how much you remember of our childhood."

James shook his head. "I don't want to talk about what I remember. I want answers."

"Please. I'll tell you everything. I just . . . want to know."

"That doesn't seem very fair," I said. "James just wants to know, too."

"It's all right." James sighed. "When we were nine, we got in trouble for swimming in the Saint Shumway fountain. Your idea, of course. And when we were ten—"

"What about before that? Before the One-Night War?"

"That's hazier. But we were young." James frowned, focusing inward. "I remember your seventh birthday party when Lord Roth gave you the pre-wraith spyglass, and we hung out the windows to get a good view of Indigo Order training. I fell and broke my leg. I vaguely remember lessons, before I went to the Academy. Hours and hours of tutors talking about history and mathematics. We were always sleepy from our sword training."

"What about any memories without me?"

After a brief hesitation, James shook his head. "No. But we were together so much then. We always have been."

"You're right," said Tobiah. "We have. But there were times you visited your mother's holdings without me. Do you remember that at all? Before the One-Night War."

"No. I just know I went there."

Tobiah's face was tight with discomfort. "You don't remember because I wasn't there. Because I couldn't tell you what happened."

James and I waited, and finally it came:

"I made the bridge earlier today." Tobiah gestured at the window, a fluttering, fleeting motion. "And ten years ago, I made James."

FORTY-ONE

"I CAN EXPLAIN." Tobiah's voice was rough.

"I hope so." Muscles tightened around James's jaw, and he never looked away from Tobiah. He hardly blinked. "Because right now it sounds like I'm a piece of a bridge. Something you can make appear and disappear."

"No, that isn't it at all." He shoved his fingers through his hair, all the way to the back of his neck, which he massaged for a moment. "This isn't the way I meant to tell you."

"It sounds like you meant to *never* tell," James said. "Saints, Tobiah. The wraith boy knew. He told me months ago that I wasn't human, that I wasn't what I claimed to be. The *wraith boy* told me the truth, but you've been hiding it for a decade."

Silence.

"What am I?" James whispered.

"You're my cousin. My best friend." Tobiah sat on the edge of the desk and kept his voice soft. "That will never change."

"Maybe you should start from the beginning." I pulled out the desk chair and offered it to James. He stared at it for a heartbeat, like he might refuse, but then he collapsed into it. I rested a hand on his shoulder.

"I need to preface it by saying this was the worst point in my life. Even with everything that's happened recently, this is the worst." Tobiah slumped and stared at the ceiling. "The night I was abducted, James, you and I were spying on my father's meeting with Aecorian diplomats, and a man in a red uniform caught us. General Lien." He glanced at me, but there was nothing to say. I already knew General Lien had kidnapped Tobiah and brought him to Aecor to use as leverage.

"What then?" James asked.

"You knew something was wrong when we saw General Lien in the hall. You didn't trust him, so you stayed in my room that night. To protect me." Tobiah's voice caught. "When the general came for me, you were there, armed with one of our wooden practice swords. It didn't stop the general. He crashed into my room and threw you aside. You were unconscious. I fought, but I was so worried about you I couldn't defend myself."

James sat straight and tall, eyes never leaving Tobiah.

"Other men came into the room, just two or three. The general said to take both of us so it would look like we'd run away or were playing a game. Our parents wouldn't know we were missing until morning. I think there was some kind of explosion in Greenstone that night, something that distracted the Indigo Order and police. We were put in a wagon and taken from the city. I don't remember much of that. Just that there weren't many people with us. General Lien wanted to move quickly."

A knock sounded on the door. We all paused and looked over, but no one moved until Oscar's voice came, sending the person away.

"Once we were out of the city, General Lien bound us to a horse. We were gagged, but I could hear you breathing in my ear. You were still unconscious. We rode for hours like that, mostly at a gallop. The general wanted to be as far from Skyvale as possible before dawn."

I barely breathed myself as I looked between the boys. James was ashen, his eyes wide and afraid.

Tobiah blinked away tears. "It wasn't quite light out when I felt your body go slack. You'd stopped breathing."

My skin prickled with a surge of horror. "No."

James looked as though he was struggling to stay upright, and I squeezed his shoulder in a pale measure of support.

There was a pause, like we were all thinking about small James, hurt and kidnapped. And small Tobiah, unable to help his best friend.

"I started screaming around the gag." Tobiah raked his fingers through his hair until it stood on end. "No one heard me over the horse hooves. There were birds chirping and everything was waking up—except for you. After an hour, maybe, they noticed us. We stopped and they took you off the horse. You were pale, bruised. But still limp. They said you were cold, except for the front where you'd been leaning against me. You didn't have a pulse."

Horror crawled over my skin.

"The general had his men throw your body over a cliff."

I pressed my fists to my mouth, but I couldn't look away

from the boys, couldn't stop listening as the story grew worse.

"What happened?" James spoke in a whisper, as though anything more would shatter the spell of memory. "Because I'm not dead."

"A lot of that is a blur now. I know we changed horses. We stopped for a few hours so the soldiers could rest. I was in and out for most of that. The next thing I really remember is waking up in an office, and a girl freeing me from where I'd been tied to a chair."

Tobiah's eyes locked on mine, haunted and dark. "You showed me your magic," he said. "And after my father's people came to rescue me, I remembered it."

"But I can't"—I glanced at James—"bring things back to life. I tried once. There was a stillborn kitten when I was a girl. Nothing happened."

"I know." Tobiah swallowed hard and looked down. "Saints. I wish I could stop there."

"I deserve to know," said James.

Tobiah smoothed his hair down with both hands, and linked his fingers behind his neck. He let out a strained sigh. "Wil, do you remember the trip to the Indigo Kingdom?"

"Not really." Was he about to tell me how I'd died, too? "Some of it, I guess. The way the wagon jumped over rocks. The other children crying. Trying to calm the babies. I don't remember much until the orphanage." I'd just seen my parents slaughtered in the courtyard, cut open by one of Tobiah's rescuers. Everything after that was a wash of nausea and terror.

"The journey back to the Indigo Kingdom was slower." Tobiah turned back to James. "I kept getting questions about you—whether you'd been with me. But I couldn't answer. On the second night, when I was alone in my tent and wishing I didn't have to tell your mother what happened. Or my own. Or anyone. I wished so hard that you were still with me, and then—"

Silence rang through the study as Tobiah caught his breath. He couldn't even say it. So I did. "You wished so hard, and then he was there."

Tobiah closed his eyes and hung his head. He seemed to deflate. "Yes."

"You're a flasher," James whispered.

"Yes." Tobiah crossed his arms, shoulders hunching. "You were just there. I wondered if I'd somehow transported your body from the cliff, but you weren't scratched up or broken."

A new James. He'd made a new James.

"I didn't know what to do, so I went to find the only person I knew who might be able to help. The girl who could bring things to life, and make them do what she said. The animator."

Me.

More voices sounded in the hall, some raised, but Oscar held them off. When it was quiet again, Tobiah continued.

"Wil, I sneaked through the camp to find you. You didn't want to use magic, but I insisted it was an emergency. I was exhausted from using my power. That must have convinced you." Tobiah licked his lips and looked at me like he was waiting for me to remember, but I couldn't. I didn't remember that at all. "You said you couldn't wake the dead, so I wasn't sure if it would work—whether I'd made something new or transported something to me—but I asked you to try anyway. You did. You said, '*Wake up. Be Tobiah's friend and cousin. He is the one who commands you.*' And that was it. You'd transferred control to me, just like that, and James was awake. Alive. After that, Wil, I took you back to the wagon and never saw you again. Not that I realized anyway."

James spoke quietly. "I'm not real."

"You are." Tobiah's attention snapped to James. "You *are* real. You're my best friend. You always were."

"No, he was. *He* was your best friend, that boy General Lien threw over the cliff. I—I don't know what I am." James surged to his feet, blinking rapidly. "Do I even make my own decisions, or do I do everything you say, like Wil's notebooks or the cathedral? Am I any different from the wraith boy? Just a little more tame. More useful."

"You're my friend. My best friend."

"No, I'm not." James strode out the door without a backward glance.

Tobiah started after his cousin, one long stride and his hands curled like claws.

"Don't." I reached, but didn't touch him. "Let him go."

"I need to explain." He faced me, looking desperate and haggard. Red rimmed his eyes.

"You've already said everything. Now let him absorb it."

Tobiah dropped his gaze. "I never wanted to hurt him. I didn't want him to feel like a replacement."

"Give him time. One day he'll understand that nothing has changed. He'll forgive you." He would. There was no one James loved more than his cousin. They'd work it out.

"Will it be his choice? His question was legitimate: has

anything been his choice? What if I've been unconsciously commanding him all this time?"

Like the wraith boy sensed my wants. It was a fair question. "Maybe if he doesn't forgive you and you really want him to, that'll be proof enough."

"Or because I know I don't deserve it." He lifted his eyes to watch me through his lashes. "What about you? I took advantage of your power. I hunted you and other radiants. All along, I had a secret of my own."

It would have been so *easy* to condemn him for his hypocrisy, but I wasn't angry with him. Curious, concerned, and confused: yes. But not angry. "I don't want to fight."

He closed his eyes and exhaled. "Me neither."

"I want to hear all about it. Your power."

A weak smile warmed his face. "It's funny. I've seen you struggle so hard to suppress yours. It's like tying a hand behind your back. You have it. Your natural inclination is to use it, even though you know how dangerous it is. You accept it as part of you."

"Sometimes I wish I could change that," I said.

"But for me, magic is the opposite. I learned to suppress it early. After James—" He glanced at the door. "I wouldn't make James go away, but I didn't want to admit that I'm a flasher, too. That's probably why I fought so hard against magic in Skyvale."

"Sometimes we hate others for the things we hate in ourselves."

He nodded. "Once, you accused me of going after radiants. You were right."

"Such is the curse of being me." I watched him from the corner of my eye. "So that's your power? You make things appear?"

"Appear and disappear. I've only done it a few times, and rarely anything big."

Same as I usually animated only small things. "James and the bridge are exceptions, then? You let go of the bridge pretty quickly."

"Too many things, or too big, and it takes a toll."

Oh, how I understood that. "A boy who makes things appear and disappear, and a girl who brings things to life."

"What a pair we make," he said. "I don't know how you've managed. James, the wraith boy, plus all the things you've animated in addition to that. You must be incredibly strong."

I didn't know about strong, but I'd definitely grown accustomed to the stress of magic. "Keeping him alive." I shook my head. "That's not how my power is supposed to work. But James *is* alive. Chrysalis, too."

Slowly, the puzzle pieces began to fit together.

"But maybe magic things are different," I mused. "Maybe I brought Chrysalis to life because he's made of wraith. James because he's made of magic."

"The Cathedral of the Solemn Hour was made with magic."

"*With*. Not *of*. The materials were mined and shaped with magic, not conjured from nothing."

"But James was." Tobiah glanced at the door, anguish heavy in his eyes. "I wanted to ask for so long, but that would have meant admitting the truth about James and myself." He leaned his weight onto the desk and hung his head. Strands of hair fell over his eyes, and he heaved a long sigh. "That was cowardly of me."

"It was," I allowed. "But also completely understandable. Saints, Tobiah. You know the things I've done—or not done—because of fear."

A cold, uncomfortable silence followed, like the memory of Meredith's lifeless body on the chapel floor.

"I need to talk to James." He looked up at me, eyes red with stress and exhaustion and grief. "He's my best friend. Magic or no magic, that never changed."

"You're a good man, Tobiah Pierce."

"I want to be." He touched my hand, a faint brush of his knuckles over mine that warmed deep into my stomach. "I'll find you later."

I lingered in the study for a few more minutes, wondering if I actually needed to return to the ball. But how would it look if I abandoned it completely? Tobiah had avoided dozens of social events so he could go out as Black Knife, which left his people believing he was lazy and unfriendly.

No matter what I *wanted* to do, I *needed* to fulfill my duty as queen. Which meant dances and dinners, in addition to the real work of running a limping kingdom.

Grudgingly, I started toward the ballroom again, Oscar at my heels.

"Your Majesty!" Sergeant Ferris raced toward me from the opposite end of the hall.

"What is it?"

"Prince Colin," he said, gasping. "He's attacking Aecor City."

FORTY-TWO

"PRINCE COLIN? YOU'RE sure?"

Sergeant Ferris nodded. "He has part of the Indigo Army and Aecorian loyalists."

I'd suspected that much, but I hadn't expected his attack to come immediately.

"Where is his army now?" I asked.

"The lowcity, engaged with the Red Militia."

"The Red Militia?"

Sergeant Ferris dipped his head. "Yes, Your Majesty. The Red Militia is also attacking."

"Saints." That was just what I needed—both enemies attacking my city at once. "Let them fight it out for a while, but clear the civilians. Move them into the castle if you need to. Fill the ballrooms and staterooms. Just get people to safety. Coordinate with Captain Rayner." I frowned at Ferris's and Oscar's uniforms side by side. "I suppose Patrick's people are wearing red, and Prince Colin's are wearing blue?"

Sergeant Ferris nodded. "I'm afraid so."

For ten years, my world had been red against blue, but I could no longer tell my enemies by the colors they wore. "We need something," I said. "Something that's just ours."

"Not ospreys, then?" Oscar crossed his arms.

"No. I wouldn't be surprised if the Red Militia is using that. We need something else." I hesitated, but it was the only thing. "Black knives. Use paint, ink, pitch—I don't care. Put them on the fronts, backs, and sleeves of all of our people's uniforms. We need to identify our friends."

Sergeant Ferris's eyebrows lifted toward his hairline. "Your Majesty—"

"When we first met, you asked if I was Black Knife." Noise from the ongoing ball punctuated my pause. "Yes. I am Black Knife. And so is your king."

Oscar's mouth had dropped open, and Sergeant Ferris turned ashen.

"You have your orders, Sergeant. Live through this and you can change that to lieutenant. I know the queen and king."

"And Black Knife, apparently," Oscar said as Sergeant Ferris ran through the hall. "What do we do next?"

"I need you to gather the Ospreys and get them ready for what they do best. Paige can prepare the castle. Connor and Ronald need to be in triage to help the physicians. Put the others where you see fit. Some should help paint knives on our army so we're ready."

"I should stay with you. I'm your bodyguard tonight."

I rolled my eyes. "Oscar Gray. I have taken care of myself for ten years. I've let you and others follow me around for the last few months because that's what queens do, but right now you're needed elsewhere."

He scowled. "What will you be doing?"

"I'm going to talk to Patrick. He knew Prince Colin was going to attack tonight. I'm going to find out what else he knows."

"I'll send someone for you when I can."

"Don't you dare!"

But Oscar was already trotting away.

With the skirt of my gown hiked up, I ran for the prison.

Patrick had answers.

I shouldn't have put off his warning.

I could apologize. Admit he'd been right. Anything to make him tell me everything he knew about Prince Colin's plans.

As I descended the stairs, a sense of wrongness crept around me. I slowed and listened.

The prison was *quiet*. No guards grumbling that they were missing the ball. No prisoners muttering that they were being mistreated. Just the faint acrid scent of wraith and blood.

When I reached the lower stairs, the copper stench grew stronger. I swallowed a few times to keep everything down.

And then I stepped off the final stair and into the guard room.

Sergeant Wallace and two others were slumped over their desks, blood dripping onto the floor. It came from their fingers, their desks, their hair. No one moved. I hardly breathed as I scanned the room, but nothing else was out of order.

Just the three dead men.

The door to the cell block hung open, only relative darkness waiting beyond.

I kept one eye on the door as I moved from guard to guard, checking for pulses I knew I wouldn't find. They'd all been stabbed in the back of the neck with some kind of large, messy weapon. They hadn't had time to call for help or defend themselves.

I'd have to tell Theodore Wallace's mother.

I blinked away a tear as I slipped into the cell block, lit only by half-empty oil lamps. Listening hard for movement, I pulled two lamps off the wall and held them away from my body. They weren't much of a weapon, but if there was someone here, I could do some damage.

But every cell I passed was empty. The rustle of my dress was the only sound.

And then, a gasp. "My queen! You're here!"

The shock made me reach for a dagger that wasn't on me, and I dropped my lamp. Oil gushed from the broken glass, and flame *whoosh*ed up and around me.

Chrysalis erupted from Patrick's cell and scooped me away from the fire. The other lamp shattered as I tried to scramble away.

"Be *careful*," Chrysalis scolded as he released me in the guard station. Then he noticed the bodies. "Did you do this?" His tone fit somewhere between alarmed and impressed.

"No." I shoved him away and moved toward the stairwell. Heat bloomed from the back of the cell block. The fire was contained there for now, but it would grow if I didn't find someone to extinguish it. "I was going to ask you if you'd killed them."

"No!" He looked offended. "You don't like it when I kill people, so I'm trying to stop."

"Then what are you doing here?" I gestured around the room. "Three dead guards. Empty prison cells. What happened? Where's Patrick?"

Chrysalis pressed his mouth into a line. "Patrick called for me. I heard him, even though he was only whispering my name. He whispered that you were in danger, but he could help. We talked."

My stomach dropped. Just what I needed: two people who'd do *anything* for me to have a discussion. "What did you talk about?"

"He said Prince Colin was coming to get you, and he knew where all Colin's people were going to be. He just needed to get out so he could coordinate."

"You could have come to me, Chrysalis."

The wraith boy shook his head. "I wanted to, but Patrick said you wouldn't do what was necessary to stop them. But he would. He said he'd be the one who did bad things so you didn't have to—and so I didn't have to. He knew I didn't want to disappoint you."

I closed my eyes for a moment.

"He said you'd finally taken your crown, and he was going to help you keep it no matter the cost."

"Saints," I muttered.

"You're not happy that he cares about you that much?" The wraith boy frowned toward the hall where smoke was just beginning to billow out. "He said you liked his help."

"No. Not for a long time. I don't like the things he does."
The smoke grew thicker as it poured from the hall. "Let's go. Up
the stairs."

I'd taken three steps when I realized Chrysalis wasn't following.

"What are you doing?"

He was busy scowling at his feet, and for the first time I
realized he still wore the white tailcoats from the coronation.
"I wanted to make you happy. I let him out of the cell, and all
his friends, because he promised he was going to help you stay
queen, and that's what I wanted, too. I agreed to wait here and
tell you his message because he knew you'd come to see him. But
I was wrong. I did something bad."

"It's fi—" I exhaled through my teeth. It wasn't fine. It was
better that Prince Colin and Patrick were fighting each other,
certainly, but this reborn kingdom with its untested queen and
heartbroken king didn't need a battle against two armies.

"I'm going to make it right." Chrysalis looked up at me, an
idea bright in his eyes. "I know how to stop them."

"What are you going to do?"

"You'll see."

Chrysalis vanished.

FORTY-THREE

A PAIR OF Queen's Guards discovered me just moments after Chrysalis vanished. Matthew went for help, while Cael announced he'd escort me to my room.

"No, I'm needed elsewhere."

"It's for your own safety." He motioned at the knife painted onto his uniform, as if I needed proof he was on my side. "Oscar Gray promised you'd come without issues."

Oscar Gray was going on floor-scrubbing duty for the rest of his life.

"I don't need to be safe. I need to find the wraith boy. You have no idea what he'll do." Neither did I, though, and that was the most terrifying thing of all.

"All the more reason to make sure you're safe."

That was terrible logic, given Chrysalis listened only to me, but I let out a resigned, annoyed sigh, and went with him.

My vermilion cape fluttered behind me as I strode through

the halls, which were filling with people wearing black knives on their uniforms, suits, and ball gowns; no one wanted to be mistaken for an enemy. When they saw me, whispers spread like fire.

"Black Knife," they murmured. "The queen is Black Knife."

"One of them anyway. Can you believe . . ."

"Is it true?" asked Cael. "That you and King Tobiah are Black Knife?"

I eyed him askance. "Hand me your sword and find out."

He felt his hip for his weapon, but I'd already unbuckled the sheath and had the blade half drawn before he noticed. "Please don't tell anyone you did that."

"As long as you understand the only reason you got me here was because I let you." I opened the door to the queen's suite and handed back his sword. "I'll be out in a few minutes. We have a lot of work to do."

"I should check the rooms to make sure there's no danger."

"If you must." Unbelievable how much unnecessary work went into making sure I was safe. But I allowed Cael to glance through the chambers, and when he left, I caught the expected *clank* of the door being locked.

That was pointless, because the lock was on my side.

But that was followed by a *thump* as he wedged a doorstop into a crack at the bottom.

"Hey!" I flipped the lock and pushed at the door, but that only forced the stop tighter. "What if there's a fire?"

"Then I'll remove the doorstop." Cael patted the door. "Oscar Gray's orders."

I kicked the door and rattled it again, but my protest was

useless. There was nothing that would inspire him to release me. Not when everyone in the kingdom had worked so hard to get back their queen.

"This is ridiculous." I marched to the center of my parlor and glared around, but there was nothing even remotely like a battering ram. I could slide something under the door to remove the wedge, but perhaps it was best to let him think he'd won for now.

After a few weak attempts to open the door, I put on a show of giving up, and then moved deeper into the queen's suite, making my own inspections inside the wardrobes, under the bed, and up the chimney. There was no one, but sending someone to keep me occupied wouldn't be beyond Patrick.

I shimmied out of my silk ball gown, piece by piece. Cape, bodice, skirt. The whole thing puddled on the floor like blood. Next, my hair came out of the bun, and went into a plain, tight braid.

Finally, I dragged my bag from under the bed and put on the only color I wanted to wear tonight: black.

The soft fabric slid cool over my skin, familiar and comfortable. Stockings, trousers, and knee-high boots followed. I put on my belt and baldric, and secured the sword on my back.

This felt right. I felt like myself. Like Black Knife.

Mask and gloves in hand, I strode toward the balcony door. And stopped short.

The doors between the king's and queen's suites were open, and Black Knife stood there with his sword across his back and his mask tucked into his belt.

"It's like looking into a mirror," he said.

"Except I comb my hair occasionally."

He smirked and brushed a dark strand from his eyes. "Are you going somewhere? And do you want company?"

"It might be awkward that we're wearing the same outfit."

"These are my best clothes."

"I agree. As nice as you looked earlier this evening, I prefer you like this. Much handsomer. You're invited."

His lower lip pushed out in a pout. "You only like me because of my sense of fashion."

"Now that doesn't sound like Optimistic Knife." Tension eased inside me. I'd missed this. I'd missed *him*. "I guess you heard about the pair of armies down there"—I waved toward the balcony—"and immediately got sent to your room."

"Hundreds of years ago, kings and queens rode into battle with their people. Now when there's danger, monarchs are shuffled away, too precious to risk breaking. But what makes us leaders if we don't lead?" He strode to the balcony and pulled open the door. Cool wind whipped inside. I ducked out first.

"Did you find James?"

His tone darkened. "No. I'm not sure where he is."

"Probably securing the castle against invasion. The good news is that I think you made him invincible."

"Perhaps. As long as he has you to awaken him." Tobiah paused. "And both of us to keep him alive. I don't know what happens to him if either of us dies. Maybe he'd drop lifeless, or disappear completely."

I opened my mouth, but there was nothing to say. I didn't know about Tobiah's power, but I knew what happened to animated objects when their masters died.

I busied myself putting on my gloves.

"Do you remember the last time we were up here together?" Tobiah slipped past me and stood at the balcony rail. Being Black Knife gave him strength and focus.

I knew, because it did the same for me.

"I remember," I said.

"You had just saved my life."

"And you were about to save mine."

"We were so young." Black Knife—Tobiah—leaned toward me. His arm brushed mine.

With both of us dressed like this, it was so easy to forget that we weren't still friends trying to pretend we were enemies. It would have been so easy to think of myself as a thief with a flair for forgery, and him as the annoying vigilante who'd done me the biggest favor in the world.

He dropped his eyes to our hands, black gloves on stone, our small fingers barely touching. "This feels like ten years ago. Both of us up here. My people down there, fighting yours. I hate this, our lives coming back to what people will do for a prince, or a queen."

"Or just someone they love, no titles necessary." I couldn't imagine Patrick actually loving anyone, let alone me, but the wraith boy possessed terrifying devotion. Where was he now?

Aecor City spread below, lights blazing under the cold starlight. People surged through the streets and castle courtyard, but not to fight. They wanted refuge.

"We have to go down there," I said. "We have to stop the fighting."

He faced me, one hand on the mask tucked into his belt.

"This is your city. Where do we start?"

"The lowcity. There." I pointed toward the marshes in the east. "That's all the information I managed to get. You said Prince Colin had about five thousand men. It's hard to guess at the Red Militia's numbers, unless we find Claire."

"Your Militia informant."

"That's right. She was to join the Queen's Guard this afternoon, but—"

"I showed up. Sorry."

"Don't be." I wanted to say more, but no words would come. Not when our relationship was so uncertain. "Let's start near the lowcity gate. There are several courtyards and parks in that area, appearing every time old buildings collapse. The ground is too unstable to support new buildings without magic."

"A likely battleground." He slipped his mask from his belt and started to put it on.

"I should warn you," I said. "Four armies. Two colors. I needed a way to identify our people, so I told Sergeant Ferris to paint the same symbol on all of his soldiers' fronts, backs, and sleeves."

Tobiah lowered his mask. "And?"

My heart thumped, and I hated myself for giving away his secret. "I told him to use a black knife. It was my only idea. Now everyone is painting knives on their clothes, even civilians."

His eyebrows lifted, and his scowl shifted into a grin. "That means there are *thousands* of Black Knives moving toward Colin's and Patrick's armies?"

"In a way." He wasn't angry?

No. He was *laughing*. It was a soft, weary laugh, but it

470

warmed his face and eyes. "That's wonderful, Wil."

"Really?"

"I always wanted Black Knife to become a symbol of hope in Skyvale. I didn't want others to take up vigilantism, which did happen on occasion, but I wanted to inspire people. I wanted them to know someone was watching over them. They didn't have to know who it was, just that someone cared." Wind caught his hair, and he smoothed it back. "I was glad when you took it up. It was a relief knowing Black Knife was still taking care of my city."

Now that city was gone, but we still had a chance to save mine.

I pulled my mask over my face. "Time to go, Optimistic Knife."

"As long as no one else takes *that* name." He grinned as he put on his mask. But before we could start down the wall, an acrid-scented heat rolled in.

White wraithy mist poured over Tangler Bay and the Red Bay, smothering the southern tip of the highcity within seconds. A deafening *crack* sounded, like bones snapping, and hundreds of thousands of glass shards exploded into the air.

The cliff-side mirrors had done nothing to protect the city. Nothing at all.

"No." Tobiah swayed on his feet, and his breath puffed out his mask in small bursts. I took his shoulders to steady him, and he turned his face against my neck with an angry sob. "Not again."

"It's Chrysalis." My words tasted like ash. "He's returned."

FORTY-FOUR

"CHRYSALIS." TOBIAH SPAT the name like a curse, but his anger didn't disguise the tremor in his voice. "Why is he out there? I thought he was secured—"

"He was, but Patrick tricked him. When he realized he'd done wrong, he decided to make it right."

"With more wraith?" His breath rasped.

"He thinks he can protect me. He thinks he can control it."

"Can he?"

"I don't know."

The bank of wraith mist coalesced into a thick band that twisted just above the city like a giant worm, stretching as far north as the castle curtain. I had to drop my head all the way back to see the end of the boiling mass. Heat and stink pushed off it in waves, nauseating.

Then it spread into the sky, blocking out the moon and stars for a moment that seemed like eternity. Tobiah's arm squeezed tight around my waist, as the wraith shifted and plunged toward the southeast corner of the city.

Wraith splashed up and rained over everything in small, glowing flecks that lit the night.

"Oh, saints." My voice sounded small under the screams that rose from the streets.

Panic erupted across the city as eerie white lights drifted through the hot sky, lighting the lowcity as bright as the wraithland, and for the first time, I could see evidence of the battle between Patrick and Prince Colin.

Columns of smoke towered over the lowcity beyond the factories—close to the gate where I'd guessed the fighting would be. That was where Chrysalis would be, too.

"Let's go." I released Tobiah, but his grip on my waist only tightened.

"It's the Inundation all over again."

"No." I faced him and pulled him close enough to lean my forehead on his. "It's going to be different this time. I'm going to find Chrysalis. I'm going to stop this."

"I've already watched one city fall to the wraith." Sweat made his mask stick to his skin. "If Aecor City falls—"

"Aecor City won't fall. We won't let it. Right? This is what Black Knife does."

He dragged in a heavy breath and pulled back a fraction to focus on me, on my eyes behind the mask.

"There's still a chance for Aecor City. We have to find Chrysalis and make him send away the wraith."

"It will just come back."

"We have a barrier. We'll put it up before the wraith returns."

He hesitated, like he wanted to argue that the barrier was only a stopgap, but at last he nodded. "We have a barrier."

"Good." I found my grappling hook. "Let's go, Black Knife. We have a city to save."

He moved toward the opposite corner of the balcony, his grapple and line in hand. "Together?" he called over the shouts from below.

"Always."

I climbed over the rail, giving him a second to do the same, and as one we rappelled down the castle wall. People scattered out of our way, making a pair of perfect half circles below us.

"It's Black Knife!" Someone pointed up at me.

"There are two!"

The news of Black Knife's identity hadn't spread out here, yet. And in the face of fighting and wraith, a foreign vigilante didn't matter much. But as my boots thumped the ground, the panic shifted into excitement.

"Black Knife will save us!"

I loosened my hook and gathered my line, searching over heads to meet Tobiah's eyes. His posture was stiff and serious as he pushed his way through dozens of people, toward me.

But the people pressed closer. Fingertips grazed my sleeve. Others tugged at my mask.

I jerked back, reaching for a dagger out of habit, but Tobiah was there, his hands on my shoulders.

"It's all right." With the noise all around, I felt his murmur of comfort more than heard it.

"What is that glow? Wraith?" asked a man.

"Yes." Tobiah's answer came hard.

"Are you going to stop it?"

"Yes," I said. "We are."

Someone gasped. "That's the queen's voice. And the Indigo king's."

There was no obvious communication, but a few people in our path stepped back and out of our way. Then more until there was a clear line to the city.

The whispers rippled down the ranks of people: "Black Knife will stop the wraith" and "The heir to four Houses" and "Queen of the vermilion throne."

Their words became waves of sound as Tobiah and I raced toward the fighting and wraith.

At the top of the courtyard wall, Melanie was waiting in the same place I'd run into her the first time I sneaked into the city.

"About time." She finished tying her hair into a ponytail; the shorter strands fell around her face. "We thought you'd never leave that balcony."

"We?" I moved my line out of the way and offered a hand to Tobiah. His fingers tightened around mine as he swung himself over the parapet.

She motioned down the walkway where five people crouched in the shadow of stonework. One by one, they stood and came to meet us. James, Oscar, Kevin, Theresa, and Sergeant Ferris all had swords buckled at their hips, and long black knives painted down the fronts of their uniforms.

"I told Oscar that sending you to your room was both pointless and rude," Melanie said.

"We're not letting you go out there alone." Theresa cocked

a hip toward the lowcity. "There's a minor war."

"Plus the wraith," said Oscar. "Is that Chrysalis's doing? His guards reported him missing half an hour ago."

"Unfortunately." I glanced at Tobiah, who was trying not to look at James. "There's no point in ordering them to go back. We may as well let them help."

Tobiah gave a swift nod. "Keep up. We can't afford to waste time."

Everyone agreed as Melanie stepped forward and tugged my mask off my head. "Put this away. Your people need to see your face."

"Fine." I thrust my mask into my belt and rappelled down the other side of the wall.

There was no easy way to travel; jumping from building to building wasn't an option in this part of the city, with the roofs pitched so steep even Black Knife and I would have trouble. That left the ground, though from the wall, I'd had a quick view of bodies packing Castle Street and all the surrounding roads so tightly it was a wonder anyone could breathe.

Moving against the flow of bodies was almost impossible, so I led my team around the edges, keeping to the walls of buildings where I needed only one elbow to keep people from my space.

"This is more annoying than I thought it would be." The din nearly drowned Theresa's grumble, even though she was right behind me.

I started to laugh, but a commotion in the street stopped me.

"The wraith is here!" A man threw himself into a cluster of boys, knocking one over. Others around him staggered and turned on him with angry shouts.

I raised my voice. "Kevin! Take care of that!" I glanced back long enough to see him snap and thump his chest, and then he pushed through the crowd to follow orders, and I had to dodge someone vomiting in the path ahead.

We forced our way opposite the crowd for what seemed like hours, pausing to help where needed, but it couldn't have been more than thirty minutes before we turned a corner and suddenly broke through the crush. Now that there was room to move, I staggered and braced myself against a brick wall, gasping in the wraith-hot air. Sweat poured down my face and neck and spine. My clothes clung uncomfortably.

The others came around the corner, sweating and panting as much as I was. Tobiah took off his mask and swiped his forearm over his face, but paused halfway through the motion, and stared up. "It's snowing."

Flakes the size of my splayed-out hand drifted from the wraith-lit sky, sticking where they hit the ground. When I knelt and held a hand over one, I could feel the heat even through my gloves.

I stood. "Don't touch it."

Melanie scowled at the sky as the number of giant white flakes doubled. "Oh, that shouldn't be hard at all." She smoothed back her hair, sweat sticking it to her skull.

I waved the group onward. "Hurry. We have to stop the fighting."

"What about the wraith?" Sergeant Ferris strode ahead, checking around a corner before I reached it. "Can you stop the wraith like you did in Skyvale?"

Tobiah, James, and I exchanged an awkward three-way

glance. "No," I said. "It might kill me. It would make everything worse."

Chrysalis would be wraith mist, and James would be the lifeless shape of a boy.

"If I can find Chrysalis, I can tell him to send the wraith back." Maybe if I just *wanted* it enough, he'd do it without my order. But I couldn't count on that; he was unpredictable at the best of times.

And this was not the best of times.

We picked up speed as the streets cleared closer to the lowcity. The eight of us took up a steady trot, with Tobiah and me in the center, and the others around us like the points of a star.

"You should have announced yourself back there," said Kevin. "They'd have made way for you."

"Maybe." Melanie waited a few steps before continuing. "Or the royal presence would have caused even more calamity."

"*You're* the one who made her take her mask off." Theresa huffed. "Make up your mind."

Melanie flicked her little finger in Theresa's direction. "Masked figures are equally exciting."

"I told you." I smirked at Tobiah. "The best mask is a face no one will remember."

He managed a faint smile as we darted around a flurry of snowflakes clumping together.

As we entered the lowcity, threads of white drifted through the streets, twining around buildings and statues and trees. Gardens withered, and houses grew eyes. Bits of wraith clung to everything, making corners of buildings rot, storefronts melt, and paving stones liquefy. A handful of bodies—both in red and blue—sank into puddles of wraith, and vanished.

We hadn't even reached the biggest mass of wraith. Not nearly.

Several times, we stopped to dispatch wraith beasts: cats and dogs, even birds. Nothing was safe from the toxic effects.

"Chrysalis," I whispered. "Where are you?"

"Here." The wraith boy appeared directly in front of me.

I skidded and crashed into him, but he didn't budge. He grabbed my shoulders and held me upright while I found my balance.

Around us, everyone else stopped and stared. James moved close to Tobiah, who looked at the wraith boy with murder in his eyes.

"Where have you been?"

He tilted his head. "Trying to stop Patrick. Isn't that what you wanted?"

"No!"

Chrysalis took a step away from me. "I'm sorry. I thought—"

"Send away the wraith." From the corner of my eye, I could see James muttering to Tobiah. The lengths of everyone's drawn swords gleamed in the wraith light. "Send it away now."

The wraith boy cringed. "My queen—"

"Do it!"

He took another small step back and glanced over his shoulder where the hulking line of factories loomed like a wall between us and the fighting. Screams, gurgles, and pleas for help sounded in the distance.

And suddenly: silence.

"I'm sorry," said Chrysalis. "I've lost control of it."

FORTY-FIVE

EVERYONE LUNGED FOR the wraith boy at once.

He dropped to the packed-dirt ground, covering the back of his head and neck with his hands. Rocking side to side, he angled his face toward me and whispered something over and over, inaudible under the sound of my friends' weapons being drawn.

"Wait!" I stepped closer, my arms outstretched. Everyone backed off.

"Wil?" Tobiah shot me a wrecked, confused look. His sword stayed in guard position, ready and deadly, but statue still.

I grabbed Chrysalis by the collar of his dirt-streaked jacket and hauled him to his feet. Sweat matted his hair, and small burns dotted his face, as though the snowflakes had injured him. "What were you saying?"

"It won't hurt you," he repeated. "The other wraith won't hurt you. I told it not to."

"What does that mean?" James's voice was rough; he stood close to Tobiah, protective as always, no matter the ten-year secret raw between them. "That's all wraith does—hurt people."

Chrysalis glanced at Tobiah, something like shame crossing his face. "I know."

"What do you mean, the wraith won't hurt me?" I asked. This wasn't the time to discuss the past.

"I told you I wouldn't let it hurt you, so it won't." He touched the small red welts spotting his face. "It hasn't hurt *you*."

I mirrored his movements. It was true; I hadn't been burned, though the others showed evidence of injury. "How, when you've lost control over it?"

"Control, yes. That's lost. But not yet influence."

Not yet.

Which meant I had to act quickly.

"The whole kingdom needs protection." I looked beyond him, toward the now-quiet battlefield on the far side of the factories; the silence was deafening. *Something* had happened, and the wraith was likely responsible. "What happened there? Are the soldiers dead?"

He shook his head. "Not yet."

My stomach dropped as I motioned at Sergeant Ferris and Oscar. "Go look."

Ferris glanced at Tobiah for direction, but his king didn't shift his glare from the wraith boy.

"Go!" I said.

Sergeant Ferris and Oscar took off at a run toward factories.

I turned back to Chrysalis. "You need to regain control of

the wraith. Those people need to survive. The *kingdom* needs to survive."

A heavy flake of snow drifted between us, then toward me at a gust of wind. I moved away, but heat touched me—and then nothing.

The wraith boy nodded solemnly as a small burn appeared on him. "I will do as you wish, my queen."

He flickered and vanished.

Melanie lowered her sword and rushed for me, while Tobiah staggered back and seemed to collect his thoughts. James didn't leave his side.

"He took it." Theresa's voice was eerily loud. "When the snow struck you, the burn went on him."

"It won't hurt you," Kevin murmured. "Because it will hurt him instead."

Tobiah still gripped his sword, the leather of his gloves stretched taut around his knuckles. "Use it while you have it, Wil. You heard him; his influence won't last."

Ahead, Oscar and Sergeant Ferris disappeared around the corner of the water purification factory. Wraith light hung gloomily over the building, making odd shadows that shifted into the shapes of disproportioned hands and arms.

"This way. Stay close." I didn't wait for affirmation, just sprinted toward the factory. If I could get them out of the snow and tendrils of wraith for even a few minutes, that would be something.

At my approach, the wraith skittered away, making a path for the others.

The factory door hung open.

"Are we going in?" Kevin asked.

"Yes." I checked the street. There was no sign of Oscar and Sergeant Ferris yet, but they'd return shortly. I hoped. "You and Theresa stand guard in the doorway and wait for the others. I don't want anyone left alone."

The pair saluted, and I led the remaining three inside the building where lights burned, both gas and wraith.

Queasiness made me sway as I took in the room. Pipes had grown talons or feet, and their claws scraped at the floor. Barrels had turned into feathers. Walls rippled like silk sheets in a breeze.

"It's ruined," I rasped. "The lowcity needed this plant, and now it's ruined."

Melanie's voice came hard. "They won't need it if we can't all pull ourselves together and stop the wraith. Now let's go."

She was right. We had work to do.

In the main room, we found Claire. She'd been trussed to a wooden chair and abandoned, surrounded by a pool of blood.

Her foot sat in the blood, detached from the rest of her.

"*Saints.*" Melanie rushed to untie her. "Who—Patrick?"

Claire was pale, her sweat-dampened hair stuck to her face and neck. "Patrick." She closed her eyes, and her head dipped as though she might faint. Someone had wrapped the stump on her leg, but not well. Blood dripped from the bandage.

"Is there anyone else here?" James asked, his sword at the ready.

"No. Everyone's gone to fight. But I haven't heard them in a few minutes. It's so quiet now." One of her eyes was bruised and swollen, and her mouth was split. "I meant to go to your coronation. I wanted to accept your offer. But the Militia got to me

483

first. They knew I'd been talking with you. They held me until Patrick arrived." She lifted her chin high, but the act didn't fool anyone. "That's why they took my foot. For straying."

I motioned at the boys. "Check the rooms. Find anything that might help Claire. I want her taken to the castle. Connor might be able to heal her."

"There are blankets in that office." Her hands free now, Claire pointed to a nearby opening; the door was gone now. "And wood beams all over, though the wraith—"

"We'll find something." Tobiah waved James with him.

"Mel, grab another chair. We need to put her"—not her foot; that was on the ground—"leg up so she doesn't lose more blood."

I pulled Claire and her chair away from the puddle of blood and knelt so I could prop her stump on my knee. The bandage was soaked, so I drew a new one from my belt and tied it over the old, like Connor and the Gray brothers had taught me.

"Here." I gave her a packet of powdered herbs to numb the pain. It wasn't enough, but it was something.

Claire accepted the medicine and dropped her gaze to me, her voice low and slurred. "He planned to go after Colin tonight. That was his goal all along. But Colin moved against you."

Prince Colin wouldn't risk his nephew's life, that much I trusted. But he'd malign and defame the vigilante king, if that meant he could take the throne. The Indigo Kingdom. Aecor. Either one. He just wanted power.

Melanie returned with a second chair and helped me arrange Claire's leg. The movement was too much, and she lost consciousness.

"We can't linger here," Melanie whispered into the oppressive silence. Where was Chrysalis? Had he regained control of the wraith?

I shook away the questions. "Four need to go back with Claire. Two to carry her, one to carry"—I pointed toward her foot—"that, and one to defend."

"James and I won't leave you," she said.

"Fine."

Claire roused herself and blinked. "The Red Militia wants to defend your right to the throne," she said. "They'll destroy Colin for you."

"I know they will. But they shouldn't." I straightened as Tobiah and James returned, their arms full of blankets, ropes, and wood beams. "Good, let's make—"

Footfalls sounded from the purification room.

Oscar and Sergeant Ferris marched in, Theresa and Kevin on their heels. Everyone's face was grim.

"What's the news?" Melanie moved to meet them in the middle. "What did you see?"

"Both armies are there," Oscar said. "Some of ours, too. Plus wraith beasts, mostly domesticated animals that were transformed."

Tobiah and I shared a quick glance. "Then why is it so quiet?" I asked, unless the wraith had smothered all their sound or . . .

"They're frozen." Sergeant Ferris was ashen. "They're frozen like the people you saw near Mirror Lake."

FORTY-SIX

"THEY'RE STILL BREATHING," said Oscar.

"The wraith hasn't solidified the way you described at Mirror Lake." Sergeant Ferris knelt to help build the stretcher for Claire. "But they can't move through it."

My head buzzed with horror. The wraithland, here in my city. "Did you see Patrick or Prince Colin?"

"No, but we couldn't get a good look. Oscar tossed a pebble into the mist, and it stuck. If they're with their armies, they're trapped."

If Chrysalis regained control over the wraith, everyone would be moving again. We had to find Prince Colin and Patrick first, force them to agree to call off their armies, and somehow send away the wraith.

"All right." I rose to my feet. "You four, take Claire to the castle. Get her to Connor."

"I don't like leaving you," said Theresa.

"Please, do this. And after you deliver Claire, take all the barrier pieces up to Radiants' Walk—the overlook above the Red Bay."

Oscar nodded. "The barrier will be there."

"Good. Guard it with your life." I dragged in a long breath, heavy with the heat of wraith and stink of blood. "Melanie, James: you're with us."

Outside, Melanie and James moved ahead, their weapons drawn, though the street was unnaturally still; even the snow had stopped, and was steaming in piles against the buildings.

"The wraith is changing everything so quickly." Tobiah's voice was low.

"Chrysalis brought it as a weapon." Now that we were so close to the battleground, haze blocked out the moon and stars completely, but the flecks of light cast enough illumination to see by. "Chrysalis doesn't think about consequences when he acts. I don't know if he can. I want to hate him for doing this, but I know him now. I'm learning the way he thinks. It's almost childlike."

"He's no child." The words were a growl.

"No, he's not."

"But he loves you. He wants to protect you."

"I don't think he has a choice." I waved the topic away. "We can discuss Chrysalis and his dubious humanity another time. Right now, we need to focus on making this city safe."

"You've said it a hundred times: we'll never be safe."

Maybe not. But right now, we both needed hope. "We have to make it safe. If not for us, for the people who come after us."

"Right." He wiped his arm across his face, leaving a streak

of sweat and dirt. "You were giving a lot of orders back there. Do you have a plan?"

"Yes."

"Do you want to share?"

"No."

"I see. You don't want to be embarrassed if everything goes awry."

I twitched my little finger at him. "Just because you have impeccable taste in clothes doesn't mean you know everything, Black Knife."

"Oh, nameless girl. When will you learn to trust me?"

"I do trust you." I bumped my elbow against his, a pathetic attempt at levity, but he caught me, turned me, and held me in place. We stood dangerously close. "It's myself I don't always trust," I whispered.

"That's strange." He released my arm and took a step backward. "I trust you, but I don't always trust myself."

"This seems to be a problem with kings and queens."

"I think it's a problem with people." He smiled faintly, and we hurried to catch up with Melanie and James. "I always believed I was a monster hunting other monsters." His voice remained soft.

Knowing what he'd done to bring back his cousin in a society that condemned all magic, I could imagine the cycle of self-loathing that must have taken hold.

"I never saw *you* as a monster, though. A criminal, yes. Definitely a troublemaker. But even when I learned you were a radiant, I didn't see you differently. I thought maybe you were like me." He didn't meet my eyes. "Since then, I've fought actual monsters. Not just wraith beasts or glowmen, but the kind of people who come out of hiding when the world falls apart. I've traveled through the wraithland of my own home. I've seen things I couldn't begin to describe."

"Like this?" We'd come to the battleground: a huge park surrounded by shops, taverns, and food stalls. I'd been here once before; people had been planting trees and beginning the frame of some kind of stage or platform. Now vines covered the brickwork, growing every second. Broken glass windows glimmered like teeth.

"Dear saints." Melanie pressed her hands to her mouth.

Mist writhed between thousands of men and women caught mid-fight. Wraith beasts, too, had been trapped with their claws raised or their jaws clamped around a leg.

Many of our people were turned away, identifiable only by the knives painted on their uniforms, but I caught a few faces I knew. They blinked and gasped, and struggled against the solidifying mist, but it was futile.

I stepped toward them, as though I could help.

"Don't get too close." Melanie raised her arm to bar me from proceeding. "Remember what Ferris said happened when they threw in a pebble. It's there."

Indeed, a small piece of rock hung in midair.

"You heard Chrysalis. It won't hurt me." When I lifted my palm to the mist, it seemed to melt. It was still wraith, but simply the kind that changed things, rather than trapped. With another step, the floating pebble hit the ground with a faint *clack*. "I have to free our people while this immunity still works. Maybe they know where Patrick and Prince Colin are."

"Fine." Melanie crossed her arms. "In the meantime, we'll just stand here, useless."

"Don't be foolish. Find a building to climb up and get a good look at everything. Or go around the edges and look for Patrick and Prince Colin there. Just don't touch the mist." That wasn't a useful instruction; there was mist *everywhere*. "Look, you can see how this mist is different. It sheers off at the edge of something, and there's a shimmer to it."

"I see it." Melanie scowled.

My smile was forced. "Take James; that way we'll each have a boy to look after."

James and Tobiah shot each other unamused looks, but after a moment, Melanie and James went off together, discussing their best course of action.

I took another step into the mist, which melted at my nearness. "Watch my back, Black Knife."

"Intently."

Another step, and then another. I reached the nearest soldier with a black knife on her uniform. She'd been trapped in a silent scream, someone's blade coming toward her from behind. I'd seen her before. Met her once. Her name was . . . Denise something.

"It's all right, Denise," I murmured. "I'm going to free you."

Her eyes widened as the mist cleared away. Her mouth moved. She dropped from the wraith's grasp and pointed behind me.

I drew my sword and spun, letting the mist scatter and melt around me.

A figure in a shredded indigo uniform limped around a corner. Blood poured down his cheek and neck, and his skin shone with sweat. He kept one arm tucked against his chest.

"Uncle." Tobiah moved toward him, but stopped as Prince Colin hefted a sword with his good arm.

"I should have known I'd find you with her." Prince Colin's glare cut from Tobiah to me, his eyes narrowed. "Flashers. Filthy creatures. You deserve to die in this stuff, not my people." He brought his sword around, cutting through banners of wraith accumulating around him. It didn't help.

"Is that why you attacked the city?" Tobiah sidestepped so that he was between his uncle and me. "Because of Wilhelmina's magic? Or because you don't want to give up Aecor?"

Denise was kneeling in the muck, silently gasping, but recovering. I moved toward another black-knifed soldier, freeing him while Tobiah had Prince Colin distracted.

"You planned this." Prince Colin shuddered as heat blasted through the street. "The coronation. Patrick Lien's release. The wraith destroying us both."

"We didn't plan anything." Tobiah's voice was firm. "Do you really think I want to see another place become wraithland?"

"I wish I could believe you." Prince Colin edged away from the shimmer mist, closer to a shop where vines grew around columns. Leaves fluttered and fattened, reaching for him. "But you're dressed as a vigilante and keep company with a flasher."

Tobiah moved again, not blocking me anymore, but herding Prince Colin away from the vines that slithered down from the buildings. Like green snakes, they crossed the walkway, heavy leaves catching air like sails on a boat. "Come back to the castle with us," Tobiah said. "Someone will help you. Is your arm broken?"

"I won't go anywhere with you."

Quickly, I freed two more of my soldiers, whispering for them to stay close. I had to assume the wraith would solidify again when I moved away.

"Come on, Chrysalis," I muttered.

The soldiers crowded behind me as I moved toward the edge of the wraith shimmer. Those still trapped looked at me, pleading with their eyes. They were afraid I was leaving them. "I'll free you," I whispered. "I swear it."

Near Prince Colin, the vines reared up to throw themselves around him. Tobiah brought his sword down with uncanny speed, cutting the thick greenery in two just before it reached his uncle.

There was no time for relief; another vine zipped in from the opposite direction. "Watch out!"

My warning came too late.

The vine wrapped around Prince Colin's throat and tightened. His sword fell to the cobblestones as he tried to tug off the wraith vine, but more twisted around his body, pinning his arms in place.

Tobiah lunged forward, drawing a dagger to free his uncle, but Prince Colin's face was already red and purple. He writhed in place, struggling against Tobiah and the vines.

I had to help. "Hurry," I called to the soldiers, and we started to run. As soon as they were away from the wraith shimmer, I sprinted toward Tobiah.

Prince Colin's eyes bulged. His mouth moved.

"Keep him still." Tobiah shoved his uncle onto his back.

I dropped my sword and knelt close, and that was all the

proximity the wraith needed. The vine loosened and fled; Chrysalis's influence still held.

Prince Colin curled inward and turned to one side, gasping and coughing. "Wraith queen." The words were garbled, but I'd heard them enough. I knew.

"How can we help?" Denise asked. The others stood behind her, shaky, but well enough.

"Guard Colin." I glanced at Tobiah. "The former overlord is officially a traitor, same as Patrick."

The four moved in just as the horrific noise of screams and metal exploded behind us—and silenced only a second later.

In the wraith shimmer, everyone had shifted. Just slightly. Just enough. One reached for us now, close to where I'd freed Denise. The one who'd been about to stab her in the back had fallen forward. Another was suddenly on his knees, trying to curl into a ball.

It happened again.

The wraith melted for a heartbeat, people lurched and gasped and cried out, and then everything stopped.

"Chrysalis." Tobiah glanced at me. "He's regaining control."

Slowly. Horribly. But he was trying.

"Wil!" Melanie's voice came from a rooftop down the street, and both she and James pointed—

A *thud* sounded as a dagger landed in the back of Prince Colin's neck. He dropped to the ground, dead.

"No!" Tobiah took up his sword and lunged for a shape emerging from a nearby tavern. Patrick. My former friend hefted a giant sword with ease, bringing it up to guard as Tobiah closed on him with an awful shout.

The blades clashed. Patrick shoved Tobiah backward, but the king regained his footing immediately. He feinted low and struck high, but Patrick knew that trick.

The two were closely matched in skill, but where Tobiah was a fast, lithe fighter, Patrick was steady. He'd wear down Tobiah, and then strike a killing blow.

But he wouldn't risk me.

"Help any of our people who escape the wraith," I told my soldiers. Chrysalis would seize control soon. I hoped.

"But Patrick—"

"We'll take care of him. Captain Rayner and Melanie will be here soon." With no more room for argument, I took my sword in one hand and a dagger in the other, and joined Tobiah.

Patrick swore. "I don't want to hurt you, Wilhelmina. I promised I wouldn't ever strike you again, but you're making that a difficult promise to keep."

Around us, lightning bursts of chaos hit—Chrysalis fighting the wraith.

"You can keep your promise." I swung for his side; he blocked. "You can choose to end this."

"Aecor won't be free until the Indigo presence is eradicated." Patrick raised his sword against Tobiah.

Before he could attack, I jumped between them and blocked with my dagger. "Stop, Patrick!"

"I can fight, Wil." Tobiah was at my side, sword ready.

"He will kill you. He won't hurt me." I didn't take my eyes off Patrick. "Once I wondered if a dead queen was better than a defiant queen, but I know better now. Patrick won't harm me, because he knows the power of my name. He's nothing if he's not fighting for me."

Tobiah backed off, but Patrick pursued, forcing me to work to keep myself between them. I blocked and redirected blows, chest burning with the effort. Heat poured over the street, and sweat made my clothes cling to my skin.

The rapid noise and silence of Chrysalis's wraith-control effort made my head spin, and banners of mist had fallen in our space. They were glowing.

"Stay close," I told Tobiah. "The wraith won't attack if you're near me."

He grunted behind me, followed by the *twang* of his handheld crossbow firing. "I am in awe of the way you inspire such loyalty. Nevertheless, the wraith has us surrounded."

I couldn't look away from Patrick to confirm, just strike and block and move and block and thrust and block. "Well, maybe"—I gasped—"you should do something."

"I just shot a streetlight in the eye. What more do you want from me?"

My sword arm shook with strain as I attacked again. Patrick blocked me with ease. "You won't last much longer," he said. "When you're finished with this, I'll kill the foreign king and hang his body from the castle wall. I'll say this is what the vermilion queen and her Red Militia do to enemies."

"You will *not*." I lunged for Patrick, and when he moved to parry, I stepped inside his guard and thrust my dagger into his stomach.

Blood poured from the wound as he staggered back. "Wil?" Patrick clutched his gut with both hands, his face filled with surprise and hurt. For a heartbeat, he was the same boy who'd given me writing supplies in the old palace, swearing to help me reclaim my kingdom.

No matter the cost.

"I'm sorry, Patrick." I made myself watch as he fell to his knees, his eyes locked on mine. Around us, the bursts of din grew longer as people broke free. Tobiah stood at my side, and a line of my soldiers at my back. On the street behind Patrick, I caught Melanie and James running toward us. "This was never what I wanted. Our problems have always been so much bigger and more complex than what you saw."

"You're wrong. You need me." Patrick scraped his sword off the ground and lunged.

Tobiah moved toward me at the same time I grabbed him and pulled him to safety, a breath away from the sword point.

Patrick's blade clattered on the ground. He grunted and fell forward. Behind him, James pulled his sword free of Patrick's heart, and Melanie looked on with a cold, distant expression.

Patrick was dead.

Heavy moments stretched as we stared at Patrick's body on the ground. Prince Colin's body lay close by. A faint numbness settled over me. Something I'd always thought was impossible had just happened. And I'd lost another Osprey in the process. Another person I'd once called a friend.

"Your Majesties!" Denise dragged my attention back to the park and the chaos within.

Chrysalis had recovered control of the wraith, so the battle had resumed. Blades clashed and people screamed. Everywhere I looked, there were bodies on the ground, and others trying to flee.

"We have to stop this. Come with me." Tobiah took my free hand and pulled me toward a tall building. We threw our hooks and climbed up the side of an old, pre-wraith structure. Melanie and James guarded from below.

On the roof, we could see the whole battleground, all the reds and blues intermixed, and those with black knives on their uniforms struggling to contain the fighting. Wraith beasts plowed through, growing with the heavy concentration of mist.

"People of Aecor!" Tobiah called. "People of the Indigo Kingdom!"

No one heard.

I touched his hand. "What do the people call you, Tobiah Pierce? What do they whisper about you?"

"The heir to four Houses?" He shook his head as understanding dawned. "No, I don't think I should. There's already so much wraith."

"And *it's* what's causing the panic right now. Contain it. I know you can."

He sucked in a heavy breath and braced himself with one hand on my shoulder.

A mirror appeared on a storefront across the way. Then another to our right. And another beneath us.

Dozens of mirrors popped into existence. Round, oval, rectangular, octagonal: they appeared in a hundred shapes and sizes, fixed to the walls and lying on the streets. They were all bare, sharp glass.

Tobiah stood at my side, his face upturned and his eyes closed in concentration. His skin was pale and slick with sweat, but mirror-reflected wraith light shone onto him. Us.

Wraith shrieked and spiraled upward, but Tobiah's mirrors caught it—for now. Even the beasts were motionless, trapped in their reflections.

Everyone looked at us.

"People of Aecor!" I called, same as Tobiah had. "People of the Indigo Kingdom!"

Tobiah steadied himself and gazed over the crowd. It was impossible to say how long we had before the wraith escaped his mirrors, so we had to hurry.

I lifted my voice. "Colin Pierce is dead. Patrick Lien is dead. The battle is finished. Aecorians: your queen, the rightful heir to the vermilion throne, has won. Citizens of the Indigo Kingdom: you are all refugees, and by coming to Aecor, you agree to obey my laws. With me, I have King Tobiah, Sovereign of the Indigo Kingdom, House of the Dragon. He, too, is a ward of Aecor, per the Wraith Alliance."

Tobiah made himself tall and proud, and in mirrors all across the park, I caught reflections of the two of us: black-clad vigilantes standing side by side. "Queen Wilhelmina has graciously taken us in. Indigo Army, you will submit to our queen. Aecorians who followed Prince Colin's rule, you will submit to our queen."

My heart thundered when he said my name. When he said *queen*.

I fought to hide the tremor in my voice as I spoke. "Our problem now is the wraith. It surrounds you. These mirrors won't hold it forever, but I will take action to fix that upon my return to Sandcliff Castle."

Thousands of eyes gazed up, some with anger, but more with hope.

"I *need* you all to work together. Protect one another. Every one of you is valuable." I stopped myself before looking toward Patrick and Colin; we could have used them, too. The sense memory of my dagger entering his gut still echoed in my fingers.

Tobiah took my hand and squeezed the sensation out, though it probably wasn't meant to be comforting, but a reminder. Hurry.

"You have your orders. Those who refuse to obey will be arrested and put on trial. Those who wish to throw out their former allegiances will be pardoned."

Immediately, people began moving, calling orders, looking for guidance from their comrades. I let them be, keeping my head high as I strode toward the side of the building to climb down again.

A faint keening rose up, inhuman and piercing.

Tobiah stood where I'd left him, his hands clenched at his sides and his jaw tight.

"What is it?" I walked back to him. The noise grew louder, humming like bees. Below, everyone was looking around, moving more quickly.

Tobiah met my eyes. "Wraith."

With a sharp *crack* and flash of light, every mirror in the park exploded.

FORTY-SEVEN

GLASS AND LIGHT shot upward in a thunderous explosion, but as the shards began to rain down, they vanished.

Tobiah was sweating, shaking, gasping. "It escaped. It broke free of the mirrors."

He'd gotten rid of the mirrors before they caused people harm. That was something. But now the wraith mist was free; it swirled and shrieked, spinning through the park with a blinding glow. Mist burst outward, stretching farther into the city.

I took Tobiah's hand and hauled him toward the edge of the building, where Melanie and James waited on the ground. "Down we go!"

We rappelled as quickly as possible. People ran from the park, others killed wraith beasts, and some attempted to make arrests. The brilliant light of wraith silhouetted my friends below, making my eyes water. I blinked away tears and looked for a place to land among the crush of people and screaming wraith.

Melanie took me by the ribs to steady me. "What happened?" She stepped back to give me room, elbowing others aside. "I thought Chrysalis had control."

"He did." I stashed my grapple and line and wiped my stinging eyes. "Now he doesn't. Maybe because of the mirrors; it's hard to say. Regardless, we need to go to the castle *immediately*."

"Right." Melanie shoved me close to Tobiah so James could watch both of us, and she began rounding up soldiers with knives painted on them. "Protect the queen!" Her voice carried over the din. "Protect the king!"

A small chorus took up the call. "Protect the queen! Protect the king!" The words spread and people circled us, creating a human barrier. Melanie and James led the group out of the lowcity.

We plowed through the confused disorder of people struggling to escape the park, but it was too slow. We'd never make it to the castle if we were forced to walk like this.

I leaned toward Tobiah. "Can you make more mirrors?"

He gave a swift nod, and a heartbeat later, a giant mirror appeared on a factory wall ahead of us, reflecting the blinding light of the park.

Tobiah staggered with the effort; I lunged to support him as more mirrors came into existence.

James glanced back.

"I've got him!" I matched my steps with Tobiah's, directing him and taking as much of his weight as possible while he closed his eyes and called a hundred mirrors into being. A thousand, maybe; the wraith wasn't contained in the park anymore, and if he wanted to stop it all, every wall in the lowcity needed mirrors.

But the wraith did stop. It trembled in its own reflection, buzzing angrily.

Tobiah's breath rasped by my ear.

"How long can you keep those?"

"Until we don't need them anymore. Or until the wraith breaks free." His tone was grim, determined. It was hard enough to believe he'd remained standing after creating the bridge this afternoon; that he was still functioning through two manifestations of mirrors . . .

I tightened my grip on him. "That's good. We'll make it."

With the wraith contained, the crowd moved faster through the lowcity and the line of factories, but it wasn't enough. Tobiah couldn't hold these mirrors for long. We had to do something.

Ahead, a clatter of hooves and voices rang out. "Mel!"

I scanned the crowd to find Oscar riding in with a squad of black-knifed soldiers.

The perimeter of guards paused and broke open. Oscar leapt off his horse, Sergeant Ferris close behind as they spoke to James and Melanie.

I aimed Tobiah toward the nearest horse, a familiar chestnut. "Ferguson!"

"That's not his name," Tobiah groaned. "Like all military horses, he was given a name before you decided to steal him."

"He's Ferguson to me. Now climb on." I steadied Tobiah as

he tested his weight on the stirrup, then lifted himself onto the saddle. I pulled myself up after him, awkwardly swinging my leg over Ferguson's neck.

Tobiah looped his arms around my waist, pulling me close.

From atop Ferguson, I had a better view of the mirrors that shot wraith light everywhere, illuminating panic and terror. Rivers of people poured north.

"Melanie!" I directed Ferguson toward her. "We're running. He can't hold these mirrors long, and I need to get to Radiants' Walk."

"Go!" she called. "I'm right behind you."

"Hang on, Tobiah." I kicked Ferguson into movement, shouting at the people ahead. "Watch out! Make way!"

Ferguson seemed reluctant to trample anyone, but he nosed people out of the way, snorting and nipping when they wouldn't let him through. Soon, more riders joined us: Melanie, James, Ferris, Oscar, and a handful of Queen's Guard.

At last, we broke through the worst of the crowd and all our mounts slipped into a gallop. I hunched low over Ferguson's neck.

The thrum of hooves and drone of voices filled my ears as we made straight for the castle, its towers and ramparts rising over the city like hope.

Behind us, glass shattered as the wraith broke free. Tobiah screamed, raw and wrecked as he pressed his forehead against my spine. His whole body shuddered, and his fingers dug into my sides hard enough to bruise.

I pressed my heels against Ferguson and urged him onward. He knew this. We'd done this before. He pushed ahead of the other horses, grunting and snorting as the inferno of wraith gained on us.

Blinding and boiling, the wraith grew brilliant with shining mist and stink.

"Mirrors, Tobiah!" I hated to force his magic, but we'd never make it if he didn't do this.

Tobiah leaned over me, his arms tight around my waist. His breath came hard and ragged, but he didn't let go.

Ahead, a handful of new mirrors glimmered to life on shop walls. Tobiah gasped with the effort, but the force of wraith behind us paused. One of the guards riding alongside us cheered, but James shushed him.

"It's not stopped," James shouted. "We aren't safe until the barrier is up."

We turned onto Castle Street and rode for my home with everything in us. Drumming hooves, Tobiah's ragged breath, the screams of people fleeing wraith—these sounds filled my head as I kept my eyes on the castle. The overlook was visible from here, a wide, flat surface lit with dozens of gas lamps.

Closer. We were closer.

The street ahead was clear. I urged Ferguson faster and faster.

The crack and shatter of glass blasted again over the pounding and the blood rushing through my head. Tobiah groaned and his hands slipped around my middle. His weight pulled away from me.

I reached around and pressed my hand on his back, trying to keep him from slipping off. But as Ferguson picked up another burst of speed, Tobiah slid backward.

James rode up alongside us and heaved his cousin back into place. "We're almost there! Just hold on a little longer."

Thin tendrils of wraith slipped up behind us, nipping.

One of the horses shrieked and a soldier cried out, but there was no time to look back. Tobiah groaned and shook himself conscious once more, his grip tightening on me when he realized we were still in transit.

"More mirrors?" James kept his hand on Tobiah's shoulder, a feat while we ran at full speed toward the castle.

Tobiah's answer was faint. "No."

There was no other option, then.

As we reached the castle rampart, I reined Ferguson hard, pulling him to a stop at the thick gate, left open for our return.

Other guards thundered by before they realized what I'd done, but James was still beside us. "What are you doing?"

"The only thing left." I stripped off a glove and dug Connor's small, silver mirror from a pouch on my belt. Dented, tarnished, but still reflective. "*Wake up*," I whispered, and the mirror began to shine in my hands. I pressed it against stone. "*Wake up, stay here, and grow. Grow until you cover the entire wall.*"

Dizziness swarmed through me, filling my sight and stealing my balance, but Tobiah kept his grip on me, and James added his strength, too. I breathed through the magical exertion as silver rippled outward, spreading across the stone.

All across the city, wraith halted.

"James, the overlook." My words felt slow. "Get us there now."

* * *

The overlook stairs were nearly impossible to climb.

Tobiah and I staggered up the narrow passage, James and Melanie at our heels.

"We couldn't get the carts through," Paige said from the rear, "so Rees and I improvised. People carried the barrier pieces in baskets and scarves, anything they could find. Is that all right?"

"As long as the pieces are there." I lurched up the last steps to find a huge glittering pile of barrier scales in the center of the overlook, and a small crowd of nobles and military.

Stumbling forward, I caught Queen Francesca's eye, Kathleen Rayner's, even Chey's. Near them stood the Corcorans and a handful of other Indigo Kingdom nobles, all watching with frightened expressions. Many of them still wore their ball gowns from earlier this evening.

It seemed like ages ago.

The Ospreys were there, too, with Aecorian nobility and the remainder of the Queen's Guard. Claire leaned against the railing, both feet attached.

I glanced at Paige. "Why is there an audience?"

"They're afraid," she said. "They want to know what's happening."

"Then they'll have to wait until we're finished. We can't delay." As Tobiah and I marched toward the barrier pieces, Melanie and James flanking us, I wondered what they saw. A king and queen, dressed as vigilantes? Or two young people, thrust into power before they were ready?

The castle shuddered as wraith strained against Connor's mirror.

"What's your plan?" Melanie took my arm to steady me.

"Don't even ask," Tobiah muttered. "She hates telling people her plans."

"Do you remember when I told you about Mirror Lake?" I knelt at the pile of barrier scales, shining in the light of gas lamps and wraith. Our audience moved to hear, but guards kept them back. "And the other night, you, James, and I talked about creating a barrier ring around Aecor."

Her mouth dropped open. "You're going to turn the Red Bay into a bigger Mirror Lake." Her eyes were wide as she gazed at the massive pile of scales.

"Not just the Red Bay. Tangler Bay, all the way through the Hand River and Grace Bay and the Wildern Sea. Yes. All of it." I glanced from Melanie to James to Tobiah. "Mirror Lake didn't just hold back the wraith for longer than the barrier, but *normalized* everything that touched it, everything that reflected over it. We'll need to remove the wraith that's in the city, but once it's gone, we should be able to hold on for a few more years."

Someone in the crowd asked, "Will this be enough?"

The pile of barrier scales here stood taller than my head. There were thousands of pieces. Hundreds of thousands.

"I can't even consider that we won't have enough." There hadn't been many pieces in Mirror Lake, but this was so much larger. I bent to take a scale from the edge of the pile; it was warm, but not as warm as those from Mirror Lake had been. Though maybe with the wraith heat pouring over the city, everything else felt cool by comparison.

"They won't be *alive*, will they?" James stood at Tobiah's

side. "Like Chrysalis or"—he lowered his voice—"me?"

I shook my head. "They have magic in them, but they're not magic, or wraith. They're just pieces of metal formed in a very specific way."

And if they did become truly alive, we'd know right away, because I'd be dead.

The castle shuddered again, making our audience shriek. Guards pushed them back.

It was just the four of us now. Tobiah, Melanie, James, and me—and this immense pile of silver scales that could be our salvation, or could ruin everything.

If I died, the mirror would fail. Chrysalis would revert. James would die.

Tobiah lifted his eyes to mine, something desperate and hopeful in there. "Are you sure?"

I repeated the words I'd told Melanie before I ventured into the wraithland. "If I'm not willing to take risks for my people's well-being, I don't deserve to be queen."

He bowed his head. "I'd make the same choice."

"*Wake up.*" I squeezed the barrier piece in my ungloved hand. "*Wake up and when I command one piece, I command you all. Do this exactly: scatter in the water, circle the entire peninsula, and hold your position. Refuse to wash out with the current. Resist being swallowed. Don't let yourself be buried.*"

The expected dizziness came, making me sway. I breathed through it. Maybe that was all. Then black fuzzed the edges of my sight and my temples gave a single warning throb.

Everything spun. I groped for something to hang on to as I dropped forward. Hands grabbed for me—I caught the shapes of James and Melanie in my fading vision—and they held me upright.

"It's working." Tobiah sounded far away.

"Go into the water," I commanded. *"Follow my orders."*

Silver shimmered and people shouted. Barrier pieces slithered across the overlook, waterfalling into the Red Bay below. I clutched my piece, my connection, and peered over the edge of the cliff.

"Hold her!" Tobiah shouted. "Don't let her fall!"

The hands on me tightened, but faintly I could see the shine of the barrier as it surged into the water, through the dark depths, and vanished.

Then the world faded.

FORTY-EIGHT

"IT'S NOT GOING to be enough." That sounded like Chrysalis.

My head throbbed as I climbed back into consciousness. Melanie's hands were cool on my cheeks and throat as she checked my pulse, which meant I couldn't have been out for long. A few minutes. My head rested on her knees.

"What do you mean?" Melanie looked to her left, and the breeze caught her hair. "It has to be enough." Her face was fuzzy.

No matter how deeply I breathed, I couldn't clear my vision of the blackness simmering at the edges, fading into gray in the center. It would be a miracle if I could stand.

"You poured magic into the barrier, but not enough." Chrysalis stood on the wall around the overlook, staring into the dark waters of the bay below. The white suit he'd worn to my coronation was battered and bloody, torn in a hundred different places. "This won't work without more magic."

I pushed myself into a sitting position, swaying. "When did you get here?"

The wraith boy flashed a smile my way. "Just a moment ago, my queen. I'm glad you're awake."

"Then this was pointless?" Melanie jabbed a finger at the bay. "Magic went into the barrier while the metal was molten. *Now* what do we do?"

I pried my hand open, stretching my fingers around the anchor scale.

Dizziness still swarmed my head, but my vision cleared a little. Around us, guards, nobles, and Ospreys stared on, their expressions a mix of fear and uncertainty. The queen mother and her sister moved to the fore of the crowd, closer to their sons.

Everyone was scared, which meant I should stand up and take charge.

James and Tobiah edged closer so that when I climbed to my feet and let them take most of my weight, it wasn't obvious I needed help.

Chrysalis stepped off the rail and strode toward me, his movements mimicking mine after all this time spent together. "My queen." An odd gentleness filled his voice. "I promised to protect you from the wraith, that I'd never let it hurt you."

"I remember." I brought my fingertips close to one of the burns on his face, but didn't quite touch. He went so still he was nearly lifeless. "You did protect me tonight. When I told you to control the wraith, you did that, too."

His eyes never shifted from mine. "But you also said it isn't just you anymore. It's the entire kingdom, and you need to protect everyone here, too."

"That's right." I dropped my hand and stepped backward, carefully, because my balance was still weak. Behind me, one of the boys breezed his hands over my shoulder and waist, keeping me steady.

Chrysalis seemed to study me, or memorize me, and then he said, "I can do it. If you want."

Yes, of course I wanted him to protect Aecor.

"I'm made of wraith," he said. "Same as the beasts they used for the barrier. If I—" He shifted his weight and lowered his eyes. "You gave me life for a little while. I had the chance to experience something incredible, even though I made everything harder for you. But maybe this time I could help you get what you want—what you *truly* want."

Silence fell across the overlook as people realized what he meant.

"You would sacrifice yourself for Aecor?"

"I would sacrifice myself for *you*, my queen. If that's what you want." Chrysalis tilted his head. "I've made many wrong decisions in my desire to serve you." His gaze flickered toward Tobiah. "I've done many things that, now, I understand were bad. Even tonight, freeing Patrick and bringing the wraith. I thought only to help you. I thought I could control something uncontrollable. I don't want to make more mistakes. I don't want to cost you anything else."

"So you're waiting for me to order you to do this." My throat tightened.

He nodded as the castle shuddered again. "I know you will make the right decision."

No.

It was an impossible order to give.

It was the kind of order queens had to give all the time.

But I'd *made* him. I'd brought him to life. Unwittingly, yes, but now it was my responsibility to teach him and care for him and ensure he did the right thing.

"I won't make you," I whispered. "When I bring something to life, it's never sentient. Almost never. It never has a choice but to do what I order."

Clothes brushed behind me, like James and Tobiah exchanging glances. But I wouldn't look. I wouldn't give anyone here a reason to question Captain Rayner and his miraculous life. It was his secret to tell, when he was ready. If.

A low rumble filled the air: the wraith still struggling against my mirror.

"You're sentient, Chrysalis. You have a choice. You said you've made wrong decisions in the past, and I know you have. Many of us have paid the price of those decisions. But this one is about you, and your life. I won't take that decision away from you." He was a person, not a tool. I could no longer treat him as one.

The wraith boy bowed his head. "You honor me."

"We don't have much time," someone said.

I lifted my hand, signaling the crowd to be quiet.

Chrysalis pressed his palms to his chest. "I'll do it. For you."

Someone breathed praise to all the saints.

"But I won't be enough. Not to make the kind of mirror you need."

A small noise escaped me. "What?"

His shoulders slumped. "I can make myself part of the

barrier; you've already linked it all together. But it wouldn't last. Liadia poured so much magic into their barrier and I can provide only a fraction of that. I'm just wraith, after all. I'm more about destruction than anything." He lowered his eyes. "I'm sorry I can't be more."

Someone in the crowd was crying. Another cursed him for offering false hope. And all around us, the castle rumbled and wraith shone bright across the city, waiting, straining. There was no way to know how much longer the mirror would last.

"What about me?"

Everyone looked at James.

"What?" Tobiah grabbed his cousin by the jacket. "Don't say that."

Murmurs fluttered through the crowd. *"What's he talking about?"*

"The king's cousin is made of wraith?"

"No!" Kathleen Rayner pushed through the crowd. "James—"

He placed one hand on his cousin's shoulder, and the other on his mother's. "This is a very long story that Tobiah will have to tell."

Tobiah shook his head. "I won't let you."

"Why not? What makes me any different from him?" James pointed at the wraith boy.

"You're my friend. My cousin. I still need you."

"Your friend, maybe, but not your cousin. That boy died ten years ago."

Lady Rayner's eyes went wide, and tears dripped down her cheeks. The queen mother joined the group, standing by Tobiah's side. "What do you mean that boy died?" she asked.

My heart climbed into my throat as I looked between them. In the audience, people pressed their hands to their mouths and whispered uncomfortably.

"You made me because you missed the first James." A faint, sad smile pulled at the corners of his mouth. "You asked Wilhelmina to bring me to life because you needed me, and I've spent every day of my life protecting you, because that was my purpose."

"*What* are you talking about?" Lady Rayner grabbed James's arm. "You're my son. You're my child. You're not like that creature at all."

Chrysalis dropped his head. "He's not like me, but he's not human, either. He's made of magic. He's stronger than I am. Better."

"*Shut up*," Tobiah growled. "Don't encourage him."

"Is that true?" Francesca asked. "Just—just explain, please."

Tears shone in James's eyes as he repeated a shorter version of Tobiah's story, outing the king's secret, my involvement, and his own existence. "That's why I healed so quickly after the Inundation. Because I'm not human. Not really."

Others tried to close in, but Melanie and a handful of guards held them back. I wanted to help, but not all the buzzing was from the wraith; my head spun with magic being sucked out of me. James, Chrysalis, the mirror, the barrier: something had to go.

Sandcliff Castle shuddered in agreement.

"Earlier tonight," James said, "I asked if I made my own decisions. You said I did. Let me make this one now."

"I can't lose you too, James."

"It's not just you anymore, Tobiah." James glanced at me, Melanie, and everyone standing on the overlook, praying for a miracle to stop the wraith. "It's the entire kingdom. There's only a little of the world left. Someone has to take care of it."

Tobiah looked at me for help. "Say something."

"I can't." A sob lodged in my throat. "I don't want to lose him, either, but what kind of queen would I be if I gave Chrysalis a choice, but not James? What kind of friend?"

"A friend who doesn't want to lose one of the people they love most?" Tobiah lifted his palms in supplication. "I need your *help*, Wil. Command him. Change his mind."

I shook my head, just slightly. Everything spun. "He's not mine to command. He never has been. He's a person, Tobiah."

Tobiah hissed through gritted teeth, lifting his eyes to the sky.

"Would I be enough?" James asked Chrysalis. "If I did this with you, would Aecor be safe? Would the barrier work like Mirror Lake?"

Chrysalis bit his lip.

"Tell the truth," I said.

The wraith boy nodded. "The two of us, yes. We'd be stronger. There's so much magic in you after all these years. You don't know half of what you could do."

"No." Lady Rayner let out a long, low wail. "No, James."

Tobiah blinked back tears. "How can you even know that?"

"I'm made of wraith." Chrysalis offered him a sad smile. "I know what I wouldn't touch."

"All right," James said. "What do we do?"

Tobiah grabbed James's shoulders. "No. I forbid you. You can't."

516

The queen mother and her sister urged James to listen to his king, but his focus was all on Chrysalis's instructions.

"We jump. We dive in and grab the barrier, and we push. My queen will need to command the barrier to accept us."

Tobiah spun toward me. "Don't do it. Don't tell the barrier anything."

James pressed a hand on his king's shoulder. "Then I'll be dead for nothing. It's a long drop."

"You've already been impaled. A drop won't hurt you."

James snorted a laugh. "I'm going to say good-bye, cousin. Please don't deny me. Please."

Tobiah threw his arms around James's shoulders, squeezing him tight. "I can't say good-bye."

James hugged him back, both of them unguarded in this burst of affection. "Then say, 'You're welcome.' You and Wil gave me ten years of life. You gave me family. You gave me purpose."

"Then you're welcome," Tobiah murmured. "And thank *you* for—for everything. You were always there when I needed you."

Quickly, James hugged his friends, his aunt, and his mother, pausing to whisper something in her ear. I couldn't hear it, and the angle was wrong for me to read his lips, but whatever he said, she just touched his cheek and said she loved him.

He came to me last. "I think Oscar will make a good replacement for head of castle security. Or Ferris, if you want to send Oscar off to his estate when this is over."

"Shut up." My jaw trembled with exhaustion and grief, but I hugged him and kissed his cheek. "You were always real to him.

To me. To everyone who knew you."

"Thank you." He pulled away, unbuckled his sword sheath, and pressed it into Tobiah's hands. Without a word, he moved toward the edge. "Coming, Chrysalis?"

The wraith boy had barely moved through all this, just stood there and watched. No one had wanted to hug him.

I did. Gently, I wrapped my arms around him. "If I could do it again," I whispered, "I'd get to know you better."

He didn't respond, just joined James on the ledge, whispering instructions or assurances. I couldn't tell.

Tears streaked down my face, cold against the wraith-heated night. Tobiah pressed himself against my side, and Melanie on the other. Everyone gathered around us, many openly weeping. We left a space between James and Chrysalis and us, like moving too close would shatter the moment as they stepped onto the railing.

"I can't watch." Tobiah spoke so that only I could hear.

"You must." I slipped my ungloved hand into his, and the barrier piece pressed between us. "James's biggest desire was always to protect you. That's what he's doing now. You must honor him."

Tobiah gripped my hand so tightly it felt like my bones scraped together, but neither of us looked away as James and Chrysalis stepped off the rail and leapt into the Red Bay.

"*Accept them,*" I whispered to the anchor scale. "*Let their magic be spread throughout the ring. Make their sacrifice matter.*"

A double splash sounded.

The scale turned hot in my palm, scalding, but the sudden

relief was immeasurable. Burden lifted. The slow drain of magic I'd lived with for so long—it was gone.

My knees buckled, but Tobiah and Melanie held me up as white light speared the sky.

It stretched from the Red Bay, north to Tangler Bay, illuminating Snowhaven Bridge from beneath, and then beyond my sight. Cool, clean air came off the water, and thousands of stars appeared in the sky as the mirror cut through the haze of wraith.

"You did it." Melanie lifted her face to the sky in wonder. "Between your mirror and the barrier, even the wraith in the city is burning away."

It was glorious, yes, but as we all huddled together on Radiants' Walk, I could only think about everything this victory had cost.

FORTY-NINE

I KNOCKED ON the door between my room and Tobiah's.

"I'm here."

Cautiously, I opened the door to find Tobiah sitting on the bottom corner of his bed, staring toward the balcony window. The curtains had been pushed back to reveal a spectacular view of the city.

"The wraith is gone," I said.

He dropped his gaze to James's sword lying across his knees.

"Colin's and Patrick's people were arrested. They shouldn't be a problem anymore."

Silence.

"Not that Melanie trusts we've seen the last of them. She'll root out any lingering opposition."

He didn't move. He hadn't bathed, or even changed out of his Black Knife clothes. He just sat there, slumped as he steeped in his grief. Tear tracks shone on his cheeks.

"This morning, I took a boat with Mel and Lieutenant Ferris. There's a sheered-off edge on the opposite shore of Tangler Bay. It worked. The wraith can't return." I'd seen refugees crossing Snowhaven Bridge, taking rescue boats where the bridge hadn't yet been repaired. "The castle wall is still silver. When I told Connor's mirror to go back to sleep, it just stayed there."

Now there was nothing magical draining me but the barrier; I couldn't risk letting go of that without being sure the pieces would never be disturbed. It'd been simpler in Mirror Lake, which wasn't connected to an entire ocean. But here, anything could happen to the scales.

So I held on to them, keeping the anchor scale in a pocket so I'd never forget.

"Did you sleep?" I asked.

"I can't." He curled his fingers around the sheathed sword. "Part of me wishes I could blame you. Or Chrysalis. Or anyone besides James, but it was his choice in the end, wasn't it?"

My dress rustled as I crossed the room to stand beside him. "You've lost so much. It doesn't seem fair that you should lose James, too. But yes, it was his choice. I think it was his way of proving he was real."

"It's interesting that he didn't feel like the real one," Tobiah said after a few minutes. "I knew him longer than I knew the first James. We got in trouble together. Had parties together. Complained about our parents together. When my father died, he was there for me, and when he was shot, I couldn't leave his side. How he came into my life never made a difference. I cared only that he was *there*."

"He's still there. I know it's not the same." I touched his

shoulder and hated my own inadequate words. "Of course it's not the same. But James was made of our magic, and you know the most basic law of magic."

"It's never created or destroyed. It simply changes forms."

I nodded. "So that's James out there." I pulled the anchor scale from my pocket and unfolded my fingers around it. "And this is James in here. Just another form. And he's doing the same thing he did for the last ten years: he's protecting. You. Me. The kingdom."

"We didn't even win. Patrick and Colin are gone now, but the wraith is still out there. The Indigo Kingdom is gone, and so is everything beyond it. We didn't stop the wraith, just found a way to hold it back."

"Sometimes that's as much as we can ask for," I whispered. "We didn't ask to inherit this world with its too-big problems, but it's the world we have. There's going to be wraith as long as there's magic, and magic is in us. It's part of us, whether we want to deny it or embrace it. Maybe our parents and their parents did the best they could, but it's up to us to do better. We'll change the world."

Tobiah leaned forward and rested his face in his hands. "I'm so tired of losing people."

"I know. I am, too."

He didn't move or indicate he needed me to stay, so I smoothed a strand of his hair and left.

I filled the rest of the afternoon with council meetings to ensure refugees were cared for, city repairs were under way, and everything was moving as smoothly as it ever had.

When I returned to my room and peeked through the adjoining door, Tobiah was nowhere in sight.

That had to be a good sign.

Dusk fell. A fire already burned in the fireplace, throwing warmth into my parlor. I turned on a gas lamp and found my notebook, the black one Patrick had given me years ago.

There was only one blank page remaining.

I lingered over the ritual of preparing to write, choosing a pen and ink, considering the handwriting I wanted to use, and finally dipped the pen and touched the tines to paper.

> When I was only nine years old, I began this diary to chronicle my return to my kingdom. I've carried it through kingdoms and battles and wraithland.
>
> I'm home at last, but everything is different from how I imagined.
>
> Friends are lost: some to death, and some to differences we were never able to overcome. Some because they sacrificed everything for what they believed.
>
> I don't know if I'm ready to be queen. I don't feel ready. But maybe queens never do.
>
> All I know is this: I'll give it my best.

Tobiah stood at my elbow, watching with those dark eyes. He'd washed up while I'd been out, and now he wore a clean black suit. He tapped the corner of my notebook. "You use this handwriting a lot. Whose is it?"

The hand was a mix of my favorites, the best parts of each. "It's mine."

"I like it." His smile was faint, but it still existed. There was hope after all. "And these"—he touched the small stack of papers near my work—"are our letters from Skyvale? You kept them?"

I blew on my writing to dry the ink, and then closed my diary. "There aren't many things I've ever really thought of as mine. This notebook. The signet ring my father gave me. My weapons. These letters are important to me."

"Right up there with your favorite daggers?"

I shrugged. "Almost up there."

He shifted his weight and touched the pale blue notebook I'd enchanted. "After you left the Indigo Kingdom, I looked for your letters every day, even when I didn't have time to respond. Or want to. But as the days passed, and suddenly I was thrust out of my city, your letters became what kept me whole. I reread them all the time. They made me feel close to you. I celebrated your triumphs, cursed your struggles, and spent whole nights wondering about this handwriting you kept using. I relied on those letters. I needed them."

My heart turned as I touched the leather cover, ran my fingers over the braided designs on the edge. "I looked for your response every day. I didn't stop hoping. Not until—not until the news came."

He nodded, head low. Hair breezed over his eyebrows. "I know. When I saw your final letter, I thought it would kill me. I wanted to reassure you, but it was impossible if I wanted to ensure your queenship."

We'd both sacrificed so much.

And so much had been ripped away.

It was a wonder there was anything left at all.

"What are you going to do with your diary now that it's finished?" He kept his gaze on me, steady and warm and seeing everything. "Will you start a new one?"

"Once I find a notebook I like as much. In the meantime, I'll put this one away." I walked to the bookcase filled with the diaries of queens before me. "I'll leave it so those who come after will know what I did to reclaim Aecor—the good and the bad. Maybe my descendants will make better choices where I failed."

"Your descendants?" He took my chair and pen, not bothering to ask permission as he found a sheet of paper and began writing. "Are you planning on having a lot of descendants?"

"One day I'd like a whole army of tiny vigilantes."

"A worthy goal."

We stayed in the quiet for a few more minutes, him writing, and me reluctant to interrupt him. It was good that he was here. Reaching out. Not alone.

Finally, he blew on the ink and handed the paper to me.

It was a list, and almost looked as though it were written in my handwriting. A fair approximation anyway.

Reasons we should get married:
Because I love you.
We both look good in black boots.
I spent some time without you, and I didn't like it.
You make me happy.
I make you laugh.
I like the way you fight.
You see through my masks.

I really love you.

You love me, too. (Though you've mostly said this while yelling, so perhaps I should have double-checked.)

Army of tiny vigilantes. (I have name ideas.)

Various political reasons that make sense but don't fit with the theme of this list.

I'm holding your handwriting hostage. You can have it back when you say yes.

When I looked up, his expression was earnest. Hopeful. "It doesn't have to be right now. We can wait. I just want to know you'll be ready one day."

My heart knotted as I reread the list. For all I wanted him, there were still barriers. One, especially. "What about Meredith?" I let his list hang limp in my fingers as I strode toward the fireplace. "Chrysalis was my responsibility, and I didn't stop him when I should have."

On the mantel behind me, the clock ticked away seconds.

"During the ball," he said, "you avoided this conversation." He pursued me across the room, taking my waist in his hands. His body was only a breath away from mine. "But it must happen. Surely you know that."

I dropped my eyes to the hollow of his throat. "I'm listening."

"Finally." His hands relaxed, but he didn't move away. That was good. "After I announced the wedding date, I would lie awake every night and think about that time in the breezeway, and the mistake I'd made."

The mistake of kissing me.

"I would think about how for ten years, our lives kept

touching, tapping, but we never seemed to stay on the same course. The One-Night War. The streets of Skyvale. Your time in the palace. And when we kissed in the breezeway, I knew, I *knew* I wanted to be with you, and that I'd never be satisfied any other way. But I still chose her because I'd promised my father— who wasn't even alive to care. That was my mistake."

"Oh." The word came as a breath.

"Wilhelmina Korte, from the moment we met, you challenged me in ways I needed to be challenged. In ways I *want* to be challenged. I've known it all along.

"When I chose her, I chose wrong. Oh, I'd have done my best to make her happy. I cared about her. But I'm just as responsible for her death, and I've spent the last months learning to accept that." Tension ran from his shoulders and he stepped back, firelight glowing across the planes and angles of his face. "And I don't want to ignore how much I feel for you, either. There's an undeniable gravity between us. I know you feel it, too."

"Yes."

And it seemed as though everyone else sensed it, too. James. Melanie. Chrysalis. Meredith. Even Prince Colin.

"We keep drifting toward each other." Tobiah's eyes were steady on mine, so familiar in the faint light. "No matter the masks we wear, we always end up together."

"I'm tired of wearing masks."

"So am I." He cupped his hands over my cheeks. "Wilhelmina. I know we have a lot to work out, but I can't deny that I want you."

My heart beating so hard made my chest ache. His list slipped from my fingers, floating, skimming across the floor a little ways before it settled.

Tobiah's fingertips brushed against my face, cool and gentle. "I want every part of you. The nameless girl. The Osprey. The vigilante. The queen. Wilhelmina, you have a hundred identities and I love every one of them."

I couldn't stop my smile. Maybe I didn't have to understand *how* he could love me after all the things I'd done, just accept that he *did*—and that maybe, probably, he felt the same way about my love for him.

He bent so his forehead rested against mine. "A few times now you've told me not to kiss you anymore. Do I have your permission this time?"

"You have enthusiastic permission." I cupped his face in my hands, keeping him in place as I tilted my head to kiss him. Softly, at first. A brush of my lips against his.

"Again?" His eyes were closed, but he was smiling.

"Yes." When we kissed, the muscles of his jaw flexed under my fingers, and the shape of his body fit with mine. His arms fell around me, drawing us close. His hands pressed against my waist and hips and the small of my back. His mouth moved against mine, deepening the kiss until we were drowning.

He'd been right about gravity. We'd spent our lives falling toward each other, and now he was in my arms. I was in his.

"Wil," he breathed. "Wilhelmina."

With my hands on his face, fingertips tracing the lines and curves of his jaw and cheeks, I could *feel* the way he said my name.

My name.

We were no longer vigilante and thief, or sullen prince and

hidden princess, or only half aware of the other's identity. This was love without masks.

I pushed my fingers through his hair and kissed his mouth and chin and neck and the hollow of his throat. He dropped back his head in surrender as heat from the fireplace washed over us in waves.

The world fell away. I breezed my hands down his back, mapping the ridges of muscle beneath his clothes. He kissed a trail down my jaw and neck and shoulder. We breathed in time with each other, like we were one.

A door clicked and footsteps sounded, but I didn't pay attention until Melanie said, "I guess this means Paige should prepare the castle for a wedding."

Tobiah kissed me again and drew back, just enough so I could see the smile that warmed his face. "One day."

"One day," I agreed.

Melanie stood in the doorway, a packet of papers in one hand, and holding the fallen list in the other. "For propriety's sake, I'd bolt the doors between your rooms and take the keys, but you're both disreputable enough to pick the locks."

"Definitely." Tobiah grinned at me.

"Did you come here to tease us, Mel?" My heart still pounded with Tobiah's nearness. "Or was there something else?"

"I brought good news." She offered the packet to me.

The top sheet was a map: Aecor, shaded in red, and the barrier around us, silver. The north and south were still questions, but in the west, the Indigo Kingdom was marked with the familiar colored bands of wraith movement. The bands covered the entirety of the Indigo Kingdom.

Tobiah's shoulders curled in.

"Mel—"

"Look at the next page."

I obliged, but it was the same thing. Just another map showing how isolated and alone we were on this peninsula. But . . .

"What is this?" Tobiah skimmed his finger down the eastern coast of the Indigo Kingdom. It was just a narrow space, but there was no color to mark wraith. He looked up. "Are these backward?"

"Look at the next page," she said again, grinning.

On the third map, the wraith-free band was a breath wider.

I could hardly breathe. "The wraith is retreating?"

Melanie shook her head. "We've had people monitoring the Indigo shore since the barrier went up, and they all agree it's not retreating. But when it reaches the bay, it changes. It's healing."

Healing.

"How quickly?" Tobiah whispered.

Melanie nodded at the maps in my hand. "These were from the last day. Since the barrier went up."

Hope thrummed in my chest. "We could make more barriers and send them farther inland, to lakes and rivers. We could heal the land from within."

"Maybe."

Or maybe it wasn't simply the barrier pieces, but the strength of James and Chrysalis and their decision to do anything to protect the people they loved most.

I knew Tobiah was wondering the same thing.

"What should we do now?" Melanie took the papers from me and laid them on the desk.

"We should tell someone." I took Tobiah's hand and Melanie's hand and pulled them to the balcony. "We should tell everyone."

Outside, a gibbous moon lit the sky, surrounded by a scattering of stars. Reflected light glowed over the courtyard below; Connor's silver mirror still shimmered across the wall, an undeniable reminder of that night's events, and the truth about mirrors.

I pushed my voice to project as far as possible. "Citizens of Aecor!"

People began to stop, one by one, and look up. Waiting.

I squeezed my friends' hands and pulled them close. "None of us were here when the wraith problem began. But for the first time in a hundred years, there's hope. Hope that we will be here when it ends."

ACKNOWLEDGMENTS

Writing this book felt a lot like stopping the wraith. Most of the time, it seemed too big, too impossible, and I definitely wouldn't have been able to do it without the aid and encouragement from many, many people.

Lauren MacLeod, my agent, whose faith was unwavering, who always championed me, and who reminded me (several times) that I'd written difficult books before and I would write this one, too.

Laurel Symonds, my editor, who should be awarded sainthood for her patience and hard work on this book. I don't think there's any way to properly thank you for sticking with me on this, but know that I am grateful every day.

Katherine Tegen, Queen of KTB. Thank you for giving Wilhelmina a home with all the remarkable books you publish.

Alana Whitman, Lauren Flower, Rosanne Romanello, and Margot Wood, Ladies of Marketing and Publicity. *book shimmy*

Amy Ryan, Erin Fitzsimmons, and Colin Anderson, the amazing team responsible for the Orphan Queen series covers (including novellas!). They are the prettiest things I've ever seen.

All the love to the best friends a girl could have, including Christine Nguyen, C. J. Redwine, Gabrielle Harvey, Jaime Lee Moyer, Jillian Boehme, Kathleen Peacock, Myra McEntire, Stacey Lee, and Wendy Beer, for always having my back; Brodi Ashton and Cynthia Hand, my amazing *My Lady Jane* co-authors who never fail to make me laugh; and Joy Hensley and Valerie Cole, who endured many long hours of listening to me talk about this book. *The Mirror King* wouldn't be what it is without every one of you.

Special thanks to C. J. Redwine (again!) and Danielle Paige, who said such nice things about *The Orphan Queen*.

Love to Hayley Farris, the most joyful person I know. Cookies to Alexa Santiago, my pretend assistant who always keeps our pretend office stocked with pretend cookies. The #OQSupportGroup, who not only supports other readers upon reaching the end of OQ, but the whole series as well. I hope you still like me after you read this book.

My mom, who's read everything I've ever written and always believed in me. My sister, who called me to scream the moment she finished *The Orphan Queen* and was one of the first people to read *The Mirror King*. My husband, who made sure I had plenty of cookies and emotional support.

God, with whom all things are indeed possible. Including writing this book.

And, as always, thank you to my wonderful readers. Librarians, teachers, bloggers, and people who lurk in bookstores—I hope you love this book as much as I do.

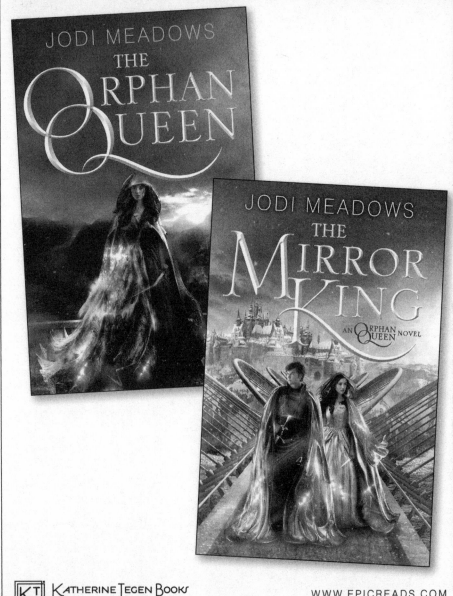